PRAISE FOR *A TASTE OF MAGIC*

'*A Taste of Magic* is a delicious mix of second-chance romance, baking show chaos, and spellwork gone hilariously wrong. With crackling chemistry and plenty of heart, Lyra and Rabbie's love story proves that the sweetest magic is the kind you risk your heart to make'

Jenn McKinlay, NYT bestselling author of *Witches of Dubious Origin*

'I adored this slow burn, second-chance witchy romance. Loved spending time in this cozy magical community—meeting Lyra and her sisters who are close and witches, and also Ruth, Lyra's adorable familiar. Lyra is coming into her powers and they are a bit rocky—which adds to the fun'

Pamela Kelley, USA Today bestselling author of *Nantucket Second Chances*

'Tricia O'Malley never fails to disappoint, and *A Taste of Magic* is no exception. Sweet, charming, and deeply romantic, it's the kind of book you fall into and don't want to leave'

K.F Breene, USA Today bestselling author of *Magical Midlife Madness*

'A perfectly delicious sequel novel that delivers on every front!'

Jill Shalvis, NYT bestselling author of *Simply Irresistible*

ALSO BY TRICIA O'MALLEY

Love's a Witch

TRICIA O'MALLEY

THE SCOTTISH CHARMS SERIES - BOOK 2

A TASTE OF *Magic*

SIMON &
SCHUSTER

London · New York · Amsterdam/Antwerp · Sydney/Melbourne · Toronto · New Delhi

First published in the United States by Gallery Books, an imprint of
Simon & Schuster, LLC, 2026
First published in Great Britain by Solstice Books, an imprint of
Simon & Schuster UK Ltd, 2026

1 3 5 7 9 10 8 6 4 2

Simon & Schuster UK Ltd, 7th Floor
199 Bishopsgate, London, EC2M 3TY

Simon & Schuster Australia, Sydney
Simon & Schuster India, New Delhi

www.simonandschuster.co.uk
www.simonandschuster.com.au
www.simonandschuster.co.in

The authorised representative in the EEA is Simon & Schuster Netherlands BV, Herculesplein 96, 3584 AA Utrecht, Netherlands. info@simonandschuster.nl

A CIP catalogue record for this book is available from the British Library

Paperback ISBN: 978-1-3985-4955-5
eBook ISBN: 978-1-3985-4956-2
Audio ISBN: 978-1-3985-4957-9

Interior design by Julia Jacintho
Printed and Bound in the UK using 100% Renewable Electricity
at CPI Group (UK) Ltd

FSC www.fsc.org MIX Paper | Supporting responsible forestry FSC® C013604

TO ALAN—
"LET 'EM SAY WE'RE CRAZY . . .
WHAT DO THEY KNOW?"
I'D TAKE A CHANCE WITH YOU
IN A HUNDRED LIFETIMES.
MO GHRÀDH.

GLOSSARY OF SCOTTISH WORDS/SLANG

- **bit o' banter**—Scots love to tease each other; banter is highly cherished
- **blethering**—complaining, talking too long
- **bloody**—a word used to add emphasis; expletive
- **bonnie**—pretty
- **brekkie**—breakfast
- **brolly**—umbrella
- **buttery**—a traditional savory, flaky bread roll
- **cèilidh**—a social event with Celtic folk music and dancing
- **chippy**—a fish-and-chip shop
- **eejit**—idiot
- **faff**—spend time on unnecessarily time-consuming things
- **greet**—to cry (to have a wee greet)
- **hen**—woman, female
- **Highland coo**—a cow, a hardy breed of Scottish cattle
- **ken**—know
- **och**—used to express many emotions, typically surprise, regret, or disbelief

- **plaster**—a Band-Aid or bandage
- **skelp**—knock across the room
- **tea**—in Scotland, having tea is often used to refer to the dinnertime meal
- **tetchy**—crabby, cranky, moody
- **wee**—small, little
- **wheesht (haud your wheesht)**—be quiet, hush, shut up

A TASTE OF *Magic*

CHAPTER ONE

Lyra MacGregor

Magick runs in my blood. So does bad luck.

One second, I was hurrying down Briarhaven's main street, my head ducked against the light mist of rain that had shadowed the early autumn days of late. My mind was fixed on Mystic Munchies, and the nerve-racking question I was about to ask when I slammed into something solid. Some*one* solid, that is.

I barely had time to gasp before I was knocked off my feet, landing hard in a puddle.

"Bloody hell, Lyra."

That voice.

I blinked up, and my breath was stolen as Rabbie Barclay loomed over me, offering a hand I wasn't sure I wanted to take. My first love. My biggest regret.

And then, as if the universe wanted to drive the moment home, the skies opened.

Rain pelted my skin, soaking into my dress, and I squealed, furious with myself for not bringing my brolly with me. I'd lived in Scotland long enough to know that I should always have something with me to protect from the rain. Although, at times, the rain literally fell sideways, and nothing kept you dry in that.

"Are you hurt?" Rabbie's voice, with a soft rasp like he'd just woken, sent a shiver down my spine.

It had always been this way.

Well, maybe not for him.

Clearly *not* for him, I silently amended as I dropped his hand and stepped back. But not before he'd started to brush me off. We both froze as his hands touched my backside, burning through the fabric of my dress, their heat seeping through the wet cloth to my skin.

His touch. Imprinted on my brain. Seared into my heart.

"Sorry, I just—"

"I'm fine, Rab. It was my mistake for not watching where I was going. Good day." I nodded briskly to him, refusing to notice that even in the increasing darkness from the moody clouds and sleeting rain, I could see the tiny flecks of gold glimmering in his green eyes. Tearing my gaze away, I dashed down the block toward Mystic Munchies, determined to see my task through, since it had taken me ages to work up the courage to go there today.

"Good day," I muttered to myself, shaking my head. What was I—a prim Victorian schoolteacher? Would I ever cease embarrassing myself where Rab was concerned?

Smiling brightly at a random man on the sidewalk who rushed to cover my head with a brolly, I stopped at the door of Mystic Munchies, Briarhaven's eclectic bakery.

"Thank you so much, sir. I appreciate it." The man's cheeks flushed bright pink, and he stuttered something unintelligible as I breezed up the walk to the bakery. At the last moment, I glanced down the street to see Rab standing under the awning to Pixie Dust Apothecary, glaring in our direction. Hoping it would annoy him, which was a side of myself that I didn't normally indulge, I blew a kiss at the man I'd left on the pavement fumbling with his brolly and swept inside the bakery.

Warm scents of vanilla and cinnamon immediately swirled around me, and the tension that banded my shoulders eased as I stepped farther inside. Mystic Munchies was an institution in Briarhaven, run by one very intimidating forest elf, Marcie.

Who, at the moment, was doing something I'd never seen her do before.

"Lyra!" Marcie crowed, a mile-wide smile on her face. With hot-pink hair plaited down to her bum, muscular arms the size of tree trunks, and a fierce countenance—smiling was an unfamiliar concept to Marcie.

And yet.

There it was.

Revealing two canine teeth a touch more pointed than was human, and showcasing crinkles at the corner of her eyes, a big, fat smile sat on Marcie's otherwise stoic face.

I was completely unsure what to do with this turn of events.

In fact, maybe today was *not* the day to ask Marcie my question.

It might be best if I just eased out of the shop slowly, pretending like I hadn't seen a thing, because one could never be certain if a smile contained joy or malice. Maybe today was the day that Marcie finally cracked, fed up with one too many tourists who didn't understand the complexities of the baked goods she offered.

Briarhaven had officially undergone a makeover several years ago, transforming itself into "Scotland's Most Magical Town." In doing so, Knox Douglas, the forward-thinking provost and boyfriend of my older sister, Sloane, had done something most had previously thought impossible—he'd given magickals a safe space to live out in the open. Now tourists descended upon Briarhaven in droves, convinced they were simply at an amusement park, and magickals like Marcie didn't have to hide the more fantastical sides of their lives.

"Come in, come in. Throw the lock for me, would ye, hen?" Marcie called, waving me forward, and I winced, knowing that I could not evade whatever was about to go down. Turning back to the glass door, I gingerly flipped the sign and cast a glance to the darkening sky. The streetlights, driven by solar power, winked on in the absence of daylight.

Odd.

I hoped it wasn't a harbinger of whatever had Marcie smiling like she'd eaten too much fairy floss. I wanted the old Marcie back, the one who grunted out answers and only gave her clientele what she thought they needed, *never* what they ordered. I sidled closer to the counter, keeping one eye on my escape route, and took a deep breath.

"Marcie, I wanted to—"

"Lyra, you'll never believe it. I'm not even believing it myself, and yet I just spoke to them. They picked me. Me! Can ye even believe it?" Marcie untied her apron and came around the counter to pace in front of the glass case that housed her magickal baked goods. Mystic Munchies lived up to its name with a wildly colorful mural of mushrooms, flowers, and rabid-looking forest animals peeking out from psychedelic trees and blooms splashed across the wall. The decor always made me think someone had dropped one too many hits of acid, but Marcie insisted it soothed her and made her think of home.

If home was full of neon flowers and forest creatures with far too many teeth, that is.

"Picked you for what?" I asked, distracted.

"Here."

I jumped because Marcie, who had previously been on the other side of the room, was now standing right in front of me, holding a towel.

"Um."

"You're wet. Dry off." Her tone brooked no disagreement.

"Yes, ma'am." I bent and wiped the rain and mud that dripped down my legs, still annoyed that I'd run into Rabbie of all people. My main goal since moving back to Briarhaven had been to avoid the man at all costs, and yet for some reason, the universe seemed determined to poke me every chance it got.

Once I was tidied up, I handed the towel over and then glanced back outside, where it was as dark as night. Worry twisted.

"Marcie, do you see—"

"*Bewitching*," Marcie said, and I turned back to see her, hands clasped at her heart, eyes wide, that scary smile still on her face.

"What's bewitching?"

"*Bewitching Bake Off*," Marcie breathed, her tone reverent.

"The reality show?" I was a huge fan, so if she wanted to discuss the latest episode, I'd be more than happy to settle in for a wee chat. It had been a particularly dicey episode, with not one, not two, but *three* explosions. I was gasping with laughter by the end. The premise of the show was to pair one experienced baker with a novice, and they'd have to follow a magickal recipe for each challenge. As can be imagined, chaos often ensued. And the contestants never knew who their partners would be until the day of the first show, so the drama of often mismatched personalities only added to the hilarity. It was bingeable reality TV at its finest, and I was addicted. "I *love* that show."

"Me too," Marcie said, her eyes now bordering on manic. "Lyra. I'm dying. *Dying*."

"What? Oh my goddess! Have you been selected to be on it?" I finally clued in to what may be happening here.

"No. Even better. I can't believe it. I can't honestly believe it. Surely this will be the best thing to happen to Mystic Munchies. Or Briarhaven. This is a huge win for us." Marcie whirled, her pink braid flying with her, and she paced again. Muscles bunched in her arms as she punched the air, emphasizing her words with each throw.

"Tell me!" I was bouncing up and down now, equally as excited as Marcie.

"They're coming to Briarhaven. They plan to film their Christmas special. Here. At Mystic Munchies."

My mouth dropped open.

"No. Freaking. Way." This had to be the coolest thing to happen to Briarhaven, and I'd seen a car turn into a dragon before. "How will they film it? Isn't it too warm out? It's only September. Who will they pick? Is there even room in here?"

"They'll shoot the judging in the main part of the shop and the baking in my test kitchen, where I teach classes."

"I didn't know you taught classes." I tried to imagine Marcie as a teacher. She'd either be terrifyingly effective or scare people into never baking again. It was a toss-up, really.

"When the mood strikes." Marcie went to the counter and opened a huge leather-bound ledger and flipped through a few pages. "They want to start filming in two weeks."

"What? That isn't all that far away. Have they cast this season already?"

"Nope, and here's the kicker. They want to pull contestants from Briarhaven. I'm supposed to make a list of people who might want to be on the show, as well as spread the word about the auditions. It will be a limited cast, since it is just their Christmas special and not a full season. Auditions will need to be sent in by the end of the week."

"That's . . ." I had a million thoughts. My heart pounded in my chest. *I could do this.* I'd come here to ask for work, to see if Marcie would take me on, as I was dying to learn some of her secrets of how she infused her baked goods with magick. But this? This could skyrocket my career. I'd been running a fairly successful YouTube cooking channel for a while now, but sometimes I wondered if people really came for my recipes, or just to see what cute outfit I was wearing that day. More often than not, the comments centered on my looks and not on what I was making. And while that *could* be flattering, I wanted people to take my cooking seriously.

Still. *Bewitching Bake Off*? This could be huge.

"Sign me up, Marcie. I'd love to audition."

"Och, the camera would love you. I'll get you all the information you need, hen." Marcie glanced around the bakery. "I have so much work to do in here. I'll need to clean this place top to bottom and make room for the production crew."

I saw my opening.

"Actually, that's why I stopped by today. I was hoping you'd be interested in taking an intern on."

"An intern? Do you know someone looking for work?"

"Aye. Me." I held my chin high as Marcie turned and glanced at my dress and heels. I knew what she was thinking. It was what everyone thought when they saw me. *Beautiful girl with not a brain cell in her precious wee head.*

"What kind of butter would you use for a croissant?"

"A higher-fat one," I answered, my eyebrows winging up my forehead.

"Why would a cookie be dry and crumbly?"

"Too much flour," I said automatically.

"And burn too easily?"

"Not enough flour." I grinned as she gave me a considering look. "I have a YouTube channel where I share my recipes. But I'm not a very proficient baker, *yet.* Though I really love it. I just know I have so much more to learn. And I think I can do that. Here. With you."

"I don't like too much chitchat," Marcie warned.

Hope bloomed. I bobbed my head.

"Understood."

"And I won't be able to train much until after this show is over."

"Of course."

"No perfumes in my kitchen."

"Got it."

"No boyfriends either." Marcie glanced pointedly at the window, and I turned to see three different men, all strangers, who were lined up outside the glass door. "Men don't line up here like that for me."

"Oh." I winced and turned back. "I can't help—"

"It's not your fault you're beautiful, Lyra. We'll figure out a way to keep any creeps at bay. Now, give me your email, and I'll send the audition information, as well as the employment forms, over to you."

"Wait, you'll hire me? I'm okay with just interning if you're not certain."

"Do I look like I don't know my own mind?" Scary Marcie was back, muscular arms crossed over her formidable chest. I gulped.

"No, ma'am."

"Then I'll see you tomorrow. Five in the morning. Don't be late."

"Five—"

Marcie glared and I swallowed the rest of what I was going to say.

"Right, I'll see you then. Thanks, Marcie. I won't let you down."

"I don't expect that you will."

Surprised but cheered by her confidence in me, I flipped the lock and stepped outside, studiously ignoring the men who tried to speak to me, and sailed down the sidewalk, a smile on my face.

A chance to be on my favorite reality show *and* a new job?

Despite the mud that stained my favorite dress, running into *him*, and the odd darkness that cloaked the midday sky, today was officially my new favorite day.

CHAPTER TWO

Rabbie Barclay

Bloody hell, but she'd felt amazing.

Her scent was just as I remembered, a heady mix of citrus and vanilla, and it had taken everything in my power not to drag Lyra behind a tree and kiss her until our painful memories were eradicated and only tomorrow mattered.

Sighing, I slammed my laptop closed and whirled in my chair, leaning my head back against the smooth leather as I rubbed my eyes, replaying the scene like I had a thousand times before.

Thunder sounded in the distance, a low rumble shaking the thin panes of glass in my bedroom window. A warning.

A tapping sound caught my ear, and at first I ignored it, head bent over my books, focused on studying for my upcoming finals. When the sound grew louder, I whirled, a smile springing to my lips. Lyra stood at the window, bundled into a rain slicker, impossibly beautiful.

And crying.

Racing over, I slid the window open and reached for her, but she ducked back. Tears streamed, and her lavender-blue eyes were wild in her face. She reminded me of a mouse, cornered and scared, and I swung one leg out of the window to go to her.

"No, Rab. Just stay."

"Tell me what's wrong." My heart hammered in my chest. I'd never seen this expression on her face before, and I'd do anything in my power to erase it.

"It's my mum. She . . . I heard them fighting. Again. This time she means it. She's having us pack. We're leaving in the morning."

I'd never really understood the expression "my heart stopped" before, because logically it didn't make sense, but in this moment, I swear mine did. It was like time stood still, and all I could see was the world of pain in Lyra's endless eyes.

"She can't mean it. Surely she's just taking the piss out of him?"

"No, Rab. She's serious this time. Dad's gone. Mum's packed up. She's never packed up before. Not like this."

I swung my other leg through the window and slid to the ground, reaching for her. This time, she didn't step back, instead leaning into my arms, her shoulders shaking against my chest.

Lyra was my world. My everything.

I didn't care that everyone thought this was just "puppy love."

I knew, in every fiber of my being, that Lyra MacGregor was meant for me.

"They can't just make you leave, Lyra. Screw them. Listen to me . . ." I pulled her back, my hand clutching her chin, forcing her eyes to meet mine. "We can do this. Without them. You just have to stay."

"How, Rab?" Lyra's voice rasped, and thunder boomed, the threat closer now. "I can't just . . . stay. Where would I stay? What would I do?"

"I've been saving money—"

"Rab, no. It won't work. I'm too young."

"So what? I'm almost old enough to leave school." I held her when she tried to pull back, needing her to see. "Old enough to get a job. To get insurance. I've been saving money for years now."

"For a car, Rab. Not to take care of me."

"I'd walk the rest of my life if it meant I got to have you by my side." I pressed my lips to hers, my conviction burning through me.

"It's too—"

"It's not." I grabbed her hands when she pulled back, willing her to see. I could make this work. "It's not too hard. I can do this. What I can't do is lose you."

"Rab." Lyra's eyes were glossy with tears. She'd been hauntingly beautiful. And so, so, desperately sad.

"You have to believe, Lyra. I can't do that for you. I'll do everything else for you. I'll find you a home, make sure you finish school, help you get work as a chef. Anything you want. But I can't make you believe in us."

"I believe in us." Lyra pushed out her lower lip, her chest rising and falling as she struggled to stop crying.

"Then meet me. First thing tomorrow. I'll be packed and have a place for us." Already my mind scrambled for ideas, but it didn't matter. By tomorrow, I'd have a plan. I wouldn't fail her.

"But—"

"Rabbie!" my mum called from just outside the room. "Rain's coming. Come help with getting the washing in."

"Aye, Mum. Coming."

"Rab—"

"Shhh." I placed my lips ever so softly over Lyra's, silencing her. When I pulled back, she gave me a watery smile. But for the first time since she'd come, hope stole across her face. "Tomorrow. First thing. Meet me at the barn." An old barn just outside of town was our favorite place to escape from the world.

"Aye, Rab. I promise."

"Rab!" Mum's voice was closer now, and I jumped back through the window. Glancing over my shoulder to make sure Lyra was out of sight, I pasted a bland expression on my face when both my parents stepped into my room.

"I was just closing the window," I explained. I gestured to the desk. "Sorry, was studying."

"Rab." Something in my dad's face caused my stomach to twist.

"Rabbie." My mum walked forward and wrapped an arm around my shoulders. "We heard. We didn't mean to, but we were taking the washing in."

"I—"

"You can't do this, son. You're too young." My dad, as usual, cut to the thick of it, his tone stern. "You think you're in love, but it's just . . . hormones. Everyone thinks they're in love at your age. I know it feels all big and real right now, but it will pass. And you can't throw away your future for some lass."

"She's not just some lass! I love her," I said, my voice trembling with the vehemence of youth and certainty.

"Aye, so you think you do. But it's impossible, what you're suggesting. Lyra isn't old enough to leave her family. To come live with . . . you? Where? Here? We wouldn't agree to that. Nor are we even sure it's legal." My mum's brow furrowed when she smoothed a lock of my hair, and I pushed her hand away.

"You're about to sit exams, Rab. You've got an incredible future ahead of you. Promise me you won't throw it away. Not for just a bonnie lass. Not for . . . a MacGregor. Of all people. You could do better for your future than to saddle yourself to a family riddled with curses. They're a blight on this community." My father's eyes bored into mine, and for the first time in my life, I lied outright to my parents.

"I suppose it was foolish, wasn't it? To think we'd have a future. I guess . . . I just got caught up. You're right. Lyra's nothing special. She's just a pretty face." I shrugged one shoulder, pretending like I was agreeing with my parents when everything inside me wanted to scream.

"That's a good lad. I knew you'd see it our way. It's hard, I know. But in a year, this won't matter at all." With a curt nod, my father left, the matter decided as far as he was concerned.

"Rab, honey." My mum pulled me in for a hug, and I let her, staying ramrod straight, fury working its way through me. She leaned back and looked at me, concern on her pretty face. "I know you care for her. I'm proud of you for offering to help her, I am. It means I've raised a good son. But, honey, it's time for the MacGregors to move on. It's become too hard to keep their curse at bay. In the long run, even though I'm sure this hurts now, it's what is best for you and for Briarhaven as a whole. Sometimes we have to sacrifice for the greater good. You ken?"

"Aye," I said, my nails digging so hard into my palms that they sliced the skin. "I need to get back to my studying."

"Don't stay up too late." Mum squeezed my shoulder and left, closing the door behind her.

The skies opened, the wind sounding like a woman wailing, and I shut the window. My pulse picked up, and I gulped several deep breaths before I could even think straight. Glancing once more at the closed door, I dug out a small duffel bag and packed. And in the wee hours of the morning, I slid from my window, like I'd done so many times before, and raced through the wet fields to wait for the love of my life at our special place.

And I waited.

And waited.

Far past the time when the bells rang for school.

Far past the time when I would be at lunch.

And finally, as the light drew long over the hills, and hunger clawed at my stomach, I hoisted my bag over my shoulder and left the barn, defeated. Taking the long way home, I walked past Lyra's house, but I already knew.

She was gone.

It had been years since Lyra MacGregor had torn my heart out of my chest and stomped on it, proving my father right that our relationship was no more than puppy love. At times I couldn't tell what I'd hated more—Lyra leaving or her proving my parents right—but either way I'd been heartbroken.

And now she was back—had been back, in fact, for a while now—and living in Briarhaven suddenly felt like trying to navigate a minefield. Still, out of some sort of asinine need to punish myself, I took her grandmother, Broca, for walks every week. Sometimes Lyra was there, stomping up the stairs and studiously ignoring me, and other times she was nowhere to be seen. Yet still, I hung on to every glimpse of her that I could get, like a dying man desperate for a drop of water.

Not that I'd ever admit it to her.

It had taken me years to be rid of the seething disappointment and then anger that she hadn't stayed with me. In my early twenties, I'd finally seen how ridiculous my offer had been. *How could I have tried to take care of her at such an age?* Logically, my parents' "advice" had eventually made sense.

But I'd been grounded for a month for attempting to run away with her, and throughout that time, my father had told me repeatedly why to *never trust a MacGregor*. And somehow, his words had eventually turned my heart bitter. Toward Lyra. She'd proven it—hadn't she? Not only had she left me without another word, but she'd never once tried to contact me since.

Her return to Briarhaven had unleashed every feeling I'd been convinced I'd long since buried, and I was still mad about it. I'd even briefly entertained the possibility of a friendship with her when she'd returned, but she'd immediately rebuffed me on first sight.

There was no other way around it.

No way to gloss over the truth.

Lyra MacGregor made me blindly, searingly *angry*, and as far as I was concerned, she was a menace to this town. It certainly didn't help that she'd grown into a blazingly beautiful woman, the kind who made men and women alike stop in their tracks when she walked by. Nor did it help that I was told her YouTube followers increased in multitudes by the day, simply because it was impossible not to look at her.

And still, much to my deep frustration, I found a part of myself rooting for her, even when she'd carelessly thrown our love away.

But I would do so . . . from afar. I didn't wish her harm. Or have a deep need to seek any vengeance for breaking my heart, never once contacting me again, and teaching me that women could never be trusted.

I only wanted peace.

Which was a word that was not synonymous with the MacGregors, that much I knew. Instead, I was stuck in this purgatory of knowing Lyra was close by, but understanding that being with her only led to a broken heart.

And yet.

The feel of her body against mine had triggered some core memory in me, and I'd been an absolute mess since—even now, hours later. I couldn't think straight, and all I could do was lose myself in the promise of a future that had never come to be.

My phone rang, a welcome distraction, and I swiped the screen to see Knox's name.

"Hey, mate, how's it going, then?"

"Yeah, well enough. Business is good, but things will slow a bit as we head toward the end of the year." I was an accountant for most of the small businesses in town, and I loved my job. I loved numbers, the way they just made sense, all neat and orderly in tidy little rows.

"That's actually great to hear. Because I've got a favor to ask you."

Knox and I had been best friends since high school, and our relationship had only grown stronger through the years. He rarely asked for anything, and he'd done nothing but help Briarhaven, so I was inclined to say yes before I even knew what he was going to ask for.

"So there's this reality show coming to film in Briarhaven—"

"Nope," I said, standing up, amused that he thought he'd even have a chance of convincing me. "No. Full stop. Not me."

"Mate, please? It's going to be a huge promotional opportunity for Briarhaven, and you're the prettiest one of my friends."

"Don't tell Liam that." I snorted. Liam owned the pub in town and arguably was equally as handsome as me. Not that I much noticed, but the *ladies* certainly noticed him. "Speaking of . . . He'd love this shite. Ask him."

"Can't. This is a busy time of year for him. And you already admitted you weren't busy."

"Bloody hell, Knox. No."

I ended the call, because I was not going to sit there and listen to all the reasons he thought I should go on a reality show.

I liked my life quiet. Predictable.

Even my magick, though incredibly strong, was predictable. My family had strengths in transmutation and activation spells, both areas that made life significantly easier—when I chose to use it.

Like now. When my phone rang again, Knox's name flashing on the screen, I pointed a finger at it and muttered a spell under my breath. In seconds, it had morphed from a ringing phone to the latest crime thriller, and I smiled, pleased with myself.

A wee dram and a quiet night with my new book were exactly what I needed to forget all about my disconcerting run-in with Lyra.

Or so I hoped.

CHAPTER THREE

Lyra

"I got a job!" I squealed, banging the door open to the house.

"I thought you *had* a job?" Nova asked from where she was slumped in a chair, sketch pad in hand. Nova was my younger sister, the exact opposite of me, and one of my favorite people in the world. Despite her annoying habit of using logic and sarcasm to navigate her way through life.

"I mean, I do. But that almost feels like a hobby I've been able to monetize." My YouTube channel had really developed from just that—a hobby I loved sharing with the world—to a viable stream of income. But I'd never actually had a real job before, not one where I had to show up on time and work under an actual boss, due to the pesky nature of the curse that plagued the MacGregor bloodline.

A curse I was doing my damnedest to ignore.

For years, my sisters and I had lived like nomads, packing up every three to six months and fleeing town after town. Running—that's the more honest word. A furious witch had cursed our ancestor, Bonelle MacGregor, and every MacGregor since had been unable to put down roots. No matter how badly we wanted to belong, the curse made every new home unbearable within months.

We'd recently returned to our childhood home in Briarhaven, and miraculously, Sloane cracked a third of the curse, buying us, and the town, some breathing room. The Charms, our local coven, had been working nonstop ever since to keep the rest of the curse from coming back.

I'd like to say I was helping, too, but fate had decided to play a mean trick on me because my magick never showed up on my twenty-fifth birthday like it did for every other witch we knew.

"And somehow you thought it would be *more* fun to work for someone else?" Nova arched a brow at me, pulling me from my thoughts. She wore ripped jeans and a Pixies T-shirt, and had her dark hair wrapped into two space buns on either side of her head.

"Of course it will," I trilled, dropping my handbag onto the side table and skipping across the room. Bending, I kissed Nova's cheek and then gravitated automatically toward the kitchen—my happy place. "I mean, Marcie's terrifying. But she knows so much. Just think of what I could learn from her. And you know I learn better by being hands-on."

I crinkled my nose. A memory of throwing schoolbooks against the wall in frustration flashed through my mind. Seeing the look on my face, Nova winced. She'd witnessed my frustration with paying attention to lessons in school. It was one of the reasons why I'd flourished when I had finally been able to work for myself. It was best if I did things on my own terms and at my own pace.

"So long as she's nice to you. I'm not sure I can win in a fight against her."

I laughed. It had always been this way—my sisters and me against the world.

"I don't think you'll need to throw down. In fact . . . I even saw her smile today."

Nova gasped, almost dropping her sketch pad, and I nodded in agreement. Reaching into the fridge, I found a ripe tomato and a fresh ball of mozzarella and pulled them out to put on the chopping board.

"I have *never* seen that woman smile. She just . . . doles out baked goods with a militant efficiency that would make my heart warm if I wasn't scared of showing emotion around her."

"I swear to the goddess, Nova, I almost turned tail and ran. If she hadn't asked me to lock the door seconds after I'd seen the smile, I might have."

Intrigued, Nova tossed her sketch pad onto the table and swung her legs to hang over the side of the chair.

"Why in the world would Marcie ask you to lock up at this time of day?" Nova glanced at the Apple Watch on her wrist and then squinted in confusion at the window, where it was dark as night outside. "Wait—"

"Oh, good, you're both home." The front door swung open, bringing with it a sharp gust of wind carrying the smell of damp earth. Sloane, my older sister, dressed in leggings, UGG boots, and an oversized jumper, carried her emberwolf, Blue, through the open door. Broca, our grandmother, glided inside after her, wearing houndstooth culottes, caramel knee-high boots, and a mossy knit jumper. There was barely a hitch to her step, as she'd almost fully recovered from her hip surgery. Her falcon, Iris, sat on her shoulder. "We've got a problem."

"Wait, I want to know why Marcie locked Lyra in the bakery," Nova protested, pushing her lower lip out.

"She locked you in the bakery?" Sloane's voice sharpened, and I laughed, putting my hands in the air. Blue struggled from her arms and took flight, landing clumsily on the countertop, his tongue lolling from his mouth. Blue looked mostly like a gray Boston Terrier would, aside from the gorgeous dragon wings that were tucked at his back. His favorite food was cheese, and his eyes were currently glued to the mozzarella on my cutting board.

"Stand down, soldier." Pulling out my favorite knife, I sliced the mozzarella and handed a delighted Blue a piece. "She asked me to lock the door behind me so she could quietly freak out about some most excellent news."

"What news?" Broca asked, pulling her leather driving gloves off and putting them in a bowl on the side table by the door. Iris flew from her shoulder to her favorite perch at the top of the kitchen cabinets, where she could watch everyone below her.

The main floor of our wee house was one large open room. The kitchen stood at the back of the house, anchoring the room, and a couch and two faded armchairs were tucked under a large picture window that looked out over the street. On the other side of the front door, a long dining table lined the wall. Two pillars stood in the middle of the room, the foundational supports my father had been unable to get rid of when they'd renovated the space into one big room, and they still bore the marks of our height growth through the years.

"They're going to film *Bewitching Bake Off*'s Christmas special here in Briarhaven in two weeks!" I squealed, bouncing on my feet. "And I get to audition for it!"

"No way!" Sloane beamed at me and crossed the room to give me a hug. "That's cracking news."

"Oh, Lyra, you'll be perfect for this." Broca joined us in the kitchen and pressed a kiss to my cheek. "You're just a natural for television."

"Thank you," I said, doing a little shimmy. This news was far too exciting to sit still over. Sloane leaned away from the knife I still held in my hand.

"Easy there, killer."

"Och, right." I laughed and returned to the cutting board. "But Marcie has agreed to hire me to work at the bakery. So maybe she can teach me the magick she uses in her recipes, or at least some of it, before filming starts. If I get cast, that is."

"You'll get cast." Sloane heaved herself up onto the counter, next to Blue, reminding me of all the times we'd sat like this—Nova sketching in her chair, Sloane on the counter—while I put together meals for our wee family.

"But we do need to talk about your magick." Broca put the kettle on and reached for her favorite teacup, one with dragons etched in gold on the side. "Have you looked outside?"

We all turned to look out the front window where darkness blanketed the street.

"Oh." My stomach dropped. While I'd noticed the strange darkness, I'd been too caught up in my excitement over the reality show and my new employment to give it too much thought. It wasn't entirely unusual for Scotland to go gray and murky in the fall, so it hadn't really pinged my radar as being something more ominous.

A knock sounded, sending Blue into a cacophony of barking as he took flight toward the front door.

"Expecting someone?" Nova asked, catching Blue and cradling him to her chest before opening the door.

"Emergency Charms meeting," Sloane said, and my cheerful mood plummeted. The Charms were the coven we'd inherited legacy seats on when we'd returned to Briarhaven. Sloane had resisted their help and sisterhood, yet somehow had found herself president by the time her side of the curse was broken. I'd always been more open to embracing our witchy ways, and being a part of a coven had excited me.

Until the focus had turned to me and magick. Or lack thereof, apparently. We'd been trying to think of ways to bloom my magick, but so far, nothing had worked.

As a witch? I was a failure.

"Hiya, Tam, Felicity," Nova said, ushering two women inside. Tam, a lanky woman with short, cropped hair and a penchant for early-morning runs, followed Felicity, a blowsy mum with an overly stuffed tote bag, into the house. Nova peeked her head outside. "No Deidre or Raven?"

"Both are at work. But with most of us here we should be able to crack on all right, no?" Tam asked, reaching out to scratch Blue's ears.

"What about Mandy?" I asked. Everyone in the room stilled. Mandy Meadows, the previous president of the Charms, had been formally voted out when our grandmother had invoked an emergency coven ordinance. Since that time, Mandy had refused to attend another coven meeting, and despite our attempts to reach out to her, she'd largely become a shut-in. Which, technically, made running a coven a touch tricky without all members at our disposal. I liked to believe in the good in everyone, and though Sloane was more than happy to ignore our former president, I couldn't help but feel bad for her. The Charms had been Mandy's entire world.

"Mandy was unreachable." Sloane hopped off the counter and motioned for me to join them at the dining table. Quickly, I chopped up some basil I pulled from a pot by the back window, drizzled some olive oil and balsamic over the tomato and mozzarella, and then added a few wedges of focaccia to the side. Carrying it over to where the women chattered around the table, I put the tray down, away from Blue's excited face, and dropped into a chair.

"Oh, this looks delicious." Felicity shoved some loose hair back into her scrunchie and reached for the cheese.

"No protein in sight." Tam shook her head sadly.

"Cheese *is* protein," Felicity argued, indignant.

"It is, but is it quality protein?"

Blue lunged forward and snuck a piece from the plate, and I swallowed a laugh.

"He seems to think so," Broca said, waving a pink-tipped finger in the air. "Ladies. Enough. The darkness?"

We all hushed and turned toward the window. There was no disguising the lack of light outside as bad weather or just a storm blowing through, particularly because even from here I could make out the stars pricking the inky sky.

"What time is it again?" I asked, worry gnawing at my gut.

"Just past eleven," Nova said, checking her watch. *In the morning.*

"We're still going to have the Mabon festival this weekend, right?" Felicity's eyes rounded as she turned to Sloane. "I'd promised the kids they might get to see dragons."

"Surely there's more important—"

"Yes, we'll still be hosting the festival," Broca said over Sloane, who sighed and slumped back into her chair. She, much to her annoyance, as she wasn't much of a party planner, was hosting a Mabon festival for Briarhaven. It was being held up in the hills, near where our father lived with the dragons, and the entire town was buzzing with excitement over the prospect of their first proper party with the dragons.

"I'm really looking forward to it," I said, reaching out to squeeze Sloane's arm. "It'll give us a chance to connect with Dad more. And who knows? Maybe being around the dragons will help my magick come to the surface."

"Still nothing?" Felicity asked, a sympathetic expression on her face. My shoulders hunched as I gave a sad shake of my head.

"That would be epic to finally get your magick during a dragon party. Maybe you'll shoot lasers out of your bum," Nova said, and I slid her a baleful glance.

"If so, I hope they shoot sparkles everywhere," I deadpanned, and she grinned.

"I'm calling you Sparklefarts from now on," Nova said.

"Fine by me, *Shorts*." Nova's eyes rounded as I used a nickname I had sworn to never use again after an unfortunate food poisoning incident had caused Nova to soil a favorite pair of shorts.

"Ew," Sloane said, closing her eyes, clearly recalling *that* particular day.

"Ladies!" Broca clapped her hands, and we snapped back to attention. "Can we pay attention to the darkness?"

"I don't like the way you say it. Like it's the plague or something." I shifted in my chair, uncomfortable.

"Are the wards not holding anymore?" Tam asked. Last year, we'd placed wards with the fae who lived in the hills around Briarhaven to help shroud Sloane's curse. So far, together with the Charms working their spells, the wards had held, and everyone in Briarhaven had enjoyed a relatively curse-free year.

"They're not, no. With the loss of Mandy's help, they've slowly waned in strength. And if this is truly what we think it is, well, it's going to be even harder to disguise from the news than the snow was with Sloane's curse." Broca gave me a sympathetic look. The last iteration of our curse had come when Sloane had stepped into her powers and constant and unrelenting snow had been unleashed on Briarhaven.

My breath caught. "The show."

"What show?" Felicity reached for another piece of cheese and blinked at us.

"They're going to film *Bewitching Bake Off*'s Christmas special here."

Felicity shrieked and Blue tumbled off the table, catching himself before he hit the ground and soaring around the room, barking hysterically.

"Sorry, I'm sorry. *Sorry*, Blue." Felicity held a hand to her heart, bouncing in her seat. "Seriously, though? That's my favorite show."

"Mine too." Felicity and I shared mutual looks of understanding across the table.

"It's most magickals' favorite show," Broca said. There were communities like Briarhaven all over the world, a magickal network of those who lived their lives on the fringes of society, and apparently, *Bewitching Bake Off* was a hit with them all. "Which means . . ."

"We have a massive problem," Sloane said, and my excitement fell off a cliff.

CHAPTER FOUR

Lyra

I was getting tired of being the one everyone made excuses for.

After the Charms meeting, where we weren't able to come up with any solution for the darkness that now shrouded Briarhaven, I needed a moment to myself. Stepping outside to my wee garden, I took a deep breath, and then another, allowing the soft scents of damp earth and herbs to soothe me. Aside from the kitchen, my garden was my happy space, a place where I could work in peace—where nobody was judging me. Between the Charms, the watchful eyes of Briarhaven, and my YouTube channel, I had very few spaces in my life that weren't open to outside scrutiny.

It had been a few weeks since my birthday.

And somehow, my magick hadn't managed to manifest. At least not that any of us could see. We'd tried it all: levitation, freezing, transmutation, healing, and so on. But nothing had worked. It was like my magick was stuck, buried deep inside me, and somehow unable to stretch its wings to fly. I *felt* it. I knew it was there. My magick hummed beneath my skin, but no matter how many times I reached for it, I couldn't quite manage to use it in a spell.

Broca assured me, over and over, that some witches were late bloomers when it came to their powers.

I was just frustrated, and frankly, a bit gutted.

I'd been so excited for my birthday, and ready to step into my new powers, and now, with the Charms unable to hold off the next iteration of our curse, I felt more like a failure than ever before.

Maybe it was true. Maybe I was just a pretty face, as much as the thought made my stomach turn, but at the moment, I wasn't bringing much else to the table. Certainly not any magickal powers that could actually *help* Briarhaven, that was for certain.

Sighing, I bent to examine my garden in the dim light of the lantern hung outside the back door and pulled back, blinking in confusion.

All the weeds were gone, the brambles neatly trimmed back, and a neat pile of cucumbers had been pulled and stacked for me.

"What on earth?" I murmured, tilting my head in confusion. Picking up one of the cucumbers, I examined the end. It had been evenly sliced, not torn from the root, and cut with precision.

If it's not harvested to your satisfaction, I, of course, can do so differently.

I dropped the cucumber and shrieked as a ball of lavender sparkles fluttered in front of my face. Warding my face with my hands, I ducked as the back door swung open.

"What's the problem, Sparklefarts?"

"Glitterbug! Glitterbug!" I shrieked, racing to the back door where Nova stood, gaping at me.

"What's a glitterbug?" Nova asked, grabbing my arm.

"I don't knooooow," I wailed, not a huge fan of bugs, or really *anything* that flew at my face unannounced.

I wasn't told you would be so dramatic.

I blinked as the glitterbug slowed its movements and came to rest on a fence post.

"You're not a bug," I said, stating the obvious, as Nova and I gaped at the new arrival standing on our fence, small sword raised in the air.

"She also comes with weapons," Nova observed.

It seems your basic observational skills are working. The creature rolled her eyes, and I started, realizing that I was hearing her voice in my head.

"Can you hear her?" I turned to Nova, whose eyes widened. Slowly she shook her head.

"She's absolutely enchanting," I breathed, now that I'd had time to adjust to the new arrival. She was essentially a lavender-colored mouse, with sparkly fur, and on her back were the most gloriously intricate golden wings. They looked like lace come to life, butterfly wings encased in gold, and she shook them out as she padded across the top rail of the fence toward us, sheathing her sword.

"Hello, gorgeous," I whispered, holding out my palm.

She lifted her head and then took my invitation, fluttering over to land in my palm. I gave Nova a look like I was dying inside from the cuteness of it all, as she stood and saluted me with a paw to her forehead.

"What are you, sweet thing?" I asked. I was certain I'd never before seen such a creature equally as enchanting as she was fierce.

I'm a fluttermouse. Her voice was soft, like gentle wind chimes in a spring breeze.

"I can hear her," I said, turning to look at Nova. "She says she's a fluttermouse."

"And she's armed. Even better." Nova nodded her approval.

"Do you want to come in and meet the family?" I asked her, dying for Broca to take a look and tell me if this was what I thought it was. Hope bloomed and I blinked down at the wee gorgeous fluttermouse, my heart hammering.

Had my familiar finally arrived? I'd been aching for one, but unlike when Blue was ready for Sloane right on her birthday, I hadn't been gifted a familiar. Broca had informed me that sometimes it took time for the magickal world to find the right fit, and that the right one found you at *just* the right time. But thus far, not a single magickal creature had approached me.

Until now, that is.

Aye, it's important that I meet your people.

A smile tugged the corners of my lips as the wee fluttermouse nodded. I gave Nova a look—*Can you believe how cute she is?*—

and then stepped back inside, where Sloane was busy slicing off thin scraps of cheese for Blue to chase around the room and Broca had settled back into her lounge chair, ready to gossip about the Charms meeting.

"Look! Look who I found in the garden!" I said, all but bouncing in my heels, and held out my hands so Broca and Sloane could see. Blue launched himself from the counter, but Sloane was quick and plucked him from the air before he could dive-bomb me and the new arrival.

But I want to see.

Shock filled me as I glanced over at Blue.

"Was that Blue? Did I just hear him too?" The voice had been very different from the fluttermouse's, and wonder made me a touch giddy. Was my magick finally coming in?

"I'm not sure. Blue, tell Lyra a joke."

What do witches put on their bagels?

Blue looked at me expectantly, his tongue lolling out of his mouth.

"I have no idea? Lox?"

Scream cheese.

Blue chuffed out his little laughing sound, and I couldn't help it, I laughed too.

He's quite proud of himself, isn't he?

I looked down to see the fluttermouse peering up at Blue, but with an indulgent expression on her face. It was true. I could hear both of their distinct voices in my head now. Excitement washed through me, making me just a touch dizzy, and I dragged in a deep breath to calm myself.

"Do you have a name? What should I call you? I suppose I should introduce myself. I'm Lyra." I held the fluttermouse up to my face so she could look into my eyes. "And this is Nova, Sloane, Blue, and Broca."

Pleased to meet you. I'm Ruth.

The fluttermouse stood in my palm and gave a little curtsy.

"Oh, her name's Ruth. That's a grand name, isn't it? You're just gorgeous, aren't you?" I couldn't take my eyes off her shimmering wings. They looked incredibly delicate, like thin gold threads spun together, an intricate spiderweb of lace, and I couldn't imagine how they'd hold her weight.

Thank you. So are you, it seems. We match, don't we?

Ruth twirled in my palm, and I realized she was comparing her fur to the unique color of my eyes. For some reason, having a matching familiar made something click inside me. Like finding a missing piece of a puzzle.

"Are you . . . are you mine?" I whispered, barely able to contain my excitement.

Aye, lass. I'm yours. And it's glad I am to finally be with you.

"She's mine," I said, bouncing up and down in glee and then gasped when Ruth went flying from my hand. She caught herself and took flight, and Blue squirmed out of Sloane's arms, meeting the fluttermouse midair.

"Blue, careful . . ." I lunged forward, but no warning was needed.

Blue sniffed Ruth and then gave her a delicate "boop" with his nose before the two took off in a fun game of chase. Ruth flew like a butterfly, darting in all directions, while Blue waddled after her like wobbly pigeon just learning to fly. I just stood, hand at my heart, in awe of the both of them as they wheeled in circles around the living room.

"A fluttermouse," I breathed, turning in excitement to Broca. "I've never even heard of such a thing."

Iris flapped her wings from above, and Ruth raised her sword.

Is she . . . ?

"Och, that's Iris. Broca's familiar. She's fine." I gave Broca a look, and Broca waved a finger in Iris's direction.

"She'll not harm the wee one, I promise."

"Her coloring is gorgeous," Nova said, sketch pad already in hand. "Those wings . . ."

"Look how she sparkles," I gasped as Ruth flew beneath the beam of light from a lamp and both her wings and fur glimmered in the light. "Do you see? She *sparkles*."

"A sparkly gift for Sparklefarts." Nova smirked.

Ruth darted across the room and bopped Nova on the forehead with one wee paw, and I gasped.

"Ruth!"

She's being quite rude.

"She's just joking. I promise. It's fine."

"Okay, okay." Nova held her hands up gently, her tone soothing, as she kept her eyes trained on the tiny assassin fluttering in front of her. "I'm sorry. I'll retire that nickname. I like your attitude, Ruth. Small but fierce."

"It appears you shouldn't underestimate her," I said, my heart warming. Ruth flitted back, landing on my shoulder, and nestled into the crook at my neck. Reaching up, I stroked a finger over her silky fur and smiled. Her weight was light, barely noticeable, and yet her small body hummed with energy.

"This is quite a welcome arrival. It supports the research I've been doing on your magick, Lyra. Did you know that fluttermice come from the Hebrides and are born from a very specific sect of witches?" Broca's lips twitched when my eyes widened.

"Does that mean—"

"Aye, lass. Ruth's arrival supports my suspicions. I know what your magick is."

"You do?" I bounced and then caught Ruth as she tumbled from my neck with a squeak. "Oh my goddess. Ruth. I'm sorry. Sorry! I am not used to having you there."

You're very bouncy. Ruth slanted me a look, and I giggled. It was true, I tended to be a touch exuberant with my enthusiasm.

"It's about damn time," Nova said, and I glared at her. She blew me a kiss, softening her words.

"Haud your wheesht, Nova. It's not about you. At least not today. Give Lyra a chance to hear what's to become of her," Sloane said, cradling Blue in her arms.

"Really, just a lovely way with words." I rolled my eyes at Sloane as Ruth toddled about in my palms. "You make it sound like a death sentence."

"Please tell me she's going to be a troll, please tell me she's going to be a troll." Nova screwed her eyes shut and crossed her fingers.

"You nasty witch," I gasped at her. Trolls were decidedly beastly, and frankly, quite gross looking.

You're a hearth witch, Ruth said, and my breath caught as I looked down at where the wee fluttermouse wiped her sword with a small cloth.

"A hearth witch?!" I exclaimed, and Broca's face dropped.

"Damn it. She beat me to it." Broca sighed but then shifted and smiled gently at me. "Aye, my dear. You're a hearth witch. Of hearth and home. It's a lovely, welcoming, nurturing type of magick you'll have, and one that I think suits you precisely."

My jaw worked, but nothing came out.

A hearth witch. I peered down at wee Ruth, whose warm brown eyes seemed ancient and all-knowing. *Of hearth and home, your magick is born; with steady heart, your gift is sworn.*

"Of hearth and home, your magick is born; with steady heart, your gift is sworn," I repeated, and I felt it.

I *felt* it.

Magick unfolded inside me, as though awakening from a long nap, stretching and unrolling as it curled through my body until the tips of my fingers tingled. Excitement raced through me, and I cradled Ruth close as I danced around the room.

"I can feel it. I can feel it. It's here—my magick is here." My entire body quivered with energy, and I was more exuberant than I would have been finding a sample sale on Louboutin heels. Today was the beginning of the rest of my life. I skidded to a stop. "Wait, what does a hearth witch do?"

"Maybe she cleans?" Sloane suggested, and I whirled on her, my mouth dropping open.

"How dare you!"

"What's wrong with cleaning?" Sloane raised her hands, hunching her shoulders.

"I don't need magick to clean," I protested. "You know I'm careful with my things." It was true too. Every handbag I owned was tucked in its dust bag, shoes were kept in their original boxes, jewelry was categorized and secured. My makeup table was a thing of beauty—aesthetically pleasing, portable, *and* functional.

I had just hoped that my magick would be something a touch more special than simply enhancing mundane everyday tasks like cleaning. I mean, Sloane could travel through fire if she wanted to and talk to baby dragons. Speeding up my Sunday chores with magickal assistance certainly paled in comparison.

"A hearth witch commands the domain of her home, as well as the kitchen. She'll be able to set magickal protection wards, infuse her food and drink with spells, and craft comfort rituals for those in need."

My mouth dropped open, and then I squealed and raced to the kitchen. Gently, I placed Ruth on the counter before flinging my arms wide and doing a dramatic shimmy.

"If we were closer to town, there'd likely be a three-car pileup outside," Nova observed.

"Indeed." Sloane laughed.

"Does anyone fancy a bite?" I rubbed my hands together, almost vibrating with excitement.

"Maybe just a wee scone or a touch of soup?" Broca suggested, pulling a tartan blanket off the edge of the couch and tucking it around her lap. "There's a bite to the air, isn't there?"

"Shall I put the fire on?" Sloane asked, but Broca waved it away.

"No sense now. Tomorrow, yes, if the cold snap keeps up. It's early this year, isn't it, though?"

"How about a wee cheese toastie and a bit of veggie soup?" Easy enough to make, but it would allow me to test my magick. Blue's head shot up at the word "cheese," and he scrambled across the room to land in a heap next to Ruth, who darted out of the way seconds before he would have landed on her.

"Sorry about that, Ruth. We're still working on landings," Sloane said. Blue's mouth hung open in a happy smile, and he didn't seem the least bit bothered by the fact he'd almost squished my familiar.

He's a bit uncouth, isn't he? Ruth sidled closer to me and tilted her head at Blue's mile-wide grin. *Charming, though.*

"That's probably most men," I said, lining my ingredients out on the counter. Ruth let out a squeaky little laugh, and I turned to her, charmed myself.

I can help.

"How?"

Picking up my knife, I sliced the corner off the block of cheddar and tossed it across the room, and Blue gave chase. Sloane, with her powers of levitation, took it up, and a keep-away game ensued with Blue zooming around the room after the bit of cheese while I began the meal prep uninterrupted.

I can chop.

Ruth reached between her wings and pulled out her sword again. She swished it back and forth in the air, so fast the movement was just a blur, and I gaped at her.

"Bloody hell, Ruth. You'd be an absolute menace in a fight, wouldn't you?"

I've been known to hold my own.

I was afraid to ask just what Ruth had been forced to hold her own against. Instead, I pointed at a carrot. "Chop that to bits if it's not—"

Thwack!

Ruth slammed her wee sword down, and it sliced cleanly through the carrot and forever eradicated the word "cute" from my description of Ruth.

"Is she really helping?" Nova asked, crossing the room to peer over the breakfast bar to where Ruth's sword was now a blur of movement, perfectly chopped bits of carrot piling up next to her.

"Incredibly so," I said, admiring her movements. "She's like a sous chef on speed."

"No kidding." Nova whistled in appreciation. "She's a wee beastie, isn't she, then? Tiny killer in the kitchen."

Already Ruth was moving on from the carrot to the celery I'd taken out, and we watched in fascination as she moved with precision through her task.

"Right, let's just crack on with this, shall we? I guess I'll just . . ." I paused, realizing that I no clue how to proceed. In one sense, I understood what it meant to infuse food with magick, but in another, I really had no idea. I usually considered magick to be used for highly specific and directed intentions. For example, if someone was sick and needed a magickal brew to cure them. But just to test magick for magick's sake? The task felt too broad, like it wasn't rooted in anything that made sense in my mind. I looked over at Broca, a helpline. "I don't really know what I'm supposed to do here. Automatically, I just want to make the meal the same way that I always would."

"Magick doesn't always have to have a purpose." Broca paused, raising one hand in the air. "Actually, that's not entirely true. See, your magick is a tricky thing. Imagine it like . . ."

Sparkles appeared in the air in front of Broca's outstretched hands, and I clapped in appreciation. I was a sucker for anything that glittered.

"See, now, imagine this is your magick, you ken? It's waiting for direction." The sparkles swirled in a formation over Broca's head and then formed the words "Welcome, Ruth."

"Aww, that's lovely," I said.

"My magick needed my intention to make it work. So the purpose it served was to follow my lead. All magick is based on intent. But not all magick must serve a higher purpose, if that makes sense? You can use magick to help you cook. To speed a recipe along, or to convert one ingredient into a missing ingredient. Not every spell has to be in service to others. In fact, it's better that it's not, at least while you are learning. You can't go and heal someone with your medicinal broth if you haven't had a chance to work with your magick for a while first. So we start small. My suggestion? Bring your broth to a boil quickly."

"Oh!" I turned to the stove, delighted. "That's a great idea. Simple, easy, but will speed up the cooking process. I understand now."

"Your magick *wants* to be used," Broca agreed.

"Oh, slutty magick, I like it," Nova said, and I snickered.

Sloane finally gave Blue his cheese, and he collapsed on the couch, winded, while she wandered over to the kitchen to watch.

"So Lyra's got slutty magick and a tiny terror in the kitchen?" Sloane asked.

"I do not have slutty magick—"

"I mean, you might, you don't know that yet," Nova said, leaning her elbows on the counter, a teasing grin on her face. "You're a hearth witch. That covers kitchen and home. And a home has bedrooms. Sooooo . . ."

"So her magick can make the bed after she shags her date?" Sloane wondered, reaching over to grab a piece of carrot and popping it in her mouth.

"Or clean the sheets," Nova said.

"Can we focus, please?" I turned to my sisters, hands on my hips. "I don't have slutty magick. And even if I did, we wouldn't call it slutty magick because it's 2026 and we embrace a woman's right to choose who she wants to shag. 'Slutty' is a patriarchal concept."

Feminine power. Ruth raised one paw in the air, looking like a little militant feminist warrior with her glittery purple fur and sword at her side.

"Aye, that's it. Feminine power. And I am using mine to boil this damn broth."

Turning, I added some stock I'd made earlier that week to a pot and put it on the stove. Flipping the burner on, I stood back and focused on the pot.

"A watched pot never—"

"Wheesht," I hissed at Nova, waving a hand behind my back at her.

"Och, just you wait, Nova, you're going to be an absolute mess when your power comes in," Sloane said.

"Like you were, Miss Control Freak?" Nova asked.

"So what if I like to have things planned out?" Sloane countered.

Stomping my foot, I turned.

"Seriously?"

Ruth fluttered up in front of them, brandishing her sword.

"Sorry," Sloane and Nova said in unison and retreated farther into the living room.

Sweeping the neatly chopped vegetables into the pot, I stood back and clasped my hands in front of me. Closing my eyes, I took a deep breath and then focused on the image of the pot in my mind. I wasn't really sure how to do this magick thing, but I was going with what felt right to me.

Keeping my eyes closed, I allowed the current of magick that rippled through me to flow out and toward the pot on the stove.

"Boil, boil . . ."

"Toil and trouble?" Nova asked, and I sighed, opening my eyes.

"You know, Nova, you're really getting on my last nerve."

Should I cut a finger off?

Both my eyebrows hit my hairline as I turned to my wee fluttermouse.

"No, no, I don't think that would be the appropriate response here, Ruth."

Of course. Anything you wish, Lyra.

"I don't need you to maim her. But it would be nice if she could hush up for once so I could—"

I stopped. The pot looked peculiar. Stepping forward, I gaped down at it.

"It's frozen."

"Oh no." Nova came into the kitchen, giving Ruth a wide berth, and hugged me from behind. Nuzzling her chin onto my shoulder like she had so many times before, she swore. "Bloody hell, I was just playing. I'm sorry I screwed up your spell."

"Maybe it's me. Maybe I can't make it work." Nerves kicked low in my stomach and I shrugged one shoulder. Nova's arms tightened around me.

"No, it's not. It's just a first try. Give it a go again. I'll be quiet. I promise."

But no matter how many times I tried, the soup stayed frozen solid. Helpless, I pulled out of Nova's arms and looked at Broca.

"I can't do it."

"You can, but there may be other works at play here," Broca reminded me, and I gaped at her.

"Oh no." Sloane gave me a stricken look. "Like what happened when I got my magick?"

Until Sloane had been able to break part of the curse, she'd dealt with a new magickal power each day. It had almost driven my control freak sister through the roof.

"Maybe," Broca conceded, and my shoulders slumped.

"So I can't even learn my magick? Because it will be something else tomorrow?"

"We don't know what's going on here, Lyra." Broca gave me a sympathetic look, and my stomach twisted.

"But—"

Try doing it the other way.

"What do you mean?" I looked down at Ruth.

Reverse it. Think of freezing the soup.

I didn't want to insult my tiny familiar, not when we'd just met and she'd already threatened to maim people on my behalf, so I just shrugged and closed my eyes. I wasn't sure why I was closing my eyes, but again, it just felt right in the moment. I wasn't entirely sure how I was meant to freeze frozen soup harder, but I just went with it.

"Oh, shite," Nova breathed, and I opened my eyes to see the soup bubbling merrily in the pot.

"What . . . what does this mean?" I looked down at Ruth, who just shrugged.

It could be an inversion affliction.

"An inversion infliction?" I winced and automatically moved to turn the burner on the stove down. "Like . . . if I say cold, it goes hot?"

"Och, she may have the right of it," Broca said.

"I guess . . . I guess I'll just have to figure it out. I mean, I can still cook without using magick, right? Like I have for ages now, anyway?" I turned to Sloane, eyes wide.

"Lyra, honey, it's going to be fine. We'll get this sorted." Sloane rounded the counter and reached for me.

"But—"

My phone dinged with a text message, and I grabbed it, my panic escalating. Who would send a text message this late?

Sorry for the late message. But!
Congrats—you've been picked to be on
Bewitching Bake Off. I couldn't wait to tell you.
This is so exciting!

"Oh no." My throat tightened, and my phone clattered to the counter. Gripping the edge of the countertop, I forced myself to breathe.

"What is it?" Nova asked.

"*Bewitching Bake Off* got back to Marcie. I made the show."

"No way!" Nova shouted but stopped when I glared at her.

"But . . . but how am I supposed to cook? Everything requires . . . measurements. Heat. Cold. All the things." I gulped for air, feeling like I was going to hyperventilate. "I can't do . . . fractions. Inversions. It won't . . . make . . . sense in my head. I can't do it. I just . . . can't."

"Yes, you can," Sloane said, hooking an arm over my shoulders and forcing me to look up at her. "We're going to figure this out."

"No, I really can't. The show starts filming in, like, a week. If my magick inverts, how the hell can I go on there—a self-professed expert with her own YouTube show of all things—and have everything go to hell?"

"Maybe you could get away without using magick?" Nova leaned on the counter and sliced a piece of cheese. Chewing it, she scrunched up her nose as she thought. "It's not like you've used magick on your own platform. That's just normal recipes and whatnot. So why not just cook without it? You know, like let your partner use the magick and you're just quality control?"

"But I don't know who my partner will be. If I'm the experienced one, they'll be in worse shape than I am. This is such a mess. I can't believe I signed up for this." I gulped in air and tried to calm my racing heart.

You're not alone, Lyra. Ruth bowed to me. *I will stand for you in this competition.*

Despite the nerves that were currently twisting my stomach into knots, I smiled at my sparkly wee warrior. "I wish. Familiars aren't allowed to participate in the show."

That's stupid, Ruth decided.

"It's gonna be fine, Lyra. I promise. We'll figure it out." Both of my sisters hugged me at the same time, and for a moment, I was transported back to all the times we'd burrowed together like this, in this very house, while our parents raged at each other.

It hadn't been fine then.

And I wasn't so certain it was going to be now.

CHAPTER FIVE

Rab

Coffee was very much needed today.

Coffee *and* delicious breakfast pastries were an even better idea, so I veered down Main Street toward Mystic Munchies. I was on my way to meet with Liam at his pub, the Rune & Rose, to go over the accounts. Despite my relaxing night in with my book and an episode of *Taskmaster*, I'd struggled to sleep, and I'd woken this morning groggy and out of sorts.

My sleep had been haunted by lavender-blue eyes, and I'd promised myself, once again, that I was going to give Lyra MacGregor as wide a berth as I could in such a small town.

Blurrily, I checked the Apple Watch at my wrist and blinked up at the sky. It was just past eight in the morning, and, by all accounts, the sun should be shining. Or at the very least, it should be daylight. Had my watch broken? Pulling out my phone, I checked it.

Nope, it was definitely eight in the morning.

And dark as night out.

Cars drove slowly past, their headlights bright, and the streetlamps flickered off and then back on again, as though they couldn't quite decide what to do with this new development. Around five years ago, Knox had transformed Briarhaven into a theme town of sorts, where magickals could live in the open and regular humans could visit for entertainment. Now, I spotted a group of tourists sporting Briarhaven-branded witch hats, peering dubiously up at the sky.

My stomach dropped. Did we have another problem on our hands?

"Good morning, Rab." I turned to see Felicity, one of the members of the Charms coven, hoisting an overflowing tote onto her shoulder.

"Morning, Felicity." I lifted my chin toward the sky. "Know anything about that?"

"Och, it's the MacGregors' curse. Back at it again." Felicity shrugged one shoulder as though to say there was nothing that could be done about it.

"Darkness? Just . . . no sun at all?" I asked, realizing that it *had* been darker than normal yesterday. I'd been so lost in my thoughts about running into Lyra that I hadn't taken much note of it at the time.

"Aye, seems to be the way of it," Felicity said as we came to the door of Mystic Munchies.

"But . . . but how will we hide that from the tourists? What are we going to do?"

"That's an excellent question, Rab. One we don't have an answer for at the moment. That's just the way of life with MacGregors around, isn't it?"

Deciding not to comment, at least publicly, on the MacGregors, I held the door open to the bakery for her, and she beamed.

"Have you heard the news? *Bewitching Bake Off* is going to film their Christmas special here. We're all just so excited," Felicity gushed, her eyes bright.

So *that* was the show that Knox was trying to cajole me into joining. I rolled my eyes. I was an eat-a-can-of-beans-for-supper type of guy, not a chef. What had Knox been thinking?

"Well, some of us like it." Felicity glared at me, and I realized she'd misinterpreted my eye roll.

"No, I'm sure it's a grand show. I just remembered some work I'd forgotten for my meeting this morning," I lied smoothly.

Felicity squinted and then sniffed, unimpressed.

"It's always men that put down our reality shows. Think they're all high and mighty with their war movies. But let me tell you, I'd take a Real Housewife into battle any day before I'd take some young lad accountant with no clue how to fight, Rabbie Barclay." Felicity turned, nose in the air, and joined the queue at the counter. I had no idea what she was saying to me, or what a Real Housewife was, but they sounded formidable.

Also, I could fight. I may have been an accountant, but that didn't mean I couldn't fight if I needed to. Annoyed, and unsure how this conversation had gotten away from me, I turned back to my phone.

Laughter had my head going up, like a wolf scenting his prey, and I froze as Lyra came out of the back room with a bright white cake box in her hand. Her hair was pulled back, a pink bandanna covering it, and she wore a frilly pink apron over a swishy blue dress.

When did she start working here?

She looked as delectable as the cupcakes artfully displayed in the glass cases. My mouth went dry, my throat tightening, and I turned to leave.

"Going somewhere?" Knox beamed from where he blocked the door. We were equal height, and both worked out regularly, but it had been a few years since we'd scrapped. I was still certain I could take him in a fight, though. Lifting my chin, I stepped closer, ready to push him out of the way.

"Aye, *mate*." I glared at him when he refused to move. He knew full well what he was doing. "Late to a meeting at the Rune & Rose."

"What a coincidence. I'm heading there as well." Knox grinned and clapped his hand on my shoulder, turning me back around to face the counter. Imagining several inventive ways to murder him, I straightened my shoulders and met Lyra's eyes over the counter.

The smile fell from her face.

I used to be the one who made her smile.

Shoving that thought aside, I pointed to the sausage rolls. "Two sausage rolls and two black coffees."

"Please," Knox added behind me, digging a finger into my ribs.

"Please," I said, annoyed at myself for not saying it first *and* at Knox for pointing it out.

A faint flush crept across Lyra's cheeks, and her teeth sank into her full lower lip as she nodded and turned to the case. Her generous curves shifted under her apron, and I tore my eyes away as she bent over.

"Aw, mate, are you getting me a roll too?" Knox's grin widened when I narrowed my eyes.

"It's for Liam. My only real friend in this town."

"Och, sure and it's a brutal lad you are, Rab." Knox pretended to clutch his heart.

Sighing, I turned back to order another.

"And—"

"Ma'am? Our coffees?" An annoyed tourist waiting on the other side of the bakery interrupted me.

"Aye, coming right up." Lyra flushed and turned, tray in hand, the corner catching the door of the case. Sausage rolls went flying and Lyra's hands flew to her mouth as the tray clattered to the ground. "Oh no! I'm so sorry."

"We'll get it sorted." Marcie zoomed out from the back room and quickly collected the rolls from the floor, while the line of people waiting grumbled in frustration. Lyra's cheeks pinkened, and her eyes took on a sheen I'd seen before. Despite wanting nothing to do with her, I discovered that I still hated to see Lyra flounder.

"Calm down, everyone," I said, turning to address the line of complaining tourists. "It's not that serious, and this is her first day of work. Give her a chance, aye?"

"Well, well, well," Knox murmured softly at my side, and I ignored him, and Lyra, for that matter, instead glaring at the line of people waiting until they all shifted under my stare and stopped their complaints. In moments, Marcie had the mess cleaned and a fresh tray of sausage rolls in the case, and Lyra handed out takeaway bags with an apologetic smile.

It was the smile that won everyone over, I was sure of it. It was impossible to stay mad at Lyra, unless, of course, she ripped your heart out of your chest and tossed it in the garbage bin.

By the time she handed me my takeaway bag and coffees, I'd replayed the reasons why she was dead to me twenty times in my head, so when she gave me a shy smile and a softly murmured "Thanks," I just shrugged in acknowledgment and turned away.

I would have done it for anyone, not just Lyra. My actions were simply the result of me being a decent person.

Or so I told myself.

Without a backward look, I left the bakery, Knox falling in step next to me.

The arsehole said nothing.

Instead, he whistled a cheerful song.

"Bloody hell, mate, I'm going to throat-punch you soon if you don't fucking shut it."

"Och, he's a tetchy one this morning, isn't he, then?" Knox laughed, and I almost crushed the bag of sausage rolls in my hand.

"Shouldn't you be the tetchy one?" I nodded toward the dark sky. Clouds hung low, shrouding Briarhaven, and the streetlights cast pools of golden light on the pavement. Spooky music played from the speakers built into the black wrought iron lights, enhancing the magickal feel of the town, and several of the stores had already started putting out Halloween decor. "This doesn't strike me as normal."

"It's not." Knox made a low sound of disgust. "It's that damned curse. Sloane's been poring over old books in the library, but we haven't been able to find the next step in breaking it."

"Because it's Lyra's, isn't it?" I asked as we wandered down Main Street, nodding to people we knew. Small-town living generally required extra time when running errands, to account for people stopping you for a chat. It was why I tried to run errands only once a week or so. I wasn't a particularly chatty type.

Unlike Knox, who kissed every baby and hugged every gran he came across. Getting anywhere with him was an exercise in patience, and I stopped in front of Pixie Dust Apothecary while he spoke with a neighbor concerned about the darkness.

"Knox doing his knightly duties?"

I turned to see Raven, owner of the apothecary, leaning in the doorway. A bonnie lass, she'd always reminded me of a wildflower on a fresh spring day.

"Per usual." I grinned. "How's business? Is this darkness causing any issues?" Raven was a client of mine, and though her business was in the black, she still needed the rush of Halloween and Christmas sales to boost her through the slower months.

"Aye, a bit." Raven shrugged, glancing toward the clouds. "The Charms have called in some help. Though how long it will hold, it's hard to say."

"The clouds? That's your doing?" I asked as Knox assured the disgruntled man that they were working on the issue.

"Somewhat. The forest fae have helped as well."

"How long?" I asked.

Raven shrugged, fingers twiddling a crystal that hung on a long chain around her neck. "It's anyone's guess. If we're lucky, Lyra's magick will finally manifest. Poor thing's been having a rough go of it without her magick. Such a shame, really."

"Hmmm." I refused to be drawn into a conversation about Lyra. It was her family's curse and her problem, not mine. There was a time in my life I'd been willing to put everything on the line for Lyra MacGregor, but years of silence from her had deadened any of those inclinations.

"Coming to the Mabon party this weekend?" Raven asked as Knox finished up, patting the man on the shoulder and assuring him everything was under control.

"I don't much care for dancing."

"Och, that's a lie, isn't it, then?" Knox snorted and Raven laughed, the sound like wind chimes.

That was the other thing about small towns, and friends you grew up with—they knew you too well.

In truth, I was an excellent dancer.

"You're brilliant on the dance floor." Raven gave me a steady look that seemed to see all the things I wasn't saying.

"I didn't say I was a bad dancer; I just said I didn't much care for it."

"Does this have anything to do with the MacGregors hosting—"

"Listen, I really have to run." I held up the bag of food in my hands. "Late for an appointment with Liam. We need to go over his books before he opens for the day."

At Liam's name, Raven's expression softened.

"Hold on just a second. I've got a wee gift for him." Raven ducked back into her store and returned with a small satchel. "A tea. Tell him to not argue about it and just take it. For his back pain."

"Will do." Knox took the satchel, and we headed down the street toward the Rune & Rose, the main pub in town. Painted a soft cream color, with a red door and large arched windows, it was the perfect mix of magical and cozy. Though Liam had been young to take ownership, Knox had bankrolled him when Briarhaven had gone through its magickal makeover. The Rune & Rose was now hugely successful, with both locals and tourists alike, and the highlight was Liam's inventive magickal-themed drinks, many in honor of historical women who were tried and executed as witches.

We found Liam at a table in the back, sleeves rolled up and his ledgers in front of him.

"Sausage rolls," I said, dropping the bag on the table and shrugging my coat off. It had been unseasonably cool this year, enough that I'd taken to a wearing a coat when I usually preferred not to. I pulled out a chair. "And coffee."

"A brekkie I don't have to work for. I'll take it." Liam flashed a smile. With light brown hair, blindingly blue eyes, and Celtic tattoos snaking up his arms, Liam had more than his share of women and men alike coming on to him.

But, much like me, since dating was troublesome in a small town where many people were clients, he largely abstained.

"A gift from Raven." Knox sat and placed the satchel on the table. Liam's eyes warmed. I'd always suspected Raven was another big reason why he didn't date much, but he'd never once spoken a word to us about her. And with my own doomed love life, I wasn't one to pry. "For your back."

"Och, my back's fine. She's always blethering on about taking care of myself." Liam shrugged, though he did take the bag and tuck it away in his pocket. "I'm not old yet."

"Can't imagine lifting all those kegs is great for your back," I pointed out and took the cover off my coffee to blow on it. "I'm guessing she's just being friendly."

"It's fine, it's fine." Liam swatted my words away and dug in the bag. "These Marcie's? I hear Lyra's working there now."

I pressed my lips together, not wanting to talk about Lyra.

"She sure is. And guess who came to her rescue this morning?" Knox put his hands under his chin and fluttered his eyelashes at me. "Our sweet Rab. A true knight in shining armor."

"You know what, mate? I can still gouge your spleen out with this." I held up the wooden spoon that had come with the coffee.

"Spleen? Why his spleen?" Liam wondered, breaking off a piece of his roll.

"Because I don't want to kill him, necessarily, and you can live without a spleen." I shrugged and took a sip of my coffee and sighed with satisfaction. *Perfect, as usual.*

"But you're fine with me being in horrible agony from tearing my flesh open with a spoon and removing an organ?" Knox raised an eyebrow at me.

"Och, aye. Toughen you up."

"Brutal," Liam observed, his lips twitching in a grin. "But, perhaps deserved. Knox, why are you interrupting my accounts meeting?"

"I knew you weren't meant to come here," I grumbled, annoyed at Knox.

A grin flashed on his face, and Knox leaned back, coffee cup in hand.

"A few reasons, but the first is that I'm staging a coup."

"A coup? Whose country are we taking over?" Intrigued, I reached into the bag for a sausage roll, my stomach already grumbling in anticipation.

"Maybe it's an intervention, then?" Knox squinted as he considered it.

"Why? Has one of us taken to drugs?" Liam looked at me, and I shook my head at him, bewildered.

"Basically, I need someone to go on this reality show, and it has to be one of you two," Knox spit out, pointing a finger between me and Liam.

Liam leaned back and hooted with laughter.

"Mate, if you think for one second I'm going to leave my pub—during a busy season, mind you, with the added bonus of an entire production cast of a reality show being in town to film and needing food and drink—well, you've lost your damn mind."

Both men swiveled my way.

"No," I said, taking a bite of my roll, and closed my eyes in bliss. Marcie never missed. When I opened my eyes again, my two friends were staring at me. "'No' is a complete sentence, by the way. I don't have to elaborate."

"But it has to be you." Knox sighed and crossed a boot onto his knee, his fingers tapping against his thigh.

"No, it really does not."

"Aye, but it does. They want someone in your age range, handsome, and with their magick firmly under their belt." Knox looked out the front window of the pub, where a pair of tourists struggled with an umbrella in the rain that had snuck up since we'd been inside. "There's not many of us who fit that description in town. And nobody else who owes me a favor."

"Damn it, Knox." I jerked in my chair, surprised he was calling in the favor I owed him. It had been a big one too.

He'd denied the license for my father's chippy, causing my parents to take their fast-food chain to other villages. With the remodel of Briarhaven into a theme park of sorts, Knox had wanted curated and individual restaurants, and my father's chippy hadn't fit the bill.

It could have, with some work, but Knox had come to me first, knowing the difficult time I'd had with my father after Lyra had left. I still struggled with guilt sometimes that I'd given Knox the go-ahead to deny their permit. But *I* hadn't asked Knox to make that decision; I'd just given him the go-ahead, even though I'd still promised him I'd owe him someday.

The result had been my parents moving two hours away, giving me room to breathe, and their business had exploded, so no real harm was done.

"Listen, Rab. This will be huge for Briarhaven. You know we're kind of the laughingstock of the magickal world, and I just feel like everyone's favorite reality show being filmed here will give us added validity. And if I can have some control over who is on the show—like someone who won't embarrass us—that will also help." Knox gave me a pointed look, and I sighed, pinching the bridge of my nose with my fingers.

Though the makeover of Briarhaven had been hugely accepted by the inhabitants, other magickal communities around the world had different views of Knox's decision. They felt Briarhaven was making a joke of magickals and sacred practices and often referred to us as sellouts. I was just happy that most of us could largely live freely and that it provided a safe haven for many who hadn't been able to find a spot to welcome them in the world.

"I don't cook," I pointed out, my resolve crumbling, and Knox's eyes took on a gleam as he leaned forward. I'd had no interest in learning my father's business, instead burying my head in books.

"Don't have to. The setup is that one seasoned baker will be paired with a novice."

"And you use magick to make food?" I asked. I had never seen an episode before.

"Magickal challenges. But you'll still use real ingredients, and the food has to be edible. It's quite fun," Liam said, and I gave him a surprised look.

"You watch *Bewitching Bake Off*?"

"Aye, mate. It relaxes me at the end of the day. Plus, sometimes I get some ideas for something I want Chef to try in the kitchen here." Liam shrugged, unbothered by my look.

"Please, mate? Sloane's on me about all the Mabon festival preparations, and I need to submit some names to the production team, like, yesterday."

"Fine," I said, squeezing my eyes shut. I was going to hate every second of this. "If I'm lucky, I'll get paired with Marcie and won't have to do any work."

"Or—" Liam began.

"And the festival? You're both coming? Don't leave me hanging, lads," Knox interrupted.

"I highly suspect I'm not welcome," I pointed out.

"Everyone's invited. It's a festival for the town. Not only will most of your clients be there, but we might get to hang out with dragons. So why not come?" Knox shrugged.

"Because I need to catch up on *Stranger Things*?" I said. Knox rolled his eyes.

"Just come," Knox said, finishing his sausage roll and standing.

"No."

"I'd come if I were you," Liam said, raising his eyebrows at me.

"Why?"

"Because if you don't, then it's going to make it look like you're bothered about Lyra being back. Particularly since her sister is throwing this festival at their father's place in the woods. Your absence will speak louder than your presence."

Knox gave a low whistle and then clapped Liam on the shoulder. "The lad's got it right. You cannae argue with him."

He was right. I hadn't thought about the festival in that light, but now that I did, I knew it would set tongues wagging if I didn't go.

"Bloody hell," I cursed, draining my coffee cup. "Sometimes I hate living in a small town."

"Only when all eyes are on you. The rest of the time, it's quite nice. Gotta run, lads. Need to see a witch about breaking a curse."

"Yeah, yeah, bye." I waved Knox away and looked at Liam, my shoulders slumping. "I'm going to hate every second of this, aren't I?"

"What? The show or the festival?"

"Both."

"Aye, lad. But you know, as they say . . . what doesn't kill us and all that."

"In that case, time to look at spreadsheets." I gave Liam an evil grin as he groaned and slipped my laptop from my bag. "Now, do you want the good news or the bad news first?"

CHAPTER SIX

Lyra

I was not remotely fine.

I'd spent two days trying to sort out my magick in the hours after my shifts at Mystic Munchies, and to my dismay, nothing was working. If anything, things were only getting worse. No matter how hard I tried, I couldn't seem to magick my way through a simple recipe.

Everything went wrong. It was basically Opposite Day in my kitchen.

If I needed a half teaspoon of cinnamon, it put a whole teaspoon in.

If I needed seventy-five grams of butter, it put in a hundred and fifty.

If I wanted something melted, it hardened.

If I tried to make something sweet, it went spicy.

But . . . but . . . I had found that Ruth was right. If I thought about the opposite of what I wanted, then I could muddle along, though the doubling measurements were tricky. The problem with that was it required me to do so for every step of a recipe. Which was not only deeply chaotic, but also impossible for me to keep straight in my brain. I was used to cooking by loosely following a recipe, going on instincts alone, and now I had to carefully read each step and then try to pick apart what the reverse would be.

This was never going to work.

It'll be okay.

Ruth curled into a ball on the windowsill, peering out into the darkness, her wings shimmering in the overhead light.

"You keep saying that, but I'm having a hard time seeing how it will be. At the very least, I can't go to the Mabon festival like this. I'm supposed to help with food for half the town tonight. I'm going to be the laughingstock of Briarhaven *and* reality television."

No, you won't. Everybody falls in love with you.

"How would you know that? You've only been with me for a few days."

It's easy enough to see. Plus, we're connected, Lyra. You've got a good heart. That trait makes you pretty damn lovable. Ruth pulled out her sword and began to file one of her nails. I winced.

"I don't know how you can be equal parts scary and adorable at the same time."

Ruth flashed me a mousy smile that really was just baring her teeth, adding to the more terrifying aspect of her personality.

I like to keep people on their toes.

"Well, I'm glad you're on my side. I just really don't know what I'm going to do. The festival is literally about balance and harvest and gratitude. I'm over here freezing soup and exploding cakes."

"What you're going to do is get pampered," Sloane said from the couch, having stayed over last night because she knew I was stressing out.

A soft knock sounded at the door.

"Who's that?" I asked.

"Your glam squad for the Mabon festival," Sloane sang. She trailed to the door and opened it to reveal Raven, massage table in her hands, Tam holding a makeup kit, and Felicity with about a bazillion hairbrushes and hairpins overflowing in her bag.

I zeroed in on Tam. Her skin glistened like she'd run here, and I'd never once seen her wear a dab of makeup in the entire time I'd known her.

"*You're* on makeup?"

"I dated a girl once who was a makeup artist. Just because I don't wear it doesn't mean I don't know all the tricks." Tam winked at me. "You're the High Priestess of Snacks tonight. Can't have you turning up to the festival looking like you've wrestled a bag of flour."

"Stop it," Felicity breathed, hand to heart, as she bent and brought her face close to Ruth. "Aren't you just the most darling, sweetest, cutest little . . . Eeeek!"

Ruth brandished her sword, and Felicity jumped back.

"A ninja mouse? Badass." Tam gave Ruth an approving nod.

"She's a fluttermouse. Her name is Ruth, and she is equal parts cuddly and terrifying. What she is to you depends entirely on how you treat her."

Raven put the table down, drew her hands together like she was praying, and smiled. "It's an honor to meet you, Ruth. Blessed Mabon."

I like her.

"Aye, Raven's a good one," I said.

"I've always liked mice," Tam observed, bringing two fingers to her forehead in a salute. "Smart, empathetic little creatures. Excellent taste in swords."

I like her too.

Raven unfolded the massage table, moving it so it ran alongside the dining table, and pointed to it.

"Make yourself comfortable, our champion baker. I hear we've got some tension to work out before you go feed the entire village under a full moon."

"And then we're going to make you the prettiest forest fairy in all the land." Felicity beamed and looked over to the discarded ingredients that lined the kitchen countertops. "No brekkie on yet? No problem, no problem. I'll just get that sorted, if you don't mind."

I waved her to it. It wasn't like I was going to be of any use in the kitchen if my magick kept misfiring.

Swallowing down the fear that threatened to make panic choke my throat, I pulled off my jumper and climbed on the table in the leggings and tank I wore, burying my face in the open circle at the end of the table.

"This good?" I asked.

"Aye. No need to get naked with the whole crew running about. This isn't that kind of harvest festival," Raven said dryly.

In moments, Broca's and Nova's voices joined the conversation, disco music took up in the background, and the scent of bacon wafted through the air. Raven's hands were like magick at my neck, and slowly the tension began to ease from my shoulders.

We were heading into the forest tonight, and I was already regretting my decision to help Sloane with the food preparations.

Outside the kitchen window, the trees at the edge of the Briarhaven woods danced in the wind, leaves tipped with the first hints of autumn gold. By tonight, those same trees would be wrapped in twinkle lights and floating candles, the whole forest transformed into a glowing river of celebration. The Mabon festival hadn't happened for several years now, and Sloane was determined to bring the tradition back, even if it meant she had to host it herself. It was a great excuse for the town to drink mulled cider, dance until their feet hurt, and pretend the witches weren't vaguely terrifying.

This year, though, it was more than that. It was also the first time the town had invited the dragons who lived in the hills outside Briarhaven to join the party and they'd accepted. Dragons. At our festival. Doing a fire-breathing light show as the grand finale. And I just had to keep everyone fed.

No pressure.

"Hey, Lyra. Wake up."

I started, realizing I had drifted off. Turning, I blinked up as Raven's face blurred and then came into focus.

"Wow, your hands are magick. I can't believe I fell asleep."

"You clearly needed it. Hopefully that helped and you'll feel better for tonight." She squeezed my shoulder. "And if your magick acts up, we'll improvise. It's what witches and bakers do."

Sitting up, I swung my legs over the side of the table.

Not only did I feel rested, but my optimism had returned. There was no point in panicking about something that I couldn't control . . . yet. Everyone was right. Things were going to be just fine. I just needed to take it a day at a time, or in my case, spell by misfiring spell.

"You know what I think my favorite part of tonight is going to be?" I asked everyone in the room. Half the people were sitting at the dining table, while Sloane and Nova were sprawled on the couch.

"What's that?" Nova asked.

"Seeing Sloane's reaction to her festival dress."

Sloane's face dropped and she groaned. "Damn it, Lyra. I hope you're not putting me in something scandalous. It's chilly out there. I refuse to freeze my arse off for aesthetics."

"Oh, I'm one hundred percent putting you in something scandalous. It's a sacred sister duty. I want Knox to swallow his tongue when he sees you in the firelight." I chuckled as Sloane's expression swung between annoyance and curiosity.

"First, brunch," Broca instructed, bringing my attention to the food on the table. "Then we tart Sloane up for the equinox."

"Ohhh, tart." Nova looked at me. "Is that acceptable or is that another tool of the patriarchy?"

"I'll allow it." I grinned at Nova and slid off the table. "But only because tarts are delicious."

By the time everyone had their dresses on, I'd mostly pushed my worries aside. It was hard not to, between the mimosas that someone had poured, the music bouncing around in the background, and the endless gossip about everyone in town—we'd had ourselves a proper pre-festival girls' day. Even Deidre, one of our busier Charms members, had shown up at one point, taking a break in between house showings, and had promised she'd make it out to the clearing later. The only coven member not in attendance was Mandy Meadows, and Felicity just shrugged when I asked after her.

I made a mental note to go visit her this week. Enough was enough. It had been some time since Sloane had taken over running the Charms. Mandy needed to stop hiding out.

"Oh, Lyra." Broca gasped as Nova finished tying the laces of my dress and I turned to the room. "You look stunning."

My festival dress was different from the sequined ball gown I might have worn to a castle party. I'd gone full forest witch.

It was off-the-shoulder, the bodice a deep, rich plum that hugged my curves before flaring into layers of tulle and chiffon that shifted between blackberry and smoke. Tiny embroidered leaves and stars trailed down the skirt like falling constellations. I'd had it specially made after calling in a favor from an ex-boyfriend of mine who worked at a high-end fashion house in Italy. It wasn't always easy to find clothes that suited me as a plus-sized woman, but he had always championed my body.

"It's not the body's job to show off the clothes, *dolcezza mia*," Anton had told me once, espresso in hand. "It is the job of the clothes to show off the body."

He'd been one of the first to convince me that confidence overruled anything else when it came to how I presented myself to the world. My size never mattered. Since then, I'd dressed my body how I liked, and didn't give another thought to thick thighs or wobbly arms.

For tonight, I'd paired the dress with a sheer black cloak scattered with tiny golden moths. The hood framed my face, and when I pulled it back, my hair—twisted by Felicity into a complicated crown of braids and curls—tumbled down my back with bits of copper leaf pinned throughout.

With it, I'd paired delicate lace wings that shimmered with golden crystals, and a matching half mask that covered my eyes and nose in filigreed vines. Ruth and I would match . . . all forest mischief and feral glitter.

As for my makeup? Somehow Tam had managed to make me look both ethereal and a little dangerous, with smoky eyes and lipstick that looked like I'd been eating raspberries all morning.

"Your brushwork is exquisite," I told Tam, who looked edgy and sexy in a fitted moss-green suit coat and slim black trousers, with no shirt under her coat, and a slinky necklace in the shape of a snake sliding down her décolletage. Tam rolled her hand and took a bow, and we all cheered.

"I can't wear this," Sloane said, peeking her head out from the top of the stairs.

"Yes, you can," I called up. We'd gone over this several times today.

"Nope. Can't do it. It's see-through, Lyra. The town will judge me."

"Ruth?" I asked, and Ruth snapped to attention, drawing her sword. In seconds, she'd flitted upstairs, and after one shriek from Sloane, she returned with her sword sheathed.

She'll be down shortly.

"Lovely." Turning, I clapped my hands. "I think this is the best you all have looked. Seriously, thank you so much for coming over and for doing . . . all this. If I didn't have you lot, I'd be rocking a flour-covered apron and stress-crying into my batter."

Steps sounded behind me, and I turned, bringing my hands to my mouth in anticipation.

I'd put Sloane in silk, with a sheer overlay of the most intricate netting of crystals. Every step she took made her softly shimmer, and the silk moved with her curves beautifully. I'd chosen a deep bronze gold, the color of bonfire embers, so that under the festival torches she'd look like she was carved from living flame.

"This makes me look naked," Sloane protested.

"Holy hell, Sloane." Nova whistled. Tam fanned herself. Felicity's eyes were wide as saucers.

"I suspect we won't see much of you once Knox gets his eyes on you in the forest," I said.

Sloane's cheeks heated, and she turned, revealing the dropped back.

"It's not too much? Or . . . too little . . . I should say? This is a town festival, not an orgy."

"Och, no. Look at me." I pointed to my cleavage, made even more formidable by the boning of the bodice. "I've got everything spilling out every which way in this dress. Between the two of us, we're basically providing heating for the event."

"And I will speak on behalf of every man in town, and a few of the women as well—we are grateful for it," Tam said, winking at me.

"Thank you." I laughed, running my hands down my body. There was just something about a well-fitted dress that put me in a great mood.

"Well, ladies? Shall we?" Broca asked, sweeping her cloak dramatically around her shoulders. Her own dress was a riot of orange and red, like a walking pile of autumn leaves.

"I feel like we're some ragtag band of Charlie's Angels," Nova observed. She wore a leather sheath dress with intricate cutouts at her sides, paired with an armful of bangles that jingled when she moved.

"That works for me. I mean, I may not know any ninja moves, but I've got Ruth to take care of things for me now."

"She's terrifying," Sloane hissed as we walked to the lane, where Knox had arranged for vans to pick up festivalgoers from town and ferry them to the forest edge. The Mabon clearing was deep enough in the woods that we didn't want drunk villagers trying to navigate the paths alone in the dark. "Did you know she threatened to trim my split ends with that sword?"

"She was bluffing," I said, although . . . I wouldn't really put it past her.

I glanced up at the clear sky, stars winking against inky darkness. Worry burst through my excitement, and my stomach twisted in knots. I twisted the ring on my hand, biting my lower lip.

"That's not for today, Lyra." Sloane curved her arm through mine as we climbed into the van. "Tonight is about honoring the turning of the wheel and reminding the town that the MacGregors aren't a walking disaster. I promise you I'm working on finding out more about the curse. We've made friends here. The town doesn't hate us so much anymore. We can do this. But for tonight? Let it all go, okay? Promise me?"

"Aye, I will. Or I'll at least pretend very convincingly. You can give me an award afterward."

The van jolted into motion, fairy lights strung along the ceiling swaying gently, and I leaned my head against the cool glass, watching Briarhaven's stone cottages slip past. Lanterns burned in windows, casting warm pools of light that made my chest ache with the sheer *home* of it all.

By the time we'd reached the edge of the woods and followed the lantern-lit path to the main clearing, I'd managed to push most of my worry down.

The forest had been transformed.

Warm golden orbs floated among the trees, bobbing gently as if moved by some unseen current. Twinkle lights were strung in swooping arcs from trunk to trunk, and hundreds of glass jars filled with candles were clustered on mossy logs, tree stumps, and low tables brought out just for this event. The scent of woodsmoke, mulled cider, and damp earth perfumed the air. Between the trees, stalls had been set up, with local artisans selling charms and knitwear, carved wooden dragons, jars of preserves, and delicate glittering crowns and masks for those who wanted to add to their costumes.

At the center of it all stood a massive bonfire, a carefully built tower of logs and branches and twisted vines. Around it, a wide circle had been cleared for dancing. A small wooden stage had been erected off to one side, where the band tuned their instruments, fiddles and pipes already weaving bright strands of music through the clearing.

And above us, beyond the black silhouettes of the pines, the sky loomed huge and clear. I could practically *feel* the dragons out there, restless, circling above their remote ridge, waiting for their calling.

The line of people on the path paused, creating a pocket of space, we were ushered through like we were a special procession, and I beamed as Knox strode out from between two trees, looking devastating in his kilt and a dark cloak, a simple black mask over his eyes.

"Oh, wow. I . . ." Sloane trailed off as she gaped at Knox. "The mask is . . ."

"Hot?" I supplied, and Sloane swallowed, nodding.

"Who would have thought?"

"Me," Nova said, laughing as Knox came to a halt, his gaze landing on Sloane.

An almost feral look crossed his face, and he audibly swallowed, suddenly unable to speak.

"Dear goddess, please let a man look at me like that," I whispered, putting my hands together like I was praying.

"Oh, hush, they all look at you that way." Nova elbowed me.

"No, not like that," I said, nodding to where Knox held out his hand, drawing Sloane forward onto the pine-needle-strewn grass. She wrapped an arm around his shoulders for balance, and he turned his face into the crook of her arm, tracing his lips over the inner skin of her bicep. She flushed, laughing up at him.

"Och, aye, I get it." Nova and I leaned into each other, sighing as Knox whispered something in Sloane's ear and her cheeks flushed again. I could hardly blame her. Knox could easily be a Disney prince, carrying his knightly duties with ease. Seeing her happy with him made my insides go all ooey-gooey with delight.

"Ladies." Knox finally looked up, cheeks a touch flushed as well. I considered my work here done. "You both look ravishing. Blessed Mabon, Lyra."

"Thank you," I said, accepting his hand as he helped me over a gnarled tree root. Once in the clearing, I hurried toward the long trestle tables already laden with food, a sharp breeze chasing me and making my cloak billow dramatically.

At the edge of the clearing, Henry—Knox's butler—stood by a smaller cooking fire, dressed in a proper tuxedo with a tartan scarf thrown over one shoulder.

"Oh, stop, this is beyond cute," I said, skidding to a halt as I looked at the animals at his side. Knox had two familiars, a blind cat named Oswald, and Haggis, a mini Highland coo with a birth defect who used a wheelchair. Both sported tiny autumn-leaf wreaths around their necks, while Blue sat dutifully next to them, wearing a blue tartan bow tie.

"How on earth did you get them to sit in a row like that?" I demanded.

"Extreme bribery," Henry said serenely. "Might I say, you look enchanting this evening, Miss MacGregor? Very Mabon chic." He inclined his head, candlelight glinting off his glasses.

"Thank you. Can you just help me with my wings?" I'd taken them off on the walk in case they snagged on every twig in existence, and Henry obliged, sliding the harness over my shoulders and tightening the buckles for me.

"There. Now you're the true forest princess of the festival."

"I do feel like one." I laughed, and Haggis wheeled forward to butt his nose against my leg.

"You three look fantastic," I said, crouching to scratch Haggis's ears.

You look the prettiest. Haggis tilted his head so I could scratch behind his ears.

I'll take his word for it, Oswald said dryly, rolling onto his back and showing his belly. He still looked vaguely disinterested.

Pretty Lyra, Blue sang into my mind, his mental voice bright as a bell.

All three of their voices clamored in my head, and I gasped, loving that I could hear them all talk now.

"That's Rab arriving," Nova murmured, suddenly at my elbow. Instinctively, I stiffened. She never asked me any questions about him, understanding in her own way that I didn't want to discuss it. For as much as we poked at each other, my sisters still showed up when it mattered.

Like now. I glanced over my shoulder to see Rab, looking incredibly dashing, leading Broca toward where some dancers swayed by the fire. They had a special bond, the two of them, but to her credit, Broca had never once tried to interfere with my non-relationship with Rab.

Nova hooked an arm through mine and steered me toward the long tables where I'd be setting out my desserts later, using the excuse of "helping" to guide me past the arrivals before I could get stuck in the line of greetings.

Between the trees, more people flowed into the clearing, lanterns swinging from their hands and cloaks swirling. Music lilted, a jaunty wee tune, and snatches of conversation and laughter floated our way.

"Much fancier than the Mabon festivals we had when we were growing up," Nova said, leaning into me, as we waved at a few people who smiled brightly at us. It was a far cry from the way people had first reacted when we'd returned to Briarhaven. The response had been lukewarm at best and the mood wary. Since then, we'd basically gone on a publicity tour of the town, slowly winning our way into everyone's hearts.

Well, not everyone's. Mandy still hated us.

But now the clearing was packed with people dressed in their finest gowns and cloaks, and to my delight, everyone had gone all out. There were antlers and flower crowns, painted faces and rune-etched masks. Fae wings, witch hats, and even a man dressed in an elaborate crow costume that made him look like he'd flown out of some goth fairy tale.

In moments, people surrounded me, and the evening took on a blurred quality. I slipped easily into hostess mode, helping Henry set out the platters of harvest breads, cinnamon-sugar twists, honey-roasted nuts, and the berry tarts I'd managed to bake *without* accidentally burning the house down. But only because I'd forced myself to not use my magick at all, no matter how much it called to me.

We moved along the trestle tables together, arranging dishes under lantern light while townsfolk drifted over with warm smiles and full mugs. Mrs. Kerr complimented my blackberry crumble and pressed a crocheted acorn charm into my hand for good luck, elderly Mr. Murphy insisted I try a sip of his allegedly award-winning equinox tonic—which nearly singed my eyebrows—and a trio of teenagers played a game of fetch with Haggis. For the first time, instead of feeling like an outsider passing through, I felt woven into the very fabric of Briarhaven—laughing, chatting, refilling platters, until warmth prickled at my back, and I turned to see my father watching me from the edge of the clearing, pride softening every line of his face.

"Dad!" I crowed, delighted. I hadn't been sure he'd be able to make it down from the ridge where he would be helping with the final act of the festival—the dragon flyover.

"I'm so glad you were able to make it down here," I said, leaning into his hug. The rough wool of his cloak scratched my cheek in the best way. "I know how hard it is for you to get away. The dragons don't exactly like to share you." My father had been working for years for the dragons, one of the few humans they trusted fully, and we had slowly been working on rebuilding our relationship after his absence in our lives.

He huffed a laugh, eyes crinkling. "They can be bribed with sweets or sparkles if the occasion's important enough." He stepped back, gaze soft as he took me in. "This felt important. It's the first time the dragons are formally flying over Briarhaven in my lifetime."

"It does feel special, doesn't it?" I couldn't bring myself to tell him about my worries about my magick.

"Listen, Lyra, I have something for you. A belated birthday gift. Consider it . . . an aid."

"An aid?" My heart kicked. "For what? My chronic inability to fold fitted sheets?"

"For your magick, imp." He reached into an inner pocket of his cloak and drew out a small charcoal-gray pouch, soft as smoke, tied with a bit of braided leather. "Broca told me that it's finally come in, but you're struggling. And, well, the dragons insisted."

"The *dragons* got me a present?" I clapped my hands together under my chin, bouncing on my heels as he handed me the gift. "Can I open it now?"

"Of course." Russell's lips quirked.

Excited, I opened the soft pouch and drew out a delicate gold chain. On it nestled a pendant in the shape of a bloomed rose. I studied the pale pink petals, which shifted in color beneath the festival lights, and the faint glow of magick that seemed to pulse from within.

"What is this flower made of?" I looked up at him, confused and awed. "This is . . . exquisite. Really, *really* beautiful, Dad."

The smile widened on his face.

"It's dragon scales."

My mouth dropped open.

"No way," I breathed. My fingers tingled where they brushed the petals. Power hummed against my skin.

"Aye. They gave me permission to collect the dropped ones." Pride warmed his voice. "I've been fiddling about with how to make the idea I had in my head. Once they caught wind of it, everyone wanted to chip in. So I should say, this is a gift from me and the dragons. For you. Hopefully to help with your magick."

"Dad," I whispered.

"The scales are from different dragons," he continued. "Some strong in fire, some in air, some in the steadiness of stone. Woven together, they hold balance. When you wear it, it should help you find your center when your spells want to do the opposite of what you ask." His mouth twisted. "Call it a . . . magical stabilizer. Like training wheels, but shinier."

Dragons were fiercely loyal to those they loved, so this was no small gift.

"Och." I waved my hands in front of my face as my eyes filled. "You've got me going."

Instantly contrite, my dad shoved his hands in his pockets, awkwardness making his shoulders jerk. "I didn't mean . . . I thought you would—"

"No, no." I waved his words away and turned, baring my neck to him, lifting my hair. "Please. Can you put it on for me? My hands are shaking too much, and I'm worried I'll drop it. What a stunning gift."

As soon as the necklace slid around my neck, clasp settling at the nape, I could feel the power humming through it. Warmth spread down my sternum, a gentle press, as if someone had rested a hand just over my heart.

There was no other way to explain it, but I just felt *love.* It was as though the necklace would be a constant reminder that I was loved, even if not always in the way that I needed. The sheer enormity of the present—birthday gifts had been rare growing up—caused the tears to spill over.

"Dad, you're the best," I said thickly. "I'm just going to pop to the springs to collect myself and make sure I don't ruin the very expensive artwork on my face." I turned and leaned up to kiss his cheek. My father looked relieved, and I squeezed his arm before slipping away, weaving among clusters of people and ducking under a line of hanging lanterns.

Sometimes my feelings were just like that. Too big. Too all-encompassing. They'd take over and I'd need a moment to sort through the thoughts in my head, making sense of the scramble of emotions.

A quiet moment alone was all I needed, and I'd be back, ready to watch dragons set the sky on fire.

The path away from the main clearing narrowed, pine needles soft under my boots. To the left, laughter and music faded, and to the right, the forest deepened into a hush broken only by the crackle of distant fires and the occasional shout. The coven had set up small reflection glades off the main clearing. They were places for offerings, for meditating, or, in my case, for trying not to bawl like a baby.

I followed a trail of floating will-o'-the-wisp lights to the small spring that fed the stream running past town. It shimmered in a hollow between moss covered stones, the surface reflecting the lanterns that had been hung in the branches overhead. Someone had placed flat stones around it in a rough circle, and on one side a small standing stone had been carved with runes that glowed faintly blue.

Untying my mask, I fanned my face as I walked, dragging in deep breaths to calm myself. The cool air off the water kissed my flushed cheeks.

How did you not become emotional when your father and a bunch of dragons gifted you something so . . . priceless?

He was a good man.

How close we'd come to not giving him the second chance he so deserved.

I sank down on one of the flat stones and closed my eyes, pressing my fingers lightly to the pendant. The warmth pulsed under my palm in steady, reassuring beats. Gradually, my breathing eased.

I was not alone.

I knew it a second before I heard footsteps and the sensation of being *seen* pricked along my skin. My eyes flew open.

Across the spring, someone stood in the shadows, half hidden by the standing stone. The lantern light caught on a familiar jawline, stubble, the edge of a tartan, the glint of a mask.

Rab.

Of course it was Rab.

We stared at each other across the water, the spring reflecting our faces back in distorted smears of color.

"What's wrong?" he asked. His voice was rough, like he'd had to drag the words out. "You bolted like the bonfire was about to explode."

"Och, nothing. Just had a wee moment." I shrugged, angling my face away from him. In fact, I was trying to look everywhere but at him. At the moss on the stones. At the reflection of the lanterns in the water. At the faint glow of the stars between the leaves on the trees.

But finally, my eyes landed on his face. It was impossible not to look at his face. That gorgeous, stupid face of his.

"You look . . ." He cleared his throat. "Really pretty, Lyra."

I bristled. "Don't."

"Excuse me?" His brows shot up.

"You cannae call me pretty," I blurted. "Not you."

The way I said "you," as though he were something I'd scraped off my shoe, had his jaw tightening.

"Ah, I see. Not good enough to be kissing your feet, am I?" His mouth twisted. "You fancy the posh men now, do you? The ones that shower you in gifts and whisk you off to luxurious trips and don't live in wee Scottish villages with muddy boots?"

"It has nothing to do with that," I snapped, the old hurt spiking. I whirled and began to pace the edge of the spring, skirts swishing. The lantern light fractured on the water, making the whole world look slightly off-kilter.

"What, then?" he demanded. "Because from where I'm standing, you've spent the last decade collecting every fancy man in Europe like they're stamps in your passport."

I froze. "Have you been keeping tabs on me, Rab? Should I be flattered? Or concerned that you're listening to the gossip?"

"Hard not to hear the stories when every time someone from Briarhaven travels they come back with another tale of 'Oh, I saw Lyra in Barcelona or Paris or bloody Prague. She was on the arm of a bloke with a yacht.'" His eyes flashed. "Meanwhile, some of us were here, scraping winter ice off the same car window every morning."

"What would you have had me do?" I demanded. "Sit at home and hide myself because a stupid curse has made it impossible for me to stay anywhere for long? Or actually go out and live my life?"

His lips parted. "That's not—"

I took a step toward him, ignoring the sting of tears. "You have no right to be angry that I built a life. That I took what I could get in the scraps between towns as we ran from a curse."

He stared at me. For a heartbeat, something like regret flickered across his face.

Then his gaze dropped, catching on my bodice, the pendant, the way my cloak had fallen open when I stepped closer. Heat slid through his eyes.

"Just . . ." He swallowed. "You look pretty tonight, Lyra."

"Don't," I repeated, louder this time. "I already told you. Not that word. Not from *you*."

I'd craved his compliments once, my tender young heart hanging on his every word. Even now, I felt myself stepping closer, the magnetic force of Rab making it impossible for me to turn away.

Instead, I took a breath, trying to steady myself, fingertips brushing the dragon-scale pendant as if it might magically supply emotional regulation.

The air around us prickled.

My magick, which had been humming quietly, suddenly surged, reacting to the thick knot of longing and hurt between us.

My fingers twitched.

Something in the air popped.

Rab jerked, his eyes widening. His glass vanished from his hand with a soft *whoomph* of displaced air, and in its place was something warm and prickly and decidedly alive.

I shrieked. Rab almost dropped the . . . thing . . . before catching it and cradling it reflexively close to his chest.

"What the hell?" he hissed, looking down at the hedgehog now curled into a terrified ball between his palms. Tiny feet. Tiny nose. Tiny, outraged eyes.

"Did you do this?" he demanded, looking up at me.

I stared, equal parts horrified and secretly delighted. "I . . . I don't know."

"What do you mean you don't know?" He lifted the hedgehog in the air and held it under my nose. "Did you or did you not do this?"

"I don't *know*," I repeated, stomping my foot.

"How can you not know?" The hedgehog uncurled slightly, poking its nose out and sniffing the air before rolling back in, and Rab instinctively tucked it back against his chest. His voice gentled. "Hey, buddy, it's okay. You're just fine. I've got you."

"I just don't, all right?" Frustration laced my voice, underpinned by old shame. It reminded me of all the times I'd struggled with my homework, unable to explain why numbers refused to behave in my head.

"Okay, that's fine," Rab said after a beat, injecting a soothing note into his voice that still tugged at something soft inside me. "We can—"

"There's no 'we,'" I cut in, fisting my hands. "There is no 'we,' and there never will be a 'we' again. Just leave me alone, Rab."

His mouth dropped open as I stormed past him, cloak snapping behind me like a banner.

"Och, isn't that rich?" he yelled after me. "Here you are. Running away again. Just like you did before."

The words slammed into my back like a shove.

I didn't turn around.

If I did, I might throw him in the water. Or kiss him. Or both.

The forest swallowed me up, the sounds of the main clearing growing louder with each step. I shoved my mask back on, squared my shoulders, and walked toward the lights.

Ruth flew to my shoulder and nestled in. She must have followed me to the clearing.

So, hedgehogs, huh?

"Not a word, Ruth. I don't even know what to say."

CHAPTER SEVEN

Rab

"Nae bother, lad," Henry said some time later, beaming down at the hedgehog he now cradled in his hefty palms. We'd retreated to the edge of the clearing near the mulled cider cauldron. "We'll get this wee beastie sorted out. Won't we?"

The hedgie blinked up at Henry, nose twitching, and, I swear on my ancestors, *beamed* at him. The two were in mutual accord, and I breathed a sigh of relief. There was no way I was carrying a hedgie around with me all night. Not that I much wanted to stay at the festival, but I'd barely spoken to anyone, and despite being annoying, Liam was also right. People *would* talk if I didn't show my face.

My thoughts whirled, my emotions a scrambled knot in my chest, and I reached for another glass of cider from the tray of a passing volunteer. I took a sip, the liquid a burst of spiced warmth on my tongue, and studied the glass in my hand.

She'd changed my drink into a hedgehog.

Which meant transmutation was one of her abilities, whether she knew it or not, and wild swings of emotion could set it off. Particularly in witches new to their abilities.

I still remembered one tricky moment when I'd changed my beer into a photo of Lyra, infuriating my father and bringing tears to my mother's eyes. It had been on one of the rare family get-togethers, a trip to Pitlochry for a Christmas play, and I'd been new to my magick.

"I can't believe you're still thinking of the lass . . . after all these years," my father had seethed, turning away from me in disgust. He'd always been a hard man, his thinking falling in black and white, with no comprehension of the grayer areas of life.

"I hadn't even been thinking of her," I'd protested. Had I? Maybe not consciously. But we'd stopped at a table of baked goods being sold outside the theater, and I'd briefly remembered how Lyra had once brought me a tin of Christmas mince pies, carefully wrapped with a pretty bow. She'd made them herself and had held her breath as I'd taken a bite. I'd devoured the entire tin.

"Clearly you were. When will you move on? Look how Briarhaven has thrived since the MacGregors have been gone."

"What do you care about Briarhaven?" I'd shot back. "You don't even live there anymore."

"And the better for it. Look how well my business is doing now." My father had patted the pockets of his waistcoat, a gold watch winking at his wrist, clearly happy with the direction his life had taken since leaving Briarhaven.

"There's more to life than a profitable business. Isn't there, Mum?" I'd turned to my mum, but once again, she'd cast her eyes down, refusing to disagree with my father. Over and over, since Lyra had left, I'd looked to my mother for support and advice, but she'd never been able or willing to help me. It was as though something in her had changed the day Lyra left, or maybe it was my perception of her. I'd always thought I could rely on her to have my best interests in mind, when instead she'd become a quieter echo of my father, parroting his ideas, never standing in her own stead.

Perhaps that had fueled my distrust of women.

"A healthy business leads to a healthy home," Mum had said, her hands gripped tightly in front of her, and my shoulders had slumped, defeated.

There'd been no use arguing or trying to change their minds when it came to the MacGregors. The worst of it was that time had, infuriatingly, proven them right.

Lyra had never really cared for me.

At least, that's what I told myself on the nights when the memory of her laugh wouldn't let me sleep.

Biting back the taste of bitterness that curled in my mouth and pushing the memory aside, I took another sip of my drink and watched as dancers began to gather in the cleared space around the bonfire. Lanterns swung from branches, casting moving patterns over the ground.

"There's the lad." Liam materialized at my side, Knox in tow. "We've been wondering what happened to you. Got lost in a maze?"

"Just stepped out for a wee minute," I said. I wasn't about to say a word about my run-in with Lyra. Largely because I was still trying to make sense of it.

For a moment, at the spring, there had been *something* in her eyes.

And I hated just how much I wanted to figure out what emotion was hidden behind her disgust toward me.

"How are you holding up?" Knox asked, his grin far too knowing for my liking.

"Fine. Why wouldn't I be?" I asked lightly.

"Because Lyra looks like a radiant forest goddess and nobody can take their eyes off her," Knox said, turning back to look toward the dance circle. "Except me, of course. Have you seen Sloane? I'm counting down the minutes until it's acceptable for me to steal her into the shadows."

I didn't say anything, my mouth going dry as Lyra accepted the arm of a man in a well-cut coat, a dark mask concealing half his face. I glanced down at my own kilt—worn, familiar, a bit frayed at the edge. Respectable enough.

Was that the type of man she wanted now?

It was impossible not to notice that every head turned when Lyra walked past on the street. Flowers appeared on her doorstep.

Men offered umbrellas in a light mist of rain. She'd traveled all over Europe, and judging by her clothes, she was well used to luxury.

I was just a simple accountant in a small town in Scotland.

Albeit one with magickal powers. But was that ever going to be enough for a beautiful creature like Lyra MacGregor? As much as it burned, the truth was my father had been right to try to stop me from a future with her. Either way, the path had always been meant to end in disappointment.

A soft sound beside me made me turn. Liam's mouth had dropped open. Following his gaze, I saw Raven emerging from the trees.

She looked ethereal, her hair tumbling in soft waves down her back, her dress flowing like liquid moonlight. A wreath of rowan berries circled her head.

"Och, there's a bonnie lass, aye?" I nudged Liam. "She looks like an angel fallen into the wrong forest."

"Go on, Liam." Knox elbowed him. "She's needing a dance partner. See? She's looking around."

"I can't," Liam whispered, but his eyes never left Raven, longing clouding his expression.

"Aye, you can." I took his glass from his hand. "After she brought you that tea for your back? Don't be rude."

One more shove from Knox and Liam stumbled toward the clearing, drunk on the sight of her. Knox moved closer to me.

"Och, there he goes, our wee fledgling. Think he'll be ready to fly yet?"

Despite the ache twisting in my gut, I laughed. In Scotland, banter between mates was our safety net.

"One can only hope. Unless he trips over his own two feet."

We watched as Raven's face lit with a soft smile and she threaded her arm through Liam's to take their place in the reel.

"The clearing looks great," I said as the band struck up a lively tune. I tapped my foot to the beat, ignoring the tug in my chest urging me forward. In a cèilidh-style dance, I'd be switching partners every few steps. It was inevitable, if I went out there, that I'd end up paired with Lyra.

And I wasn't sure my heart could take it.

"Aye, Sloane and Henry did it all," Knox said. "Those two together are terrifying, with their lists and spreadsheets." He gestured to the canopy of garlands and fairy lights twined overhead. "Do you know how many conversations I had about leaf-color palettes? Leaf-color palettes, Rab."

"Far more than I'd care to," I said, eyes tracking Lyra again as she spun beneath her partner's arm, the gems on her dress catching firelight like stars.

Maybe I'd been here long enough.

"I think I'm going to head out—"

"Och, bloody hell. These two." Knox groaned as Haggis hurled himself into the dance circle, wheeling through pine needles at an alarming speed. Oswald streaked ahead like an offended chaperone, tail fluffed.

I choked on a laugh. "What is he doing?"

"He can't help himself." Knox sighed. "The wee coo loves a dance. Any dance. Every dance."

"Look at him go." I grinned as Haggis spun in circles, his wheels spraying bits of moss. Blue darted overhead, with a small creature—a tiny, glittery menace—flitting at his heels, sword glinting dangerously.

"A fluttermouse," I murmured. "Isn't that something?"

Lyra broke away from her partner, laughing, and bent to muss Haggis's fur before joining the dance again. She glowed bright as summer, and I hated how instantly my chest tightened.

Then her gaze caught mine.

For a heartbeat, time stuttered. She dipped her head, and for one second, the smallest, softest smile flitted across her face, so achingly familiar it split me open.

And something in me snapped.

Screw it.

Before Knox could blink and before I could talk myself out of it, I strode toward the dance.

Lyra's eyes widened when I stepped into the reel opposite her. She drew in a breath, her impossibly gorgeous breasts rising in the dress as she did, and I almost closed my eyes at the sheer wash of need that rushed through me.

How long would I lie to myself about this woman?

How long would I use anger as my shield to protect my sad, wounded heart?

Even now, with the whole town watching, all I wanted to do was kiss her.

The music surged, and we moved . . . hands clasping, bodies brushing, our steps in beat with each other. It had always been this way with us. Perfectly in tune. Every turn brought us closer and then pulled us apart, before spinning us back together.

Her fingers slid across my palm.

Heat bolted up my arm.

She looked up at me with her lips parted, eyes shimmering, and for one dizzying, impossible moment, the world narrowed to the inch of air between us. Her breath mingled with mine. Her lips tilted upward . . .

I bent my head, and our mouths drifted closer, instinct driving us.

And just as my heart slammed against my ribs—

The dance shifted.

We were forced apart, spinning away to new partners. The moment shattered like thin glass.

My pulse crashed. Cold clarity followed.

And I remembered.

How she'd left.

How she'd lied.

How I'd begged her to stay and she'd walked away anyway.

I dragged a deep breath into my lungs, the taste of almost kissing her still heavy on my tongue.

When the reel ended, applause rose through the trees, and I stepped back before she could turn toward me.

Before I could be tempted again.

“Aye,” I rasped to no one. “That’s me off, mate.”

Knox called my name, but I only shook my head as I turned.

Above me, the sky flickered with the dragons preparing for their big display.

But I didn’t look back.

If I did, I wasn’t sure I’d be able to make myself walk away.

CHAPTER EIGHT

Lyra

By the time the dragons finished their fire-breathing light show, my cheeks hurt from smiling.

They'd come in from the north, black shapes against the stars, wings spanning what felt like half the sky. The town had collectively gasped, every head tilting back, the murmurs and chatter dimming to nothing.

One by one, the dragons had circled the clearing, hovering far enough away not to set us alight, close enough that we could see the ripple of muscles under scales. Fire streamed from their mouths in spiraling arcs, weaving patterns of light through the dark, like galaxies briefly birthed in the Briarhaven sky.

My dragon-scale pendant had pulsed in time with their roars, warmth flaring every time a jet of flame painted the air. It had been like standing under a sky full of living fireworks, only these fireworks were intelligent, temperamental, and very particular about sparkly gifts.

When the final dragon swooped low and let loose a curtain of shimmering sparks that fell like golden rain around the clearing—harmless sparks, that is, dissolving before they hit the ground—the entire town had erupted into cheers.

Now, hours later, the festival had slid into that soft, fuzzy stage where people either danced like they'd never have to get up early again or slumped happily by smaller fires with mugs of mulled wine.

I'd danced until my feet ached, until my skirt was dusty with pine needles and my curls were coming loose. By the time I finally let Nova drag me away, my throat was scratchy from laughing and singing.

We caught one of the last vans back to town, Ruth tucked in the crook of my arm, her little body warm against mine. Through the window, I watched the dark outline of the woods recede, occasional flickers of light marking the last of the festival fires.

"I'll get the gifts inside," Knox's driver said when we pulled up outside the cottage. The back of the van was piled with covered trays, leftover pastries, and a handful of small, wrapped parcels people had shoved into my arms as they said good night. Mabon was a time of giving, and I'd been surprised with how many people had brought me a small token of thanks for helping with the food for the festival.

"Thank you," I said, meaning it. I stepped inside, leaving the front door open for the driver.

"Let's get you upstairs so I can get you out of that dress, and then I'm going face-first into my pillow," Nova muttered, rubbing at her eyes. Her winged eyeliner had smeared, but somehow she still managed to look effortlessly edgy, like she'd meant to create smudged smoky-eye makeup.

"Agreed." Though I wasn't nearly ready for sleep. I was too keyed up after the night I'd had, excitement still thrumming through my veins along with my magick and the echo of dragon roars.

Nova quickly helped me out of my dress, both of us laughing as we peeled me out of the layers like some kind of glamorous onion. I left my hair and makeup mostly intact, pulling on a soft jogger set instead. The moment the fabric hit my skin, my body sighed in relief.

Joggers, my new magickal necklace, and residual dragon glitter on my shoulders. It was giving peak witch.

Nova trudged off to bed. I scrambled back downstairs to wave the driver away and lock the front door. Popping my head in Broca's room, I saw she was long asleep, having returned home far earlier in the evening than Nova and me.

With a soft sigh of contentment, I lit a few candles around the room for ambience, and the cottage filled with warm, flickering light, shadows puddling in the corners. I put the kettle on for a wee cup of tea, the familiar ritual settling me.

Did you have fun?

I turned to see Ruth sitting on the edge of the counter, her wee feet dangling over the side. Her wings drooped slightly with tiredness, sword resting beside her.

"I had the best time, Ruth. I truly felt like a princess in a spooky forest fairy tale. That dragon show? To die for. Did you see all the patterns they made? The peony might have been my favorite."

You should have seen it from above, she said smugly. *All florals and crystals and twinkling lights and teeny excitable humans. Really, really stunning. You looked happy.*

"I am."

Are you? She tapped a paw on her wee chest and studied my face. *I get the sense there is a strain of sorts. Do we need to talk about the hedgehog?*

"It's just . . ." I exhaled. "Old hurts. A boy I'd once thought would be my future is now a man who makes me sad about my past."

But you want to know him again?

It was almost three in the morning, a time for truths that couldn't be spoken during the day, and I pursed my lips as I poured steaming water into my mug.

"I . . . I don't know. He pulls at me, Ruth. Maybe that's just the way of first loves. They carve themselves in your heart, you ken?" I hated to admit it, having kept the walls around that old hurt particularly high.

Or maybe you still love him? she said gently.

"How?" I turned and laughed, shaking my head. "I was just a teenager. Who's to say what was real then is real now?"

This makes you sad, Ruth observed.

"Aye, a bit. It's not easy getting lost in the ghosts of your past, I guess."

I know what will cheer you up. Ruth stood and pointed toward the pile of parcels and little boxes now sitting on the dining table. The driver had stacked them neatly. *Let's open some of your Mabon offerings.*

My wee familiar wasn't wrong. I did so love a good prezzie. Plus, for the first time—if we could continue to keep the curse at bay, that is—I might be able to keep the gifts without thinking how I could travel with them.

"That's a grand idea." I took my mug and followed her, Ruth fluttering ahead like a tiny, bossy lantern.

"I've never really been to a festival where people brought me things," I admitted as I sat. "This is nice, isn't it? Like maybe they're saying they want me to belong?"

The pile was a hodgepodge of packages, with some parcels wrapped in brown paper with string, some in bright tissue, a couple in repurposed tea tins. Locals had handed them to me throughout the evening with murmured thanks for my baking and muttered comments about their hopes that for the MacGregor lasses, may this year be kinder than the last.

Has it been hard? This curse of yours? Ruth asked, settling on the table with her knees tucked up, wings draped.

"It's not been great," I said, picking up a slim package wrapped in silver paper with a card tucked under the ribbon. "Briarhaven was the longest we'd ever been able to stay in one spot. Turns out, the Charms had been helping keep the worst of the curse away from Mum so she could raise us here. But even when they were at their most powerful, they couldn't stop it from hurting the town. It didn't help that my mum wasn't much interested in helping them. She's what I would call a chaos demon."

A chaos demon? Ruth brought her paws to her nose in shock.

"Not a real demon. Just that . . . she bred chaos. Thrived in it. The type of person who liked to break things just to hear them shatter."

Ah. Sounds . . . toxic?

"Quite." I smiled wryly and slid my finger under the ribbon, unwrapping the silver paper to reveal a gilded book, each page a recipe card meant to be filled. A sweet note from Raven was written on the inside cover.

"Isn't this lovely? It's a recipe book."

Very pretty. Ruth nodded.

I picked up another package that looked book-shaped, this one wrapped in plain brown kitchen paper with twine. No note was attached, just my name scrawled messily across the front.

"But then Broca had a vision and called us to come home," I continued. "So here we are, back where we started, and with that comes having to run into my first love in the woods like a tragic ballad." I unwrapped the paper to reveal a book with a pretty blue cover that shimmered softly in the candlelight. Something niggled at the back of my brain, a memory I couldn't quite pull free, and it slipped away before I could grasp it.

You've had no other loves? Ruth asked. *No other men, or women, since Rab?*

I laughed at my progressive wee familiar and set the book aside.

"I've dated quite a bit. Men, as that's where my particular taste runs. But it's hard to establish a lasting connection when you know you'll have to leave town in a matter of months. Instead, I guess I threw myself into every relationship with the enthusiasm of a backpacker taking their gap-year trip. Love as if every day counts because you know you'll be leaving soon." I smiled, thinking back on the past men in my life. They'd all been wonderful, if fleeting, connections.

But none were willing to come with you? Ruth asked.

I stopped, struck by the question. The steam from my tea curled up between us.

Rab had been the only one who'd offered to come with me. Or at least, that's what I'd thought he'd been offering. The only one who'd looked at the chaos of my life and said, *I'll figure it out if it means being with you.*

"No," I said quietly, shaking my head. "Most knew the score. Many of these men were quite worldly. Neither of us were looking for long term, just to live in the now. It suited me at the time."

I reached for another parcel wrapped in ruby-red paper. Pulling the ribbon apart, I unwrapped it to find a twin set of gold hair combs with tiny butterflies encased in crystals.

"Aren't these pretty?" I held the combs up for Ruth's inspection.

They'll look gorgeous in your hair, she said, stifling a yawn.

"Should we save the rest for tomorrow? I think I'm finally starting to wind down," I said.

Just one more, she pleaded, tiny paws clasped.

"Okay, one more. What about you, Ruth? Any love for you? Family?"

My family are mostly with their witches now, she said. *We're trained from a young age to take on the role of familiar. It's a great honor, you ken?*

"But what about love? Do you need it? Or seek it?"

Not particularly, she said after considering. *I find great satisfaction in finally being able to fulfill my life's goal, which was meeting you and becoming your familiar. I'm not sure I'll ever need or want love. At least not in the sense you crave it.*

"Maybe that's for the better," I murmured, and paused when I saw the name on the card of the package I held.

Rab.

He'd gotten me a gift.

My stomach swooped.

I unwrapped the package, my hands suddenly shaky, to find a pair of knit socks with cupcakes all over them.

My mouth dropped open.

It was a silly gift.

But he'd remembered.

As a teenager, I'd had a favorite pair of socks I'd worn endlessly, covered in ridiculous pastel cupcakes. They'd snagged on a nail in the old barn we'd once spent all our time in. I'd tried to mend them, but over time the hole had grown too large, and the socks hadn't survived our next move. I'd mourned them for weeks.

The memory hit me like a soft punch. Rab sitting cross-legged in the barn, carefully trying to darn the sock for me while pretending he wasn't terrible at it. The two of us laughing when the mending turned the pattern into something that looked more like an abstract crime scene.

More confused than ever, I held the new socks to my heart, unsure what the gift meant.

You're pleased, Ruth said, standing with her paws on her hips, head tilted in concern. *But sad?*

"Aye." I swallowed past the lump in my throat. "That pretty much sums up my relationship with Rab too. I think it's time for bed," I said, my heart shaky.

Be well, sweet Lyra, Ruth said softly as she fluttered up to my shoulder. *Mabon is a time of balance and new beginnings. Your new life starts now.*

I carried my tea upstairs, the socks clutched in one hand, the dragon-scale pendant warm against my chest, wondering how I would ever fall asleep.

But I did.

Cupcake socks warming my feet and dragons' fire still painting my dreams, for the first time in ages, I slept dreamlessly through the night.

CHAPTER NINE

Lyra

It had been over a week since the Mabon festival, and though there had been plenty of disasters in the interim, no more hedgehogs had appeared.

I considered that a *very* small win.

I also couldn't stop thinking about Rab.

I hated that he still had an effect on me. I hated that my eyes were still drawn to him, and when he was near, I found myself leaning toward him, as though we were two magnets pulling each other closer.

I hated that after all these years, I still cared what he thought of me.

It shouldn't be that way.

I should be over him.

Past thinking his opinion of me mattered.

And yet, as much as I tried to ignore it, I still found that he got under my skin.

I hadn't told anyone about my run-in with Rab. What would be the point? My sisters would grill me with a million questions that I wouldn't be able to answer, and I was too embarrassed about the hedgehog incident to tell them.

Because, upon further reflection, I had an idea of what had triggered the champagne-to-hedgehog pipeline, so to speak.

And if my hunch was true, well, then I could basically just never see Rab again.

Which was fine by me.

Sighing, I pulled another tray of almond croissants from the oven. There had been this moment—actually, there'd been *several* moments—in my interaction with Rab that had dominated my thoughts this past week, but when I'd noticed he still carried the pocket square that I'd made for him? And really looked at him? Not as a boy, but as a devastatingly handsome man who'd really grown into who he was as a person?

I'd wanted him.

Desperately.

I'd wanted to crawl into his arms and never leave. I'd wanted to kiss him for hours like we used to, lying in the fields, our future dreams ahead of us.

And because I couldn't look him in the eye, at least not while thinking such thoughts, I'd stared hard at his champagne glass instead.

Which had subsequently turned into a hedgehog of all things.

Transmutation hadn't been on my bingo card for my magickal powers, and it had surprised me as much as it had him.

I also hadn't been able to replicate it since. No matter how hard I tried, it was thus far impossible for me to turn an inanimate object into a sentient being.

So why him? Why that?

It frustrated me and made me feel foolish, a feeling I deeply tried to avoid at all costs.

True to her word, Marcie had been an impeccable, albeit largely silent, boss. I found I didn't mind coming into the bakery in the early-morning hours, when the streets of Briarhaven were quiet and stars still twinkled softly in the sky. This morning I'd noticed the leaves had begun to change, their colors shifting from green to golden to ruddy orange.

I loved this time of year. Not just because we were saying goodbye to summer and looking toward the holidays, but because there was something so special about the change of seasons, when nature began to quiet and put itself to bed for a while. If you were in the Northern Hemisphere, that is. I tried to imagine Christmas with sunshine and palm trees and laughed quietly to myself, shaking my head.

"What's funny?" Marcie asked from where she piped frosting onto cupcakes.

Mostly, Marcie enjoyed listening to murder podcasts first thing in the morning, and though initially I found them jarring, soon I was equally as invested in the stories as Marcie was. Today she'd put on classical music, which was also a far cry from the usual death metal she enjoyed. When I had questioned her about it, she just shrugged and said, "Today the music must soothe."

"I was just thinking about Christmas with sunshine and palm trees." I moved the croissants to a cooling rack. "It must feel so different."

"It does. But also fun. I dated a merman for a bit. He was a wild ride, let me tell you." Marcie paused and gazed into the air, her eyes closed. "Glorious in bed. Absolutely rigorous, just—"

"Right, okay, and where was this?" I was desperate to get the image of Marcie and a merman shagging out of my head.

"Antigua. And Christmas is still fun. Twinkle lights look great on palm trees too. If you do them right. Otherwise the tree just looks like a huge penis."

"Damn it, I wish I'd caught that on film." We turned to see a handsome man with dark hair, dark-rimmed glasses, and a flannel shirt standing in the door, a clipboard in hand.

"Do you, though?" I asked, laughing, and dusted my hands off. This must be the executive producer that Marcie had said was coming around this morning to check out the bakery before filming commenced.

In two days.

Nerves churned low in my gut, even though I pasted a sunny smile on my face and automatically went into charming mode.

"Oh, I really do. The unexpected always makes for the best television." The man cocked his head and studied the both of us. "And you two are . . . very unexpected. Are you a couple?"

"Like she could handle me." Marcie snorted, and my eyes widened. I wasn't sure if I should be insulted or not. But then, upon further reflection, Marcie was likely not wrong. In every part of the world, she was a terrifying woman, so I imagined she would equally be so in bed.

And now I was back to thinking about Marcie in bed.

Mentally slapping my forehead, I pressed my lips together and raised my eyebrows at the man.

"I'm Marcie, owner of Mystic Munchies," Marcie said as she wiped her hand on a towel and shook the man's outstretched hand so hard he jerked forward a step.

"I'm Vaughn Culloch. Executive producer of *Bewitching Bake Off*."

"And an elf." Marcie sniffed, looking him up and down in approval. "What clan?"

"Ah, of the streams. Aberdeenshire."

"Good folk out there. Sit. You'll eat." Marcie pointed to a table, and Vaughn blinked at her before seeming to realize that resistance was futile. He cast me a *help me* look, and I smiled, dusting my hands off and pouring him a cup of coffee.

"Milk or sugar in your coffee?" I asked.

"Just plain. Thanks."

Pouring myself a cup as well, I went over and joined him at the table. It was still well before the bakery opened, and there was a short lull in time between when things went in and came out of the ovens. Usually, Marcie took her cup of tea in her office, poring over receipts from the day before, during this time, while I tried to memorize the newest recipe she'd given to me. So far, I hadn't had any success with my baking, but Marcie was surprisingly patient. She knew I had the learning curve of all learning curves at the moment. The curse had settled its claws into me, making it virtually impossible for me to use my magick, and Briarhaven still suffered from darkness all day long.

"Welcome to Briarhaven," I said, putting the coffee down in front of Vaughn. He blinked at me, a smile hovering on his lips.

"Please tell me you're not on the show so I can ask you out to dinner."

My smile widened.

"I'm Lyra MacGregor, one of your contestants."

"Damn it." Vaughn's face fell, but then he brightened. "At least it's just a Christmas special. It won't take all that long to film. Can I ask you out to dinner after the show wraps up?"

"Um—"

"Can I ask if you like having your fingers broken, one by one?" Marcie asked, her tone mild, as she punched a mound of dough on her butcher-block counter.

"No, I can't say that I do," Vaughn said, wincing.

"You will not put my staff in a compromising position," Marcie ordered, shooting him a disapproving look over her shoulder.

"Yes, ma'am."

I bit back a grin. Marcie paused her dough punching and brought us a plate of pistachio-crusted croissants.

"Eat."

"Yes, ma'am," Vaughn said again, and shot me a pleading look across the table.

"You'll enjoy these," I promised. "Her pistachio croissants are a house favorite. And she doesn't always serve them along with the threat of bodily harm."

"Oh, so I'm lucky, then?"

I laughed. Vaughn was actually really cute, and if Marcie hadn't interrupted his advances, I might have actually considered going on a date with him. Since we'd returned to Briarhaven, I'd abstained from dating. I remembered what it was like to live in a small town where everyone was always in your business, and the last thing I needed was the busybodies discussing my dating life.

But this? This could be an opportunity to date again, at least when filming was over. Vaughn didn't live here, which meant it wouldn't be anything too serious, and I could enjoy being in the company of a handsome man again. I had to admit, a part of me did miss being wined and dined. There was something to be said for dating men who put you on a pedestal.

It was far better than ones who threw you away.

Shaking my head before my thoughts went dark, I took a sip of my coffee and waited while Vaughn took a bite of the croissant.

"Och, Marcie. This is brilliant," Vaughn said, holding the pastry in the air in a salute to Marcie. She nodded. He wasn't telling her anything she didn't already know.

"So, Lyra. What brings you to Briarhaven?" Vaughn asked, taking another bite of the croissant, his face creasing in pleasure at the taste. "Have you always lived here?"

"She grew up here, traveled for a bit, and now she's back." Marcie glowered from where she had resumed her dough punching.

"Right." Vaughn's lips quirked, and he flipped through a few pages on his clipboard. "So, we'll start contestant interviews today, just to get some backstory for when we film, and the production crew will be in to set up cameras, run wiring, make sure lighting and everything is in place. We'll need to block things out, make sure we have our angles, that kind of thing."

"Today?" The color drained from my face. I'd wanted to back out of this a million times since I'd gotten my magick, but everyone had convinced me to stay in. But now that it was all happening, I felt the urge to throw up.

"Aye, today. We start filming this Monday."

"And when do we meet our partners?" I asked, hopeful for some information. For a small town, there had been surprisingly little gossip about who else had been picked for the show. Which, I'll admit, was decidedly annoying.

"On the first day of filming. As usual." Vaughn winked at me, and I groaned.

"I'm dying to know."

"Everybody always is. That's why we want to catch your reactions on camera. We like things unfiltered. Unpracticed."

"Hmpf." I dropped my chin into my palm.

"I do hope you're not getting the jitters. I can already see the camera will love you, and we'd hate to lose you from the show."

"If she wants to leave, she can leave," Marcie cut in.

"I—"

"I agree, Marcie. But I hope she doesn't leave, because I think our viewers will love her."

"Why?" I asked, curious. "You barely know me. I could be absolutely vile."

Vaughn's smile deepened. "I highly doubt that. You've been nothing but smiley and welcoming since I came in. Plus, not to state the obvious, but you're knockout gorgeous."

"Which she well knows. You think you're first man to be mooning about in here over the lass?" Marcie asked.

I winced. "I swear there aren't that many men."

"If there aren't, there will be. After the show airs. We'll make a star of you." Vaughn beamed and polished off his croissant, and I took a sip of my coffee, gulping down the nerves that caught in my throat.

I'd used to think that was what I wanted. But now that my magick wasn't working, my life had been turned upside down. What had been something I was excited about now loomed as my biggest fear—being made to look like an idiot on television.

CHAPTER TEN

Lyra

"Ow!" I blinked awake to see Ruth fluttering over me, tweezers in her paws instead of her normal sword. "What are you doing?"

Plucking your eyebrows.

"I'm certain that's not in your job description," I grumbled, rolling to pull the blanket over my face. Ruth bopped me on the forehead with her tiny fist.

"Hey!" I grumbled, squinting at her. "I thought you were on my side."

I am. Which is why you need to get up. We've got to get you ready for your first day of filming.

Butterflies filled my gut. It had taken me far too long to fall asleep the night before; instead I'd spent the time opening the rest of the gifts I'd received at Mabon and writing out thank-you cards. I had to hand it to Briarhaven, they'd certainly shown up when it came to presenting interesting gifts. Aside from the touching necklace that hummed with power around my neck, I'd received magickal ornaments, a talking mirror, a variety of charmed baking instruments, and even a certificate for pottery-making classes.

But my fierce wee familiar was correct. I did need to get up and get started on my makeup. There was no way I didn't have bags and dark circles under my eyes after a largely sleepless night. Sighing, I pulled the blanket down and rubbed my hands over my face.

I think you should wear the red or the purple.

I turned to look at where I'd hung three dresses out as options to wear for my first day of filming. Even though I'd be in an apron for much of the show, they wanted to do some introduction interviews and confessionals, and that would be just wearing a normal outfit. I'd been instructed to stay away from patterns, and that bold colors showed up well on film.

"Red. I think. It is a good power color."

My door banged open, and I shrieked as Nova and Sloane bounded in, Blue wheeling in an arc over their head.

"What the hell?"

"Och, there's a bonnie lass ready for her first day of filming." Nova took on a deeper accent and gave me a lewd wink.

"Seriously?" I groaned, covering my face with my hands.

"We're just here for moral support. We know we can't go in with you to filming today, but wanted to be here while you got ready in case you needed to talk about anything," Sloane said, sitting on the corner of my bed. Blue slammed into the comforter next to her, bouncing once, before tumbling over to me, stomach up. He turned his head to me, tongue falling to the side, a hopeful look on his face.

"Hey, buddy," I said, reaching out to scratch his tummy, and his eyes closed in bliss.

Everyone needed an emotional support emberwolf, I decided. I cast a look to where Ruth was neatly lining up my makeup at my small vanity table across my room. I'd learned that my wee familiar dearly loved order, so she was always arranging everything *just* so. It was like having a tiny militant housekeeper following me around at all times.

"How am I going to do this?" I whispered, my gaze going between Nova and Sloane.

"Like you do everything else . . . one recipe at a time."

"One ingredient at a time," Nova amended, coming over to slide an arm around my shoulders.

"Listen, we've discussed this. There's nothing in the rules that says you have to use magick in every step of the challenge. Plus, your partner is going to have magick. Just lean heavily on them for the magick aspect of things, and you do your charm and glamour thing to win the judges over. Once you meet her, you can have a wee chat and come up with a game plan. I'm sure it's going to be fine."

"You're right. I know you're right. She's going to want to win. Because who signs up for these things unless they want to win?" Feeling better, I nudged Nova aside and swung my legs out from under the blanket. "Right, I'll just pop in the shower and get ready."

"I'm on brekkie," Sloane said, and Nova threw her head back and laughed.

"I hope you're ready for a fortifying breakfast of Ritz and Primula," Nova said.

"Just tea. A spot of tea would be lovely." I was too nervous to eat anyway. Sloane's preferred breakfast of crackers and spreadable cheese was not exactly enticing.

Two hours later, I was sitting in the passenger seat of Sloane's car, frozen.

"There's . . . so many people," I whispered. I guess I hadn't known what to expect, but the sheer amount of activity swarming around the bakery was beyond anything that I'd dreamt of. There were cameras to shoot the exterior, lighting, boom microphones, chairs set up in front of what looked to be TV screens on wheels. People bustled about, coffee cups in hand, others with wires over their shoulders or reading clipboards. It all looked incredibly professional, and the low dredges of panic seeped into my stomach.

"That's showbiz, baby." Sloane glanced over to see my face and immediately changed her tune. Reaching over, she grabbed my hand. "Hey, look at me."

I turned, meeting her eyes. She looked her usually rumpled self, but her eyes were fierce in her face. Mama bear mode activated.

"If you want to leave, we leave. No questions asked. I've been telling you to go ahead with it because it's what I thought you wanted, but if you don't, I truly do not care. This is only about what is best for you, Lyra. Just tell me and I'll turn this car around and we can all go back to bed."

Sloane. She'd always been a constant in our chaotic life. She'd borne the brunt of criticism when we'd first moved back to Briarhaven, and would do so again if needed.

"No, you're right. I do want this. The magick not working has thrown me off is all. But that's fine. It's all fine. I've gone twenty-five years without magick, as you've said. I'll figure it out."

"And if you blow anything up, well, it makes for great television," Nova said from the back.

Swiveling, I glared at her. Ruth fluttered up, sword in hand.

"Hey, hey. I was just kidding." Nova held her hands in front of her face. "Call off your minion."

"No, I don't think that I will," I mused, and Nova shrieked as Ruth fluttered closer.

"Can you not scream?" Sloane hissed as a few people turned to look at the car.

"Easy for you. You're not the one with a wee assassin coming after you."

"Lyra." Sloane sighed and pinched her nose.

"Ruth, come here. Are you okay going in my bag? I'm bringing you in with me."

Ruth gave Lyra one more warning look and then flew to my lap and crawled into my Loewe tote bag, gifted to me by an enthusiastic admirer in London. I didn't keep the man, but I did keep the bag.

"Oh, look, they're getting the set ready." Sloane pointed to where they were bringing a Christmas tree up the walk and into the store. A switch flipped, and the outside of Mystic Munchies lit up. It looked like Christmas had thrown up all over the building. Twinkle lights fell in curtains over the stone facade, and evergreen garlands were wrapped around the doors and windows, with lights intertwined among the leaves. Elaborate bows in red, gold, and silver were wound through the greenery, and I gasped as snow began to fall.

“They brought in a snow machine,” Nova said. “Jeez, they should have filmed this when Sloane’s curse was working at top speed. No need for a machine then.”

“And likely no real ability to film. The streets were almost blocked for weeks,” Sloane reminded her. Her iteration of the curse had brought endless snow to Briarhaven, along with the anger of most of the residents.

“And now it’s just complete darkness. How are we going to explain it?”

“As of now, Knox has met with the production crew and informed them we’ve purposely magicked the town this way in order to showcase the Christmas lights to their best effect for filming.”

My mouth dropped open, and I turned to Sloane, my eyes wide. “That’s such a good idea.”

“Isn’t it? Proud of myself for that one.” Sloane patted her own shoulder, looking pleased with herself. “But it’s not the production crew we’re really all that worried about.”

“It’s the normal people.” I let out a sigh and smoothed a wrinkle in my skirt. So far, the wards had been holding, and the clouds still clung to Briarhaven, creating a somewhat feasible explanation for the darkness that shrouded the village. But even so, it would be hard to explain the lack of light for long. Even the cloudiest of days were rarely cast in full darkness. The rumblings of discontent had started to spread through Briarhaven, as people feared losing out on the lucrative tourist business as we neared the holiday season. Tourists came in droves to buy enchanting gifts and treats from the shops, but they wouldn’t if they thought the town was *actually* haunted and posed any real danger.

“But that’s not for you to worry about,” Sloane said, injecting a cheerful note in her voice. “At least not for today. The festival committee is on it, and we’re all brainstorming solutions.”

“The festival committee composed of you, Knox, and Henry?” Nova asked.

“And Blue.” Sloane glared over her shoulder.

"Ladies. Please continue all bickering later. I'm going." I cracked open the door and a gust of wind slid inside the car.

"You got this, Lyra!" Nova and Sloane shouted all kinds of encouragements at me as I checked on Ruth, hitched my bag on my shoulder, and slammed the door, muffling their words. It was a good thing I hadn't done anything fancy with my hair. I bent my head to the brisk wind and walked up the pavement until I spotted Vaughn.

"Lyra, great to see you." Vaughn had a headset around his neck, a clipboard in hand, and was bundled into one of those poofy jackets that made him look a bit like a marshmallow. "We'll just get you through here to the back of the building, where we've brought in a few trailers for hair and makeup and all that. We'll film your introduction in"—Vaughn glanced down at his watch—"twenty minutes."

"That quick?" My voice hit a high note.

"Aye, we like to knock them out quickly because then we need to introduce you to your partner. Otherwise it gets too hard to coordinate when everyone is arriving to set if we need to keep things a secret."

"Oh, sure. That makes sense." Fingers crossed my partner was a professional baker who excelled in magick. I would work the judges; she could work the spells.

It was going to be fine. I was sure of it.

Twenty minutes later, I was convinced this was the worst decision I'd ever made.

Everything was just so . . . professional. From the lighting to the microphones, the massive cameras, and the whole "Quiet on set!" right before they started filming. The inside of the bakery had been transformed into a Christmas wonderland. They'd draped the walls in a deep evergreen brocade fabric, entirely obscuring the manic mural with the furious beasties. I couldn't say I blamed them, as filming with that in the background would be more than a touch distracting. A trio of Christmas trees exploding with ornaments and lights were clustered in the corner, and boughs and garlands were draped in every available space. I hoped the test kitchen where we'd be actually baking wasn't as decorated as this, because it would make it hard to move about if it was. Not to mention, it was highly flammable.

I'd seen enough explosions on the show to look gingerly at the silver tinsel that dripped from the ceiling as I took a seat in a solo chair in the middle of the room.

Vaughn followed my gaze.

"Don't like the tinsel?"

"No, it's lovely." I flushed when I realized the cameras were on. "And also highly flammable."

Vaughn chuckled as he took the seat across from me, outside the range of the cameras.

"Spoken like a true baker."

I shrugged one shoulder, crossing my legs and smoothing my skirt down over my thighs. I'd gone with the deep red dress with a sweetheart neckline, sleeves to my elbows, and a skirt that dropped to mid-calf. The dress looked great on me, and Ruth had been right: It was a power color.

Still. It was hard to not feel nervous when three cameras were pointed at my face and a group of people I hadn't met yet stood behind Vaughn, all staring at me.

"I've watched the show enough to see that things don't always go to plan." A grin spread across my face. "Like the sticky toffee pudding incident."

Everyone in the room laughed. It was impossible not to. One baker had mistakenly attempted to speed up the baking time with a new spell, and the pudding had grown legs, exploded out of the oven, and raced around the room and out the back door, never to be seen again.

"So, Lyra," Vaughn began, checking the notes on his clipboard. "You grew up in Briarhaven? How have you found the new look of the town?"

"I love it," I said, pleased I could give an honest answer. "Granted, I was a bit surprised when we first returned to town last year, but not only has the entire town gotten a fabulous makeover, it's also become a lovely spot for tourists and locals alike. It's incredibly charming, so if you get a chance to visit, I highly recommend it." I beamed at the camera. There, that should make Knox happy.

"There you have it, folks. Briarhaven's best cheerleader." Vaughn grinned at me. "And since we're going to be celebrating Christmas with this challenge, I have to ask, what was your favorite Christmas? Were you one of those wee ones who was peeking down the staircase to see if Santa had arrived? Or was it the food for you? Did your mum make a special meal for tea?"

I froze. Christmas had always been a tricky time in my family. Mum had been unpredictable at best, and money had sometimes been an issue, so fights were the usual fare served at Christmas. More often than not, my sisters and I would spend the morning together in one of our rooms, making up games and trying to avoid the arguments downstairs.

"Lyra?" Vaughn prodded, and I blinked, shaking my head and clearing my throat.

"I . . ." *Focus, Lyra.* I shook my head slightly. "My best Christmas was actually spent with my high school boyfriend."

"Ah, young love." Vaughn perked up. "And what was his name?"

"Rab," I whispered, surprised I'd brought it up. I hadn't thought about this in years.

Vaughn glanced at a woman next to him, raising an eyebrow, and she shook her head slightly.

"And what did young Rab do to make your Christmas so special?"

"It . . . it had been a rough day at home." Between the blinding lights and the shock of this being the first memory that had come up, I stumbled through my words. "My dad had lost his job, money was tight, and Mum wasn't happy about it. There were a lot of arguments. But our gran made it as fun as she could."

"But . . ." Vaughn encouraged me to continue. I closed my eyes briefly. I'd watched enough reality television to know that this was the deal. I would have to be vulnerable if I wanted people to root for me. Still, now that I was here and being asked these questions with cameras trained on my face, I realized just how tricky it was to be forthcoming.

"But . . . it still was a pretty dismal day. Until Rab surprised me, that is." I sank back into the memory, pulling it out like a comfort blanket. "He surprised me at the end of the day, tossing pebbles at my window, and I snuck out with him."

"Naughty," Vaughn said, a twinkle in his eye.

"Och, I was known to get into trouble once in a while." I laughed and flipped my hair back, warming to the memory. "But he told me to bring my sisters this time. There was an old barn outside town, and he'd decorated it for Christmas. He'd brought in lanterns, hot water bottles, and loads of blankets. We all piled under the blankets, and then he gave us presents he'd picked out for each of us." My eyes misted at the memory.

"That sounds really sweet," Vaughn said, encouraging me to continue.

"It was." I swallowed, looking down at my lap. "And then he brought out sweeties and a thermos of hot cocoa, and we played a vicious game of UNO. It was, honestly, perfect. A perfect Christmas."

The room grew quiet, and I glanced up to see everyone staring at me, the cameras still recording. I winced. Perhaps I had been a touch too vulnerable. It was best that I put my walls back up.

"That sounds really lovely, Lyra. And what happened with the lad?" Vaughn asked, and I pulled my walls around me like a cloak.

"We moved." I pressed my lips together. That wasn't even remotely the real story, but there were some wounds that weren't open for public scrutiny. "Mum and Dad split up, and we moved to the States."

"Och, I'm sorry to hear that, Lyra."

I needed to turn this around before my entire interview was depressing. This was supposed to be a fun Christmas show, not Lyra's depressing childhood memories.

"One of my favorite things about moving was that I got to experience cuisines from all over the world. It really fueled my love of cooking, and it's why I started a YouTube channel focused on trying out recipes I've found from around the world." I handed Vaughn a new topic.

"And, since you just turned twenty-five recently, you're still fairly new to your magick. Care to share how that's going?" Vaughn winked at me and gave a subtle shake of his head, discouraging me from answering. Taking the hint, I put a flirty look on my face.

"That's for me to know, and you all to find out."

"You heard it here, friends! The lovely Lyra is fresh to her magick, has traveled the world testing out recipes, and is ready to make brand-new Christmas memories. Welcome to *Bewitching Bake Off*, Lyra—we're excited to have you on the show!"

I smiled at the camera until the light blinked off and someone called, "Cut!"

"Great job, Lyra." Vaughn stood and came over to shake my hand.

"It wasn't too depressing?" I asked, worried.

"Nope, it was just the right amount." Vaughn chuckled. "The reality is, not everyone always has a great Christmas. I think a lot of people will relate to your experiences. Now, I hate to hustle you out of here, but we do need to interview the next participant. Debbie here will take you back to the trailer. Once our interviews are done, we'll film the next portion."

"How many teams are there?" I asked, curious.

"Four teams. Eight participants. Less than our usual twelve since it's a holiday special." Vaughn looked up and nodded at someone, and then back to his clipboard. "Great job this morning. We'll see you shortly."

And just like that, I was ushered out and through the hallway and deposited into a trailer.

Told to wait, I plopped down on a bench and stared at the wall.

Are you okay? Ruth crawled out of my tote, where she'd been napping, and fluttered to stand on the table next to me.

"Um, that's hard to say, really." I shrugged one shoulder and took a deep breath, reaching up to cup my hand around my dragon-scale necklace. Instantly, a cooling wash of calm worked its way through me, and I sighed, releasing some of the tension. "It's just that . . . I brought up a memory on camera. About Rab and me."

The boy you cared about.

"Well, he's not a boy anymore."

And you still care about him.

"I . . . It doesn't matter, Ruth." I shook my head, turning to gaze out the darkened window of the trailer.

It had been years since I'd thought about Rab and the sweet Christmas he had given me and my sisters. And once I did, other memories started to flood back. Like the summer night we'd stayed up and played with the hedgehogs scrambling through the garden, feeding them and laughing at their little squeaks and grunts. Or the time we'd snuck out and watched a meteor shower from the roof of the old barn.

Shaking my head, I pushed those memories down.

I needed to keep my mind in the game and focused on the competition, not on my past. Sure, Christmas was a nostalgic time, but at the end of the day, what I needed to do was keep my eyes on the prize. I wanted to win *Bewitching Bake Off* and show the world that the MacGregor sisters weren't the laughingstock of the magickal community.

CHAPTER ELEVEN

Rab

I was fairly certain my first interview had been a disaster.

And I suspected the producers knew that I was doing *Bewitching Bake Off* against my will.

"That Vaughn lad," I said to Knox. He'd joined me in my trailer, allowed on set since he was provost of the town. "I don't like him."

"You barely met him," Knox said, kicking his feet out in front of him and crossing his legs at his ankles.

"He was nosy."

"That's his job, mate. The viewers want to get to know you."

"Why?" I asked, genuinely bewildered. "Aren't they watching to see recipes and shite like that?"

"Och. Mate." Knox slapped a hand to his forehead. "Please tell me you watched at least one episode of this show like I asked."

I'd meant to but had been distracted by quietly obsessing over my run-in with Lyra at the Mabon festival. Every time I tried to read or watch a show, my thoughts drifted off, and our almost kiss haunted me. What would have happened if we'd kissed? And why for a moment had I thought I'd seen longing in her eyes?

Because you're deluded, lad, and that's the way of it.

"I was busy," I mumbled, and Knox sighed.

"The reason reality television is successful is that the viewers also get invested in the contestants and their real-life stories. You have to be relatable."

I glowered at him. "I'm relatable."

"Are you?" Knox gave me a disbelieving look.

"I am. I'm an accountant. What's more relatable than that? Everyone's heard of my job. Many people have worked with one before. There's literally nothing interesting about my life."

"And that doesn't bother you at all?" Knox quirked an eyebrow at me.

"Why should it bother me? I like predictability. I don't like to be surprised by things. I'm a man of routine. It's what makes me a great accountant," I pointed out, leaning forward to pick up my cup of coffee.

"And an incredibly boring reality show contestant."

"Fine by me." I shrugged, unbothered. "I didn't even want to be on this damn show."

"You could put a little bit of effort in," Knox grumbled.

"It's your fault. You picked me, remember?"

"I expected you to at least try."

"I answered the questions, didn't I?"

"With, like, two words."

I shrugged. "Why was he asking all that stuff about my love life? You didn't sign me up for a dating show, did you?"

"No, Rab. *Bewitching Bake Off* is not secretly moonlighting as a hidden dating show. At the very least you could pretend like you're not being tortured."

"This *is* torture. They put makeup on me!" I pointed to my face, where a belligerent woman had dusted powder across my nose before I'd pushed the brush away.

"It's just to stop the shine under the big lights." Knox leaned forward. "Just promise me you'll be nice to your partner. Whomever they are, it's likely they'll be super excited to be on this show. It might be nothing for you, but it could be a dream for someone else. It wouldn't be fair to ruin that with your grumpy attitude."

My shoulders slumped. Damn it, but he had a point. My job literally focused on how to help small business owners achieve their dreams. It was one of my favorite parts of my job when I was able to help move a business into the black. The last thing I ever wanted to do was shit on someone's dream.

"Och, that's a fair point." I met Knox's eyes. "I'll do better. It's just a bit of baking. I know how to work in a kitchen, even if it's not my favorite. I promise to be an excellent sous chef."

Knox groaned. "You don't need a sous chef in baking."

"Fine, assistant. Whatever. I'll assist with a smile on my face. What could possibly go wrong?"

My words came back to me as I stood in the hallway two hours later, just off set. Everyone had hyped this moment up, and though I didn't really think it was a big deal, and this was just some baking competition, I'd promised Knox I would put my best foot forward. Even so, I didn't feel all that nervous. If anything, I was just a bit bored. It seemed like a lot of the behind the scenes in filming reality shows involved sitting around and waiting. At least something was about to happen now.

We were going to be the last team to be announced. Then we would get some time to have a quick chat, get to know each other, and then our very first challenge would start. From this point forward, I was told things would move fairly quickly, as they planned to have everything filmed and done in about ten days or so. I don't know why that length of time surprised me, as for some reason I'd expected it to carry on much longer. But I could do anything for ten days. Even if it was paste a smile on my face and hold a whisk for my teammate.

Knox was just pleased that the filming would go fairly quickly. He was in a particularly tricky spot. Not only did we have to lie to the tourists about what was getting filmed in Briarhaven since the show was broadcast only for magickals, but we also still had to explain away the constant darkness that shrouded the city. At the moment, Knox was sticking close to the truth and telling tourists that a show was, indeed, being filmed at the bakery. But he was lying and telling people it was just a documentary on the historical methods of using ancient grains in baked goods. He deliberately made it sound as dry as dirt, in order to discourage anyone's interest in learning more about the film trucks that had set up camp outside Mystic Munchies.

"And last but not least, we have our final team. Both contestants are originally from Briarhaven, and from what we've just learned . . . share a history. Come on out, team number four!"

I jerked as I realized that Vaughn was talking about me and then paused. What did he mean, "share a history"? Before I could do anything else, the aggressive makeup lady gave my shoulder a shove, and I straightened and stepped out into the bakery, blinking as my eyes adjusted to the bright lights beaming in my face.

Lyra stepped out of the other door.

For the second time in my life, it felt like my heart stopped.

Her mouth dropped open, and she brought a hand to her lips.

I froze. I couldn't say anything. Blood pounded in my ears. The world slowed, and though I knew Vaughn was saying something, all I could do was stare at Lyra, looking mouthwateringly sexy in a brilliant red dress.

"Rab?" Vaughn's voice penetrated the fog that surrounded me, and I turned, blinking at him like he was speaking a foreign language. "Are you all right, lad?"

"Aye," I said, clearing my throat when my voice rasped. I was most decidedly not "all right" as I tried to swallow past my suddenly dry throat. Sadness washed over me, as I realized I'd have to say goodbye to the nice life that I'd built for myself when I went to jail for killing Knox.

"Lyra?" Vaughn asked. Stepping forward, he hooked an arm through hers and looked adoringly down at her. I stiffened. Why was he touching her in such a familiar way? I certainly hoped she hadn't fallen for the producer. He gave me creepy vibes. "Are you ready to reconnect with your new teammate, Rab?"

"Um, yes, of course," Lyra said, pasting a smile on her bonnie face. Only someone who knew her well would see the lines of tension that banded her eyes.

"Imagine our surprise when we learned that our last team has a romantic history?" Vaughn drawled, clearly delighted with the development. All I could do was stare at the blinking red light on the camera and imagine the viewers at home eating this development up. My pain was not for public consumption, and I truly had no idea how to respond to this situation. "Who knows . . . maybe this will be the second time that Rab delivers the best Christmas ever for Lyra."

My gaze swung to Lyra's.

"She said that?" I shocked myself by asking. Vaughn, clearly pleased that I'd come back to life, seized on the moment.

"Och, she did, mate. Raved about what a brilliant job you did decorating the barn and making a sweet moment for her and her sisters."

"I don't know if 'raved' is the word I'd use," Lyra grumbled as Vaughn drew her forward to stand next to me.

"That was your best Christmas memory?" I ignored Vaughn, my eyes drilling into Lyra's. When Vaughn had asked me about mine, I'd remembered that moment with Lyra but had refused to speak on it. On *her*. Instead, I'd talked about Christmas from when I was just a wee lad, and my grandpa was still alive and had used his magick to make me float across the room like Superman.

"It's just what came out." Lyra shrugged, looking away.

"Well, you two, perhaps you can re-create some Christmas magic when we start the competition. I'm sure working together won't cause things to heat up in the kitchen . . ." Vaughn elbowed me and winked, and I turned my head slowly to glare at him. Vaughn cleared his throat. "Right, so, Rabbie, I'm told your family owned a restaurant. How would you say those skills might help you out today?"

"They owned a chippy. Not a bakery. The only thing I learned is that I'm good at taking orders."

"Sounds like a perfect partner to me," Vaughn quipped. Lyra's cheeks flushed, and she looked away.

I wanted to simultaneously hug Lyra and punch Vaughn, so I did neither, instead turning to stare sullenly into the camera.

"And Lyra? You said you're a massive fan of the show and that you cook all the time. How do you feel things will go working alongside Rab?"

"So long as he actually does what he says he'll do, I'm sure it will be fine," Lyra said, steadfastly looking anywhere but at me.

"What's that supposed to mean?" I burst out. When had I ever failed her? If anything, she was the one who had lied to me.

"Oh boy, things are already starting to heat up in the kitchen, aren't they? Let's save that fire for the first challenge, shall we? It's time to meet the other teams and get assigned to your stations. Stay tuned, everyone, as *Bewitching Bake Off* returns with the first challenge of the season."

I waited until someone called, "Cut!" and then turned to Lyra.

"What—"

"Nope," Vaughn said, stepping between us. "Save it for the cameras. This is reality TV gold."

"I'll not have my private life tromped out for public pleasure," I said, whirling on Vaughn.

"Then you shouldn't have signed up for a reality show," Vaughn said, flipping pages on his clipboard as the scary makeup lady drew close, brushes in hand.

"But—"

Someone called for Vaughn's attention, while another woman, also carrying a clipboard, came over and ushered me back toward the hallway. "Come on, then, let's get you to your station. The first challenge is going to be filmed soon."

"Wait—"

"There's no time, sir." The woman nudged my shoulder, and I cast a glance at Lyra, who was studiously ignoring me. How the hell was I supposed to film a challenge segment with her if we couldn't even talk to each other?

Caught, I stumbled through the hallway, a thousand thoughts whirling in my brain. Yet somehow the one that rose to the top was that Lyra had told the show that the Christmas we spent in the barn together was her most favorite Christmas of all time. Why would she tell them that?

Unless she knew.

Maybe this was all her doing.

Fury filled me as I realized that I was probably just a pawn in her game. A publicity grab was what this was. Lyra probably wanted to grow her brand, and what better way than digging up old drama for reality television? Knox was her sister's boyfriend, so he'd probably been in on the whole thing.

Instinctively, I knew that last thought was likely untrue. Knox had always been a good friend to me, and I had no reason to think he would put me through something like that simply to grow Lyra's YouTube channel. But I was mad. I'd been mad ever since Lyra had returned to town. And sometimes, when I was mad, logic didn't always dictate the direction of my thoughts.

So if Lyra wanted a show, well, she was going to get one.

CHAPTER TWELVE

Lyra

"I didn't know," I whispered the minute we were directed to our station.

Rab said nothing, his jaw rigid, hands jammed in his pockets. I hadn't even glanced at the other contestants, intent on making Rab understand that I'd had no part in whatever was happening here. My heart hammered in my chest, and I reached out to grab his arm, but he dodged my touch.

"Don't." His words stung. Like he had any right to be angry about this? I was just as much a victim of this scenario as he was.

"Don't?" I hissed, hands on hips. "Don't? *You* don't. I'm just as much in the dark here as you are. That's the entire purpose of this game. To pair unknown people together. Haven't you seen the show?"

When Rab didn't respond, my eyebrows shot up.

"You haven't, have you? You haven't even watched an episode, have you?"

"It wasn't a requirement for auditioning," Rab said stiffly.

"Bloody hell." I threw my hands up and stopped short of stomping my foot. Any lingering hope I had that this might turn out to be a good experience drifted away. "Great, just great. Not only am I stuck with you, but you don't even want to be here or know what the show is about. Why would you even come on the show, then?"

"Oh my goddess!" I turned at a squeal to see Felicity bouncing in excitement at her table. It was only then that it dawned on me that we were being filmed, and cameras were tucked up in every corner of the room, and I'd been so focused on Rab that I hadn't even taken a second glance around the room. But now I did, and my heart fell.

The room itself was set up much like it had been for other seasons of the show that I'd watched. There were six stations total, though only four were occupied, and each station had a stove with burners and a stand mixer. Shelves below showcased bowls, baking trays, and other kitchen necessities. The room was long and narrow, with creamy stone walls, and Christmas garlands and boughs of evergreen and birch branches were wound with twinkle lights. Contestant aprons, in Christmas-themed red and green, were folded on the stations with our names embroidered on the front.

And standing next to Felicity was Mandy Meadows.

I gaped at Mandy, surprised she would come on a reality show when she had barely shown her face in public for a year now. Not since Sloane had usurped her as president of the Charms, and certainly not in any social capacity, at least not that I'd heard about. She looked . . . decidedly un-Mandy-like. When I'd last seen her, she'd been perfectly put together, not a hair out of place, usually in a fiercely starched pink pantsuit. I'd certainly never seen her in jeans and a T-shirt before.

A black T-shirt of all things.

Her blond hair was longer now, and her eyes were lined with dark liner and shadow. If anything, this was a goth version of Mandy, and I had no idea what to make of it.

Nova would probably *love* this change in her.

Rab turned, following the direction I was looking, and nodded curtly at Felicity and Mandy. Then his gaze landed on the team behind them.

"Henry?" Rab asked in disbelief. "Knox got you too?"

I gasped and smiled, giving Henry a wee wave. He was one of the most gruffly sweet men I knew, and I'd loved working with him on the Mabon festival.

Henry shrugged sheepishly.

"The lad can be quite convincing."

His partner was Nyx, a cat sith who owned the Silver Quill bookshop who I didn't know all that well, and the last team was two people I hadn't met yet but looked delighted to be here. At least based on their matching Christmas elf hats that one of the members must have brought.

"So Knox made you do this?" I asked quietly, hoping the cameras wouldn't catch what I was saying.

"Aye," Rab said, not looking at me.

Lovely, this was going to be a great show. I was saddled with a partner who thought I was nothing special, and a goth Mandy Meadows, who was currently staring bullets in my direction.

"What?" I finally asked her, exasperated, and Mandy reared back as though I'd thrown acid in her face. "I have done nothing to you, Mandy. In fact, I've called you twice a month checking up on you. You have no reason to stare at me like that."

"My, my, my . . ." Vaughn drawled, walking up with two people I recognized to be the judges of the show. "Even more drama? I guess there's lots to unpack here with you, isn't there, Lyra?"

I whirled, uncertain and disconcerted. I wasn't used to being the problematic one. Frankly, I was used to everything just . . . going my way. I know that sounded awful to say, but once I'd gotten free from the clutches of my angry mother, life had mostly been smooth sailing for me.

Aside from our pesky curse, that is.

But even that I'd grown used to as time went on. It was kind of like how I assumed sailors or extreme adventurers felt—if you prepared for the storm, then the storm wasn't so bad when it arrived. That is kind of how I felt about our curse.

However, I also made it my life's goal to radiate optimism and kindness to everyone. I genuinely wanted to smooth things over when I saw people were stressed or hurting. I never held grudges, except for in extenuating circumstances, like with Rab. And when Mandy had been booted out as president, I'd made it a point to stop by and check on her, no matter that she refused to answer the door.

I hated to see people hurting.

But I could see the wheels turning in Vaughn's eyes, and I whipped my gaze around the room, seeing how the camerapeople were turning their cameras on me, how the producers lined up behind the camera were furiously scribbling notes.

It happened on every season.

They'd squirrel out the person with the most issues or biggest vulnerabilities and focus heavily on them.

And . . . and I'd loved it. I'd loved watching it.

But I wasn't loving it so much now that I saw what was happening . . . to me.

Between this and my faulty magick, I was screwed.

A dead witch walking.

Resigned, I closed my eyes and took a deep breath, and then opened my eyes and pasted a wide smile on my face. The one thing I wasn't was a sore loser. I'd signed up for this show, and nobody had forced me to be here. Now I'd just have to deal with whatever challenges came my way.

And so I'd give them what they wanted.

Winking at the camera, I twirled a lock of my hair around my finger. "A little bit of drama sure does add some spice to life, doesn't it?"

Rab shot me a disgusted look, but I ignored him. He didn't get to dictate how I dealt with situations.

He didn't get a say in anything in my life. *Not anymore. He lost that right many years ago.*

And yet, as much as I tried to ignore it, I still wanted him to at least like me. Couldn't we get along?

Maybe that was just how it was with your first love. They somehow managed to imprint on your soul, and you'd forever have a yen for them. I didn't know. I'd never allowed myself to feel for someone the same way I'd felt for Rab. I didn't know if I ever could. A first love was shiny as a new coin, untarnished by the wear and tear of years of use . . . crafted to last.

Did people look back on their first love, years later, with fondness? With a touch of understanding and grace toward their younger selves?

Because I didn't.

I was still angry.

Broca had told me that would fade in time, but seeing Rab again, being close to him, just made me replay his world-shattering words in my head over and over again. It also made me determined to show him differently.

That I was more than just a pretty face.

And that I was something special, no matter what he thought of me.

"So, how do you ladies know each other?" Vaughn asked, glancing between their station and ours.

"We're coven sisters," Felicity gushed, and then her face fell. "Well, we were until Mandy left because she was voted out of the presidency and Lyra's sister took over."

"Thanks, Felicity," Mandy bit out, and Vaughn's look sharpened.

"Well, well, well," Vaughn repeated, and he might as well have looked like the villain in a B horror movie, rubbing his hands together. "An ousted president and an ex-boyfriend? How do you think you'll handle the pressures of this challenge, Lyra?"

"Being a good chef is about staying focused under pressure," I said, even though I'd never worked a day in a commercial kitchen in my life. However, I'd been working front of shop at the bakery long enough now to see how Marcie stayed cool on high-traffic days.

"Spoken like a true baker. Now, let's meet your judges, shall we?" Vaughn turned and held out his hands to the two people waiting patiently at the front of the room. One was a woman with neon-green hair down to her waist, wearing checked trousers and a lacy blouse, and the other was a man with no hair to speak of whatsoever and tiny oval glasses with bright blue frames perched on his nose.

"Kelly and Nevin. Both are masters in their craft, have several successful bakeries under their belts, and have been featured on numerous programs, including our esteemed *Bewitching Bake Off*."

We all dutifully clapped, and despite the fact that I knew a bull's-eye was on my chest now, I couldn't help but feel excitement bloom. I loved Kelly and Nevin. They were the funniest pair, and their banter was first class. I had to admit, I was a bit starstruck.

"Welcome, bakers! We're so excited to be filming a Christmas special this year, and we've dreamt up the best Christmas-themed challenges for you. And just so you don't get too comfortable, the first challenge starts . . ." Nevin lowered his glasses and looked down at us. "Now."

I darted forward and pulled the apron off the table and slung it over my head, tying it behind my waist, while Rab jumped back and looked at me in confusion.

"Get your apron on. The details will be in the envelope," I said, nodding to where a sparkly green envelope with a red wax seal sat on the table, half concealed by Rab's apron.

"Rab, read out the challenge for us, will you?" Kelly asked, sidling closer to Rab and fluttering her lashes at him.

Reluctantly, Rab picked up the envelope and slid a finger under the seal.

"'Together, bake a Christmas spirit soufflé. If you are able to infuse the soufflé with warm Christmas spirit, it will levitate and sing a Christmas carol. If you fail, it will collapse and reveal one of your most embarrassing secrets.'" Disbelief crossed Rab's face. "Are you kidding me with this? Isn't this a little harsh?"

"We usually work our way up to these types of challenges, but since it's a Christmas special, we're diving right in," Nevin intoned.

"See who draws first blood?" Rab asked.

"Ah, I see you have a touch of the dramatic." Kelly winked at Rab. "Just my type."

Is she hitting on him? My brow furrowed.

Rab flipped the card.

"There's no recipe on here."

"Right," Nevin said, smirking. "We do expect our more experienced bakers to know how to make these recipes."

Rab glanced at me.

"You ever make a soufflé?"

I nodded, biting back a grin. He looked adorably irritated, his hair just a touch askew, his face set in the permanent glower I'd grown used to seeing on his face whenever he'd run into me over the past year.

"Well, then, let's crack on and get this over with."

"Some people enjoy making these recipes." Nevin stuck his nose in the air and drifted to the Christmas elves, who were already busy getting their ingredients ready.

"And some people enjoy running marathons too," Rab muttered under his breath, and I couldn't help myself, I snorted. Rab's eyes flew to my face. "Do you think this is funny?"

"Um," I said, pressing my lips together and bending to pull bowls off the shelves. "Mildly, yes."

"At least one of us does," Rab grumbled. He gestured to the table. "Well, go on, then. Make the soufflé."

"So that's not really how it works," I said, stalling as delighted shrieks sounded behind us as Team Elf crowed over their recipe.

How was I going to hide my inverting magick while we did this?

"Right," I said, grabbing eggs from the central fridge and faking a confidence I absolutely did not possess. "We need room-temperature eggs, so I'll separate them while you prep the ramekins."

Rab gave me a suspicious glance. "You sure you know what you're doing?"

"Obviously," I said, and then promptly cracked the first egg backward. I mean, literally—somehow my magick reversed the shell and yolk so the shell dropped into the bowl in a gelatinous blob while the yolk bounced neatly into my palm. I blinked down at it.

"Is that . . . an inside-out egg?" Rab asked, eyebrows raised.

"Just a little kitchen magick," I said, too brightly, tossing the mangled yolk into the compost bin and trying again.

The same thing happened. Again.

By the fourth egg, I was sweating. My hands were a sticky mess, and my thoughts scrambled.

My magick was supposed to help in small, convenient ways—whisking when my hands were full, chilling cream instantly, heating sugar to soft-ball stage without burning it. But not this. Anything but this.

I turned to grab the cream of tartar—and somehow, my magick whirled it into salt.

"You sure you've done this before?" Rab arched an eyebrow at the bowl of salt I now held in my hand.

"Yes," I snapped, too loud, drawing the attention of two nearby camera operators. I forced a grin and turned to the other bowl on the table. "Sorry! Just really passionate about properly whipped egg whites."

Rab looked at me like I was spouting nursery rhymes.

I took a deep breath and tried to stir the batter. My spoon started swirling itself—counterclockwise. The whites collapsed instantly.

"Oops," I muttered.

"Don't you dare say 'oops' again," Rab said. "That's the fourth time this bowl has curdled on us."

I faked a cheery shrug and reached for the sugar. My magick decided now would be the perfect time to heat the bowl beneath it. The sugar melted instantly into a hardened syrup crust.

"Oh, for—"

"Lyra." Rab's voice was low. Controlled. "Do I need to take over?"

"No," I said, biting my lip. "I can do this."

Except I couldn't. I couldn't even charm a whisk to rotate the right way. My magick flipped every step of the way—chilled instead of warmed, deflated instead of lifted, stirred when it should've folded. Rab kept trying to interject, but I was too determined to try to make my magick work. By the time the batter was in the ramekin, it looked like a sad, foamy porridge.

And then came the final step.

Already, I knew this wasn't going to work. I knew it. There was no way that lumpy mixture in the ramekin was going to transform into a soufflé.

I closed my eyes. I had to conjure a warm Christmas memory. Something joyful, sweet, powerful enough to bind the magick and let the soufflé rise with song.

I tried. I really did.

"Sugar, spice, and tinsel bright,
Lift this treat with yuletide light.
Wrap it warm in joy sincere,
A taste of love and festive cheer!"

But the only memory that surfaced was the Christmas my parents spent the entire day arguing over my mother's desire to take a vacation to Portugal and my dad insisting our finances couldn't handle the expense. I was eight, curled in the corner, combing my Barbie's hair, pretending I didn't hear the shouts. My Christmas dinner had been two candy canes and a mug of hot chocolate made with water, not milk.

"Wait, shouldn't I add my own memory too—"

My eyes snapped open. The soufflé gave a mighty puff . . . and collapsed with a dramatic sigh. A cloud of cinnamon-scented steam burst into the air and then—

The table glowed.

"Oh no," I whispered, but it was too late.

A voice rang out, loud and magically amplified for the whole room to hear.

"Lyra MacGregor failed her biology final because she'd stayed up all night replaying her first kiss with Rab on her pillow."

Gasps. Laughter. A snort from Mandy. Even Nevin chortled.

"This does not surprise me in the slightest," Mandy said, and I turned to see her smirking at me. "You've never been the brightest bulb, have you, dear?"

I winced. I could feel myself shrinking, just like I had all those years ago, when school had infuriated me beyond belief, and I'd tried to make myself small. Unnoticeable.

Rab just stared at me.

"You . . . failed?" he asked.

"Yup, that's me. An absolute failure," I muttered, soft enough for only him to hear.

The cameras zoomed in.

Because of course they did.

"Rab named a sick lamb after Lyra and nursed it back to health after she left and broke his heart."

I gaped at Rab as his secret was revealed and he turned away from me, refusing to make eye contact. *What? Was that even real?* Laughter welled up, surrounding me, and making me feel like I was back at school, struggling to keep up, having answered an easy question from the teacher wrong again.

I wanted the floor to open up beneath me, welcome me into the sweet, silent void, and close neatly over my head. My cheeks burned, my stomach twisted, and I could only imagine Vaughn's delight at having the first magickal catastrophe of the show. This would be killer for ratings.

"Right," Nevin said brightly, clapping his hands. "Time to tally points for round one!"

Oh, good. Now everyone could quantify my humiliation numerically.

Kelly bounced forward, green hair swishing like an excited plant sprite. "Let's start with Team Elf!"

"As you know, we'll be awarding points for taste and presentation, and the team with the most points at the end of *all* the challenges will win the entire competition," Nevin said, reiterating the rules for the cameras.

The two cheerful contestants beamed. Their soufflé hovered

above their ramekin, harmonizing a surprisingly on-key version of "Deck the Halls."

"Ten points for presentation," Kelly announced.

"And ten for taste," Nevin said, licking a spoon. "Perfectly sweet and delightfully airy."

Team Elf squealed and hugged, jingling from their festive collars. The room applauded.

"Next, we have Mandy and Felicity!" Kelly sang.

Mandy's soufflé was obnoxiously perfect. It levitated, sparkled, and belted out "Jingle Bells" like a drunk lad after a football match. Mandy folded her arms and preened like she'd personally reinvented the concept of baking.

"I'd say a nine for presentation," Nevin said, "because the glitter is a tad excessive."

"Slander." Mandy sniffed, tossing her hair.

"But ten for taste," Kelly added. "This is exquisite."

Mandy gave me a smug little smile. Felicity squealed and bounced up and down as she clapped.

"Next team!" Kelly continued.

Henry's soufflé hovered only an inch above its ramekin and warbled waveringly through the first line of "Silent Night." But still . . . singing was singing.

"Let's give an eight for presentation," Nevin declared.

"For taste . . . a seven," Kelly added, frowning thoughtfully. "A touch flavorless, but still charming."

Henry looked utterly delighted, his bushy eyebrows lifting as he accepted applause with a bashful wave.

"And finally," Kelly said, turning with far too much sparkle in her eyes, "Team Rab and Lyra!"

Oh goddess.

The judges approached our pathetic, sunken soufflé, which was basically the culinary embodiment of my emotional state. It sat there, collapsed and steaming, like it had given up on life halfway through rising.

Nevin leaned in. "Well . . . it slightly resembles a soufflé."

"And there *is* cinnamon." Kelly sniffed, clearly trying to be fair.

"Um, I'd say a three for presentation," Nevin said gently.

Three.

"Now for taste," Nevin continued, lifting a spoon.

Rab actually flinched. "You don't have to—"

Nevin took a bite.

There was a long moment where everyone held their breath. Then Nevin nodded slowly.

"It tastes like scrambled eggs had an identity crisis," he announced.

I wanted to crawl into the nearest oven.

"Right. Two points for taste," Kelly said, a look of glee on her face. They always needed someone to fail for it to be a good show.

"Thank you," I said, quietly dying of embarrassment inside.

Mandy coughed out a laugh.

Beside me, Rab stood very, *very* still.

I slid him a glance to see his jaw clenched and his fists tightened at his sides.

I'd just embarrassed him on a show that most of the magickal community watched.

Nevin clapped again. "And that concludes round one! It looks like Team Elf is starting out strong. Keep your eyes on them as we move into the next challenge in this Christmas special of *Bewitching Bake Off*!"

"And . . . cut," Vaughn called, and the room visibly relaxed, while the other teams spoke excitedly about their challenges. I just stood there, blinking at the mess on our table, completely unsure of how to proceed.

There was no way I was going to make it through this challenge. And in the meantime, I was going to bring Rab down with me. If he didn't already hate me enough, once again, I was going to remind him what an embarrassment the MacGregors were.

Turning, I fled the kitchen without another word.

CHAPTER THIRTEEN

Rab

I'd thought the soufflé debacle would be the low point of the day.

I was wrong.

The producers called for a reset, cameras pivoted, and suddenly Vaughn was shoving a fresh mic pack into my hands, smiling like we were all loving this disaster of a show. "You're doing great. Keep up the drama," he said.

I curled my lip at him in a silent snarl, and his grin only widened.

Lyra stood at our station, arms tight around her middle, lips pressed together. She wasn't crying, but she had that look she used to get in school . . . right before she shut down entirely. Back then, all it took was one teacher saying she wasn't trying hard enough, and she'd retreat into herself, ashamed and furious and convinced she wasn't good enough.

It gutted me now the same way it had gutted me then.

And I hated that she still had that power over me.

The production team was circling like sharks, cameras catching every angle, every tiny change in our expressions. And they were particularly focused on Lyra. Why wouldn't they be? She was gorgeous and impossibly bad at baking. Even I could see how this would be television gold.

I told myself that I didn't care. I shouldn't. Had she cared when she'd left me and never once called or written to me after leaving me behind?

Then Vaughn clapped his hands and declared, "Quiet on set. And . . . rolling."

Lyra flinched beside me.

"Next up we have our rapid-fire round," Kelly chirped, "and your next challenge is to create a snow globe sugar ornament!"

Lyra's mouth fell open. Obviously, it meant something to her, but I had no idea what they were saying to me.

"We're looking for a clear sugar exterior, perfectly shaped. A miniature edible scene inside. And"—Nevin flicked his fingers dramatically, sending a swirl of magickal frost spiraling across the room—"your snow globe must contain enchanted snowfall."

Lyra's hands tightened on her apron.

"And just to keep things exciting . . . you have fifteen minutes!" Vaughn announced. My mouth dropped open. Fifteen minutes? That challenge sounded intensely technical for only fifteen minutes.

"And . . . go," Kelly said, clapping her hands.

Chaos erupted instantly. Team Elf shrieked with joy, knocking over their own ingredients out of enthusiasm.

"Bloody hell," Henry swore behind me.

"Och, please. Someone get me a real challenge." Mandy sighed and rolled her eyes.

But Lyra stood perfectly still.

Too still.

I nudged her with my elbow. "We'd best start. Timer's already running."

"Right . . . right."

She snapped into motion, but I recognized the frantic energy in her movements. She wasn't focused, instead, likely slipping into a panic spiral like she'd used to the night before we had big exams.

"We need to heat the sugar syrup slowly," I said, glancing at the recipe card on the table and reaching for the pot.

"I can do it," she insisted, and took the pan from my hands. I let her, but only because I was trying not to ride to her aid.

Surely it wouldn't be so bad this time around?

I watched her dump sugar and water into the pan and crank the flame up high.

"Lyra—"

"It's fine!" she insisted.

It was not fine.

Fifty seconds in, the mixture went from clear to golden to . . . frozen? What the hell?

"Oh no . . . no . . . no . . ."

She yanked the pot off the burner so violently that the sugar sloshed and cracked.

"Warm-up batch," she said breathlessly.

"There are no warm-up batches," I muttered. "This is the challenge."

Her eyes flashed with panic before she swallowed it down. "I can fix it."

Round two seized instantly, turning into a grainy, crystallized mess that looked as appetizing as wet cement.

Round three bubbled over.

Round four? I grabbed the pot before it boiled onto her hand.

"Switch," I snapped, unable to watch another disaster unfold. "Prep the molds. I'll handle the syrup."

To my surprise, she didn't argue. She just nodded tightly and moved to line up the spherical molds with trembling fingers.

Bloody hell. She was shaking.

My chest tightened. I hated seeing her like this—on the verge of crumbling and trying to hide it. She'd always been this way. She felt things deeply. It was part of what made her . . . *her*. Or at least the person I'd thought I'd known all those years ago.

Shaking my head to clear my thoughts from my instant urge of wanting to protect Lyra, I focused on the sugar. Slowly I heated it, keeping the temperature even with no spikes.

It came out perfectly. At least from what I could tell by Lyra's murmur of approval.

"Ready?" I asked.

Lyra reached for the mold halves. "Aye."

She lifted the first one, tilting it carefully, her teeth digging into her lower lip.

The syrup blasted out of the mold as though the air inside rejected it. The hot sugar arced through the air in a perfect, horrifying line and landed with a plonk on the table in front of us, solidifying instantly into a lopsided icicle.

Lyra's face twisted.

"You've got to be kidding me. I didn't even need to use my magick for that part of it." Lyra hissed, clearly insulted by the mess on the table in front of us.

I swallowed a laugh, some of the tension loosening inside of me.

"We'll try again," I said gently.

We managed four semi-usable shells, though calling them clear would have been charitable. They looked like they'd been sneezed on by a snowman. But with time ticking dangerously low, this was what we were working with.

"Two minutes!" Nevin sang out.

I fused the shells with more hope than skill. The result was . . . well . . . a globe in the vaguest possible sense. It looked more like a slightly deflated volleyball than anything.

Leaning close, she began to whisper the enchantment. I opened my mouth to stop her, thinking maybe it was best if we used my magick, but her words flowed over me, and I stopped, caught on watching her lovely face as she went inside herself to focus on her magick.

Her voice went soft, melodic. For a moment, something in the globe shimmered . . .

And then it began vibrating.

Hard.

"Lyra—" I warned, reaching forward.

"I don't know why it's doing that . . ."

We both held the trembling sphere like it was a live bomb. I reached for my magick, trying to figure out how to counteract whatever was happening with Lyra's, when a large jagged line split the sugar surface.

Our globe cracked in two.

Bloody hell.

"Time!" Kelly shouted.

Lyra stepped back, shoulders slumping.

I felt something twist inside me. It wasn't pity, but something far more complicated that I wasn't sure I was ready to examine in great detail yet. The judges stepped forward.

Team Elf got glowing praise, of course. Their snow globe not only contained snowfall but also tiny enchanted elves caroling inside.

Show-offs.

Henry and the bookstore owner got strong marks for presentation when Rudolph danced in a circle in their snow globe.

Mandy and Felicity delivered an absolutely perfect globe that sparkled as if blessed by the Christmas gods themselves.

Then came ours.

Kelly leaned close, peering at the cracked and foggy sugar sphere. "I'd give this a four for presentation."

Lyra winced.

Mandy snickered.

Nevin broke off a piece of the cracked globe and split it, handing some to Kelly before taking a bite.

"But taste, I'd say a seven?" Kelly said, surprise apparent in her voice.

"Agreed," Nevin said.

Lyra looked up, and hope flickered softly across her face.

"Oh, please," Mandy drawled. "Seven for taste? Pity points, surely. The rest of it is a disaster." She sneered. "But then, Lyra has always excelled at . . . simple things."

Lyra went absolutely still.

"Things are really heating up in the kitchen today," Kelly crowed, clapping her hands together. "Be sure to sit tight, as we have another challenge coming your way in the Christmas special of *Bewitching Bake Off*!"

"And . . . cut," Vaughn called, standing up. "Great job, everyone! That's a wrap for today."

Lyra untied her apron with stiff, jerky motions.

She set the apron down and turned away before anyone could stop her.

Before *I* could stop her.

I took a step after her and then froze.

What would I even say?

It's fine? *It's not your fault*? *Let me help*?

None of those things were smart for my heart or my life.

So I stood there, rooted to the floor like a bloody eejit, and watched her retreat.

She didn't look back.

And I hated it. I hated that I couldn't run after her, that I couldn't bring myself to fix this for her.

Cleanup happened around me in a noisy blur.

Team Elf chattered about their victory. Mandy basked under Kelly's praise like a smug cat. Henry patted my shoulder in sympathy.

"She's had a tough go of it, lad. Go easy on her."

I barely heard any of it.

All I could see was Lyra's face as Mandy spoke. The way her expression had gone numb, like she couldn't even muster the energy to be angry.

She'd always taken things to heart. People assumed she was frivolous or flighty because she smiled easily and dressed like a fairy escaping a garden party. But I'd been the one who had held her while she'd cried over her parents' constant fighting, her struggles in school—hell, even when she'd found a kitten and her parents had made her take it to the shelter instead of giving it a home.

She cared. About everyone and everything. Too much.

Except me, it seemed.

I dragged a hand down my face, trying to scrub away the twist in my chest, indecision warring as I tried to decide if I should go after her and try to soothe her worries after the tough day of filming.

"Bloody hell," I muttered under my breath.

I wanted to help her.

I needed to ignore her.

I wanted to run after her.

I needed to turn my back on her.

Instead, I stood exactly where I was, the indecision burning like a hot coal behind my ribs.

Lyra MacGregor was still undoing me.

And I still didn't know what to do about it.

CHAPTER FOURTEEN

Lyra

"I'm going to fight Mandy." Sloane pretended to throw a punch and almost knocked her cocktail off the bar.

Liam caught the drink neatly with one hand, while finishing his pour of a Guinness with the other.

"Well done," Raven said, her cheeks pinkening when Liam winked at her.

I'd all but run out of Mystic Munchies as soon as filming had wrapped for the day, ignoring Marcie's calls to come back. I didn't want to tell her that my magick wasn't working. I didn't want to tell anyone that I was a failure.

I'd made it clear enough, hadn't I?

"Tell me, again, how you kept slingshotting yolks into your hands?" Nova squinted at me, confused.

"I have no clue, Nova." I sighed and took a sip of my pink gin and lemonade. "It was like they were determined to go anywhere but in the bowl."

"And they just . . ." Nova splayed her hand out.

"Yup. Dripped right through my palms."

Nova slapped a hand to her face, but not before a giggle escaped.

"Don't you dare," I hissed.

"I'm sorry . . . I just . . ." Nova hiccupped, and Sloane punched her shoulder.

"Knock it off, Nova."

"I'm trying," Nova said, but still her shoulders shook with laughter. "It's just . . . eggs are so gross. Like the consistency, you ken?"

Despite my embarrassment, I could smile.

"She's not wrong. It was super gross. And I had to keep dumping them in the bin and trying to wipe up the mess while Rab looked at me like I was doing this on purpose or something."

Sloane, Raven, and Nova had met me at the Rune & Rose directly after filming, when Liam had called them for emergency support. I hadn't said a word to Liam, no matter how many times he'd tried to get me to talk. Liam was friends with Rab—the enemy—and I certainly wasn't going to dump my sorrows on him.

"I can't believe Rab is doing the show," Liam said, sliding me a fresh drink. "I lucked out. Knox tried to guilt me into doing it, but I told him there was no way in hell."

"You'd look great on camera, though," Raven offered shyly.

"I don't know about that," Liam said, ducking his head. "But I do know that I'm no chef."

"Apparently, neither am I," I said morosely, and dropped my chin into my hand. All I could see was Rab's surprised look when he learned that I'd failed my finals.

"Lyra's nothing special. She's just a pretty face."

The memory of his words that awful day burned through me, and I took a gulp of my fresh drink.

"Whoa, tiger," Sloane said, leaning over and sliding the drink farther out of my reach. "You've still got to film tomorrow, and I guarantee you don't want to be hungover."

"She's not wrong. You're *so* bitchy when you're hungover," Nova agreed.

"I've had one drink," I pointed out, annoyed with her. "That does not a hangover make."

"No, but if you don't eat anything and sleep shitty, it's only going to add up." Raven dug into her satchel and pulled out a small pouch. "Here. A tea to refresh you in the morning."

"Thanks, Raven." She'd always been closer with Sloane growing up, but since we'd been home, our friendship had grown. As owner of the apothecary, Raven vacillated between fun friend and de facto healer as needed.

"I still can't get over that Mandy was there," Sloane mused.

"Oh, sure, that's what we're going to focus on? Not the fact that I've been paired with Rab and my magick is falling apart?" I glared at Sloane and she shrugged.

"I feel like we're easing you into that." Sloane patted my arm. "Just gotta lube you up a bit first."

Liam coughed and turned away, and I raised my head to level a look at Sloane.

"What?" Sloane asked innocently, and I sighed.

"Liam?" Raven asked sweetly, and Liam turned back, his eyes soft for Raven.

"Aye?"

"Go away, please."

Liam's face fell, and Raven laughed. "Sorry, this is a chat for us ladies. We can't gossip if you're listening in."

"I would never repeat what I hear." Liam held a hand to his heart.

"Lies." Nova laughed. "You're best mates with Rab. Go away."

"Fine, fine," Liam grumbled and moved to the other side of the bar. The pub was busy tonight, with many of the crew from the set grabbing food and after-work drinks.

"Lyra, darling, I say this with the utmost love in my heart for you, but"—Sloane reached over and grabbed both my hands, forcing me to look her in the eyes—"the time has come to tell us what happened with Rab. Nova and I have always respected your privacy on this matter, but we can't help you if we don't know what happened."

My throat tightened. I hated thinking about it. I hated going back to that moment, standing with my back pressed against the house, my teeth sinking into my fist as I blinked back the tears that flooded my eyes.

But Sloane was right.

Maybe teenage Lyra couldn't talk about it.

But twenty-five-year-old Lyra could.

"Lyra's nothing special. She's just a pretty face."

I hadn't left that day. Instead, I'd pressed myself against the house, listening to Rab's conversation through the window he'd left open. And as the storm had blown in, his words had shattered me like the thunder exploding in the sky above. I'd raced home in the rain, determined to never think of Rab again, and when morning came and our mum had loaded our suitcases in the car, I'd never looked back.

"I was stupid enough to think what we had was real." I shrugged and brushed off Sloane's hand when she reached for me again. "It's fine. It was a long time ago."

"It's not fine, though," Nova said. "It was a foundational part of your life, Lyra. He was, like . . . your whole world. You were devastated when we left. You didn't speak for almost a month—do you remember?"

I nodded, my mind flashing back to burrowing silently into the back seat of a car, watching city after city flash past the window outside, numb with grief.

"Just teen hormones, I guess." I shrugged. *Again.*

"I disagree." Raven leaned forward, her face earnest. "I hate when people dismiss your feelings as a teenager as not real or valid. Just because we're experiencing roller-coaster hormones doesn't mean that what we feel isn't real. If anything, I argue that we should go back to that more. We spend so much time as adults dulling our emotions, and I don't think that's a valid response either."

It was the first time I had heard someone speak about teenage emotions in such a way, and I blinked at Raven in surprise.

"You know, she's right. I guess I didn't think much about it, at least not in that manner, but when we talk about what Mum and Dad put us through?" Sloane tapped a fist to her chest. "I feel it. Like I still feel it deeply. I'm sorry, Lyra. I'm sorry you didn't feel like you could tell us what happened then. Do you think you can now?"

And so I did. I poured it all out, pushing down the tears that threatened because I refused to be seen crying in public after my disastrous day of filming.

"I know I was young"—I lifted my head and leveled a look at Sloane, needing her to believe me—"but I was ready to leave with him. Do you understand? I'd put some money aside. I had a bag packed with just the necessities. All my paperwork. I was ready to go. Nothing mattered, so long as I could be with him."

"What a coward," Nova broke out, her face twisted in anger. She slapped a palm on the bar. "To just capitulate to what his parents wanted? What a fucking joke of a man."

"Is now the wrong time to come back over here?" Liam asked.

"Aye," we all shouted at once, and Liam threw up his hands in protection and disappeared back to the other side of the bar.

"Sixteen is still young," Raven mused. "Maybe we should give him some grace. It's a big deal . . . running away with your younger girlfriend. Illegal, actually. Not only were you going to both lie to your parents, but you would also be breaking the law. It's a big decision."

"He didn't even try," I said, squeezing my eyes shut and taking a deep breath. "I thought he was . . . different than that. Stronger. And he just . . . gave up. I heard him. He said . . . I wasn't anything special. Just a pretty face."

"Oh," Nova breathed, her eyes flying to my face. "Ohhhh. Is that why you hated when people called you pretty? Remember that, Sloane?"

"I do." Sloane turned to Nova. "It took us a good few years to build your confidence back up."

I squirmed on my stool, feeling exposed in a way that wasn't very comfortable for me.

"Which, if I do say so myself, I think we did a great job at that." Nova patted her shoulder, and despite my awkwardness with this conversation, I laughed. They weren't wrong. Once I'd hit eighteen, I'd blossomed, embracing my looks and my curves, moving through the world unapologetically. The confidence had caused a dramatic shift in my life, and that was when I'd really started dating again. And I'd thrown myself into the dating pool with a vengeance.

But I always kept it light.

My lovers always knew the score going in. I wasn't going to stay long, always moving on, and I embraced the life of being sought after and savored but never held on to for long. It suited me, or at least that was what I'd told myself, until I returned home.

And had seen Rab again.

Now I turned all of my energy to building my career, trying to reconnect and rebuild the relationship with my father, and making friends in Briarhaven. I'd been on a yearlong publicity tour, determined to win everyone in Briarhaven over, because I had known that as soon as our curse surfaced again, goodwill would go a long way toward smoothing any animosity toward our wee family.

"Anyhoo, so here we are. Paired up and both of us miserable." I shrugged.

"But why is *he* miserable?" Raven wondered.

"What?" I said, confused.

"Like, I get why you're mad . . . anybody would be if they heard the love of their life speak about them that way. But why is he mad at you?"

"I . . . I . . ." I tilted my head, screwing my face up as I thought about it. "Actually, I don't know. I just thought he was mad because I'd left and hadn't contacted him since."

"But if he didn't care about you, then he would have gotten over it, right?" Sloane wondered, nodding at Raven. "You're onto something here."

"Something's off. We're missing something."

"Well, whatever it is, it hardly matters now," I said forlornly. "That ship has sailed. What matters is how I'm going to get through the rest of filming without making a laughingstock of myself."

"It's okay that you started poorly," Nova reassured me, raising her pint in my direction. "Everyone loves a redemption arc. They'll root for you."

"Or delight in my downfall." I sucked an ice cube into my mouth and chewed, trying to figure out how I was going to fix my magick.

"So you make Mandy the villain."

We all swiveled to look at Nova.

"What?" Nova asked, leaning back.

"Why would we make her the villain?"

"Because viewers love someone to hate. And if you don't want it to be you, you'd better get someone else on the chopping block."

"I don't . . . I don't want to villainize Mandy. She's finally come out of hiding," I said. No, making an enemy of Mandy was not the way forward. "This might be something that's really good for her."

"She seemed to have no problem gunning for you, though," Sloane pointed out, going into mama bear mode. She'd always been fiercely protective of us.

"She's hurting. It's fine." I held my hands up. "I'm not worried about Mandy. What I *am* worried about is my magick failing on television. And working with Rab."

"It sounds like he didn't have any clue what he was signing up for. Maybe you should go talk to him. Outside the show. Perhaps you could find a way to work together? At least for the next couple of weeks as they film," Raven said, and I looked blankly at her.

"Talk to him?" I repeated.

"Aye, you know, like adults. You're both in this together now. Maybe you could ask him for help?" Raven asked, her voice soft.

"Ask him for help?" For some reason, my brain just couldn't wrap around this idea of going to Rab and talking to him about my problems.

"It's not the worst idea, Lyra." Sloane nodded in agreement.

"When would I talk to him?" I asked. There were so many people buzzing around the set that there was no way I'd be able to speak freely to him without tipping off one of the producers that I was in trouble.

"Now?" Raven looked out the window. "I mean, it's not super late. You could just go talk to him."

"Och, what are we going to do about this darkness?" Sloane hissed, changing the subject as my mind whirled.

I could just go talk to him.

Why hadn't that occurred to me before? Because I did want to know . . . Why was he so angry with me?

"Will we still have the Halloween party this year?" Raven asked.

"I hope so. It was very popular last year." Sloane had a determined look on her face. "I don't see any reason why the darkness should deter people."

"Well, we know why *you* liked it," Nova said, reminding Sloane of how her misfiring magick had exploded glitter all over the party while she'd been snogging Knox in the back room.

"Wheesht," Sloane hissed.

But I'd stopped listening. All I could think about was going to talk to Rab. Taking one more sip of my drink for courage, I slid off my stool.

"I'm going," I whispered.

"And . . ." Sloane paused and narrowed in on me. "Wait, what? You're going?"

"Aye, I'm going. Now, before I lose courage."

"Go get 'em." Nova punched me.

"Need a ride?" Sloane asked, worry dancing across her face.

"No, I need to walk. Can you take Ruth home, though? She's sleeping in my bag. I guess the chaos of the show was pretty tiring for her today." I nodded to my tote.

"On it." Sloane stood and gave me a hug, and then I slipped out into the cool night air before I could second-guess what I was doing.

CHAPTER FIFTEEN

Lyra

I knew where Rab lived. In a town of three thousand people, it was pretty easy to learn where most people lived, if you paid attention.

And I had.

Not that I'd admit it to anyone.

I'd told myself that I just wanted to know where he lived in order to avoid running into him.

A soft breeze buffeted Main Street, but I didn't mind it. The slap of air against my face sobered me, and I admired the mix of decorations as I strolled down the eclectic cobblestoned street. Mystic Munchies was the most elaborately decorated—already in Christmas mode because the show's professional decorators had gone all out. However, the other shops were still decked out in cozy early autumn vibes, and there were a mix of magical and witchy decorations splashed across the main street. Pixie Dust Apothecary was coated in silver-and-purple lace spider-webbing, matching their packaging. The Familiar's Nest, the shop for all familiars' needs, was done up in golden leaf garlands with gourds and pumpkins tucked beside their front door. I stopped at the Dragon's Hoard, a curiosity shop, and smiled into the window.

The owner, Dorothy, a true dragon enthusiast, had gone all out. According to her, dragons loved anything shiny, and her window display was an explosion of sparkles. Disco-ball dragons swooped through the air, with striped witch hats on their heads, and a forest of glittery gold and silvery trees filled the window. The Arcane Attic, next door, had its finest Halloween costumes in the window, and Nyx, who owned the Silver Quill bookshop, had made a witchy hat out of stacked books.

Even though nerves jangled low in my stomach, walking through the town soothed me. I loved Briarhaven and had never wanted to leave. As a child, it was the longest place we'd ever lived without our curse ruining things for us, though my sisters would argue that living with our parents' constant arguments was curse enough.

Our mum had reached out to me recently. We hadn't spoken in years, Sloane fiercely protecting us from her. My parents had fought constantly when I was growing up, and no matter how many times I smiled and tried to cheer them up, they'd still broken apart. My charms hadn't been good enough to keep them together. After they'd broken up, Mum had dragged us all over the States before Sloane had gotten old enough to spirit us away from her clutches, and after that, I'd worked even harder at charming everyone that I met. I couldn't help it. I just wanted everyone to get along.

It was one of the reasons that this whole rift with Rab was so distressing to me. It just wasn't in my nature to stay at odds with someone.

And yet.

Sloane had been very clear to me that establishing boundaries wasn't the same as being *in* an argument with someone. And so I'd dutifully responded to my mum, letting her know that we were safe and doing well, but not inviting further contact. It was healthiest, all around, if we kept her out of our lives.

Never once had she put her daughters first. If anything, we'd only been a burden to her. Or an audience when she wanted to smash things. I suppose I'd inherited a flair for dramatics from her.

I wasn't entirely sure if that was a good thing or not.

Rounding the corner, I walked to the next street over running parallel to Main Street. Rab's street.

Sucking in a breath, I stopped in front of a detached two-story house that was tucked into a row of houses along the street. One side of the house had a door with a neat gold sign that proclaimed: Barclay Accountancy.

The lights were dark on that side, so I walked to the next door, painted a bright green with a lion door knocker.

Rab had tied a striped witch hat onto the lion's head.

Before I could talk myself out of it, I raised my hand and knocked.

I heard movement behind the door, and then it swung open, and my breath caught.

Why did he have to be so damn good-looking?

Rab looked adorably rumpled in a simple gray jumper and flannel pajama bottoms. He blinked at me in confusion.

"Are you real?" Rab asked, and I glared up at him.

"Have you been drinking?"

"I just can't fathom why you'd be showing up on my doorstep," Rab said. He crossed his arms across his chest, leaning against the doorframe.

Annoyance flitted through me.

The man wasn't even going to invite me in?

A gust of wind blasted the house, and I shoved past him, furious with his absolute indifference to me.

"By all means," Rab murmured, slapping the door closed behind me. "Make yourself at home."

The door opened into a hallway with two doors on either side. I veered into the room with the light on in it. Inside I found a deep-seated leather sofa, a fire crackling softly in a stone fireplace, and what looked to be a police drama frozen on the wall-mounted television.

A can of beans sat open on the coffee table, the handle of a spoon sticking out.

I whirled on Rab.

"Are you eating a can of beans for dinner?" I asked, exasperated. Turning, I snatched up the can and was distraught to find it cold.

"It's an easy meal," Rab said. "I'm not a foodie, Lyra."

"Yeah, but you can also be an adult." I glared, stomped past him into the room across the hallway, and turned on the light to reveal the kitchen. Muttering under my breath, I found a pot and put it on the stove, then dumped the beans in. Turning, I opened his refrigerator and pursed my lips as I studied the contents.

There wasn't much to go on, but I was a master at making something out of nothing. I grabbed a hunk of cheddar and found a package of dried noodles in a cupboard. Putting another pot on to boil water, I worked quickly to whip up some mac and cheese to go with his beans.

"Sit," I ordered, pointing a finger at the small bistro table in his kitchen with two chairs.

"Care to tell me why you're here ordering me around my own kitchen?" Rab asked. Instead of sitting, he reached for an open bottle of red wine breathing on the counter and topped up his glass. He hesitated and then opened a cupboard and filled a second glass. Sliding it to where I stirred the pot at the stove, he then took a seat.

I could feel his eyes boring into the back of me, and I kept my attention on stirring the beans, doing everything in my power to ignore the magick that desperately wanted to unfurl inside of me. I didn't know how to explain it, but as soon as I was in a kitchen, my magick just hummed to life, desperately wanting to be used. It took a conscious effort to not engage it at this point, but the last thing I needed was to explode boiling water across Rab's kitchen.

Third-degree burns probably were not the way to a working partnership.

My dragon-scale necklace warmed at my neck, and I reached up, wrapping my fingers around it. As I did, my nerves cooled. Considering, I turned to look at Rab.

"Do you have a cheese grater?"

Rab laughed and ran a hand through his hair.

I turned quickly, his laughter sending a warm tendril of lust down my spine, and took a deep breath to soothe myself. Instead, I found a knife and cut up the cheese.

It had always been this way with Rab.

I'd been intoxicated as a teenager in love.

And even now, the pull of him was almost impossible to ignore.

"Lyra. Why are you in my kitchen right now?"

"Because we need to talk. About the show."

"Do we?" Rab asked, and I shot him an annoyed glance over my shoulder. Dumping the pasta into the water, I dug for some milk and butter and another pot to mix the sauce.

"I think you know that we do." I was determined to muscle my way through this. Blowing out a breath, I took a sip of my wine before turning to face him as his dinner simmered on the stove. Leaning against the counter, wineglass in hand, I gave him an aggrieved look. "I need you to know that I didn't plan this. It's true what they say—you really don't know who your partner is going to be. Trust me, you'd be the last person I'd vote for."

"What's that supposed to mean?" Rab lifted his chin at me, and I turned to stir the sauce.

There was something about the way he challenged me that set a fire burning inside me.

"I have zero desire to be partnered with you, Rab," I said, my voice even.

"Aye, you've made that abundantly clear," Rab said, and annoyance flashed through me.

"Och, I'm not the one who—"

"How do I even know you're telling the truth?" Rab asked. He got to his feet, his face twisted. He gestured to the stove. "Look at this."

Distracted, I glanced at the stove, where his meal bubbled away. "At what?"

"This." Rab slapped a hand down on the counter, and I jumped. "What was that shite earlier? When filming?"

"Um . . ." I trailed off, taking a deep breath. Here was where I'd have to admit to him my magick was broken.

"You were a mess. Flinging eggs about, every step going wrong. And now this?" Rab held out his hand to the perfectly cooked pasta. "Nothing. Not a thing wrong. Why are you lying?"

"I'm not lying," I said, frustrated. Digging an elbow into his ribs, hard, I pushed him aside and opened cabinets until I found a strainer.

Dumping the boiling water and pasta out in the sink, I tossed the pasta back in with the sauce and turned the power on the beans off. "Bowl?"

Rab swore under his breath, but then bowls clunked down next to the stove.

Two bowls.

Taking that as a sign we might have a semblance of a respectable conversation, I quickly dished out some food. Forgoing the beans, I scooped a small bit of mac and cheese into my bowl, and the rest into his. I always remembered how much he loved to eat what I made for him, even if in those days it was as simple as what I was making tonight.

Turning, I leaned against the counter while he sat with his bowl and dove in. I couldn't bring myself to join him at the table. It was too . . . cozy. Already I was kind of embarrassed that I'd immediately defaulted into my pattern of wanting to take care of others. I'd just barged into this man's house, yelled at him for eating a dinner of his choice, and then steamrolled him into eating a meal that I'd made.

Sighing, I rolled my eyes at myself and took a bite of the mac and cheese. It wasn't bad, all things considered, but I would have liked there to be a mixture of cheeses and maybe some crumbled bits of bacon on top.

"This is good," Rab said, an unreadable look on his face. "Thanks."

"No problem." I put the bowl down, unable to eat more, as nerves ground in my stomach. "My magick is broken."

"What?" Rab stopped eating and looked up at me, a flash of something behind his eyes.

"It's broken. I . . ." I winced, unable to meet his eyes. "I think it's part of our curse. Sloane had it, too, when she got her magick, except for her it manifested in having different magick every day."

"She had different magick every day? I didn't know that."

I snorted and took a sip of my wine. "She hated it. Sloane's an absolute control freak, so being unable to plan what she'd be dealing with every day really set her off."

"That was right when Sloane and Knox were getting together?"

"Aye." I nodded.

"I remember now. Knox had mentioned things were chaotic."

"But he didn't tell you details?" I asked, surprised.

Rab scooped more food into his mouth. "Men don't talk like that."

"Right." I cleared my throat and shifted, trying to look everywhere else but him. The kitchen wasn't all that big, and his presence filled it.

I missed him.

Missed *this*.

Just us, alone, talking. The world hovering outside, nothing being able to touch it because this was us, and we had our whole future ahead of us. Together.

But would that have fallen apart had we stayed together?

Because now that I knew what he'd really thought of me, he would have grown tired of my . . . inadequacies. Perhaps I'd never been book smart enough for him. Was it for the best that we'd finished when we had? Would I have been miserable always feeling less than compared to him? Physically, we'd been like fire, but that wasn't enough for long term, right?

"So your magick is broken. How do you plan to fix it?" Rab's voice cut through my thoughts, and I blinked at him, thrust firmly back into the here and now.

"I don't know," I said. "It's . . . doing the opposite of whatever I ask it to do."

"Ah," Rab said, leaning back, his plate already cleared. "That explains today but doesn't explain why you could whip up this meal with no problems."

"I deliberately didn't use my magick," I explained. "I wanted to—hell, my magick wants to come out every time I step in a kitchen—but I held it back."

"So just hold it back in the competition, then," Rab said.

"I . . . you . . . can't. It's part of the rules." I looked at him, widening my eyes. "You have to use magick. That's the entire premise of the show."

"Can't we just use my magick, then? Does it have to be both?" Rab asked, his eyebrows drawing together on his forehead.

Something inside me loosened.

He was trying to find a solution.

Which maybe, just maybe, meant we might have a way forward.

"We can try. But I don't think it's just in their rules. I think that is part of the magick that controls the show. I'm not sure I can contain my use of magick when I'm cooking there."

"I . . ." Rab tilted his head as he thought about it. Getting up, he took his plate to the sink. "Actually, you may be right. Because when you were busy destroying a perfectly nice soufflé, I could feel my magick humming along, wanting to be used. I think it even began to seep out, but your catastrophic magick made it scared."

"I was not destroying it . . ." I argued, appalled.

"Och, darling." Rab turned and laughed outright, and despite my embarrassment, I found myself grinning at him. It was impossible not to. He'd been a good-looking boy, but holy hell, he'd grown into a mouthwateringly handsome man. It was like all his soft edges and gawkiness as a teen had filled out into all muscle and confidence as an adult. "You were an absolute mess."

"I know . . ." I said, my shoulders shaking so hard with laughter that tears sprung to my eyes. "Bloody hell, but I couldn't stop it. I couldn't control it. It was like a tornado in there."

"And I was just caught in the danger zone."

"I'm so sorry," I said, wiping my eyes. "I truly am."

"Och, it's fine. Now that I know what's going on, I can try to do something about it." Rab waved it away and hope sprung up.

"You're going back? To the show, that is? I was certain you'd be out after today."

Rab tilted his head, seemingly weighing his words as he looked at me, his mossy eyes drilling a hole through me.

"I can't say I haven't been sitting here considering it. But no, Lyra. I gave my word. Which is something I take seriously." Rab's jaw tightened as he looked at me, an unreadable look in his eyes.

Was that supposed to be a dig at me? It wasn't *me* that hadn't kept my word.

"Is that right? I suppose that's yet to be determined. Your track record doesn't speak well for itself."

Rab was across the room in a blur of movement, his arms on either side of me at the counter, caging me.

"I say what I mean, Lyra."

"Aye, so I heard." I lift my chin, refusing to back down.

Why did it feel like we were having two different conversations here? But as I met his eyes in challenge, something shifted inside me.

Our faces were centimeters apart, and I was so close I could pick out the tiny gold flecks in his eyes.

"That face," Rab fumed. "I've never been able to get past you, Lyra."

His words fell like acid on my skin, burning me. He didn't say it as a good thing. He said it with the deep-rooted conviction that something was bad for him.

I swallowed.

Because I understood.

I felt exactly the same.

Something fundamental in me, in my personal growth, had stalled with Rab. I was stuck, caught in the sticky web of emotions that I still felt for him.

"Bloody hell." Rab closed the distance, and his lips were on mine.

Burning, burning, and I was falling, falling into everything that I'd remembered and tried to forget about him. Rab kissed me with the urgency of youth and the confidence of adulthood, one hand coming up to grip the back of my neck, angling my mouth so he could take.

Before I could think better of it—or worse of it—his other hand found my waist and lifted. The edge of the counter pressed into the backs of my thighs as he settled me there, close enough that there was no mistaking what this meant, or how little space he intended to give me.

My fingers curled into his jumper, my knees bracketing his hips as he kissed me again, slower this time, deeper. Like he was reminding himself. Like he was reminding *me*.

Like I'd ever really forgotten. No matter how hard I'd tried to.

I mewled into his mouth, heat flashing like throwing water on a grease fire, and—

"What the—"

Rab drew back as a squeak sounded. I thought it had been me.

But it wasn't.

Not even close.

A swarm of hedgehogs filled his kitchen. Was it a swarm? I had no idea what to call it. All I knew was that there were a good twenty hedgehogs racing around his kitchen floor, squeaking and snorting, and I closed my eyes.

This was all my fault.

Without another word, I darted through an opening in the hedgehog party and out the front door.

"Lyra!"

I ignored Rab's shout, because I was done.

I was so done.

My humiliation for the day was complete.

Because I'd just confirmed my suspicions from the Mabon party.

It was true.

Apparently, when I was turned on, somehow that manifested into sentient objects shifting into hedgehogs.

This must be the universe's way of telling me to stay away from Rab. Every time I was near him, my brain just scrambled. And what was the point of finding out why Rab loathed me so undeniably? He'd said what he'd meant to his parents and for some unknown reason was also determined to be angry toward me. *I can't change the past. I can't change him.*

Just leave it be.

My lips still burned from his kiss. I pressed my fingers to my mouth, sealing the feel of him to my lips, and then dug my hands into my pockets as though I were hiding his kiss away forever.

CHAPTER SIXTEEN

Lyra

I didn't realize I was still half running until my shoulder smacked the front door.

"Ow," I muttered, fumbling for the handle, and then stumbled into the cottage like I'd been chased by wolves.

I stopped dead in my tracks. My living room was bright with candles and full of people.

Every head snapped toward me.

Sloane, Broca, Raven, Tam, Deidre, Nova, and Felicity.

All of the Charms. Well, except for Mandy, *of course*.

Brilliant. This was so not what I needed right now.

"Hi." I tried for casual and probably landed somewhere around deranged. My mind was still back at Rab's house, and my lips still tingled from his kiss. "I, uh . . . didn't realize we had a meeting?"

Nova, perched on the arm of the sofa, narrowed her eyes. "You're flushed."

"It's cold out."

"Not *that* cold."

"It's dropped a bit," I protested, reaching up to smooth my hair.

"Your hair's a mess."

"It's windy."

"Your lipstick's gone."

I shot her a look. "Do you want me to shave your head in the middle of the night?"

Nova raised both eyebrows at me and sat back with a knowing expression on her face.

Sisters are such a pain in the arse.

Ruth launched herself from the curtain rod and zipped over, landing on my shoulder with a soft thump. Her wings tickled my cheek as she sniffed at me dramatically.

You smell like lust, my friend.

"Ruth," I hissed under my breath, cheeks blazing.

Don't worry. They're too distracted to notice. Her tiny paws patted my jaw.

I glanced back at the room. Seven witches, every one of them tired and tense, stared at me like I held the answers to all their problems.

Sloane cleared her throat, pulling herself into president mode. "Lyra, sorry to do this so late, but we think it's important."

"Emergency meeting," Tam added grimly. "Felicity's found something that might help with the curse."

A knot formed in my stomach that had nothing to do with Rab and everything to do with the unbroken darkness pressing against the windows.

"Right." I shrugged out of my coat, hung it on the peg, and tried not to think about the fact that my entire body was still humming from that kiss. "I'll get the kettle on."

It's what we did in times of trouble. In times of joy. Anytime, really. A cup of tea sorted most things out. Maybe it would sort my curse out.

By the time I'd poured myself a mug and dropped into a chair next to Broca at the long dining room table, the room had gone quiet. Felicity sat on the edge of the chair opposite me, fingers twisted together, tote bag at her feet.

"Okay," Sloane said. "We all know why we're here, but for the record, Briarhaven hasn't seen daylight in a while now. The streetlamps have drained their batteries. Tourists are spooked. The locals are getting restless. Though we've built up a lot of goodwill in this town, I'm worried it will only go so far."

Deidre, who'd somehow still managed to bring both her phone and a folder of papers to an emergency Charms meeting, glanced up. "I had three viewings cancel today. One buyer pulled out entirely. He said it felt like the start of a horror movie."

"The gym's full," Tam added. "People don't want to exercise outside in the dark. I saw Mrs. Macarthy wearing a headlamp to deliver the mail."

"Maybe we can start a new fashion trend?" Nova wondered out loud, and Sloane shot her a look.

"Point is, this isn't sustainable. We can't ask an entire town to live in perpetual midnight while we faff about."

Guilt prickled down my spine. "Sorry," I muttered automatically.

"Stop that." Sloane softened. "None of this is your fault. It's the curse. Which is why"—she turned to Felicity—"you called us. Tell them what you found."

All eyes swung to Felicity.

She swallowed, smoothed her hair back, and reached for her tote. When her hand emerged, it was holding an old leather-bound book.

It made the hair on my arms stand up just looking at it.

The cover was cracked and dark, with faint Celtic symbols pressed into the leather. The pages inside were browned and uneven at the edges.

Ruth stiffened on my shoulder.

I don't like the smell of this book.

"Where did you get that?" Broca asked, leaning forward.

"In Kingsbarns," Felicity said. "There's this little bookshop called Highland Hearts. The book just fell at my feet."

"But when were you there?" Tam asked, turning to peer at Felicity.

"Och, it's been ages. But I forgot about the book once I got home. You know how busy the kids keep me." Felicity was a single mum with two very active kids, and she was always chauffeuring them to various activities.

"But you decided to read it tonight? After filming?" I asked, tilting my head at her in question.

"I was trying to wind down. It's just so exciting, isn't it? Being on a show?" Felicity beamed at me and waved her hands in the air. "Anyway, I couldn't rest, so I grabbed a book from the shelf and, well, I saw this."

She flipped the book open to a marked page and set it gently on the coffee table. We all leaned in.

The script was cramped and ornate, and very hard to read. Sigils had been drawn in the margins showing intertwining circles, thorned vines, and tiny suns and moons.

Raven's eyes lit up. "Oh, she's a beauty."

"Trust you to flirt with a grimoire." Tam snorted.

"I'll flirt with anything that has this many footnotes," Raven said. Then, more seriously, "What am I looking at?"

Felicity tapped a paragraph midway down the page. "I've been deciphering it as best I can since the writing is a bit smudged now. It's not perfect, but this section . . . It's about breaking curses of darkness tied to bloodlines. The kind that cling to families and through them, to places."

My heart stuttered.

"That . . . sounds familiar," I said weakly.

"That's kind of what I thought," Felicity said. "It mentions a bloodline that drags shadows with it wherever it goes. Towns fall into disrepair. Weather changes . . . that kind of thing."

"Wow. Love that for us." I sank back against the chair.

Just listen. Maybe this could be helpful. Ruth nuzzled into my neck.

Sloane leaned over Raven's shoulder. "Does it mention what to do about that?"

Raven scanned the page, lips moving silently. "It references, like, breaking a chain, I guess. Something about unlinking the curse from the dominant line and . . . anchoring it differently."

Tam frowned. "Differently how?"

"The wording's fuzzy. 'Line to line, root to root, burden shared and shadow soothed.' It's half poetry, half legalese. I'd need time to read this properly." Raven grimaced.

"We don't exactly have time," Deidre said. "Tourist season is bleeding out. Remember, we've got Halloween and Christmas coming up soon."

"From what I can gather, it seems that the witch at the center of the curse—Lyra, in this case—has to agree to doing a ritual. We cast the circle, and the spell . . . redistributes the darkness so it doesn't sit entirely on her line. It looks like it's supposed to unravel the worst of it." Felicity looked up at me, her eyes hopeful.

"Redistributes to where?" Nova asked, a concerned note in her voice.

Felicity hesitated.

"It doesn't say," she said, giving the table an apologetic look. "Just that it spreads the weight so it's not all crushing one branch. Like . . . like taking bricks off a collapsing wall and reinforcing the others."

There was a beat of silence.

Ruth shifted on my shoulder.

Hmm. I'm not sure about this, Lyra.

"I think we need to be careful here, Felicity. Old magick loves to hide the fine print." Broca's eyes narrowed slightly, but her voice stayed mild.

"I know." Felicity looked around the room, almost pleading. "I wouldn't have brought it if I didn't think it could work. I just felt like it sounded like the sort of thing that could help you, Lyra. And the town. I couldn't just . . . *not* say anything. Aren't we supposed to bring anything we find to the Charms?"

She met my gaze, her eyes hopeful.

Nerves in my stomach twisted; however, I did believe that Felicity truly wanted to help. She'd always been so sweet and earnest in her role as a coven member.

Sloane rubbed at her temples. "Raven? Risk assessment?"

"On a scale of one to Broca once tried to bargain with an angry river spirit who wanted to flood the town?" Raven asked.

"Och," Broca said, looking aggrieved. "I helped the drought, didn't I?"

Raven blew out a breath. "Look, anytime you're messing with bloodline curses, it's risky. The language here is murky, and Felicity's translation is working from damaged text. But the framework . . . It's not obviously malevolent. It's not a sacrifice or a summoning. It's a rebalancing."

"Could it make things worse?" Tam asked, leaning back to cross her arms over her chest.

"Yes," Raven said frankly, biting her lower lip. "It could deepen the curse instead of easing it. Or shift it unpredictably. Or just . . . fizzle, I guess?"

"Sweet, that's super fun," I muttered.

Ruth dug her claws in. *I do not like unknowns.*

Sloane looked at me. "Ultimately, it's your call. If you say no, that's it. We shelve this and go back to the drawing board."

The weight of the town's expectations seemed to press down on my shoulders.

Perpetual night. Empty shops. Worried faces.

My chest hurt.

"I don't want anyone hurt because of me," I whispered. "If there's even a chance this helps . . ."

Ruth made a soft squeak of displeasure. *Lyra . . .*

"We do it carefully," I added quickly. "The second anything feels wrong, we stop."

"Agreed." Sloane nodded solemnly.

Around the room, the others murmured assent.

Ruth was vibrating so hard against my neck I could feel it in my teeth.

Fine, she said at last, reluctantly. *But if I say "out," we are out.*

We rolled back the rug to bare the wooden floor. Broca drew a wide circle with salt and herbs, casting the spell for the circle under her breath. Raven set candles at the quarters and their flames flickered, throwing shadows up the walls. Nova fetched a bowl of water and set it near the hearth as a grounding point.

I stepped into the center of the circle, my dragon-scale necklace warm against my skin. Felicity took position opposite me, just outside the salt line, book cradled in her hands.

Ruth perched on my shoulder, tiny claws dug firmly into my dress, wings half lifted. If a fluttermouse could look like she was ready to battle a Viking, Ruth somehow managed it.

Sloane, Broca, Raven, Tam, Nova, and Deidre formed a ring just beyond Felicity, hands linked. Their combined magick hummed in the air and wrapped around me, as comfortable as a warm shawl.

"Deep breaths," Raven murmured.

I inhaled. Exhaled. Tried not to think about Rab's mouth on mine or hedgehogs or the fact that my magick currently had the impulse control of a toddler high on sugar.

"Okay," Sloane said. "We raise power as usual. Felicity, you keep your recitation slow so Raven can track structure as we go. The second something feels off, we stop. Clear?"

A chorus of "ayes" sounded around the room.

Broca began the opening chant, voice low and rhythmic. The others joined in, and the sound vibrated through the floorboards, through my bones. The air warmed. The hairs on my arms rose.

Magick gathered like a tide.

It slid through me, tugging at my own power. My magick, so very eager to be used, rushed to meet it.

"Behave," I whispered to it. "No hedgehogs."

Ruth squeezed my ear. *Focus.*

The chant shifted, rising. The circle's power locked into place with a gentle whoosh of light, surrounding me.

Felicity took a breath. "Here goes."

She began to speak.

The power in the room tightened.

At first, it felt . . . okay. Heavy, but not unpleasant. Like a storm building.

Then something snagged.

"Line to line, root to root, balance paid where balance's due . . ."

A cold prickle walked down my spine.

The magick shifted.

The gentle blanket pressure turned into a pull almost like invisible fingers hooking behind my ribs, tugging.

My breath hitched.

Ruth stiffened.

Lyra. Her voice was sharp.

Felicity's voice sped up just a fraction.

Raven's brows drew together.

The tugging increased. It wasn't painful yet, but it felt wrong, like someone rummaging in drawers they had no business opening.

"Slow," Raven said quietly.

Felicity stumbled on a word, then paused. "Right. Sorry."

Her cheeks were flushed and a bead of sweat ran down her temple as she fixed her eyes on the page.

The next phrase caught like a hook.

"Burden shared and shadow soothed . . ." Felicity intoned.

Something latched on to the threads of my magick . . . and tugged. Hard.

I gasped.

Ruth screeched.

Enough.

She shot off my shoulder in a flare of lavender light, her sword raised.

It happened fast.

One second, Felicity was reading, the circle was humming, and the magick was tugging at me.

The next, Ruth was at the center of the circle between us, wings thrown wide, with her sword drawn, glowing so brightly it hurt to look at her.

"Ruth!" I choked.

She wasn't listening.

Her tiny voice rang out, and not just in my head this time, but in the room, high and fierce and commanding.

Stop.

The magick hit her and bucked like a wild thing. For a heartbeat, I saw what looked like lines of energy twisting between Felicity and me, threads of some sort.

Ruth's sword came down through the middle of it.

The circle shattered.

The candles guttered and went out. A gust of cold wind whooshed through the cottage even though the windows were closed, snuffing every bit of flame.

The odd tugging sensation stopped.

I staggered, knees buckling. Nova lunged in and caught my elbow before I face-planted into the salt.

"Easy," she said, voice shaking.

Raven's arms were pulled tightly across her chest, hugging herself. Sloane braced herself against the back of a chair. Tam swore softly.

Felicity had been knocked backward onto her bum, book splayed across her lap. She looked stunned, eyes huge in the dim light.

Ruth hovered between us, sword still out, golden wings trembling.

This was wrong, she said, turning in the air to face me. *That spell grabbed you. It did not feel like help.*

"She says it was wrong," I said, reaching out my hands so Ruth could flutter into my palms. "That the spell tried to grab me."

Raven swallowed hard. "She's right. There was a twist in the structure. The energy wasn't just easing off the curse . . . it was . . . hooking something else onto it. I couldn't see what yet."

"It might have resolved cleanly," Felicity argued. "Sometimes old spells feel strange halfway through. We stopped too soon."

Sloane shot her a look. "Better too soon than too late."

"But—"

"No." Sloane's voice brooked no argument. "Whatever that was, well, it was wrong. I'm not gambling on my sister."

The room was quiet for a beat.

Felicity's shoulders sagged. "I was only trying to help," she whispered. "I thought . . . it sounded so perfect. Like it was written for you."

I believed her.

That was the worst of it.

She truly, desperately wanted this to work.

"It was worth trying," I said softly, even as my insides still felt like they'd been rearranged. "But if Ruth says it felt wrong, I trust her."

Ruth looked up at me, giving me a nod of appreciation, before tucking her sword back into its small leather sheath.

The spell smelled like old grudges.

Raven pushed herself to her feet, picked up the book, and turned it carefully. "I'd like to study this more," she said. "There are gaps in the text I didn't see until the power rose. Sections that look smudged or . . . deliberately obscured."

"Deliberately?" Broca asked, eyes sharpening.

Raven lifted a shoulder. "Could be nothing. Or it could be someone trying to hide the cost. Either way, it's too unstable to use as is. We're shelving this approach. Agreed?"

"Aye," came the tired chorus.

Felicity's mouth trembled. "I'm sorry," she said again. "I didn't mean to scare anyone."

"You didn't," Tam said, then grimaced. "Okay, you did a bit. But only because we are a touch on edge these days."

"You did right by bringing it," Broca said, reaching over to pat Felicity's shoulder. "Old magick's always a risk, and that's the truth of it."

A flicker of frustration crossed Felicity's face. Then she nodded, blinking fast. "Of course."

Sloane took a steadying breath. "Right. Then tonight's conclusion is that the darkness curse lives to make us miserable another day."

Chairs scraped and mugs were brought over to the sink. The Charms began to bundle themselves back into coats and boots, and everyone said their goodbyes. The door shut with a soft click, and I turned, feeling weary down to my bones.

Nova flopped back onto the sofa. "Well," she said. "That was a fun little evening. How's your soul? Still attached?"

"Barely," I muttered.

Ruth crawled around in my cupped hands, her fur still faintly bristled. I stroked a finger gently along her back.

"Thank you," I whispered.

Always, she said simply. *I don't mind trying spells. I don't even mind old spells. But that one felt like it had too many hands in the pot. Too many old arguments soaked into the ink.*

"Old arguments?" I echoed.

She yawned, showing tiny sharp teeth. *The book was written by someone who'd been angry a very long time. I don't like angry ink. It forgets who it's meant to help.*

An odd little shiver walked through me, but I shook it off. It had been a *very* long day, and I was exhausted.

"We'll find another way," I said aloud, more to myself than anyone. "One that doesn't feel like being turned inside out."

Nova nudged my shoulder. "Preferably one that doesn't require emergency exorcism by your pocket mouse, yeah."

Ruth huffed. *Pocket mouse with a sword.*

I smiled, even as the weight of the darkness outside pressed in at the edges of my awareness.

We hadn't broken the curse tonight.

But we were trying. And someday, somehow, we were going to fix this. That much, at least, I could promise myself. Even if I couldn't see the way now, I had faith in our coven. The Charms had been nothing but a blessing to us, and I was certain we'd see our way through this.

And for now? I needed to go face down into a pillow for eight hours and think of nothing else but ideas for my next baking challenge.

CHAPTER SEVENTEEN

Rab

As I had suspected, Lyra's magick ran to transmutation as well.

It was a good thing that this particular area of magick was in my wheelhouse, as maybe I'd be able to head off any catastrophe in the future, but for now I had to figure out what to do with a prickle of hedgehogs.

I didn't have the heart to turn them back into the silverware they'd once been.

"I've got a hedgehog problem," I said without preamble to Knox, sitting on the floor of my kitchen and watching as the wee beasties ran around in circles.

"And I've got an owl problem," Knox said, and I paused, pulling the phone away from my face to squint at the screen.

"Are you taking the piss?" I asked, annoyed. One particularly bold hedgehog ran up to me and then clambered into my lap. Rolling over, he held his wee hands to the ceiling, as though inviting a cuddle. Sighing, I scratched his tummy and the hedgie's eyes closed in bliss.

"No, mate, I'm bloody well not." Knox's beleaguered sigh came through the speaker. "The short-eared owl, to be specific. Apparently, it only hunts during the day."

"Oh," I said, understanding dawning. With no daylight hours, the owls would begin to starve. "That's . . . that's not good."

"No, mate, it's not. They've moved into town and are trying to hunt by the light of our lanterns. Which, as you can imagine, is creating some chaos."

"Can they see okay? Is that an issue?"

"It's more that they are hungry, so they are dive-bombing any potential food. Including cats and dogs."

"Oh no." I looked at the hedgehogs milling about my kitchen. Not an ideal time to release them to the wild, then. "Have there been any tragedies?"

"Not yet, as I've put the warning out. But we're going to have to figure out how to feed them, otherwise we're going to have even angrier neighbors than we already do." I could hear the strain in Knox's voice.

"If someone loses their cat over this . . ."

"Exactly. Then the MacGregors will be on the chopping block, because Briarhaven will once again want them gone. I'm already dealing with an onslaught of complaints. The gardening center is particularly peeved, as their plants are dying without sunlight."

"Shite."

"Exactly. Now what is the hedgehog issue?"

"Um, right. Well, Lyra was over and—"

"Lyra? She came to your house?" Interest sharpened Knox's voice. Leaning back, I banged the back of my head lightly on the cupboard door. I didn't particularly enjoy being the subject of gossip, but I also needed someone to talk to about this. What had I been thinking, kissing Lyra like that?

It was like all my frustrations had built up and the only outlet was through kissing her.

Which made no sense, really, because now I was even more furious.

At myself.

At her.

At the situation.

"Let's just say filming didn't go exactly as planned today. She wanted to talk about it, in hopes we could try to work together as a team." Remembering now that Knox was the one who forced me onto the show, my thoughts took a turn. "Speaking of . . . What the hell, man? You put me on this show as her partner?"

"You're her partner?" Knox gave a low whistle and then burst out laughing.

"Och, I'm glad you think this is funny."

"I swear, mate, I had no hand in that. I did know Lyra was auditioning, but that's the extent of it."

"You could have clued me in," I grumbled.

"I mean, it's not all that hard to find out information in Briarhaven, Rab. You could have just asked around and had a likely list of candidates for who might be on the show," Knox said, his voice unapologetic.

He wasn't wrong. But for some reason I'd never considered the idea that Lyra might have signed up for the show.

A second hedgehog crawled into my lap and bumped his nose against the other, and the two began to bicker, making soft grunting noises.

"While I understand what you're saying, that's absolute bullocks, mate. You should have told me Lyra was auditioning."

"It didn't go well, it sounds like?" Knox said, neatly avoiding taking responsibility for my current predicament.

I paused, unsure of what to say about Lyra's magick, yet knowing how Briarhaven worked, I was sure word would be out by now. Felicity never met a piece of gossip she didn't share, and Mandy didn't seem particularly fond of Lyra, so even though they were coven members, I was sure the news would have spread.

"Catastrophic, really." I sighed and pulled apart the two hedgies in my lap, which were now locked in a death grip. "Her magick went haywire and basically everything was everywhere. Yolks flying left and right, butter curdling. It was an absolute mess."

And she'd looked adorably, impossibly gorgeous, as frustration had brought pink to her cheeks and her teeth had dug into that lush lower lip of hers.

"Och, poor lass. I know how much she wanted this to be a success. She's got a YouTube cooking show, you know?"

"Does she?" I pretended I didn't have it saved on my browser.

"Aye, mate. It's her main source of income, so I'm sure she's worried about what this will do to her channel."

"I'm going to try to help," I said, nudging one of the hedgehogs away from biting a loose thread in the seam of my trousers.

"Och, that's a good lad. I was worried you wouldn't."

"I don't want to see her fail," I admitted, looking out across the kitchen.

"It's hard to tell. You never talk about it."

Silence fell, and I knew he was waiting for me to explain myself. Something I wasn't really in the habit of doing.

"I'm not a horrible person. She hurt me, and I'm angry about it. But that doesn't mean I want to see her crash and burn either."

"You still care for her." It was a statement, not a question.

Did I? If I told Knox what happened between us, would he tell me that we'd only been children and that Lyra had never really had a choice? That she had been forced to leave? Because, yes, that thought had run through my head a thousand times as well.

She could have texted. Messaged. Emailed. Yet she'd never reached out. She'd just . . . vanished.

"Never trust a MacGregor, Rab," my father said. *"They're a menace to this town and will only cause you grief."*

I pinched my nose, my shoulders tightening with tension. "As a nice human being, I don't care to see her, or anyone, make a fool of themselves on a hugely public scale."

"You still care for her," Knox repeated.

"I care about not being made a laughingstock," I said, annoyance flaring.

"You still—"

"Fine, mate," I almost shouted, exasperated. "I still care for her. Okay? Does it make you happy to hear it? Bloody hell."

"I knew it." Knox's tone was smug in the way of one who was happily ensconced in a relationship where regular sex was the norm.

"But I'm angry at her, Knox. I have been for a long time. I wish I could just turn off my feelings for her, but that's never been the case. Not where Lyra is concerned. It's better for me if I just stay away from her entirely, but now that's not really an option. Thanks to you." I glowered at the two hedgehogs in my lap, which had now curled up and gone to sleep.

"That might be a good thing."

"No, I don't think it is." I sighed, thinking about how good her lips had felt on mine, her soft body pressed against mine. How much I still desperately wanted her. Bloody hell, but the taste of her kiss was imprinted on my soul. "I don't think it is at all."

"What about the hedgehogs?" Knox asked, a voice sounding in the background. Sloane must be home. "What do I need to do, and why are they a problem?"

"Um, I don't quite understand why they are a problem," I said. I had an idea of what was going on, since I'd once been new to my powers and unable to control transmutation when my emotions went haywire. "But I have about twenty of them and need to figure out what to do with them."

"Do owls eat hedgehogs?" Knox wondered, and a sharp voice in the background had him turning away from our conversation. "*Of course* I'm not going to feed the owls hedgehogs, Sloane. I just need to find a place for them to go."

A muffled conversation took place, and then Knox returned to me.

"Sorcha. The owner of the Familiar's Nest? She'll take them. Runs a sanctuary or something of that nature."

"Got it. Thanks. I'll give her a call."

"Still not going to tell me how you got them all?"

"Nope," I said, shaking my head. Lyra already had enough humiliation on her hands; she didn't need the world to know that she turned inanimate objects into hedgehogs when she was aroused.

Because I was pretty sure that was what was going on.

Which meant two things. The first?

Lyra was still very much attracted to me. At least based on the amount of hedgies running around my kitchen floor.

And the second?

She had no clue how to harness her power, which would be catastrophic for the show.

CHAPTER EIGHTEEN

Lyra

Bloody hell!

Ruth leapt back from the windowsill and fluttered over to my makeup table, her small body visually shivering. Immediately, I dropped the blush brush I was holding and picked her up, cuddling her close to my chest.

"What's wrong, wee one?" I asked, stroking a finger down the soft fur on her back.

An owl just flew at the window.

"Really?" I craned my head to look out the window.

Really. I saw my life flash before my eyes.

"I never thought about it, but I guess you still have some predators, don't you? Do you have any defense mechanisms? What should I know so I can help you?" I stood up and walked across the room, curious about the owl.

Frankly, I was happy to have anything to take my mind off Rab.

Off his kiss, which was both the same and foreign, memories of what had been blended with what could be.

It was the type of kiss where time stopped, you forgot your own name, and all you could do was feel. I'd dated my fair share of men since Rab, always keeping things light, and I certainly enjoyed a wee make-out session and a cuddle.

But this hit different.

It always would, my heart seemed to whisper to me, and I pushed thoughts of Rab out of my mind as I peered out the window to see an owl sitting on a branch of the tree just outside my window, tilting its head at us.

"Is it magickal?" I asked Ruth. I couldn't tell, but its eyes looked intelligent.

No. Which makes it even scarier.

"What about your sword?" I asked, turning away so the owl wouldn't get any ideas about flying at the window.

I could hold off one owl, but more than one would be a problem. I'd have to alert all magickals within range.

"What does that do?" I asked, curious. I hadn't heard of this.

Most magickals will help others in need. If they're one of the good ones.

"Hmm." I put Ruth down on the other side of my makeup table, away from the window, and picked up my phone to text Sloane. "I'm just going to let Sloane that we'll need to be on alert to make sure you're protected. And to let Blue know."

Ruth snorted.

"Och, I know he seems harmless, but don't forget he can shoot fire. He'd protect you. I'm sure of it."

He's a good lad, Ruth acknowledged. She picked up a gold tube of mascara and twirled it over her head like it was a weapon before handing it over to me. *You're upset today. I can feel it.*

"I don't know if 'upset' is quite the word for it." I leaned forward toward the mirror and uncapped the mascara. "I'm embarrassed. About the mess I made on the show. And other . . . things. I'm . . . sad. I'm shaken. I'm confused. I'm all the things."

And in love.

I slammed the mascara wand back into the tube and glared at my wee fluttermouse. She'd stood up on her back two feet, and her front arms were perched on her lavender hips like she was some sort of little diva.

"I am not in love."

If you're all the things, wouldn't "in love" be one of them? Ruth studied a nail she'd painted a screaming hot pink.

"So could being 'on the hunt for a less annoying familiar.' One who doesn't make assumptions at six in the morning," I said.

Is it an assumption? Ruth crossed her arms over her chest and raised her nose at me in challenge.

"Have I mentioned how annoying you are?" I asked. I was not in love with Rabbie. I had once been in love with him, but a lot had changed, for both of us, since that time. He was different. I was different. "It's . . . complicated, Ruth. You can't love the idea of someone, no matter how much your heart wants you to."

But what if your heart is right?

"Because to find that out, I'd need to take a chance on him again. And he doesn't want that. And I don't want that."

Coward. Ruth sniffed.

"Coward? He hurt me." I jabbed my mascara wand in Ruth's direction.

The people you love will always hurt you. Being in love doesn't stop you from causing one another pain. It's the ones who hold on, who work through those hurts, that last. They know that demanding perfection of one another is an impossible ask. That's real love. A little bit of grace can go a long way, Lyra.

She sounded like a teeny-tiny wizened oracle, and I narrowed my eyes at her.

"How come you're so smart?"

I've lived many lives, Lyra. And I'm small, which makes me a constant observer of others, since I'm usually overlooked. If you're someone who sticks to the corners of the room, you see everything. And I've seen a lot of people make idiotic choices through misplaced pride.

"This is some deep life advice before I've even had my coffee," I said, leaning forward to swipe mascara across my lashes. "Much more intelligent than the sayings on the side of the tea bags."

Live, laugh, love. Ruth twirled and pretended to curtsy.

"There it is." I laughed and capped my mascara.

Smile and the world smiles with you.

"Do I really want the world smiling at me? Wouldn't it be creepy if every single person I saw walking around downtown was smiling? At the same time?"

Ruth bared her teeth at me, her attempt at a smile, and I shuddered.

"No offense, but I prefer the sword."

That's fine. Being approachable is not a metric I aspire to have.

"I could learn something from you." I sighed as I pulled one side of my hair back in a bejeweled hair comb and left the rest to tumble down my back.

Men approach you because you're beautiful. You smile at them because you're nice, but they misinterpret friendliness as an invitation. That is their problem, not yours. You can try scowling more, if you wish to dissuade them. But I prefer a more direct approach. Ruth brandished her sword.

I pursed my lips and scowled into the mirror, trying to look dangerous.

Ruth sighed. *You even look cute doing that.*

"I want people to see more than just a pretty face when they look at me." I winced. Rab's words to his parents still stung, all these years later. At that point in my life, his was the only opinion I'd really trusted. In a chaotic household, where my parents fought, Sloane was sullen and removed, and Nova was still a child, I'd leaned on Rab to be my true north.

Beauty is a tool. Use it when necessary. Think of it this way—your beauty may be what gets people to stop and watch you, but your talent is what will keep people around.

"While I appreciate that, tiny oracle, that doesn't really help when I can't even harness my bloody magick." I stood and reached for my dress. Today I was going emerald green, with a deep square-cut neckline, flouncy little sleeves, and a skirt that hugged my body. It was important to me to showcase my body, in all of its strength and softness, so that those watching would see real people represented on-screen. Once I'd regained my confidence after the breakup with Rab, I'd made a promise to myself that I would never dress unimaginatively or hide my body just because I was plus-sized. And I'd stuck to it. The reality was, people could see what size my body was; I wasn't fooling anyone. So why should I dress in boring colors if everybody could already see what I looked like?

I had been told on more than one occasion that my confidence was what had drawn men to me. Not that I was dressing for a man's attention, but when I liked what I was wearing, I felt good about myself, and that, in turn, seemed to make me approachable.

A trait that, apparently, my wee familiar spat on.

Are you sure I can't help during filming? Ruth asked, fluttering across the room to perch on the edge of the bed.

"You can't." I frowned at her. "They still have a strict no-familiars rule, otherwise, I'd have you there in a heartbeat."

That's too bad. The only suggestion I can give you? Ruth reached for the dragon necklace on my bedside table and then flew it over to me, the rose dangling from her arms. *Use this.*

"How?" I asked, taking the necklace from her and clipping it around my neck. As before, the delicate charm warmed beneath my fingers and then settled gently against my skin.

Ask it to help you channel your magick. Or to calm you. Either way, dragon scales are immensely powerful, and you're beyond lucky to have this necklace to wear. Plus, it was given with love. Use it. At best, it might dull some of the chaotic nature of your magick right now.

"Thanks, Ruth. I'll do that. I do feel . . . something inexplicable when I wear it." I cupped the charm in my hand, and it buzzed happily over my palm. "It's like it's happy to be here with me."

Of course it is. It was designed for you. And now it is home. There's nothing in the rules about not using the tools at your disposal, right?

"Not that I'm aware of."

Well, this is a tool. Use it.

Emboldened, I saluted my wee familiar, and she saluted me back, with her sword in hand, and I winced as the sword came dangerously close to the ends of my hair.

"Careful, there, Xena."

Ah, the iconic princess warrior. I like that.

"Shall I make you a wee crown?"

Obviously. Ruth gave me a look as though she was annoyed I hadn't already thought to do so.

"One crown, coming up. I'll get Broca on it. She'll have you dripping in sparkles by the end of the day."

I'll stay here to direct. I don't want to go out with the owls, even though I do enjoy some violence to perk up my morning.

"Easy, killer. No need to get stabby before coffee."

Isn't that the stabbiest time for humans?

"Ah, well, yes, I suppose it is." I laughed. She had me there.

You look beautiful, Lyra. But beyond that, you look fierce. Now all you have to do is get over yourself and tell Rab you love him.

I stopped in my doorway where I'd been about to go downstairs and turned to glare at Ruth, who was currently standing at the window, her sword raised at the owl.

"I will do no such thing. And I'd appreciate if you'd keep that sentiment to yourself."

Stupid humans. Always in their own way.

"And please stop tormenting the owl."

He started it.

CHAPTER NINETEEN

Lyra

There was no way I still loved Rabbie. I didn't even know the man anymore. He could have entirely changed since high school, gotten into a cult, and he probably thought that Chappell Roan was a type of cheese.

Plus, he ate cold baked beans out of a can for supper.

What kind of person even did that?

I wondered if he'd been able to do something with the hedgehogs. I'd felt bad, leaving him with a kitchen full of the wee beasties, but there was nothing that could be done. I didn't even fully understand what was happening, so I wasn't going to be a good source of information for him.

I'd needed to get out of there, because ten seconds more, and I would have been wrapping my legs around his waist and inviting him to butter my scone.

Still, a tiny part of me felt bad about leaving him with all those hedgies.

"Good morning, gorgeous."

I turned, a smile blooming, until I saw Vaughn approaching me, and my face fell.

"Were you hoping I was someone else?" Vaughn asked, holding a hand to his heart and pretending to be wounded.

"What? No, not at all." I shook my head in earnest. "How are you this morning? How are you finding Briarhaven?"

"Och, it's a cracking wee town, isn't it?" Vaughn smiled, leaning one elbow against the wall over my shoulder, standing a touch closer than I would have preferred. "Had a great meal at the pub but would love for you to show me around once we're finished filming."

"You can drive around the entire place in fifteen minutes. Show *yourself* around."

My eyebrows went up at Rab's voice, and I looked under Vaughn's arm to see him standing behind the producer, a glower on his handsome face.

Vaughn's lips quirked, and he dropped his arm, turning to Rab.

"Aye, mate. I'll do that. I just find exploring is always better with a local."

"Felicity?" Rab called, keeping his eyes level on Vaughn.

Felicity appeared at Rab's side, a Christmas scrunchie in her hair, looking oddly bereft without her usual overflowing tote bag on her arm.

"Good morning." Felicity beamed at us.

"Vaughn's looking for a local to show him around Briarhaven. Think you'd be up to the task?"

"Oh, I'd love to." Felicity clapped her hands and bounced a bit. "There's just so much to see. Knox really did a great job when he rehauled the place. Have you been to the Dragon's Hoard yet?"

"I have not." Vaughn gave Rab an unreadable look as he passed, and Rab's grin widened until it looked almost threatening.

See? I'd been right when I'd told Ruth it would be scary if people smiled all the time.

"Was he bothering you?" Rab asked, and I blinked up at him, confused. I'd been about to apologize for Vaughn and explain that I hadn't been flirting. Taking a step back, until my bum hit the wall, I tilted my chin up at him.

"No, it's fine. He's hoping to take me out after filming wraps up is all."

"Which you'll say no to," Rab said, his green eyes deepening in color as he stepped closer.

"Excuse me?" Initially, I had thought about saying yes to Vaughn's invitation for a date, but since he'd so gleefully thrown me to the wolves yesterday, I'd realized he wasn't the type of man that I wanted to be dating. Still, that was my choice to make. Not Rab's.

"You heard me."

"You don't get to dictate who I date."

Rab just looked at me, his gaze unwavering, and I shifted beneath his scrutiny. What was he trying to say? What did this mean? For the past year he'd done everything in his power to avoid me, and now he was telling me who I could date? And kissing me until I couldn't see straight and hedgehogs exploded around the room? Even thinking about the kiss again sent a rush of heat through me.

The coffee cup Rab was holding shifted, blurred, and then Rab was swearing softly under his breath as he tucked a hedgehog to his chest.

"You've going to have to get this under control, darling."

"Me? It's not me," I said, my heart hammering as I stared at the wee hedgie cradled against Rab's muscular chest.

"Och, lie to yourself all you want, Lyra, but this is one hundred percent your doing." Rab leaned closer, his mouth inches from my ear, his breath hot against my skin. "And I know why it's happening."

"Don't make assumptions," I stammered, stepping back and sliding along the wall until I was away from him. "You know what they say about those."

A grin flashed lightning quick on Rab's face before he turned to scowl down at the hedgie in his hand.

"It'll be our little secret." Rab turned as a whistle sounded. "I'll be right back."

"Where are you going?"

"Dropping this wee lad at the Familiar's Nest. Sorcha's watching over the lot of 'em. We can't release them with the owl infestation."

With that, Rab left, even though we were being called to set.

"An owl infestation that we have *you* to thank for." I turned to see Mandy Meadows, dressed all in black again today, her eyes rimmed with smudgy liner.

"You can't put that on me," I said, frustrated. "It's not my fault our family is cursed."

"And yet. You haven't done a damn thing to break your end of it, have you?"

"That's categorically untrue." My hands clenched. "We've been doing the research. Just everything comes up a dead end."

"Must be because the Charms suck now that Sloane is in charge." Mandy sniffed, as though my inability to break an ancient curse reflected the strength of our coven.

"That's unfair. And they *don't* suck. And you're still a part of us, no matter how much you ignore my attempts to bring you back."

"Why the hell should I come back? You're destroying what I've built." Mandy's eyes narrowed, and she hunched, bringing her face closer to mine. "You're all just playing at magick, when I was the real deal. It's why you're going to lose this competition. All of you MacGregors . . . just a blight on this town with poorly executed magickal skills."

"What the actual f—"

"If you've got a problem with the lass, then you've got a problem with me as well."

Mandy whirled to see Marcie, pink hair tied in warrior braids, slapping a rolling pin into her hand. Muscles bulged in her arms, and she'd opened her mouth enough to show just how sharp her teeth were. Mandy stiffened next to me.

"I'm not—"

"You are. I've been watching you, Mandy Meadows. You're trying to get in Lyra's head with your nonsense, and I won't be allowing it. Not on my watch." Marcie slapped the rolling pin once more, and Mandy took an automatic step back.

"Ladies?" Vaughn interrupted.

Marcie turned and Vaughn threw his hands up in the air, reading her intention accurately.

"And you," Marcie continued, marching forward. "Keep your eyes on your work, not on the contestants. And make sure everyone cleans up better. Last night I found several bowls with hardened dough stuck to them. I'll be adding any damages to the expense sheet."

"Yes, ma'am." Vaughn nodded, swallowing as Marcie stormed past. Mandy followed, not sparing me another glance.

I was seething because I'd actually cared about her. Hadn't I been the one to check on her repeatedly this past year? I'd been convinced that eventually I'd be able to help her come back to the coven.

"All good? Where's Rab?" Vaughn asked, reaching up to run a finger under the collar of his shirt.

"Right here."

I didn't turn as Rab's voice sent a shiver down my spine. He was right about me needing to get control over my emotions. If I didn't, the baking competition was about to become overrun with hedgehogs. Forcing myself to remember how he'd hurt me, and not the way his kisses had awoken something long dormant inside of me, I brushed past Vaughn to join the line of contestants waiting to walk onto set.

Felicity whispered furiously with Mandy, and they both cast me a look over their shoulders. I didn't care what they were gossiping about. If they wanted to be mean, that was their choice. I'd just kill them with kindness.

I pictured Ruth with her tiny sword and smiled. She would certainly have a different opinion on what I should be doing. But, since I didn't carry a sword, and my magick was not even close to functioning normally, I just had to fall back on my strengths.

Which were charm, more charm, and the charmiest charm to ever charm.

"So exciting, isn't it, ladies? I can't believe we coven sisters get to be on the same show." I injected my voice with syrupy sweetness and beamed at them both when they looked back at me. Felicity responded instantly to me, all smiles and bouncy excitement, whereas Mandy continued her campaign of misery.

"It's like actual Christmas Day," Felicity gushed, gripping my arm, "cooking with our family."

"Gag me," Mandy grumbled.

"Gladly." I beamed at Mandy, fluttering my lashes a bit, and she gave me snake eyes in return.

I wanted to be like Sloane or Nova, happily abrasive when the need arose, but it just didn't suit me. It felt like I was trying to squeeze myself into a too-small one-piece swimsuit. I sighed.

"Mandy—"

"All right, everyone, take your places." An assistant producer ushered us into the room, and there was no more time for talking. Once again, our aprons were folded neatly at our tables, ingredients were lined up, and Nevin and Kelly stood at the front of the room, hands clasped behind their backs.

"Sorcha was able to take the hedgie but has requested that we slow down with delivering them to her, if possible," Rab said under his breath.

I closed my eyes and took a deep breath.

He was the enemy. *The worst.* He'd ripped my heart out and—

"Quiet on set."

I snapped my eyes open and waited through the countdown before action was called. Nevin and Kelly jumped to attention and began their usual welcome spiel before turning to us.

"As we know, yesterday's challenge brought with it some, shall we say, difficulties for one team . . ." Nevin smiled creamily in my direction. "How are we feeling after the catastrophe yesterday, Lyra?"

"Just great." I beamed at the cameras. Since the judges had to taste everything we made, if I couldn't get my magick to work, maybe I'd just make something extra putrid for Nevin and Kelly to choke down. "Everyone has an off day in the kitchen, and I'm excited to see what today's challenge is."

"Rabbie, how do you feel going into today? Was it a little off-putting to discover that the supposed professional on your team was experiencing *so* many issues?" Kelly asked, sidling closer to Rab. Was she wearing an even lower-cut top today?

"Not a problem for me. I thought it was kind of fun, actually." Rab smiled, and Kelly giggled, running a finger over the neckline of her blouse.

"Oh, you're so forgiving."

"Nothing to forgive. This is a friendly Christmas competition, isn't it? We're here to try out some recipes and have some good old-fashioned Christmas cheer, right?" Rab asked, rocking back on his heels.

"I'm not," one of the people from the Christmas elf team muttered, and the cameras swiveled toward them.

"Team Elf! Out for vengeance, are you?" The hosts moved over to their table, blissfully leaving us alone, and I released a long breath.

"Don't let them get to you," Rab said, turning to me.

"I'm not." I was surprised by Rab's change of heart about the competition, but at the same time, pleased he seemed to be in a more positive mindset about it. I took my apron from the table and pulled it over my head, bending forward a bit as I tied it. When I glanced up, I caught Rab's eyes glued to the front of my dress, as I was still bent over. As soon as he saw me looking, he quickly averted his gaze.

Heat flushed.

"Marigold. Tulips. Roses. Hydrangeas," I recited to myself, latching on to the first thing that I could think of that would distract me from Rab. I could only imagine the delight on Kelly's face if I turned my mixing bowls into hedgehogs.

"What?" Rab hissed.

"Nothing," I hissed back. "Wheesht."

"Right, challengers. Today we've cooked up something extra fun for you all," Nevin announced, his eyes sparkling with mischief. "Or should I say . . . fun for us and our viewers. Not likely so great for you all."

A murmur of apprehension rippled through the room.

"Today's challenge," Kelly said, practically bouncing on her heels, "is the Trust Truffles baking challenge!"

A flurry of glitter erupted above us, snowflake-shaped confetti drifting down like enchanted dandruff.

"In the spirit of the season," Nevin continued, "you'll need to trust in your partner completely. One of you will be blindfolded and doing the cooking, while the other has their hands tied behind their back and must give explicit directions to their blindfolded partner."

The room erupted in exclamations.

"No way," I said flatly. I turned to Rab. "I can't do this. I can't even make toast with both hands and full vision right now."

"Oh, but wait!" Kelly interrupted, giddy as a teenager on espresso. "There's more! Your goal is to make a batch of Christmas pudding cookie truffles—with a molten center, a candied holly decoration on top, and a surprise magical moment infused by one partner's favorite Christmas memory."

Everyone groaned in unison.

"And the blindfolded partner," Nevin added with relish, "must be the one to handle the spell infusion at the end."

I looked up at Rab, eyes wide. My throat had gone dry. It was already bad enough that my magick was going wild, but without full capability? "This is a recipe for disaster."

He grinned. "Aye. But it could be kind of fun."

"Fun?" I gritted my teeth. The man had a concerning idea of what fun was.

"You'll be given an enchanted blindfold, a set of magical binding ribbons, and one recipe scroll. As soon as you pick up the scroll, the enchantment locks in," Kelly warned, gesturing to the golden scrolls that had appeared on each workstation.

The room went quiet. I looked behind us to see the other teams all eyeing the scroll with varying expressions of concern on their faces.

"You touch it," Rab said, bumping me with his shoulder.

"I don't wanna," I whined.

"Och, let's just crack on . . ." Rab reached out and picked up the scroll.

The paper unfurled, like someone rolling out a carpet, and a golden ribbon and red silk bandanna flew out. I gasped as the gold ribbon darted at Rab, and he dodged, but no matter which way he moved, the ribbon flew the other way until it had wrapped itself around Rab's wrists with a neat *SNAP!* behind his back.

"Ow, bloody hell," Rab said, giving me a look.

I blinked. "Wait, I thought I was going to be the one—"

The blindfold dropped onto my head before I could finish my sentence, plunging me into darkness.

"Time starts now, Rab and Lyra," Nevin called gleefully. "You've activated the challenge!"

"Oh no. Oh no, no, no," I muttered, patting around blindly.

"Don't worry, darling," Rab's voice rumbled. "I'll be your eyes. You just be my hands."

Heat flushed as I thought about his hands on me.

"Toilet paper. Paper Towel. Dish detergent. Hand soap," I recited, forcing my mind away from any hedgehog-spawning thoughts.

"That's not quite what the recipe calls for," Rab said, his voice sounding worried.

"I know how to make truffles," I said, annoyance lacing my voice. "I'm just not sure that I can trust you."

"Och, it's trusting *me* that you're worried about?" There was a note in Rab's voice that I couldn't decipher.

I opened my mouth to lay into him about just why I couldn't trust him, but then snapped it shut as I remembered the cameras, all aimed in our direction.

"Having trust issues already?" Kelly's voice drew near. She sounded gleeful, and I stiffened.

"The man eats beans straight from the can."

"Beans are a perfectly respectable source of protein," Rab protested.

"Not cold, they're not."

"Och, Rab. You're breaking every chef's heart who is watching this." Kelly chuckled. "But I'm sure there will be more than one viewer who'd happily sign up to help teach you how to . . . heat your beans."

My mouth dropped open. I couldn't help it. Was she really openly hitting on Rab, fully knowing he was my ex-boyfriend? I was going to—

"That's all right. Lyra will sort me out. Now, not to be rude, but time's running out," Rab said.

I took a deep breath, trying not to imagine the cameras capturing the flustered flush on my cheeks. I was blindfolded. Rab was helpless. The recipe was already listing itself aloud in a floaty, enchanted voice.

"Step one," the recipe intoned. "Crack three eggs into the large mixing bowl."

I put my hands out.

"Okay, Lyra, there's a bowl to your left. No, your other left. Now go forward . . . little more . . . not that much—you're about to hit the—"

I knocked the bowl off the table and it went flying to the floor with a loud clang.

Mandy's laugh rang out behind me.

"Found the bowl," I muttered.

"That's okay, there's another just next to it. Go slowly."

I fumbled around until I found the bowl, but this time managed to keep it on the table.

"There you go—that's a good lass."

"Rosemary, marjoram, pink peppercorn, cayenne pepper, sage," I recited, desperate to push the thought of being blindfolded with him saying those words to me in a very different environment out of my head.

"Nope, not going to need any of those. Eggs are up next," Rab said, sounding slightly confused. His voice was nearer to me now. "Now, the eggs are to the right. No, farther."

I edged my hand slowly across the table, terrified to knock anything else off. My hand closed around the carton of eggs, and I breathed a sigh of relief.

"Eggs seemed to be a particularly difficult step for you yesterday, weren't they, Lyra?" Nevin's voice boomed nearby, and I jumped, almost dropping the carton.

"Bloody hell . . ." I whispered, shaking my head.

"That's just fine. We'll take the eggs slow today." Rab's voice was reassuring. I knew what he was trying to tell me. He was going to use his magick to help me. Now that he knew what the problem was, maybe he'd be able to counteract it.

I felt for the rim of the bowl, put the carton of eggs down next to it, and eased the top open. I'd done this a thousand times before. Breathing in, I held up the egg and cracked it on the side of the bowl.

Sticky wet slapped my face and chest, and I gasped.

"Right, that was not the plan." Rab sounded dangerously like he was trying not to laugh.

I turned my head toward him, egg dripping down my neck, steel in my voice. "No, it wasn't part of the *plan*, was it, Rab?"

"There's a hand towel just inches from your left hand."

I moved my hand slightly to find the towel and then carefully wiped the yolk from my face.

"Right, shall we try again?" I said brightly, knowing the cameras were watching us closely.

"Why even bother? It's clear your magick doesn't work," Mandy called.

"Eyes on your own table," Rab said, his voice sharp. "That attitude must be why you got kicked out of your coven."

Mandy's gasp almost made me laugh, and I pressed my lips together while I felt for another egg.

"Now, Lyra. Focus on me. My words." Rab's voice wrapped around me, cocooning me as I focused solely on his words and the task at hand. By the time I'd cracked the egg and it had landed successfully in the bowl, I was thoroughly under his enchantment.

"I did it!" I exclaimed and turned to him in excitement. I'd been reaching for . . . well, I'd meant to high-five him, completely forgetting his hands were tied behind his back. Instead, my hand landed on his rock-hard abs.

Holy hell.

No, Rab was nothing of the boy that I remembered. He was all man now.

"Challengers . . . stay focused. Time is ticking," Kelly shouted, surely louder than was necessary, and I jumped, pulling my hand away from Rab and turning back toward the table.

"Let's muscle through this, shall we?" I said, and then winced, since muscles were clearly on my mind.

"Aye, lass. We'll get it done."

Turns out, we were an absolute mess at this challenge.

Flour exploded. Butter smeared on my elbow. Something sizzled ominously. I shouted. Rab shouted. At one point, I was ninety percent sure I'd tried to zest his hand instead of the orange.

And suddenly—despite the frustration and the absolute absurdity of it—I started to laugh.

Really laugh.

Because here we were, blind and bound, with truffle batter somehow on the ceiling, and Rab just kept going. He took every mistake in stride, listened carefully, gave me specific directions, teased me gently when I flubbed up, and never once lost his temper.

I could also hear the other teams growling at missed or splattered ingredients, which somehow soothed my issues. This would look hilarious on the show. Eventually, despite chaos in every step of the recipe, Rab claimed he thought we had it close to being finished. The truffles were rolled, what few of them I could make from what ingredients weren't splattered across the ceiling, and Rab assured me they looked beautiful. Which I seriously doubted, but at this point, I was happy to have anything on the plate at all.

It was now time to infuse the truffles with magick.

"'Now,'" Rab read from the recipe, "'infuse the truffles with a memory of Christmas joy. One that stirs the soul.'"

I reached for something—anything—not involving Rab. But the memories slid around, stubborn. The warmest ones refused to surface. Christmas had always been a tricky time for my family.

Until—

"Do you remember the Christmas we built that snow fort?" Rab asked quietly.

I stilled. "Aye."

"You almost got frostbite on your nose and pummeled me with snowballs."

"You always underestimated my throw." I smiled, remembering the snowball that had splattered across his shocked face.

"I did."

"Snow and laughter, frost and flight. Seal this treat with winter's bite," I recited, my magick rippling through my fingers. Reaching up, I wrapped one hand around my necklace, feeling the charm warm against my palm. Rab leaned in, his shoulder touching mine, and I gasped as his magick met mine, two streams converging, his stronger and directing the flow of mine.

The blindfold tightened, warmth surging down into my palms. I didn't need to see the truffles to know the magick had worked. A gentle hum filled the air. The scent of zested orange and gooey chocolate wafted up.

"Well, I'll be damned . . ." Kelly said.

We'd done it. We'd done a trust-based exercise, despite our broken history, with my complicated magick on top, and somehow had managed to work as a team.

When the round ended, I yanked the blindfold off. Rab stood there, arms still bound, looking rumpled and ridiculous . . . and heartbreakingly handsome.

I held up a perfectly formed Christmas truffle. "We did it."

"Aye, we did." Rab gave me an approving nod.

And even with chocolate batter in his hair and a piece of orange zest stuck to his chin, I thought . . . maybe. Just maybe we might be able to become something new together. *Friends,* I rushed to tell my heart, which had seemed to shiver in excitement at my thoughts. *Just friends. That might be nice. Surely we can pull that off?*

Feeling confident for the first time in this competition, I preened down at the Christmas truffle. Maybe my magick was finally working. Was it possible I could start tentatively believing in myself? I straightened my shoulders, cautiously optimistic.

Until the judges walked over.

Kelly clapped her hands. "All right, teams! Time to taste your Trust Truffle creations. We'll be judging on presentation and taste."

Nevin headed to Team Elf first. Their truffles shimmered with enchanted gold dust and puffed out a little burst of sugar snow when cut.

"Presentation . . . ten," Kelly said without hesitation. "And that flavor? Ten."

"Agreed," Nevin said, offering his hand. "Simply divine."

Of course.

Next was Henry's table. Their truffles were neat, if a bit plain.

"Nice shape," Nevin said. "I'd give it an eight for presentation."

"And I'll match that for taste," Kelly agreed.

Then came Mandy and Felicity.

Kelly sliced one open. A glossy center of gooey chocolate oozed out, topped with a tiny bit of holly made of candied peel.

"Gorgeous," she breathed. "Really well done. I'd give it a ten for presentation and an eight for flavor. Very impressive."

Felicity squeaked. Mandy just smirked like the scores were a foregone conclusion.

Then it was our turn.

Rab straightened a little. I sucked in a breath and waited, nerves pinging around my stomach.

Kelly cut into one of our truffles. And though it smelled divine, the center wasn't as smooth or as well shaped as Mandy's had been.

"Not bad, though a little rustic. The shell could have been better formed," Kelly said. "I'd give this a seven for presentation."

Nevin took a bite, chewed, and gave a brief nod. "Good flavor. Nice orange and spice. A seven for taste. Well done."

My breath left me in a tiny whoosh. We'd done it. It wasn't amazing, but it wasn't also a total catastrophe.

"Aw," Mandy drawled from her station. "Kind of like a participation award, isn't it?"

My smile withered.

Felicity bit her lip like she wanted to say something, but Mandy was already turning away, triumphant.

The cameras zoomed in because *of course* they did.

My throat tightened, and that old familiar feeling of thinking I was a failure washed over me like a cold wave.

I hated it.

And I hated that Rab, standing there with his wrists still tied behind his back, was staring at me with that look.

The one that meant he wanted to help.

But he didn't move.

And I turned away before he could say anything.

Because if he tried to comfort me . . . if he tried to say anything at all . . . I wasn't sure my fragile newfound confidence could take it.

I wasn't sure *I* could take it.

So I set my truffle down, pasted on a smile that felt brittle as sugar glass, and walked off the set before my emotions betrayed me on live television.

Behind me, I heard Rab suck in a breath like he was going to come after me.

But he didn't.

And I didn't look back.

CHAPTER TWENTY

Lyra

I slipped out the back door and practically fled to my little trailer. I shut the door behind me and sagged against it, letting the silence swallow me whole. My face burned with humiliation. Mandy's voice still rang in my ears. And worst of all . . . Rab's silence echoed like a hollow space inside my chest.

Had he wanted to come after me?

Had he been relieved I'd left?

For some reason, I didn't care as much about everyone else thinking I was a failure, but it mattered to me what Rab thought. Even if it was tough for me to admit.

The door flew open, and I sucked in a breath, hope blooming.

"Lass. You've got to get this under control." Marcie stepped in, worry on her face.

"Ugh, Marcie. You were watching?"

"Of course I was. I need to keep an eye on everyone. They're like ants running around my space, and I don't trust they won't ruin things." Marcie's brows dropped in a glower as she eased the door shut behind her.

"I don't know what to do. Should I just not use my magick at all? I'm an absolute failure," I moaned, burying my face in my hands.

"Och, no, you aren't. Nobody who tries is a failure, dinnae ken?"

"I mean, I'm not sure that's really true," I said, looking up at her.

"It is," Marcie insisted, and she had that scary look in her eyes, so I just nodded along because that's what you did when you were facing scary Marcie. "Trying is the win, Lyra. Even if the outcome isn't what you want it to be, you'll always learn something that helps you the next time around. Remember, it's those who sit on the sidelines and watch and laugh that are the real failures."

"I—"

"I said what I said, Lyra. Now listen to it. Feel it. Absorb it." Marcie tapped her chest hard before giving me one more fierce look to make sure I was absorbing her wisdom, then ducked out of the trailer.

I blew out a breath. She might be right, but did she have to be so damn intimidating when she delivered her wisdom?

I paced the small space. Stared at my reflection in the mirror until my eyes no longer looked shiny with unshed tears. I gave myself five full minutes, then another five, then one more for good measure—long enough that *surely* Rab would have finished whatever he needed to do and left the set by now.

Hopefully.

Only when I figured enough time had passed did I gather my things and crack the trailer door open a sliver.

No Rab in sight.

Good.

I stepped out, closing the door quietly behind me. I needed to find Vaughn and apologize for walking out during live filming.

Sloane was on her way to pick me up, as there wasn't much space to park near the bakery, what with the production crew needing any available space. I could have walked home, but since it was an early start, Sloane had insisted on driving me. Despite the fact that I was twenty-five years old, she still managed to feel the need to mother me. Mostly, I didn't mind it. Sloane had been the glue that had kept us together when our toxic mother had almost torn us apart.

Some mothers weren't meant for mothering.

Ours had been one of them.

"Nice job today, Lyra. It's going to be a fun episode to edit." Vaughn's voice caused me to jump, and I whirled, hand at my chest.

"Thanks," I said. "Listen, I'm sorry for walking out like that. I know the cameras were still on."

"Don't be. It makes for great television." Vaughn smiled. He looked cute with a newsboy cap pulled over his head and a waxed canvas jacket buttoned up against the biting wind.

"Say, Lyra—"

I caught sight of Mandy slipping in through the back door of the bakery, and I held a hand up, interrupting him.

"Hey, sorry, Vaughn. I just want to catch Mandy before she leaves. See you tomorrow?" I was already moving past him.

The back entrance opened into the small prep corridor that led directly into the kitchen the crew was working in. Cables snaked over the floor, leftover desserts were being sampled, and a couple of production assistants were scraping eggs off the walls. I winced at the sight.

"Mandy!" I called.

A small hitch in Mandy's step was the only indication that she'd heard me. I followed, dodging a stand mixer being wheeled past.

"Mandy! I know you can hear . . ." Annoyance, and my need to play peacemaker, caused me to speed up. I caught up with her by the big stainless steel sinks.

"What, Lyra? What?" She spun. "Why are you harassing me?"

"Harassing? Wait a minute. You're the one who has been coming after me on the show. I'm not—"

"You are!" Her voice bounced off the walls, startling one of the crew. "I haven't responded to a single message of yours. Ever since Sloane stole the presidency from me, you've been bothering me. And I've tried to ignore you. I haven't answered the door when you came knocking—uninvited, mind you—and I don't return any of your calls. When are you going to leave me alone?"

Mandy crossed her arms over her chest and pursed her lips, her bright blue eyes flaming in her face. The harsh kitchen lights cut across her cheekbones, making her look like a villain in a very chic prison drama, and my mouth rounded in surprise.

"Mandy, truly, that was not my intention in the slightest."

"I will not be mocked," Mandy hissed, stepping forward. Her hand jerked up, and for a second, I thought she might jab a finger into my chest, but she seemed to catch herself and dropped it to her side with a strangled sound of frustration.

"I'm *not* mocking you," I said, rubbing at the place she'd almost poked, out of reflex. "What the hell, Mandy?"

"I'm not like you messy MacGregors." Mandy bared her teeth, like our very name tasted disgusting on her tongue. "Do you understand me, Lyra? I don't need to parade my emotions out for the world to see. I can handle it. I *have* been handling it. On my own."

"I wasn't trying to mock you," I said, squinching my face up, confused. "I was trying to be your friend."

"My friend?" Mandy said it like I'd just offered her fried cockroaches to eat.

"Aye, your friend. I've been worried about you."

Now it was Mandy's turn to look confused. She tilted her head at me like she didn't know what to make of the words I was saying.

"Worried? You're worried about me?" She paused, then threw her head back, her laughter echoing off the hanging pots and pans. "Och, isn't that rich? *You?* The girl who can barely manage her magick? From the family whose curse is ruining all of our lives? *You're* worried about *me*?"

"Okay, so first of all . . . rude," I said, putting a hand on my hip and sticking my lower lip out in a slight pout. I'd never had someone so openly reject my friendship before, and I honestly wasn't sure how to handle it. "And secondly, *aye,* I was worried about you. I know the Charms were important to you, and it made me sad to think you were hurting. I don't like to see people hurting. Even if it's someone as barely tolerable as you."

"Listen, doll, I'm sure you think the Charms was the be-all and end-all of my existence, but I can assure you, I'm doing just fine."

I did a slow scan of Mandy's baggy jeans and dark shirt and then raised my eyes to her messy hair. The Mandy I'd known when she was president of the Charms had dripped in designer clothes, and never did a hair of hers dare to stray out of place.

Mandy's eyes narrowed at my perusal.

"I'm trying out a new look. You should consider it sometime." She sniffed and gave my fitted dress a pointed once-over.

"Mandy, I've been checking up on you because I'm concerned, and I think there's a way we can resolve these issues. You're still a part of the coven. Sure, you made a mistake, but we all do. Why can't we just put it behind us and move on?"

"My goddess, I knew you were the sweet one, but you're just blindly optimistic, aren't you?" Mandy rolled her eyes and turned back to the counter, snatching up a stack of mixing bowls. "Some things you can't just glitter over and call it healed, Lyra."

Before I could respond, Felicity came through the door.

"Hey, guys, coming through!" Felicity said, her voice bright and breathless. She backed through the door, arms loaded with a precarious pile of baking trays, chopping boards, and a long narrow knife roll balanced on top. "Vaughn said we need to clear all this before the crew can switch out decorations."

"Careful, Felicity, the floor's wet," one of the PAs called as they left the room.

"I've got it!" Felicity sang out, which were, historically, the most worrying three words in the English language.

I moved automatically to help, stepping around Mandy. "Here, let me take—"

Everything happened at once.

My boot hit a slick patch of suds. My foot skidded. I flailed, reaching out instinctively for the counter, for the trays, for anything. Felicity, seeing me pitch forward, tried to twist out of the way and at the same time catch me, her arms jerking to compensate.

The top tray slid sideways. Something long and gleaming shot free as Felicity's body followed it, slamming sharply into me as we both toppled to the ground.

The pain hit me before my brain caught up to what had happened. A hot, searing line along my side that stole my breath.

I froze.

The clatter of metal rang around the kitchen as the rest of the trays crashed to the floor.

I rolled, pushing myself up from the floor as Felicity tried to extradite herself from my limbs.

"Shite," I gasped.

We all froze and gaped down at where a chef's knife had sliced directly into my side, the fabric of my dress already darkening with blood.

"Lyra," Felicity whispered, the color draining from her face. "Oh gods. Oh gods, I—"

"Don't move," Mandy snapped, her voice low and fierce. She grabbed the edge of the stainless steel table with white-knuckled hands, like she needed to hold on to something solid. "Felicity. Go get help."

"I . . . I stabbed her," Felicity breathed, stumbling to her feet.

"It was an accident," I croaked, though I wasn't sure if I was trying to reassure her or myself. Fiery pain licked up my side as I instinctively pressed my palm to the wound, trying to keep the world from tilting.

"Felicity, go." Mandy crouched at my side.

That jolted her. She spun and bolted for the back door, nearly slipping herself as she pelted out into the alley to find anyone with a functioning adult brain cell.

My knees trembled.

"Come on, let's go." Mandy slid an arm around my shoulders, surprisingly strong as she lifted me up, guiding me toward the door. "Keep pressure on the wound."

"Bloody hell, this really hurts," I whispered. Spots danced at the edges of my vision.

"Just breathe. In . . . out . . ." Mandy ordered. Her face was pale, but her voice was steady.

Mandy pulled me through the open back door and into the alley leading to the front of the shop, and I heard a car engine and a familiar horn.

"Lyra?" Sloane's voice carried faintly over the chatter of noise around me. "What's going on? You done? Why is Felicity waving her arms like a demented windmill?"

I must have made some sort of noise, because Ruth flew to me and landed on my shoulder.

Lyra? she squeaked, sensing the wrongness in me. *What's happened?*

Felicity was in the middle of the narrow lane, hands flapping as she tried to explain to Sloane, whose car idled at the far end with the window rolled down.

"I didn't mean to. She slipped . . . and then—"

"Ruth! Watch out!" Sloane shouted.

Above us, on the eaves of the bakery and the neighboring shop, half a dozen owls had gathered, drawn by the lights and noise. They swiveled their heads in eerie unison as Ruth shot out into the open, sword raised, tiny wings beating furiously.

You hurt Lyra? Ruth shrieked, furious on my behalf. Diving through the air with astonishing speed, she drove her wee sword into Felicity's arm.

"Ouch!" Felicity screeched and whirled, trying to knock Ruth out of the air. "You bloody eejit!"

"Ruth, no!" I wheezed as the screech of an owl made my blood run cold.

To the owls, a glittering, shrieking fluttermouse with a sword must have looked like dinner.

One owl dropped from the roof, wings spread. Then another. And another.

They were a squadron of feathery death planes.

And they all had eyes on Ruth.

Ruth darted left, then right, trying to find cover, panic spiking through our bond.

Too many. Too many, she gasped.

"What the hell is happening?" Sloane shouted. "Ruth! Watch out!"

Before I could scream again, a familiar howl split the air. Flame burst at the entrance to the alleyway.

"Duck!" Sloane shrieked as Blue threw himself through the open car window, wings flaring open. Fire billowed from his mouth, lighting the alleyway with a whoosh of heat that rolled over my face.

I crouched as best I could, wincing as the movement tugged at my side, and Ruth arrowed straight for me, wedging herself in the space between my chin and my neck. I slapped a hand over her, curling it protectively, while my other hand stayed clamped over the wound in my side.

Another blast of flame rocketed over our heads, more warning than weapon, singeing the air just high enough that no owl was actually flambéed.

A feather drifted down in front of my face, turning lazily in the heated air. Above us, the owls wheeled and then broke formation, flying high in indignant retreat.

"I think we're clear," Sloane finally said, wide-eyed as she took in the feathery chaos, Felicity's stricken face, and my hunched form.

I couldn't bring myself to unravel from my crouch. I was scared to let go of Ruth, in case another rogue owl dove from the sky, and I needed to keep pressure on my wound.

"Lyra?" Sloane asked, a worried note in her voice. She rushed down the alley to my side. "What's wrong? Is it Ruth?"

"There's been an incident," Mandy said tightly, stepping back to give Sloane room.

"With you around? Shocking. What did you do to her?" Sloane demanded, furious, automatically assuming the worst.

"It was me," Felicity blurted, voice wobbling. "It was an accident. I was trying to tell you. I dropped my knife and she . . . she slipped and . . . I stabbed her."

"You *what*?" Sloane's voice leapt an octave. "You bloody eejit."

"It was an *accident*," Felicity cried, tears streaming down her face. "I was trying to grab her. The floor was wet, and everything just—"

"What Lyra needs is help, Sloane. This isn't the time for accusations," Mandy cut in sharply.

"Sloane," I said weakly, and Sloane immediately folded back to me, dropping into a crouch.

"Tell me what you need," she said. "We'll go straight to the hospital."

"Take Ruth. Please. I can't worry about her getting hurt," I whispered. Though it comforted me to have her warm, furry body tucked at my neck, her nervous trembles were only making me more anxious about taking care of her and me.

Love you, Lyra. I'm sorry I couldn't protect you in time, Ruth whispered.

"You're a brilliant wee warrior, Ruth. Don't worry. I'll be fine." I had no idea if that was true. I couldn't remember another time I'd been in so much pain. Blood dripped through my fingers, and I cringed, knowing that this was really bad.

"I've got her." Sloane gently coaxed Ruth from under my hand and tucked her into the front pocket of the hooded jumper she wore. Ruth's ears poked out, furious but obedient.

"Let's get you in the car." Sloane hooked an arm around my shoulders, and to my surprise, Mandy stepped to my other side, bracing me as I tried to straighten without screaming.

"This doesn't mean we're friends," Mandy muttered.

"Noted," I said through gritted teeth as they half carried, half walked me toward the car.

"But I also don't want you to die."

"Never harm, always charm, right?" I almost rolled my eyes, but instead winced as I tried to shift myself into the car. Finally, with their help, I hoisted myself onto the back seat. The movement jarred the wound, and a sharp gasp tore from my lips. Mandy hovered by the open door while Sloane sprinted around the bonnet of the car, her phone already at her ear.

"I'll call Raven," Mandy said, pressing her lips together as she looked down at the blood staining my dress. Felicity stood behind her, hand held to her own shoulder where Ruth had nicked her, tears still flowing. I knew I should have said something to reassure her—to tell her I wasn't mad—but too many scary things had happened in a very short amount of time, and my brain just couldn't get past the white-hot pain.

Blue flew dangerously close to Felicity's head, his wing clipping her in the face as he dove through the open front window and landed with a plop on the front passenger seat. Immediately, he clambered so he was half hanging between the front seats, his tongue lolling as he looked back at me, eyes wide and worried.

"You're the best, buddy," I whispered. "Thanks for saving us."

"We're going to the castle, Lyra," Sloane said, swinging into the driver's seat and slamming the door. "The hospital's too far away, but we can get you there fast if we need to. We need to assess how bad it is. Henry has healing powers, and Knox is calling Raven." She swiveled to look at me, eyes bright with fear. "Unless you think straight to the hospital?"

"I . . . I don't think so." I could still breathe, so it wasn't like she'd punctured a lung. Not that I had any medical training to discern that fact. "Castle will work. Henry's good."

Mandy shut the back door gently, her face caught in shadows.

"Right," Sloane muttered. "Drive sensibly, don't kill anyone, don't crash the car." She recited it like Knox had made her take notes.

"Nova and Broca?" I asked, leaning my head back and closing my eyes. I took shallow breaths, keeping my hand clamped over my side, and tried not to think too hard about the wound.

"Knox is calling them as well. I've been told my only job is to *drive safe*," Sloane said, pulling out onto the road.

"Ruth?" I asked.

I'm here. I'm all right, she said from Sloane's pocket. I felt a soft whoosh of air by my neck as she wriggled free and scrambled back up to perch on my shoulder, as if she'd simply refused to be anywhere else.

"Scary night. For all of us," I murmured.

"What the hell happened?" Sloane asked, doing that thing people do when they're internally freaking out—inflecting their voice with a cheerfulness that doesn't match the words. "Why were you guys all huddled in the alley like that? It was weird. I was looking for you out front."

"I followed Mandy into the kitchen," I said, adjusting slightly on the seat, moving the seat belt so it didn't press so hard into my side.

"Why?" Sloane was not the least bit bothered by Mandy's absence from the Charms. She'd never warmed to the ex-president and was almost certain Mandy was some sort of fembot.

"Because I've been trying to get a moment to speak with her," I admitted. "I just feel bad. I was hoping to—"

"Smooth things over, make nice, and welcome her back to the Charms?" Sloane guessed.

"Something like that."

"And she stabbed you for it."

"No, she did not. Felicity did," I said quickly. "And it really was an accident. I slipped, she tried to catch me, the knife went flying . . . I'm kind of confused on how it happened. One second I was talking to Mandy, the next second Felicity was coming through the door like a human avalanche of bakeware."

"Seems really odd. Who doesn't secure their knives?" Sloane griped.

We paused.

"Felicity," we said in unison, and despite everything, we laughed.

"Ouch. Don't make me laugh." I hissed as pain shot through me with the movement.

"We're here. It's okay. Took your mind off the drive. Everything's going to be fine," Sloane said, more to convince herself than me.

I opened my eyes to see the castle lit up against the night, and people running to meet Sloane's car.

Just rest, Lyra. We'll take care of you, Ruth murmured at my neck. Reaching up, I patted her soft fur.

"I know you will. I know."

Henry's worried face was the last thing I saw before I blacked out.

CHAPTER TWENTY-ONE

Rab

Once a week, when the pub was closed, I met Liam and Knox at the Rune & Rose to play darts and bullshit about life in general. They'd been particularly excited to meet this week and hear about how filming was going, while I'd almost canceled on them because I was still annoyed Knox had made me do the damn show. And depriving those two busybodies of their favorite dessert—gossip—was well worth it to me to just be a little petty.

But in the end, after a quick hot shower and scrubbing all the residual food from my hair, I'd made my way over to the pub.

"Och, there he is. The baker himself," Liam said, reaching for a pint glass.

"Hopefully a champion baker." Knox grinned. His phone rang, and I rolled my eyes as he reached for it automatically. The man was always on call.

"Why don't you both piss off?" I asked.

"A pint, mate?" Liam held up a glass.

"Guinness, please." I took a deep breath and rolled my shoulders, hoping some of the tension would ease from them. Today had been . . . a day. A day that I wasn't quite sure what to do with.

Lyra had been . . . everything.

With her blindfolded, I'd been able to watch Lyra without her knowing. Hell, the task had required it. And I'd loved it. She was just so damn beautiful, even with a blindfold covering half her face, and it had taken everything in my power to keep my mind on the task and not how good it had been to taste her kiss the night before. After I'd delivered the hedgehogs to their foster home, I'd spent the night obsessing over every moment of our kiss, wondering what the hell that meant. What had I been thinking? I was setting myself up for heartbreak all over again. I'd—

"She's hurt? How bad?"

I jolted from my thoughts at Knox's sharp words.

Who? I mouthed, trying to get his attention. *Sloane?*

Knox was already reaching for his car keys.

"How bad? Sloane? How bad? You need to stay calm. Get Lyra in the car."

My heart stopped.

For the third time in my life.

It felt like my heart just completely stopped beating as I dragged in a breath. I sprang up from my stool.

"Where?" I shouted, and Knox waved me away, putting a hand to his other ear to focus on the call.

"Take her to the castle. Henry will be able to help. We're on the way. Yes, we'll get Nova and Broca." Knox threw a look over his shoulder to Liam, who nodded and made his way around the bar. "And Raven. Just get her there safely. Do you hear me? We're on our way. Should we come to you?"

"Are they close? Where?" I demanded, moving toward the door.

"Just let him get the details, mate." Liam held me by my arm, and I forced myself to breathe.

"Okay, you're in the car. Stay safe, Sloane. Get off the phone. Focus on driving. I'll take care of everyone else. Promise me. No phone. Just drive." Knox hung up and swore. "Liam?"

"I'm on Raven and the MacGregors."

"Grand. Rab. With me." Knox snapped his fingers, and normally, where I'd be annoyed at that, I just followed. It was clear I wasn't getting information until we were in Knox's car and sweat broke out down my back.

"Knox, tell me. How bad?"

"We don't know," Knox said, and we raced to his car, a gust of wind seeming to push us faster. An owl swooped past, landing in a tree near the car, and I stared at it as Knox peeled away from the curb.

"Tell me," I bit out, furious that I didn't have all the information.

"I don't know much, and I don't want to scare you."

"Just tell me," I repeated.

"She's been stabbed. That's all I know—"

"What the fuck?" I jerked forward, the seat belt slamming tight, my hands in fists.

"It was apparently an accident. Unclear on how it happened."

"She's—"

"She's breathing, talking, but bleeding and in pain. That's all I know. There was a lot going on, Sloane said. Something about the owls. I don't know. I just needed her to get Lyra somewhere safe."

"And Henry? You're sure he can help?"

"Henry has stitched up and set every broken bone and wound among myself, my brothers, his entire family of forest ogres, and a few injured dragons on top of it. The man is a bloody miracle. And he's also comfortable enough to say when he needs help. If he can't fix it, he'll get her patched up enough for the hospital."

"Why wouldn't they have just gone directly to the hospital?" I asked, worry a steel band around my chest.

"Hospitals need reports. Stab wounds require investigation."

I stilled.

"Are you saying you think this was intentional?"

"I have very little to go on, mate. But I know it was Felicity, she has her kids to think about, and things could get messy. Best all around to just take care of it, if we can, with the best healers we have."

"And if she needs more? More than magick can provide?" I asked. Though, if I was being fair, I'd seen magick outperform science many times over through the years.

"Then we'll get it for her. Lyra has a lot of people who care about her." Knox slid me a glance as we turned up the road to where his castle glowed, a beacon in the dark night. "Including you."

"I mean, of course I care." I rolled my eyes, affecting nonchalance. "Nobody wants to see anyone get hurt."

"Bloody hell, Rab. Cut the shite. If you can't be honest with me, at least be honest with yourself." Knox's words sliced through me, and I pressed my lips together, worry hammering in my chest.

"I care." It came out in a rasp, a sentiment I was pulling out of the shadows and dusting the cobwebs off. "I don't want to care. I didn't want to keep caring. You know that, Knox. But I still do."

"Duh," Knox said, and I turned to glare at him. He laughed. "Och, please, mate. You're fooling nobody. If you didn't care, you wouldn't have spent every day of the last year deliberately avoiding her. People who don't have feelings for someone else can be in the same room together."

"I've been in the same room as her," I protested.

"All while bloody well ignoring her. It's obvious you both still have feelings for each other."

"You think she has feelings for me?" I asked, caught on his words.

"Bloody hell, mate." Knox shook his head. "You're worse than I was."

"Och, not even close—"

"We're here," Knox said, turning through the wide gates of the castle, and I cut off what I had been saying, my focus narrowing to where I caught a glimpse of Henry hustling through the front door, Lyra's body draped in his arms.

Icy fear washed through me.

Her body had looked completely limp, her head lolling on Henry's arm.

"Stop the car," I shouted, my hand already going to the door.

When Knox's arm came out, slamming back against the seat, I whirled on him, needing an outlet for my anger.

"What the—"

"Stop it. Whatever this is, stop it. She doesn't need—"

"What she needs is—"

Knox slammed me back into my seat again.

"What she needs is a trained healer who can focus on helping her."

I froze.

He was right. Of course he was right. I couldn't help her, not in the way she needed, and if I distracted Henry, I could only make it worse.

I dragged a breath in, and then another, forcing myself to calm down. When I had myself under control, I gave Knox a curt nod. He'd always had my back—from helping me heal from Lyra leaving to opening my own business—so I knew I could trust him.

"I'm okay. Thanks, mate."

"No problem. Let's go."

Our car doors slammed, a sharp sound in the quiet night, and gravel crunched beneath our heels as we raced up the front path to the doors that had been left open.

The castle had a grand entrance with a high ceiling painted with a dramatic mural of dragons twisting through clouds, and several hallways branching off from the main foyer. I had no idea where to turn.

"He'll have taken her to the closest guest suite." Knox gestured to the right, and I veered that way, following him as he strode down the hallway. "I just want to see Sloane, let her know we're here, and then I'll come back out to run interference with Liam and the others."

We came to the door, and I had to press my nails into my palm to keep from running to the bed and trying to do anything at all to help.

Lyra was lying on the bed, her skin pale, her cheeks devoid of color. Her dark eyelashes were fanned across her cheeks, a smear of dried blood marring the creamy skin at her neck. I swallowed against the lump in my throat as I drew closer, staying out of Henry's way, and rounded the bed.

An alarming volume of blood stained the side of the dress that Henry was now cutting off. Sloane stood, a towel in hand, tears streaming silently down her face. Knox went to her and wrapped an arm around her shoulders, whispering into her ear.

"I'm here if you need anything, Henry," I said, keeping my voice low, but wanting him to know I was there.

Henry nodded, focused on his task. I winced as the dress revealed the wound. It wasn't long, but blood still seeped from it, which meant it was deep.

"Rab?" Lyra shifted, her eyes still closed, my name just a whisper at her lips.

"Aye, lass. I'm here," I said, reaching out to take her hand. A fine tremble worked through her body, and my eyes flew to Henry. "I think she's cold."

"Could be shock too. I've got the lasses on heating water bottles." Henry made a small sound of distress as he examined the wound. "Such a shame."

Turning, I pulled a soft blanket thrown over a reading chair at the side of the bed and leaned over Lyra, tucking it so it draped around her shoulders and over part of her body, trying to give her some warmth.

"You're going to be all right, Lyra. Henry's going to sort you out just fine."

Lyra's lashes fluttered, but she didn't open her eyes.

"Hurts," Lyra whispered.

"Aye, it looks it. But you'll be back to exploding eggs in the kitchen in no time."

Lyra's lips quirked, and I took that as a win. I started to ease back, not wanting to get in the way, but Lyra's hand patted around the bed until she found mine.

"Stay."

"Och, of course, love. I'm not going anywhere." I squeezed her hand, that warm tingle of connection bouncing between us. It had always been that way between her and me. We'd touch, and electricity would leap between us.

"She's bloody well lucky," Henry murmured. His eyes were closed, and his hands were glowing with a soft golden light as he gently touched the skin on either side of her wound. "It caught her just below her ribs, missing any organs. The wound is deep, and the knife has cut through muscle, an oblique, and nicked an intercostal artery."

"Her artery?" Sloane gasped.

"A lesser one. It's not as dangerous, but does bleed a lot," Henry murmured, his eyes still closed. He must be doing some sort of magickal scan of sorts, seeing his way around her wound with his mind's eye. "We're lucky. She's lucky. We'll get this stitched up in no time. I just need to start with the internal stitching."

Henry opened his eyes and nodded toward a black leather medical bag at the end of the bed. "Knox, grab that for me. I'll need the silver sutures, the mermaid's tears tincture, and the moonmoss salve."

"On it." Knox dug through the bag, and I shifted, pulling myself onto the bed so I half sat, and held Lyra's hand between both of mine.

"You're doing great. Everything's going to be just fine. Nothing major was hit," I mumbled, repeating variations of those phrases over and over.

Movement at the door, and I looked up to see Liam, Raven, Broca, and Nova all squeeze quietly into the room. Raven, a dedicated healer in her own right, stepped up and took the medical bag from Knox, moving quietly to Henry's side. Everyone fell back, giving the two room, and I stayed where I was, tracing designs over Lyra's hand.

"Mermaid's tears." Raven handed a small bottle over, and Henry carefully uncapped it, squinting as he carefully dripped a single silvery drop of liquid into the wound.

"Oh," Lyra breathed. Her grip on my hand relaxed some, and I looked up in question at Knox, who just shrugged.

"Mermaid's tears will clean and numb the wound," Raven explained, catching my look as she carefully recapped the bottle. "It's a magical antiseptic and numbing agent. She shouldn't feel a thing when he begins suturing."

Raven quickly threaded a needle, and Henry took it from her, his movements quick, and showed no hesitation as he bent over the wound. I looked away. I hated seeing her perfect skin marred by something so ugly.

"You shouldn't feel a thing," I murmured, continuing to draw on Lyra's hand, trying to take her attention away from what was happening.

"Just a tugging," Lyra mumbled. "No pain."

"Good, that's good."

I looked down to see her eyes open and focused on me. The impossible lavender blue of her irises sucked me in, as they always did, and I almost forgot where I was and bent down and kissed her forehead.

I had no idea what was going on with us, if Knox was right and she still had feelings for me, or if we could get over the heartbreak of the past, but none of that mattered. At least not right now. What mattered was that we healed her up.

Henry worked quickly, though at the same time every careful stitch felt like it took ages, and his hands continued to shine with his magick. I wasn't sure if it helped light his way, increased his speed and accuracy, or was something else altogether, but soon enough he was leaning back with a sigh of relief.

The wound was neatly closed, a jagged slash against her skin, and seeing it made me want to murder Felicity. Taking a deep breath, I pasted a smile on my face.

"Looks like he's almost done," I murmured to Lyra, who continued to just stare up at my face.

"Okay. I can't look. Is it bad?"

"Nah. You'll look like a proper badass."

"I can tell people I got into a fight at the pub," Lyra whispered.

"There ya go."

"Just the moonmoss now, please." Henry passed the sutures off to Raven, and she gave him a small tin. Opening it, Henry pressed a silvery mossy material over the wound, and then he took the bandage Raven offered him and taped it over the moss. He took his time taping the bandage, making sure it was amply covered, and then sat back with a pleased smile on his face.

"There you are, Lyra, darling. All patched up."

Lyra's eyes slid from my face to Henry's. "What's the prognosis, Doc?"

"You'll be woozy from loss of blood and shock, and you're going to be in some pain the next few days, but Raven's got a few things that will sort you out on that end. The muscle will just need some time to repair itself, but we've sped it along as best we could with our magick." Henry reached over and patted Lyra's arm. "I'm just glad it wasn't anything more serious. That was a nasty wound. Quite deep."

"Aye, it felt that way," Lyra said.

"I'd like you to stay here, at least through the night, so I can watch over you, lass. Is that all right?"

"She's staying," Broca said, stepping forward, Nova and Sloane at her side.

"Brought your comfies," Nova said, holding up a bag. Her eye makeup was smudged from crying. "We're all staying."

"Yay, a sleepover." Lyra gave a weak smile.

"Let's get you changed and out of these bloody clothes." Sloane glanced up at me, and I nodded. Henry had cut her dress away enough to treat her but hadn't taken it off her body. I'd covered her as much as I could with a blanket to protect her modesty, not that I thought anyone in this room cared.

We all just wanted her safe.

"We'll just see about sorting out some food. Soup, maybe?" I asked. Squeezing Lyra's hand one last time, I dropped it and eased from the bed. There was nothing else I could do for her now, and she certainly didn't need me hanging about while her sisters changed her.

"Aye, but we want to get her cleaned up a bit first, no?" Nova looked over at Raven, who nodded her agreement. "There's blood everywhere."

"We'll get a warm sponge bath ready," Henry said, slipping neatly back into butler mode.

I met Knox and Liam out in the foyer, and Knox took one look at my face and gestured for me to follow him. Ruth surprised me by flying out of the room and landing on my shoulder. Reaching up a hand, I stroked a finger down her back as she cuddled into my neck. She felt comforting there, as though she'd decided I was hers to look after, too, and I realized she must have been incredibly stressed out as well.

"Are you okay?" I asked.

"She says she is, but her energy is low." Knox looked back at me, his eyes soft as he looked at Ruth on my shoulder. He'd always had a strong affinity for animals, and his ability to communicate with them was one of his favorite magickal traits.

"We'll get you some food and rested up," I promised Ruth, and she snuggled in closer.

We ended up in his library, Knox pouring us each a dram, as I stared into the fire, a thousand emotions swirling through me.

"Mate."

I glanced over my shoulder to look at Liam.

"You still love her."

Goddess help me, but I did. Turning back, I stared into the fire, its flames matching the ones burning inside me.

Even though I'd felt so betrayed all those years ago, so lost in my sadness, defeated, and then anger . . . fueled by my father . . . when I saw Lyra dangling almost lifeless in Henry's arms, it had felt like a part of me was dying. *I can't lose you. Not again.* Those were the words that had looped on repeat as I'd watched her limp body disappear into the castle. And then when she looked up at me and uttered the word "stay," I knew in my heart that there was nowhere else I *could* go. There just wasn't a choice.

Because no matter how I'd tried to fight it, no matter how I'd told myself she didn't mean anything to me, the reality was that I was still hopelessly in love with Lyra MacGregor, history be damned.

"Aye, lad. I do."

CHAPTER TWENTY-TWO

Lyra

I shifted in bed, and Nova put another pillow behind my shoulders so I could prop up more, and then both my sisters crawled into bed on either side of me, cocooning me much like they had in the back seat of the car on our endless road trips as children.

"I told you I would stop calling you Sparklefarts." Nova sniffed, dropping her head on my shoulder. "You didn't need to go and get stabbed to get me to feel bad for you so I would stop."

I chuckled and then winced. Henry and Raven had done a brilliant job with managing my pain, but they'd also told me they couldn't take it all away or I'd do something stupid that could impede my healing process. It wasn't anywhere nearly as painful as it had been, but I was sore. There was an odd tugging sensation in my side, likely the stitches, and a dull pain that Raven had told me would be the muscle knitting back together.

They'd used a spell to advance my healing, and I was told I should be right as rain in a matter of days, versus weeks with a normal healing process.

I still couldn't believe what had happened.

"I can't believe this happened," Sloane said, echoing my thoughts.

"Now that things have calmed down a bit, would you mind running through it for me?" Broca asked. She was curled into the chair by the bed, a blanket on her lap, with Ruth snuggled there. My poor wee fluttermouse had returned from being somewhere else in the castle, worn out and needing a big rest. I was just grateful she'd somehow managed to remain unscathed despite the threat of the owls.

I gave everyone a play-by-play of what had happened, and to their credit, they listened without interrupting until I'd finished, and Sloane picked it up from there.

"I had pulled up in front of the bakery, and Ruth and Blue just began freaking out." Sloane's face creased with worry as she remembered. "Ruth was demanding I open the window, so I did. She darted for the alley, so I pulled the car forward and couldn't figure out what was happening. I just saw you, like, crumpled over." Sloane's voice caught, and I realized she was dangerously close to crying. Reaching over, I squeezed her knee, swallowing against the lump in my throat.

"It was scary," I admitted. "I'm sure for you too. Since you didn't know what was going on. Hell, I didn't know what was going on."

"Why the hell was Felicity carrying knives like that?" Broca wondered, shaking her head, making a small tsking noise. "That's foolish, even for her."

"It's beyond foolish. It's bloody stupid," Nova seethed.

"I mean, I don't know." I shook my head and sighed. "I . . . I can't fathom. I just . . . like, not something that sharp, not the way she had it. Every chef would know that. So it's just—"

"She's not a chef, though," Nova said.

"Och, that's the way of it, isn't it?" I nodded, agreeing. "That's part of the challenge of the show. Real people trying out baking challenges. Mandy would be the more experienced baker on her team."

"I thought Felicity was always baking stuff for her kids and whatnot," Broca said.

"I don't know. I haven't really had time to chat with them." I sighed. "I finally got to speak with Mandy, and she basically called me a stalker and told me to leave her alone."

"A stalker?" Sloane bolted up, and I grabbed my side.

"Jeez, Sloane, chill."

"Sorry, sorry." Sloane stood and paced in front of the bed, her hands shoved into the front pocket of her hoodie. "I'm just absolutely fed up with her nonsense this year. She is not a good coven member."

"Sloane. It's your job, as president, to keep the coven together." Broca's tone was mild as she stroked Ruth's back.

"Like Mandy did?" Sloane whirled. "We never heard a word from the coven until we arrived here in Briarhaven. You were taking Zoom calls with them to hold our seats, and now I'm supposed to follow all the coven protocol?"

"You didn't hear from them because you hadn't stepped into your magick yet."

"Yet Nova and Lyra could join before they got theirs." Sloane held up her hands, taking a few deep breaths. "I'm sorry. I'm just heightened right now. Today was . . . a lot. And to find out Lyra's been nothing but nice, trying to offer friendship to Mandy, and she treats her like that?"

A knock at the door was our only warning before pandemonium hit. The door swung open, and Blue flew in, all smiles, his chunky body wobbling through the air. Haggis rolled in behind him in his wheelchair, while Oswald streaked inside and bounded onto the back of the bed, an aggrieved look on his face.

Cat.

Ruth had awoken at the noise, and now she stood, sword raised, eyes on Oswald.

"I'm sorry." Henry sighed from the doorway, hands spread out in apology. "I was coming to invite the lot of you to dinner in the library. Not you, Lyra. I've a tray coming your way. But food is on. And, well, it was impossible to keep the lads away. They wanted to see you, Lyra."

Haggis's wet nose pushed onto the bed. Leaning over, I scratched his scraggly fur at his ears.

You're hurt.

I loved that I could hear him now.

"I was. But I'm better now. Henry healed me all up."

Henry's the best. He gives me scratchies.

"Yup, and he's awesome with healing. I'm okay."

Is there a mouse in here? Oswald's head was up, and he was swiveling it.

"Aye, there's a fluttermouse, Oswald. She's highly armed and will cut you if you cross her," I warned, turning to tap my finger on Oswald's head. "She's mine, and I'll be furious if you make any attempt to hurt her."

Hurt her? Why would I hurt her?

"Because you're a cat, and historically they hunt mice."

Ew. Oswald shuddered and prodded along the back of the bed until his head bumped into the tassel from the curtain tied on the four posters of the bed. He stiffened and then crouched.

"Nae, boy. You'll not ruin another . . ."

Oswald pounced, dragging his claws through the fringed end of the cord, and rolled on his back to battle it.

"Bloody hell. Every time." Henry sighed and crossed the room to untangle Oswald from the cord.

I have it under control. Oswald hissed.

"The first step in getting help is admitting you have a problem," Henry lectured the cat and took him out of the room.

"Right, Lyra, will you be fine with a tray on your own? Or we can stay."

Rab appeared in the doorway, a tray in his hand.

"Never mind," Sloane said, and before I could say a word, my family had hustled from the room, taking Haggis, Blue, and Ruth with them.

"That's quite a menagerie." Rab grinned, looking over his shoulder as Haggis raced down the hallway with Blue and Ruth flying over his head.

"Rolling deep." I laughed. Butterflies flitted through my stomach at the look in Rab's eyes. He carefully placed the tray of food on a table near the bed, closed the door behind him, and then went to stoke the fire.

The silence drew out between us.

All I could think about was how I'd come to, having been in and out from the shock, and he'd been sitting by me on the bed, my hand clasped in his.

Had he known he was tracing a heart on my hand?

It was all I could think about, the touch of his finger burning against the back of my hand as he'd traced a heart, over and over, and I was half convinced if I looked down now, I would see a tattoo of it lingering on my skin.

He'd kept my focus away from the injury and on him, and whether that had been intentional or not, I was grateful for it.

"Thank you," I finally said, breaking the silence. I pulled myself farther up the bed, grateful that my sisters had brought me a pair of sleep pants and a buttery-soft jumper to change into. At least I was no longer splayed out, half naked and covered in blood, and was beginning to feel a touch more human again.

There was something incredibly humbling about being a victim. Or a patient, I guess. It made me feel vulnerable in ways that I didn't like.

"For what?" Rab asked. He crossed to the side of the bed but didn't sit. He just stood, staring down at me, his fists clenched. His face was a mask. *Did I misread his concern? If he doesn't want to be here, why bring the tray? Why close the door?*

"For helping me. During the healing. It made a difference."

The silence dragged out and on instinct, I patted the space next to me with my hand.

"No, you should eat. Let me help you up?" Rab asked instead. My heart fell a bit, and I realized that what I'd really wanted from him was a wee cuddle.

Which was a huge shift in how I'd been feeling about him since we returned to Briarhaven last year. Had the kiss last night changed something for me? Or had it been working together through the catastrophic challenge? Laughing and being silly with each other was something we had once done so well, and it had been ages since I'd felt this comfortable with someone.

Maybe it was time for me to face what had happened between us, to ask him why he'd given up on us so quickly. Why he'd told his parents that I'd only been a pretty face with no substance . . . *That still stung.* Could he have been a scared kid, just like I'd been, trying to make big adult decisions without a support system to do so? I didn't know, but maybe it was time to get some answers.

I scooched myself to the side of the bed, and Rab was there, lifting me up and then steadying me as a wave of dizziness washed over me.

"Should I get a lap tray instead?" Rab asked, worry sounding in his voice.

"No, just need a second." I took a deep breath and the dizziness washed away. I hadn't eaten since that morning, so that also likely played a part. "I really should eat."

"Henry has prepared enough food for twenty," Rab said as he led me to the table and chairs tucked by the fire. Once I was settled in, he took the top off the tray and I laughed.

"Goddess, there's everything, isn't there?" Cheese toasties, tomato soup, chips, a salad, scones, three different kinds of meat pies, sausage rolls, a variety of biscuits, and a pickle and cheese tray were spread out before me. "Please tell me you'll help me eat this."

"Uh, sure, if you want me to stay," Rab said, clearing his throat before sitting across from me.

"I do." I looked up at him, and his shoulders seemed to relax just slightly.

I started with a cheese toastie, dipping a corner in the soup and munching as I watched the firelight play across Rab's handsome face.

"How did you end up here?" I asked, chickening out on asking him about what had happened with us, that fateful day, in our youth. Maybe it was lack of courage, or maybe it was just because I'd had a wildly emotional day, but I wasn't sure I could handle whatever he would say about the moment he'd broken my heart.

"Tonight? Or on Earth?" Rab's lips quirked in a smile. "See there's this thing called the birds and the bees . . ."

"Ha ha," I intoned, shaking the toastie in the air at him. "Tonight."

"Lads' night at the pub. I'd just walked in the door when Knox got the call."

"Ah." That made sense. What didn't was why he'd come along with Knox. "And you came with to help?"

"Of course I came to help," Rab said, exasperated. He leaned back in his chair and crossed his arms over his chest, glowering at me.

Ah, so we were back to that. At least I'd grown familiar with his glowering over the past year.

"Well, thank you. Again, I guess." Feeling awkward, I focused on eating, knowing I needed my strength.

"We need to figure out how this happened. Felicity can't go around armed like this."

"I don't think she was armed." I laughed, looking up from my food. "I think she was being stupid."

"You'd be surprised how often those two go hand in hand," Rab said, and I snorted.

"It's just Felicity," I said, shaking my head. "You can't assume malice."

"I know. I just . . ." Rab finally leaned forward and picked up a pie. "I want someone to blame for this."

"I get it. But sometimes, shite happens. This was one of those times. Let's look on the bright side, Rab. I'm hurt, but not seriously. The knife missed major organs and arteries. I don't need surgery. I should be fine in a matter of days. Albeit, likely with a scar."

"Your beautiful skin," Rab said, the words so soft I almost missed them.

I nearly dropped my toastie in my soup.

The look in his eyes was almost . . . feral. Was it need? Or was he wanting to fight someone? It was hard to understand.

I wasn't sure if I had the emotional capacity to decipher it.

At least not today.

All I knew was that it seemed some tenuous bridge had been built back between us, and what that meant, I wasn't sure. But I did know that he would be here if I needed him. Which meant, for me, at least, that I could consider Rab a friend again.

If I ignored the kiss from last night, that is.

"Tuberculosis. Meningitis. Flu. Polio. Chickenpox," I muttered, trying to ignore my body's flush of excitement when I thought about Rab's lips on mine.

"Are you worried about your wound getting infected?" Rab's eyebrows rose.

"No." I stabbed a chip with a fork, grumpy, and shoved it in my mouth.

"Lyra." I looked up to see one side of Rab's mouth lifted in a smirk. "I know why you're repeating random nonsense."

My cheeks warmed. Would my embarrassment for the day ever be complete?

"You do?" I asked, stabbing another chip.

"Transmutation is one of my powers, Lyra." Rab leveled me a look over his pint glass. "Which means, when I was learning, I went through a similar phase of understanding that strong emotional responses can trigger a transmutation."

Oh. *Oh.* Bloody hell. So he knew exactly why hedgehogs were popping up every time we were alone.

It seemed my embarrassment for the day was not, in fact, complete. Closing my eyes, I pressed my lips together and nodded.

"Can we pretend that was just my extreme dislike for you that did that?" I popped one eye open to see Rab's shoulders shaking with repressed laughter. "Cool. Cool."

"It's nothing to be ashamed of. There's a learning curve with magick."

"Which is what I'm dearly afraid of." I sighed and reached for my lemonade, needing something to cool my burning throat.

"Why didn't you tell me about failing your exam?"

"Och, Rab." I waved away the memory of the past. "Can we not? I've had enough embarrassment for the day."

"Embarrassment? You should hardly feel embarrassed for getting stabbed, Lyra. If anything, you should be pissed. I could throttle Felicity for—"

"No, I just mean . . . everything else. Like, all the explosions and messy magick at the filming. Then, after. Everybody here. Me getting stitched up. It's all just . . ." I waved my hands in the air. "Messy. Uncomfortable. I don't know. I'm just feeling very at odds with myself lately, and I don't know what to do about it."

"Growth will do that to you," Rab said sagely, and ducked when I threw a chip at his head. "What?"

"Listen to you. Like acting like you're some old, wizened sage. You're barely two years older than me, Rab."

"Och, I just meant with your magick. It doesn't immediately fit. Not with anyone. It's like, I don't know, having to break in a new pair of shoes. Just turns out yours is worse because of the curse and all."

"Ugh." I glumly spooned up some more soup.

"It's going to be okay, Lyra. You've made some progress with the curse. I'm sure, between all of us, we'll get it figured out."

"'Us'?" I said, raising an eyebrow at him.

Rab shifted, looking away. It was clear this conversation was making him uncomfortable.

"Lyra . . . I think we should talk."

Talk? As in about us? Would we finally lay everything out on the table? My heart hammered in my chest, but, unfortunately, now that I had food in my stomach, exhaustion snuck over me, burrowing deep. As I went to speak, a yawn escaped instead, and Rab's eyes snapped back to me.

"You must be knackered. Come on, let's get you back to bed."

"I can—"

"Let me help. Please, Lyra." It was the "please" that stopped me in my tracks. Something had changed with him, but I couldn't figure out the undercurrents of what was happening here. Before I could respond, Rab was up, coming around the table, helping me as

I stood. As much as I hated to say it, he was right. I needed the help. Leaning on him, I let him lead me to the bed. Pulling the warm duvet over me, Rab surprised me by brushing my hair back from my face and placing a soft kiss on my forehead.

What did it mean? Why was he being so nice to me? How was he just putting aside a year of turning his back on me? Could I even believe his actions now? Confused, and too tired to do anything about it, I let my eyelids flutter closed.

"Sleep well, darling. You're safe here."

His words drifted across my skin, just as comforting as the blanket he'd pulled over me, and I slipped into sleep.

CHAPTER TWENTY-THREE

Lyra

"They've canceled filming for the day."

I slitted my eyes open the next morning to see Sloane next to my bed, her auburn hair piled in a messy knot on her head, a cup of tea clutched in her hands. Dark circles smudged her eyes.

She'd worried.

She'd always been the worrier of the three of us.

"That's a relief, though I'm sure they were annoyed about it. They were on a tight schedule."

"Turns out, they're considering you to be one of their stars and would hate to have to film a segment without you."

I made a rude sound. "They just like watching my magick explode things. I know it because I, too, loved watching when people's recipes went wrong. It's boring when everything goes smoothly."

"But it hits different when you're the one the cameras are on." Sloane's worry lines creased more deeply, and I sighed.

"Och, I'll admit, I thought it would be a belter of a time going on the show, but it's been . . . a bit shite." I shifted, and my side tugged, and the rest of yesterday came flooding back to me.

The pain.

The fear.

The confusion.

The expression on Rab's face as he traced hearts on the back of my hand.

Before I could stop them, tears welled, and Sloane was popping her cup down on the bedside table and crawling into bed next to me to put her arms around me.

"Och, I'm fine, I'm fine. Just having a wee greet is all." I dashed away the tears with the back of my hand. "It just kind of all came back in a rush."

"Scary day." Sloane kissed my head. "Not a huge fan of you getting stabbed."

"Me either." I laughed.

"Do you have a lot of pain today?"

"No, not really. Just that sort of dull ache when you can feel something is healing. It's like a tightening up, I guess?" I wiped my eyes. "Is Ruth okay?"

"She's just fine. Had herself a lovely wee nap, woke up long enough to discover not only does Oswald not hunt mice, but he used to be friends with a fluttermouse, and the last I saw she was curled up sleeping on Haggis's back."

"I thought Felicity was going to skelp her across the alley." My mouth twisted as I flashed back to the expression on Felicity's face. She'd been furious, and it was the first time I'd seen the normally easy-breezy witch lose it. "She was really angry, Sloane."

"It was pretty chaotic, wasn't it? I imagine her emotions were running high. Hell, she'd just stabbed you. She was likely in a blind panic and then Ruth knifed her."

"Och, I forgot about that. I wonder how she's getting on?" Though my wee familiar's sword was small, it was sharp.

"She had two stitches. Mandy cleaned her up. But it's also why the filming didn't go on today. Two injured contestants, and I think they need to just make it clear to the powers that be that this incident happened after filming wrapped. Liabilities and all that."

"Did you speak with Mandy?"

"Nope, text message only. But she did inquire if you were alive or dead."

"Gee, well, now, isn't that something?" I rolled my eyes. "Eventually, I'm going to wear her down."

"I don't know why you bother. She's—"

"She's hurting, Sloane. You dethroned her. And for someone like Mandy, that's a huge blow to the ego. I think, given that it's been a while now, we can extend an olive branch."

"You've always been the best of us, Lyra. Sunshine in a bottle, you are." Sloane squeezed my shoulders.

"Aye, well, I'm not much feeling it today." I plucked at a loose thread on the sleeve of my jumper, thinking about Rab.

"Rab?"

"Aye." There was no point in pretending to my sister that he wasn't on my mind.

"He was . . ." I looked up to see Sloane shake her head slowly, her eyes distant as she thought about it. "His face, Lyra. That is a man who cares desperately for you. There's no denying it. Is it still so bad? All these years later? It's clear you mean something to him."

"I don't know." I wound the thread around my finger. "I don't know if I can trust him."

"You can't trust him? Or the boy he was?"

"That seems to be the crux of it."

"Worth a conversation, don't you think?" Sloane nudged me when I didn't reply.

"He was drawing a heart on my hand," I admitted, looking over at her. "When I was getting stitched. I don't even think he realized it."

Sloane gasped and slapped a hand to her mouth. "Och, Lyra. It's your life, and I'm not going to tell you what to do, but bloody hell. He was good-looking then, but now?" Sloane fanned her face.

"Looks aren't everything." It was a particular point of contention with me.

"Don't I know it. But he dropped what he was doing the second he heard you were hurt and drew hearts on your hand during surgery. I mean, that has to mean something, aye? And he didn't walk out of the competition when he saw you were his partner, did he?"

"He kissed me," I admitted on a rush of breath and winced when Sloane squealed and bounced in the bed.

"Not great . . ." I put a hand to my side.

"Sounds great to me," Nova said from the doorway, a smirk on her face. Today she wore leggings and a simple black jumper, and her hair was pulled back in two space buns. She looked like she was just back from her morning run.

"Oh my goddess, I'm sorry, I'm sorry." Sloane jumped off the bed, the worried look back on her face.

"I'm fine. Just a touch less exuberance next to the wound, please."

"So you finally shagged Rab?" Nova came inside carrying a tray of food. "Give me the deets before Henry gets here to change your bandage."

"I did *not* shag Rab." I swung my legs over the side of the bed and waited to see if the dizziness from yesterday would hit me. But after a big sleep I was clearheaded. I just needed to use the loo, brush my teeth, and down several cups of tea, and I'd be sorted out. "He kissed me."

"Aaaaand?" my sisters asked in unison, the word drawing out in excitement.

"And sparks flew, I turned his entire drawer of cutlery into hedgehogs, and then I ran away."

"Um . . ." Sloane paused, looking between me and Nova, unsure how to address this particular new development.

"Did you say . . ." Nova's lips were already trembling with held-back laughter.

"I just got stabbed, remember? I almost *died*. You're not allowed to make fun of me," I grumbled, wobbling toward the door. "I desperately need the toilet."

"Aye, this way. I'm coming with you. Just to make sure you're steady on your feet." Sloane swung back into mama bear mode and hooked an arm around my shoulders to lead me down the hallway.

By the time we'd returned, with one look in the mirror confirming my worst suspicions about my appearance, Henry had arrived with the menagerie in tow. Blue sat as close as he could to the table of food, his face ever hopeful. Ruth sat on Haggis's back, holding on to two hanks of his shaggy fur as reins, and Oswald was curled at the foot of the bed.

"There she is. Looking bright-eyed and bonnie this morning," Henry crowed, coming forward with his hands out to grasp my arms. "How are you getting on, then?"

"I know what I look like, Henry," I mumbled but accepted his kiss on my cheek. "Thank you for your excellent work. I'm feeling much better."

"Och, that's grand to hear. I'll just take a wee peek, change out the bandage if you don't mind, and then you can have a relaxing brekkie with your sisters."

"Nae bother." I lifted my jumper and looked down as he peeled the bandage away.

The scar was . . . not pretty. At least the slice seemed to be fairly straight, but the skin was bright pink and puckered beneath the threads of the stitching.

"It's looking grand, Lyra. I know it seems garish, but that will heal with time. We'll just keep putting the moonmoss on it and cleaning it. You'll scar, but it will be nothing like this." Henry's movements were swift and competent as he cleaned and reapplied the moonmoss before gently covering it with another bandage. "In another day or so, we'll keep the bandage off and let it heal on its own."

"That quickly?" I asked, surprised.

"It's the muscle that needs the healing. The skin will close up fast enough. You'll still want to take it slow for a few days as the rest knits back together. Our magick will hurry that along for you, lass. It's just a few days of being gentle with yourself, you ken?"

"Aye. Understood." I gave Henry a mock salute, and he grinned.

"That's me off to get rid of these bandages. Enjoy your brekkie, lasses. The others will be around in an hour."

"The others?" I asked as I sat at the table, my stomach growling.

"The Charms."

My eyes whipped up to Sloane's.

"Felicity too?"

"Aye, Felicity too. Maybe Mandy. That remains to be seen. We need to look deeper into this curse, and we need to address what happened yesterday, Lyra. Even as an accident, it needs to be smoothed over."

I took a deep breath and poured myself a cup of tea. Henry had gone all out on the breakfast, and I was beginning to see a theme here when it came to his meal choices: More was more. There was black pudding, two types of bacon, beans, eggs cooked three ways, butteries, fruit, yogurt, granola, roasted tomatoes, sausages, and a basket of toast.

"You're right. Best to crack on. I'd really like to see if we can make any headway with this curse. I'm going to have to keep Ruth with me at all times when we're outside." I ripped off a piece of bacon and slid it down to Blue, who almost expired from happiness.

Have you looked to recipe books?

I turned to look at Ruth. She was now braiding the fur on the back of Haggis's head while he wheeled slowly around the room.

"Why recipe books, Ruth?"

You're a hearth witch. The spell you need might fit with your magick.

"I don't really know my magick." I took a bite of a buttery and thought about it. "I haven't had a lot of time to learn what it wants. I just know it gets excited when I'm in a kitchen."

Magick likes to be used. Yours will always be happy when you're in your natural space.

"I can look in my grimoire," Sloane said. "Let me go get it."

"Ahem." Nova cleared her throat as she dug into her brekkie. She circled her fork in the air. "The hedgehogs?"

"I don't know, Nova. I just don't, okay? I'm such a freaking eejit. Do you know what I'm doing now?" I looked up at Nova, my eyes wide. "I am reciting random words to make myself not think lustful thoughts about Rab so I don't inadvertently turn things into hedgehogs when he's around."

"Ohhhhhhh." Nova sucked in a breath, and then threw her head back, her laughter bouncing around the room. Oswald jumped up, startled, and Haggis took a delighted lap around the room. Blue, naturally, remained focused on the prize—bacon. "You . . . you . . . Every time you get horned up, you turn random objects into hedgies?"

"Such a lovely way to put it, Nova," I hissed. But even I couldn't hold back my laughter. Blue seized the opportunity to snag the rest of the bacon from my hand and flew off to the other side of the room, his face a picture of a bliss. "Blue!"

"Och, let the wee man have it. He's a hero." Nova waved it away.

"That he is. I'm surprised he didn't take our hair off with his flames. A surprising amount of control the wee lad has," I said, looking affectionately at where Blue smiled at us from his perch on the bed.

Sloane returned, her grimoire in hand, and something prickled at the back of my neck.

"Just the most majestic wee beastie, aren't you, then?" Nova crooned, and Blue flew to her, slamming into her chest as she caught him. "Oof."

Her crooning faded into the background as I stared at the book in Sloane's hands. She sat paging through it, and my eyes fixed on the brilliant blue cover, soft shimmers catching the light. The grimoire had first appeared to her when Oswald had knocked it off a shelf at her feet, and she'd been the only one able to read it. In it, we'd learned the spell to break her curse.

It was just—

"The Mabon festival!" I stood up, bumping my plate, and Blue dove for the sausage that went flying. Catching it before it hit the floor, he skidded to a stop across the carpet and landed in front of Haggis, who promptly booped him with his nose.

"Hell, Lyra. Did you hit your head too? What are you blethering on about?" Nova griped.

"Wheesht, you silly twat." I swatted Nova's shoulder. "The book. Sloane's grimoire. It looks like a gift I received."

"You got a grimoire for a gift? And didn't say anything?" Sloane's face filled with disbelief. "How could you just ignore that?"

"I don't know if it's a grimoire." I shoved my lower lip out. "Listen, I had a lot of gifts to go through, all right? I spent most of one night opening and writing thank-you notes. Isn't that nice of me?"

"That is. I don't think Sloane sends thank-you cards for her gifts." Nova arched an eyebrow at Sloane.

"That's because I try to discourage gifts. I don't need more stuff," Sloane huffed.

"Aye, because where could you possibly find room to put it all?" Nova lifted her hands in the air and looked around the expansive guest room, one of many in the castle that Sloane now lived in.

"Can we focus, please?" I asked, before Sloane and Nova got into it. "The book, which the more I think about it has the same cover as Sloane's, was in with the pile of gifts. But there was no note."

"Was it wrapped?" Sloane asked.

"Aye. But very simple. Like brown kitchen paper."

"Right. You finish breakfast. I'll go get it and be back before the Charms meeting." Sloane stood.

"Can you get me some makeup? And some other clothes?" I asked, looking down at my clothes. I didn't want to look like I was . . . less than powerful for the meeting. I hated thinking I was a problem to be fixed and wanted to be presentable.

"Are you sure you want Sloane to do that?" Nova laughed. "You'll get leggings and a hoodie."

"Jeans and a jumper would be fine," I said to Sloane, knowing anything more intricate would fluster her. "And fresh pants and a bra."

"On it."

"So . . . back to the hedgehogs. How many? And what do you do with them?"

I glared at Nova and plopped back into my chair. Ruth flew over to me and tucked herself against my neck, while I considered various ways to make my sister's life miserable.

I'm glad you're okay, Lyra. That was scary.

"I'm glad you're okay, too, Ruth." I cuddled her in. "I would have been devastated if you'd been hurt."

I'm faster than I look.

"It was good flying on your part."

Got a good slice into Felicity too. I don't trust her.

"That's fair. I know it's your job to protect me, but I'm sure it was all just an accident."

I'll be keeping an eye on her.

"I wouldn't expect anything less."

CHAPTER TWENTY-FOUR

Lyra

The meeting of the Charms took place in the library, a room Sloane basically lived in now, and I couldn't say I blamed her. With bookshelves that went all the way to the high ceilings, three rolling ladders, several deep leather couches, a fireplace, and large paned windows that overlooked Briarhaven, it was atmospheric in the best way possible.

Though right now, all I could see through those big windows were the softly twinkling lights of the houses in town, even though it was just shy of nine in the morning.

Admittedly, I didn't stare out of this window down at Briarhaven at night all that much, but the town seemed darker to me today. Was it just my mood? Had the knife incident yesterday and subsequent interaction with Rab dulled my usual optimism? Because even though the house lights shone brightly, the streets were shrouded in a thick gloom, and from here I couldn't make out a single tourist wandering the cobblestone streets.

It could just be my mind playing tricks on me.

"Cuppa tea?" Sloane asked from behind me, where Henry had set up tea and biscuits on a long table that could easily seat sixteen people.

"Aye, thanks." I tore my gaze away from the window. "Does the town seem . . . darker to you? Or am I just not used to looking at it from here?"

"Oh no, it's definitely darker."

I turned to see Tam in the doorway, wearing dark denim jeans, a soft blue jumper, and black Sambas with blue stripes.

"It is?"

Behind her, Deidre, our resident house witch, followed with a phone pressed to her ear.

"Right, I'll get back to you with a counteroffer shortly. Yes, I understand." She wore a smart black suit with a red blouse and typed furiously into her phone as she beelined for the table. "Good morning, ladies. I'll be with you in just a minute. I have to submit a counter on a house I'm selling on Marigold Lane."

"That's a pretty street," Tam observed, coming over to give me a hug. "Hopefully some fun new neighbors."

"I don't know about 'fun.'" Deidre pursed her lips as she typed with one hand and poured herself tea with the other. "But he's a cash buyer and might open a tattoo shop here."

"He what?" Nova's head snapped up from where she was doodling on her phone.

"That's right. I'm working on more than one transaction for him. He may secure the shop at the end of main. Gilda's Gifts? They're looking to retire."

"Gilda's been leaving pamphlets for world cruises under George's coffee cup for years now." Tam smirked.

"Why is the town darker?" I asked, trying to cut through the gossip and get to how else my curse was wrecking Briarhaven. Guilt had already taken up permanent residence in my stomach, and now that the threat was escalating, it had started carving out extra rooms.

"The streetlamps are solar," Tam explained.

I closed my eyes. "Of course."

"They've got batteries, and they can store power for a while, but since it's been full dark for well over a week now, they've finally kicked it. The streets are totally dark." Tam took a seat and poured herself a glass of water. Usually, she was as optimistic as I was, but now I could see the tension lines fanning from the corners of her eyes. "It's not safe. I saw people wearing headlamps and reflective vests to cross the street today."

"That's our first order of business," Sloane promised.

"Lyra." Raven swept in in a swirl of velvet skirts and crossed over to give me a hug. "How are you today?"

"Better. Much better. Thank you so much." I squeezed her back, inhaling lavender. "Your magick is very powerful. I swear I'll be healed up by the weekend."

"As you should be. Henry's excellent, and so am I, if I do say so myself." Raven laughed, tossing her tumbling hair, then joined the others at the table.

Broca strolled in on Henry's arm in a sequined jumper and wide-legged trousers, and we all made our way to sit. Henry bowed out, promising he was nearby if we needed more food or drink, before closing the library doors behind him.

We were just settling when those same doors opened again.

Felicity slipped in first, clutching a massive travel mug, her hair in a messy bun. She looked a bit washed out but determined. Right behind her, Mandy swept through in a black tweed Chanel jacket, dark jeans, and an expression that suggested the room smelled faintly of rubbish.

"Well," Mandy said, arching a brow as her gaze skimmed all of us at the table, "I wasn't going to miss a mandatory Charms meeting, now, was I?"

Ruth, tucked into the collar of my jumper, poked her head out.

The prickly one came back. Interesting.

"Like all the ones you missed over the past year?" Nova raised a brow.

"Come in, both of you," Sloane said, giving Nova a pointed look, and then gesturing to the empty chairs. "Grab tea, biscuits, whatever you need. We're starting properly now."

I watched Sloane to see how she would react to Mandy's appearance at the meeting, but her expression gave nothing away. It was why she made a good president, I realized, pride for my older sister filling me.

Felicity hurried to sit while Mandy took her time settling, stirring sugar into her cup as if she was judging the entire coven and finding us wanting.

When everyone was finally ready, Sloane rested her palms on the table and exhaled. For a heartbeat, she just looked at us, one by one, her eyes serious.

"Okay," she said, clearing her throat. "Before we dive in . . . I just want to mark this moment."

Nova groaned softly. "Oh goddess, she's going to make a speech."

"Shut it," Sloane said without heat. "It is a big deal. My sister was seriously hurt. I'm traumatized. But we still have to mark this moment as this is the first time since I became president that we have the *entire* coven in one room. All of us. At the same table."

The words sank in. Even Mandy's posture softened a fraction.

Broca smiled, lines creasing at the corners of her eyes. "Took you all long enough."

"I'm glad you're here," Sloane finished, a little gruffly. "Whether you're thrilled about it or not."

Mandy sniffed. "Let's not get sentimental. It might stain my jacket."

But she didn't get up and walk out, and that said more than anything.

"All right." Sloane straightened the coven notebook in front of her. "Two big things on the agenda. First we need to have a quick check-in about what happened yesterday"—she glanced at me, then Felicity—"and second, the curse. The darkness. The owls. All of it."

A tense breath left me in a small woosh.

Felicity's fingers tightened on her mug. "I just want to say before anyone says anything else . . . I'm so, *so* sorry, Lyra. I know I said it last night and sent that ridiculous fruit basket and texted you but—"

"It was a very fancy fruit basket," Nova put in. "I stole the kiwi."

I'd never even seen the fruit basket, but I just nodded along with what Felicity was saying.

Felicity's mouth wobbled. "I feel sick every time I think about it. If it had been an inch higher—"

"It wasn't," I said quickly. Remembering the knife sliding into my side made my skin prickle, but I forced a smile. "You were carrying too much, the floor was wet, I have the grace of a newborn giraffe . . . it was an accident. We all know that."

Sloane inclined her head. "We do. I went over the CCTV with Henry. It looked like a slapstick sketch with a tragic twist. No one's getting punished, no one's getting kicked out, and I think that knives need to be carried with much more care. Agreed?"

A soft chorus of "Agreed!" went round the table.

I still think Felicity deserved to be stabbed back.

"Ruth," I whispered.

"What did she say?" Raven asked, eyes bright with curiosity.

"She maintains her very strong 'stab first, ask questions later' stance." I sighed.

Tam snorted. Felicity gave Ruth a wary look. "I, um, guess I can't blame her."

"Good." Sloane clapped her hands once. "We're done with that, then. Everyone's alive, mostly healed, and our takeaway is we need protective sheaths for all sharp objects. Moving on."

"See, this is why I came," Mandy said, leaning back. "I missed the part where we establish better stab-avoidance protocols."

Broca fixed her with a look. "You came because you're still a Charm, whether you like it or not. And because you love the drama."

Mandy pursed her lips but didn't argue.

Sloane exhaled and flipped open the thick, leather-bound coven book. "All right. Curse time. The darkness is starting to cause very real harm to the town."

"The solar streetlamps are dead," Tam said, leaning back in her chair and crossing her arms over her chest. "Kids are walking to school in the dark with headlamps on and carrying flashlights. The tourists think it's vaguely spooky and fun *now*, but our bookings for next week have tanked. People are canceling."

"Briarhaven's reputation is taking a hit," Deidre added. "Social media is already whispering about strange weather patterns and unnatural darkness. I've had two buyers pause their contracts."

Guilt surged again, and I folded my fingers around my teacup so tightly I was afraid it would break.

This is not all on you, Ruth said sternly in my head. *Curses are group projects. Blame the ancestor who started it, not the one who inherited it.*

"On top of that," Raven said, "the owls are struggling. Their hunting patterns are completely thrown. They relied on daylight for hunting. This endless midnight is confusing their instincts."

Some of us do not feel bad for the owls. Ruth shivered against my neck.

"We like owls," Tam said. "We just don't like them dive-bombing our familiars."

"So." Sloane leaned on her elbows. "We need ideas. Practical ones. Magical ones. Anything that keeps the town safe, keeps the tourists calm, and stops the local wildlife from going feral."

"We can get the streetlights off solar," Tam said. "That's a practical thing. Wire them into the main supply. It'll take some work, but it's possible."

"Henry's already pulled the permits form," Sloane said. "Knox is talking to the council. But that only solves the lamp problem. The sky will still look . . . wrong."

"I've been thinking about that," Raven said, perking up. "Since we can't fix the sky yet, we might be able to manage how people perceive it. If we weave a very gentle illusion spell into something communal—like the teas or the pastries at the bakery, or even the mulling spices the pub uses—we could help nudge visitors and locals into believing the darkness is just unusually heavy cloud cover."

Deidre's eyebrows shot up. "Involuntary mass suggestion. Bold."

"Not suggestion," Raven protested. "It wouldn't change anyone's thoughts or emotions. Just . . . cushion their perception. Enough that when they look outside and think, *This feels wrong*, their mind naturally supplies, *Oh, Scottish winter gloom—happens every decade or so*. We're just giving them a comfortable explanation so they don't spiral or start rumors about curses."

"That . . . actually isn't a terrible idea," Mandy said before she could stop herself. She caught me looking and snapped her gaze away. "If we're trying to keep the town from hemorrhaging tourists, this is better than letting the conspiracy groups descend on Briarhaven."

Raven nodded eagerly. "Exactly. A mild perception veil could buy us time, you know, to actually address the curse instead of putting out fires."

"We'd need the whole town on script," Deidre said thoughtfully. "If someone asks why it's pitch-black at 9 a.m., the shops and cafés can all answer the same way . . . freak atmospheric inversion, a weird solar flare bringing early winter hours . . . whatever."

Broca nodded. "People believe the truth they're most comfortable with. If ninety percent of the town treats this like an odd weather event, the other ten percent will follow along."

Tam tapped her fingers on the table. "All right. Raven's perception-cushion spell goes on the board. It'll help with morale, even if it doesn't solve the underlying issue."

"And we need morale," Sloane agreed. "Briarhaven is deeply unhappy, and we all know that, *historically*, does not go well for us."

"Light tunnels," Nova suggested. When we all stared, she shrugged. "I saw them in Norway once. Big mirrored arches that reflect any available light. We could enchant crystals and hang them along the main street. At least give people somewhere that feels brighter, even if the sky's still black."

"That could help with the owls too," Tam mused. "If we build enchanted light paths in the forest that mimic dusk, we might be able to lure wildlife there at predictable times. The owls could adjust their hunting patterns and stop stalking alleyways looking for fluttermice."

I strongly vote for the owl redirection plan. Ruth hopped onto the table in front of me and put her paw in the air.

"All right," I said. "Raven and I can look into it. I'm happy to try anything to help."

We'll try, Ruth corrected. *I am extremely good at stabbing things that threaten you.*

"Any other ideas?" Sloane asked, looking round.

"We need a PR campaign to manage public mood," Deidre said. "We need to keep spirits up. If people start talking about leaving, we're sunk. Maybe extra events at the pub. Quiz nights. Free hot chocolate in the square at noon so people still feel the rhythm of the day."

"I can ask Marcie to do a special midday menu at Mystic Munchies," I offered. "Keep things cozy."

"Perfect," Sloane said. She sat back. "Look at us. An actual functioning coven."

"Don't get carried away," Mandy muttered, though the corner of her mouth twitched.

Before Sloane could respond, the library doors swung open.

"No need for glowworms, ladies," Knox announced, strolling in. Rab walked at his side, hands in his pockets, looking annoyingly edible in a tartan flannel shirt. My heart did a little inappropriate flip.

"Why's that?" Sloane beamed up at Knox as he bent to kiss her cheek.

"See, there's this little-known magick called . . . electricity." Knox laughed and slung an arm around her shoulders. "We'll get the streetlights wired properly. I've already got an electrician lined up and the council mostly on board."

"Of course you do," Sloane said, eyes soft. "Show-off."

"Just doing my part to impress the president," he said. "Morning, Charms."

"Morning," we chorused.

Rab's gaze snagged on mine for a second, and something unreadable shifted in the depths of his eyes. My pulse skittered.

"Right," Sloane said briskly. "Then I think, for now, we've got a plan—"

She broke off, her mouth falling open as she stared at me.

I frowned and followed her gaze.

A hedgehog lay on its back in the middle of the table where my teacup had been a heartbeat ago, tiny paws curled in the air in sleepy confusion.

My gaze flew to Rab.

The corners of his mouth lifted in a slow, knowing grin.

Mandy looked between us, then at the hedgehog, and burst out laughing.

I buried my face in my hands. *Seriously? This had to happen now?* My humiliation was complete.

CHAPTER TWENTY-FIVE

Rab

"All right, all right, that's enough." I took away the tin of canned hedgehog food I'd given to Merry and Pippin, the two hedgehogs that had fallen asleep on my legs the other day. For some reason, I'd found it hard to give them over to Sorcha at the Familiar's Nest, and instead she'd loaded me up on hedgie food and enrichment toys.

It appeared I was a hedgie dad now.

The two hedgies raced around their pen, bumped into each other, had a wee bickering squabble, and then promptly rolled up in tight balls. I had to admit, the pair of them were seriously cute, and seemed amenable to being friendly with me, which wasn't usual for hedgehogs in the wild. Maybe there was something about Lyra's magick that made them like me more.

I hadn't been able to stop myself from laughing yesterday when Lyra had promptly turned her teacup into a hedgie upon seeing me. Henry had swooped into the room, picked the wee creature up off the table, and disappeared before the blush had faded from Lyra's cheeks.

Something had shifted for me. For us.

"You love her."

Knox's words came back to me. After I'd admitted it, both he and Liam had laid into me about the importance of second chances.

Usually, I took most of their advice with a grain of salt, but something Liam and Knox had echoed still resonated with me.

"You were just kids."

They hadn't been saying it in the annoyingly patronizing way people do when they dismiss your emotions. Instead, they'd both validated that my feelings at the time were real, but also the situation itself had been largely unrealistic. Some dreams could be too big. At the end of the day, I'd been asking Lyra to make an impossible decision. She'd been supposed to leave her sisters and family behind to come live with me? Where? In a barn somewhere? I'd had nothing, really, to offer, aside from my love. At the time, I'd thought that was enough, but the reality of what our lives would have been like if she'd left with me would have broken us anyway.

We'd always been destined to be torn apart. Or maybe, had my father not persisted in fueling my anger toward Lyra and all the MacGregors, I could have moved beyond the pain sooner.

So now it was on me to decide whether what we'd had back then was worth fixing or if who we were now was worth fighting for.

I knew for a fact that she wasn't unbothered by me. It was exceptionally clear she was still attracted to me. But was that enough to build from? Would she be able to start again with me?

At the end of the day, the real question was—could I trust *her* again?

It had broken something in me, and my mother's subsequent enthusiasm about Lyra's departure had created a reticence in me to believe what women were telling me. I'd once trusted my mum to be on my side, but when she'd sided with my dad against the MacGregors, it had thrown off my perception of her. She'd once been so caring and kind about my relationship with Lyra, but the minute they'd had a chance to run her off, they'd been happy to see her gone. It was an about-face I hadn't been expecting, and had added weight to my reluctance to believe in relationships. I'd dated since then, but never seriously, and anytime things did get too serious, I backed off.

Maybe I'd known that I wasn't ready for love again.

Or maybe my heart had been waiting for Lyra all these years.

I'd given her space yesterday—as much as I wanted to linger in the library with her, it was clear the coven had more business to attend to. Plus, I'd just needed some time to think. I'd walked home from Knox's castle, the wind cold on my face, Briarhaven sprawled out and twinkling below me in the darkness. It was one of those walks where I'd needed to give myself a stern talking-to, and the wind slapping my face had mirrored the truths slapping my heart.

By the time I'd returned home, I'd concluded that the fundamental truth about wounds is that they are meant to heal, and though scars could be cautionary tales, they could also serve as badges of honor. *I survived that.* I'd been living with a wound that had driven my choices, when instead I should have patted myself on the back for being resilient and trusted that I could handle what life threw at me in the future.

And life had thrown Lyra right at my feet in the form of one ridiculous baking competition.

Which was back to filming today, and I needed to get to set, I reminded myself. Making sure that Merry and Pippin's enclosure was securely shut, I locked up and walked to Mystic Munchies. It was still early, as the producers required we show up in time for makeup and all that—not that I let them dust me with too much powder and whatnot, but still we were required to be there. I'd learned that filming television required a lot of waiting. They liked to pull us aside for these candid interviews where I had to answer asinine questions like: *How did you feel when the flour for your truffle exploded in your face?*

Not all of the streetlights were back to working, but between the ones that Knox had been able to get wired and the sheer volume of twinkle lights that the houses and shops had used for decorations in order to combat the darkness, I found that my path was well lit. Knox had even managed to get string lights hung in crisscross patterns across the main street, and they served as a lovely temporary solution for ambient light. I liked them. I made a mental note to ask Knox if he'd consider keeping them up year-round.

Sometimes living in a small town could feel constraining, but in moments like this, where it was obvious the community had pulled together to make something beautiful for visitors and neighbors alike, my fondness for Briarhaven swelled.

"Good morning." Kelly strode up to me as I walked to one of the trailers parked behind Mystic Munchies. The judge had been fairly obvious in her flirtations with me, but they had all been on camera, so I suspected she had been doing it just to try to create tension with Lyra. I was very aware that the producers were angling for the most interesting reality show they could make, not just to film the person who could make the best baked good.

"Good morning," I said, nodding to her.

"How was your day off? Do anything fun?" Kelly asked, flipping her hair over her shoulder and smiling up at me.

"I helped Knox with some of the issues because of the darkness. We were able to get some more lights strung up and a few of the streetlights wired."

"Och, I heard about the curse. Such a shame, isn't it? It must make life so difficult for you all, having to put up with her curse."

Annoyance filled me. "It's not Lyra's fault. She didn't do anything wrong. It's not like she's sitting around thinking up ways to hurt Briarhaven."

"Thank you."

I whirled to see Lyra behind me, her eyes huge. She looked healthier today. I'd hated seeing her with the wind knocked out of her sails, but today she looked ready for battle in a brilliant magenta dress, hair pinned back from her face to tumble in soft waves down her back, and a deep pink lipstick slicked on her lips.

Looking at her mouth made my knees weak.

I didn't presume that she wore that lipstick to distract me, but either way, I couldn't take my eyes away from her.

"Lyra. *So* great to see you," Kelly said, though her tone suggested it was anything but. "How are you feeling?"

"Much better, thank you."

"You look bonnie today, Lyra," I said. I was rewarded with a quick smile before her eyes dropped away.

"Don't worry. We've made sure today's challenge won't require any knives," Kelly said, and I looked at her in disbelief.

"What?" She twinkled up at me. "Too soon?"

"It's fine," Lyra said, reaching out to stop me. My arm tingled where her hand landed. "There will be some point where I'm sure we'll find this funny. Just not yet."

"Have some class, Kelly," I said, and a warning flashed in the judge's eyes. I just didn't care. She should be happy that Lyra had come back to finish shooting at all, not poking fun at her for getting stabbed.

"Rab." Lyra sighed. "It's fine. She was just trying to lighten the mood. Right, Kelly?"

"Right. It was just a bit o' banter, Rab. Lighten up." Kelly flounced away, and I watched her go, not caring in the slightest that I had annoyed her. She shouldn't be making fun of someone who had been injured so recently, especially considering it could have been a lot worse. When Henry had mentioned what it had *just missed*, my anger had grown.

"Are you sure you're well enough to film today? You don't have to put yourself through this if you don't want to." I fell into step next to Lyra as we approached the trailer.

"It's fine. There's no use in delaying this. I'd rather we got back to filming anyway. I'm not sure how much longer I want to subject myself to this humiliation."

"Och, it's not that bad. Is it? Are you worried?" I stopped in my tracks and turned to look down at her. Twinkle lights reflected in her eyes.

"I mean, it's not great." Lyra laughed and looked away. "But I don't think there's much I can do to change it at the moment. Not until we make some headway with this curse. So the only thing I can do is be a good sport about it. Hopefully, if I keep a good attitude, people will still root for us. I'd hate to make you look stupid."

I tilted my head. "Lyra, I couldn't give two shites what anyone who watches this show thinks of me. Don't worry about that."

"Still. You didn't sign up to be made a fool of."

"You're not making a fool of me." I stopped her when she went to walk forward, turning her to me. "You're *not*. If it were something that I truly cared about—which is largely profit and loss statements and sound financial planning for small businesses—I would be upset. But this means nothing to me. It is important to you, though. So I'm here to help you however I can."

Lyra's face softened. "Rab—"

"Oh, good, just the people I wanted." Vaughn popped his head out of a trailer. "Lyra, you're in for makeup. Rab, you're in confessional."

"Why is it called a confessional? Isn't it just an interview? Are you a priest?" I grumbled as I followed Vaughn into the room where they filmed private interviews with the producers. Why did they ask a bunch of odd questions that often had nothing to do with baking?

"Because the point is for you to open up and tell us things that will get the audience to like you. Or hate you." Vaughn shrugged as he took his chair. "It's your call which way you want to spin that."

"How much of these reality shows are actually all that real?" I asked, plopping onto the stool and crossing my arms over my chest. "It all gets edited the way you want it to, doesn't it?"

"Welcome to showbiz, baby." Vaughn winked at me, and despite finding him annoying, I laughed. At least he was honest.

We waited while the production assistant counted us down, and then the cameras began recording.

"Right, let's just jump right into the question that everyone is dying to know. Are you and Lyra dating again?"

"What?" I dropped my arms and leaned forward in surprise. "That's the question everyone is dying to know? Isn't it something like . . . I don't know . . . how much salt to put in a brownie?"

"And do you know the answer to that?"

"I don't know. But I would say, toss a handful in there." I shrugged a shoulder. "Salt goes well with sweets. Doesn't it?"

"Aye, it does, but you certainly wouldn't want a handful. It's not the main ingredient."

"Which is why my question makes sense. Wouldn't viewers want to know the exact amount so as not to screw up their recipe?"

"You're avoiding the question."

"No, Lyra and I are not dating," I answered, rolling my eyes.

"Do you want to date her again?"

"Is this really relevant to whether I can bake a rhubarb tartlet or whatever?" I asked.

"Food is love, Rab. Baking is about passion and joy. Ever eat a meal where you were convinced the chef hated life?"

I pursed my lips, considering his words.

"I've eaten some bad meals in my life, but I think I chalked it up to an inexperienced chef."

"Or an unhappy one. Perhaps that's why your recipes are going wrong?" Vaughn arched an eyebrow at me.

"I believe that's called leading the witness, Your Honor," I said. I loved watching American legal dramas.

"Are you going to answer the question?" Vaughn sighed.

"Aye, I'd like to date her again," I said, surprising Vaughn. He perked up, straightening in his chair. Checking his clipboard, he looked up at me.

"Why?"

"Because I love her," I shocked myself by saying. But I realized I didn't care who knew it. Somewhere along my walk home last night and a long discussion with Merry and Pippin, who just kept running in circles while I sat with them on the kitchen floor, I'd realized that I was done lying about what I felt for Lyra. My love for her was nothing I would ever hide or be ashamed of again. "Do you know when it's absolutely pissing out, and the clouds have all clustered in and are moody and gray?"

"Aye, that's typical enough Scottish weather."

"And then, out of nowhere, the clouds will shift, and the loveliest ray of sunshine will pierce through all that gray. It just lights the whole world up in a way that has made poets reach for their pens and painters grab for their brushes in a desperate attempt to capture that moment of stunning, perfect light." I lifted my head and looked the camera dead on. "That's Lyra."

I stood up, not caring that we were still filming. I needed to go find Lyra and tell her to her face everything that I felt about her.

"Great, there you are, Rab. We're ready to film." A production assistant that I didn't know the name of snagged my arm and drew me toward the back of Mystic Munchies.

"Lyra—"

"She's already at your table. Everyone's waiting."

Bloody hell, but this would have to wait. Annoyed and somewhat flustered that I'd been willing to be so open on television, much to Vaughn's delight, I'm sure, I entered the test kitchen.

Felicity and Mandy stood at the table parallel to ours, instead of behind us. The producers must have decided to move them. But why? Did they think Felicity was an actual threat to Lyra? Or were they hoping for more drama to explode? Instinctively, I moved to the side of the table that would place me between Lyra and Felicity.

"No, Rab. The other side, please." Kelly pointed to the other side of the table.

"Why?" I asked, lifting my chin.

"They're hoping to distract me with Felicity being near. Or that I'll distract Felicity," Lyra murmured, moving to the side they wanted her to be on.

"So don't give it to them." I looked down at her, shaking my head. "You don't have to play into what they want."

"It's not that serious, Rab. Remember, it's just a show, right?" Lyra smiled, squeezing my arm, and everything inside me warmed at her touch. I hadn't been lying. Every time Lyra smiled at me it was like finding a warm spot of sunshine on a gloomy day.

"If you're fine with it."

"I am." Lyra turned back toward the cameras and placed her hands on the table, ready for battle.

"Right, is everyone sorted, then?" Nevin asked.

I glanced back to Henry, who gave me a wink, and Team Elf seemed enthused to be here with matching reindeer headbands on their heads today.

"And rolling in three . . . two . . . one . . ."

"Good evening, and welcome back to everyone's favorite baking show, *Bewitching Bake Off*!"

Nevin looked festive today in a tartan waistcoat and bow tie. "We have an extra-special baking challenge for you all today."

"Lovely," I said, under my breath, and Lyra lightly bumped my shoulder with hers.

I grinned.

"Today's challenge is going to get very . . . personal." Kelly picked up where Nevin had left off, the cameras following her as she walked across the room. "Because the holidays tend to be nostalgic, and many of our favorite recipes come from our memories, today's challenge is called: Whisking up the Past."

Worry niggled at the back of my neck as Kelly turned her smile toward our table.

"Contestants will drink a magickal tea that will allow them to exchange one memory of their choice with their fellow team member. Based on those memories, you'll need to come up with one holiday-themed recipe of your choice."

"Memories of Christmas morning?" one of the elves asked.

"*Any* memory from the past."

I couldn't bring myself to look at Lyra, though I could feel her practically vibrating with angst at my side. We had so many shared memories together, but there was one very important one that we had two differing viewpoints on.

I knew it was what the reality show wanted.

But, I realized, so did I. I wanted her to see that day, from my view, so she could understand just how much I'd hurt when she'd left.

"Rab, no." Lyra looked up at me, worry creasing her forehead, understanding in her eyes.

"Why not?" I asked, with a shrug. "It's what they want. And maybe it will be good for us."

"Us?" Lyra asked, raising an eyebrow.

"Us," I said, and took the tea that Kelly handed me.

"Lyra, you'll drink first. Then, Rab, drink from the same cup. You'll recite the spell after me, and you'll be brought into Lyra's memory first. And then Rab's. Once finished, you can decide which memory will inspire your shared dish."

I took the tea without hesitation.

"Are you sure?" Lyra whispered, tugging on my shirt.

"Lyra, we have a lot of great shared memories together, but what we don't know about is the day we fell apart. So why not? Why not now?" I asked, my gaze boring into hers. After a brief hesitation, she pressed her lips together and then nodded.

"Right, let's do this."

Taking a sip of the peppermint tea, I passed it to Lyra, and then we looked to Kelly.

"Recite after me." Nevin stepped forward. "By holly bright and candle's gleam, show us now the other's scene. Through winter's glass let past unfold, one heart, one sight, and a tale retold."

We recited, and then I . . . was no longer in the room.

I was staring at the old tree in my backyard, my hands at my mouth. I blinked, trying to get a bearing on my senses.

Thunder rumbled the skies and the branches shook over my head as voices carried to me through the open window.

"Rabbie." My mum's voice drifted through the window. "We heard. We didn't mean to, but we were taking the washing in."

"You can't do this, son. You're too young." My dad's no-nonsense voice followed. "You think you're in love, but it's just . . . hormones. Everyone thinks they're in love at your age. I know it feels all big and real right now, but it will pass. And you can't throw away your future for some lass."

"She's not just some lass! I love her," my younger voice cried out.

"Aye, so you think you do. But it's impossible, what you're suggesting. Lyra isn't old enough to leave her family. To come live with . . . you? Where? Here? We wouldn't agree to that. Nor are we even sure it's legal," my mother said.

My heart dropped as I realized what I was seeing.

Lyra hadn't left that day.

Instead, she'd pressed herself to the wall of my house and listened to every word my parents had said that fateful night.

"You're about to sit exams, Rab. You've got an incredible future ahead of you. Promise me you won't throw it away. Not for just a bonnie lass. Not for . . . a MacGregor. Of all people. You could do better for your future than to saddle yourself to a family riddled with curses. They're a blight on this community."

"I suppose it was foolish, wasn't it? To think we'd have a future. I guess . . . I just got caught up. You're right. Lyra's nothing special. She's just a pretty face." I cringed as I heard my own voice agreeing with my father.

"That's a good lad. I knew you'd see it our way. It's hard, I know. But in a year, this won't matter at all."

And then the landscape in front of me shifted, and we were running, racing through the icy rain that slapped our face, tears hot at our cheeks.

The memory cut off as soon as Lyra slammed through the front door of her house, suitcases piled up at the door, because what else was there to show? I'd thought I'd heard crying that day but had chalked it up to wind wailing through the branches.

My heart felt leaden. *She'd heard. She'd heard my lie.* She hadn't known that those words were only spoken to pacify my parents. *Shite.*

All these years I'd assumed she'd left me because she'd lied, because she hadn't really loved me. Not because she'd overheard me lie to my parents. Opening my eyes, I looked down at Lyra, only to be thrust directly into the next memory.

Mine.

CHAPTER TWENTY-SIX

Lyra

I closed my eyes, and suddenly I was standing in Rab's room, seeing through his eyes. It was discombobulating to say the least. We were bent over, digging through his closet, and I realized that he was packing a bag.

My stomach dropped.

He lifted his mattress and pulled out a wad of cash and tucked it inside a pocket of the duffel bag. In went socks, pants, clothes, the handkerchief I had foolishly embroidered for him when I was trying my hand at making clothes for a bit. Quietly, we tiptoed to the window and then slid outside into the night and around the house.

And then we were running. Running, with hope in our heart and excitement fueling us, toward the abandoned barn on the edge of town.

Our spot.

My heart twisted as the memory flashed through the hours Rab spent waiting in the barn.

He'd waited for me.

It had all been a lie—what he'd said to his parents about me—it had been a *lie.*

When the memory finally took us away from the barn and plodded slowly past my empty house, my heart split open.

I'd been so wrong about so many things.

I'd been convinced he'd thrown me away at the first sign of hardship, just like my father was willing to walk away from my mother. Men left. It had made sense to my teenaged brain, but now I realized just how distorted the lens I'd been looking through was.

Rab had lied to his parents. And he'd been willing to change his entire life to rescue me from mine.

Why hadn't we just had this conversation? A thousand times through the years I'd been wanting to reach out. And then when we'd come back he'd given me the cold shoulder, which had just further affirmed my belief that he'd meant every word he said.

The memory winked out, and I was left standing with my mouth open, my heart hammering in my chest as I looked up at Rab.

"My, my, my." Nevin pounced. "What do we have here? Is it a revelation? Anything you care to share with the viewers?"

Tears threatened, and I had to take a deep breath to steady myself. This changed everything.

Everything.

And somehow I needed to face the cameras and bake my way through a competition challenge.

I froze.

"Jam cookies," Rab said smoothly, taking my hand. I blinked up at him.

"Jam cookies?" I echoed.

"You know. The cookies with the jam in the middle? We'll call them 'Mended Hearts.'" Rab beamed into the cameras as I just blinked up at him, stunned. What was happening? Mended hearts? What did this mean?

"Ah, dare I ask what the memory was you two shared?" Kelly asked.

"You may ask, but it's ours to know." Rab grinned cheekily. All of a sudden he was all charm and charisma for the cameras when he'd basically growled in their direction all week. I couldn't get over the change in him, let alone the fact he'd suggested a recipe.

"Boooo," Nevin called, sidling over to me. "Care to share, darling?"

Did I? I looked up at the cameras and took a deep breath.

"It was a memory of a misunderstanding. One that could have saved a lot of heartache had I been brave enough to reach out." I swallowed against the lump in my throat.

"And now? Is it a Christmas miracle? Will you two get back together?" Nevin leaned in, the cameras all focused on us.

"What is this? A dating show?" Mandy griped from her table.

"Well, let's see how the challenge goes." I felt my lips tug up into a grin, and hope bloomed in my heart. Turning, I looked up at Rab, who had an equally silly grin on his face. "But Mended Hearts memory cookies sounds like the perfect recipe to me."

"I mean . . . are jam cookies all that hard to make?" Felicity wondered, and the cameras swung to their table.

"Ohhh, we have some trash talk from one of the other teams. You'd be surprised how tricky the jam cookies can be." Kelly strolled over to Mandy and Felicity's table. "Tell me, what are you both making?"

"A Christmas Yule log cake to remind us of warm family mornings." Felicity beamed.

"Aw, well, isn't that nice? Yes, a touch more challenging than the cookies, but we'll just have to see how it plays out. Remember, it's not just the recipe, but the taste and presentation that matter as well. Simple can often be more difficult to achieve than seemingly complicated recipes." Kelly looked around at the others in the room and raised her hands. "And . . . bake on, challengers. Your time starts now."

"Rab," I said, squeezing his hand that I still held. "I didn't . . ."

"Not for now, Lyra," Rab said out of the corner of his mouth as he bent to pull out bowls from the shelves beneath our workstation. "We gave them enough of us."

"But—"

"Later, Lyra. We have all the time in the world now." Rab glanced up at me, his eyes burning in his face, and I realized that he'd forgiven me.

Not only that, but he wanted a future with me.

Relief filled me, and so did bone-aching lust.

The bowl Rab held promptly changed into a hedgehog.

"Whoops," Rab said, and tucked the hedgie inside the cupboard, leaving the door open a small crack for air. He was still crouching, so I was certain the cameras hadn't caught the transmutation, but my cheeks burned. "I'll be back for you, wee man. Right. Stay focused, darling. We've got bigger things to worry about. Like how to make those wee jam cookies."

I laughed, glad he had given me something else to focus on other than jumping his sexy body, and I turned back to the table.

"Right. Jam cookies are often called Linzer cookies. So we'll need"—I thought about it for a second—"butter, flour, sugar, ground almonds, eggs, vanilla, and raspberries for the jam."

I reached for the butter—and immediately watched it frost over in a block of ice so solid a polar bear could've skated on it.

"Oh no," I groaned.

Rab's lips quirked, but he didn't say anything—just quietly swapped the frozen lump for a fresh one.

The flour was next. I tipped the bag toward the bowl, but it exploded into a cloud so fine it coated my hair, my face, and my apron until I looked like a ghost.

Across the room, Mandy snorted into her mixing bowl. "Snowman chic, Lyra?"

Rab didn't even glance up. "Ignore them." He took my hand—grounding me—and guided it toward the mixing bowl. The moment our palms touched, my magick stopped fizzling at the edges, like he'd clicked a switch.

We rolled out the dough together, elbows brushing, his big hands covering mine to keep my focus. The heart-shaped cutters behaved themselves . . . mostly. One tried to sprout legs and run. Rab caught it mid-escape.

"Not today, mate." He plunked it back onto the dough with authority.

The jam was the final test. I stirred, and it immediately tried to turn into raspberry soup. Rab stepped in, wrapping his fingers over mine around the spoon. "With me," he murmured. The raspberries bubbled into a glossy, jewel-red filling that smelled like Christmas morning and brand-new hope.

We baked, dusted with sugar, sandwiched the jam between two perfect hearts at a time, and arranged them in pairs—two halves, mended together.

Kelly swept over, eyes going wide. "Ohhh, these are gorgeous! And symbolic. Viewers, take note. 'Mended Hearts' from Team Mystery Memory over here."

Nevin smirked. "So . . . what's the meaning?"

Rab grinned down at me. "That sometimes the right halves fit together to make a stronger cookie."

The judges approached. Nevin took a bite—at which point one cookie puffed up like a balloon animal and floated gently toward the ceiling.

"What the . . ." Kelly looked up, wide-eyed.

"It's . . . extra flair," Rab said smoothly, reaching up to pluck it out of the air before it could hit the lighting rig. He set it back on the plate like nothing had happened.

Mandy muttered something about "show-offs" under her breath.

Kelly tried one next, her eyes widening. "Crisp, buttery, just the right amount of sweet from the jam—" She broke off as another cookie twitched on the plate and shimmied toward her hand like it wanted to be chosen.

Rab blocked it casually with the serving tongs. "Eager to please. Just like us."

The camera guys loved it, Henry laughed behind us, and the judges? They gave us the highest marks of the round.

It had been messy, but instead of being embarrassed or upset by my misfiring magick, I'd actually had fun. And I realized that was a huge part of the challenges as well. It wasn't just working under pressure or freaking out if my magick didn't work, it was about finding joy in the process. I'd made it work.

All because of Rab.

CHAPTER TWENTY-SEVEN

Lyra

"That's a wrap!" Vaughn called. "Great job, everyone. Lyra . . . a word?"

Rab grabbed my hand, and I gasped as he dragged me out of the test kitchen and toward the trailer.

"Rab!"

"Get your coat, Lyra. Let's get out of here before they corner us for two hours of interviews."

I dashed into the trailer, feeling like I was cutting school, and swallowed a nervous giggle as I ran back outside to find Rab had his coat on as well. As soon as he saw me, he grabbed my hand and tugged me down the same alleyway I'd stumbled down bleeding from my side two days prior. The lanterns glowed softly, the cobblestones were still damp from an earlier drizzle, and a mild breeze rattled the ivy on the walls. Nerves skittered through my stomach, and I let out a relieved breath when we left the alley and hurried along the pavement on Main Street. Rab was almost dragging me, he was moving so fast, and my pulse picked up to match his pace. A few fallen leaves scudded around our feet, storefronts twinkled with Halloween decorations, and happiness bloomed in my chest. It was quaint, picturesque, and I wanted to capture this moment in my mind forever—the warm feel of Rab's palm under mine, his urgency in getting me home, the giddy excitement of finding our way back to each other filling me.

"Lyra?"

I jerked my head up to see Sloane tailing us in her car. I'd completely forgotten that she was meant to pick me up after the show.

"Is everything okay?"

"Oh, aye. Everything's good. I'm sorry, I should have called." I tugged Rab's hand, a bit breathless, and forced him to slow.

"I see. Rab, dear?" Sloane called.

Rab finally stopped and turned, a quick flash of annoyance in his eyes at being stopped making me smile.

"Please be careful with her. She's still recovering, remember?"

"Och, I'm a bloody eejit. Dragging you down the sidewalk. Have I hurt you?" Rab's hand went to my side, and I went dizzy at the touch of his hand at my waist. Need filled me.

"No," I said, too loudly, and lowered my voice. "No, it's fine. Really. Their healing magick is pretty incredible."

"You're going home with him?" Sloane called.

"Bloody hell, Sloane," I said, throwing my hand in the air. "Why not announce it to the whole town?"

"Oh, sorry. Right. That's me off to my own man. Let me know if you still need a ride tomorrow."

"I'll take care of her," Rab said, and I almost melted in a puddle at the street. My magick tingled.

"High heels. Loafers. Trainers. Clogs. Chelsea boots," I recited, and Rab grinned.

"Gotta run before this entire street turns into hedgehogs." Rab dragged me away, and I waved to Sloane as we crossed the street and turned the corner onto Rab's street.

"Rab."

"Wheesht. Just let me get you inside." Rab fumbled with his key at the door. "I need—"

Rab popped the door open and dragged me inside, slamming it closed behind me. And then my back was against the door and his mouth was on mine.

It was everything.

Everything.

It felt like all of my senses short-circuited at once, my mind going completely blank, and then everything narrowing to a singular point.

Rab.

His lips on mine, the heat of his kiss searing through me, and everything in my body roared back to life, and I knocked my elbow against a picture frame and sent it falling to the floor as I reached up to hook an arm around the back of his neck, pulling his mouth more tightly against mine.

"Shite," I breathed, breaking away to try to see if I'd broken the picture.

"Fuck the picture," Rab swore, capturing my lower lip with his mouth and sucking so hard my lip made a little popping sound when he let it go. "Bloody hell, Lyra. I want to eat you alive. I don't even know where to start. I'm mad with wanting you. I can't even—"

"Rab," I gasped against his mouth as his tongue slid against mine. I broke the kiss, panting. "I'm afraid . . . I'll turn your house . . ."

"Into a hedgehog?" Rab chuckled, the sound vibrating through me, and I pressed my breasts closer to his hard chest, brushing, loving the feel of his strength against all my softness. "Bloody hell, Lyra, you're going to . . . just hold. *Hold.* One second. I know how to handle this."

"With a condom, hopefully?" I asked, and Rab buried his face in my neck, laughing. And then he nipped at the sensitive skin there and need streaked through me. Arching my back against the door, I pressed myself against him, rubbing like a cat asking for cuddles.

"Shhh, just, hold. I have a spell. A protection spell." Rab unhooked my arm from around his neck and pulled me farther into his house.

A chittering noise stopped me.

"Oh no, Rab. I've made some more already." Damn it. There was no way that we could do anything. I really would turn the entire contents of his house into one massive . . . "Wait, what do you call a group of hedgehogs?"

"A prickle," Rab said, flipping the light on to his kitchen and going to the fridge. I stopped in my tracks and started laughing.

"Seriously?"

"For real." Rab took out a can of what looked like dog food, and I stared at him in confusion. "And you somehow have managed not to make any more hedgies. I just, well, I kept two of them. From that night. In the kitchen. Our kiss."

I stared at him, floored, as he moved to a pen on the floor I'd completely missed and spooned out some food for two tiny hedgehogs that were clamoring for his attention.

"You kept them?"

"I . . . well, yeah. I wanted . . . I don't know. It's stupid."

"No, Rab, tell me. We're done keeping things from each other." I put a hand on his shoulder and he looked up at me.

"I just wanted a reminder of the moment, I guess. A piece of you to hold on to."

"Oh, Rab." My throat went dry as my eyes filled.

"Right. Take the lass home and make her cry. That's one way to her heart." Rab dumped some more food into the pen and straightened, a frustrated look on his face. "Please don't cry. I didn't mean to—"

"No, it's just . . . It's really sweet."

"Sweet? I don't want to be sweet. I want to be strong. Manly. Able to lift you over my shoulder and carry you into my cave."

I laughed and looked down at myself as he put the food away. "I doubt you could lift me over your shoulder."

Rab slammed the refrigerator door and moved toward me, a feral look in his eyes, but stopped a second away from touching me.

"The spell. First, we do the spell. It's a spell used for protection when people with transmutation skills are just learning their magick. I'd forgotten about it, but was looking through my grimoire to see if there was anything to help you with your magick and found it. Repeat after me."

I nodded, doing my best to stay focused.

Rab's lips lifted in a sultry smile.

"Darling, you're massaging my chest."

Oh my goddess, I was. I just wanted to keep touching him.

"Right, sorry."

"Hold my hands. It seems your magick likes to use me as a conduit."

"I'd like to use you as a—"

"Focus, darling." Rab laughed. "What is, shall stay . . . until I say. No shift, no swirl, no change today. By thought made firm and will hold tight. My magick rests until just right."

My magick unfurled inside me, shimmering through my limbs and wrapping around me as I invoked the spell. Once finished, I met Rab's eyes, sinking into their mossy green depths.

"Now what?" I whispered.

"Now this." Rab bent, and I squealed as he lifted me into his arms and smacked my bum with his hand.

"Hey!" I laughed, taken completely off guard that he was able to carry me like this. The smack became a caress, and my insides went liquid as he slid his hands over my bum and down my thighs, the soft strokes sending heat rocketing through my body.

Soft light spilled across a floor with a simple navy knotted wool rug thrown over golden hardwood floors. And then my world righted as Rab laid me ever so gently down on the bed.

He could have tossed me like a sack of potatoes.

Instead, he lowered me softly to the mattress, like I was the most important thing in the world to him, and then he dropped to his knees before me.

"Lyra, I have dreamt of you countless times through the years. This still feels like a dream. That I could be here. Like this. With you." Rab unzipped my boots and slid them off my feet, his fingers trailing up my stockings. "Darling?"

"Aye?" My breath hitched as he drew lazy patterns on my inner thighs with his hands, and my legs twitched, widening of their own accord.

"How attached to these stockings are you?"

"Och, not at—"

A rip sounded and cool air hit my thighs, followed by the warmth of his mouth.

"Oh." I gasped, leaning back on my elbows as he rid me of the rest of my stockings and my underwear. Desire burst through me in fizzy little pops, and I shifted against the bed, pulling my skirt up as his mouth moved higher. His breath was hot against my skin as he softly kissed his way up my thigh, and when he reached the top, he started on the other thigh, making sure both legs were loved on. It was true, he was worshipping me, I realized, and let out a soft moan when his mouth finally found where I craved him most.

He licked deeply, savoring me as if I were the most delicate of desserts, and I arched against his mouth. My thighs trembled as he lapped at me, taking his time to figure out what I liked, and I cried out as he slid a finger inside of me.

"Oh, Rab, I can't . . ." Pressure built as he circled me with his tongue, mirroring the movement with his finger, and I shattered, coming apart around him, as he laughed into me. His laughter vibrated against me, carrying little bursts of pleasure through my body, and I laughed along with him even as I gripped his hair and pulled his head up to look at me.

"I need you," I said, simply but urgently.

"Bloody hell, Lyra. You're a goddess. *My* goddess." Rab stood and stripped his shirt off, and I blinked at him.

He was so mind-numbingly handsome. Broad shoulders tapered to a narrow waist, and muscles ridged his abdomen. I wanted to touch every inch of him. Preferably with my tongue.

I reached out my hands. "Gimmee," I demanded, and his smile was wicked.

"Let's get this dress off you. I suspect you'll be less than happy with me if I rip it."

"No, I wouldn't like that. I bought this in France." I stood up and turned, pulling my hair to the side, and shivered when his lips met the back of my neck. My body felt languid and excited, little pulses of pleasure keeping my nerves alight. Rab unzipped the back of my dress, and cool air hit my skin.

"Holy . . . hell, Lyra. Are you trying to give a man a heart attack?" Rab's voice at my back was a rasp in the dimly lit room, and I looked over my shoulder at him as my dress dropped to the floor. I stepped out and turned, and Rab froze, his eyes on my body.

"What?" I asked, looking down at myself. I had a matching pale pink silk set on—well, I'd *had* the set on, but my pants had disappeared with my stockings. Delicate lace edged the silk of my bra.

"You're a miracle. A walking fucking miracle," Rab choked out.

I reached up to cup my breasts.

"You like this bra?"

"I like you. And anything you put on your gorgeous body." Rab came forward, and where I'd thought he'd rush, he slowed instead.

I saw the moment his face twisted, anger flashing.

"Och, don't." I went to cover the jagged scar at my side. The stitches had already magically dissolved, but the scar was bright pink and puckered against the creamy white skin of my side.

"No," Rab said, taking my hand away. Bending, he pressed a soft kiss to the wound, tracing his hand lightly around it. "You're beautiful, Lyra. All of you. Even this. Do you still have pain? I shouldn't have carried you."

"Sloane's going to kill you." I tried to inject some levity, but his eyes came up to mine, his face serious.

"She should. I shouldn't have been so rough with you."

"You weren't rough, Rab. Truly. I've healed up quite a bit. Aside from this, that is." I looked down at the ugly scar.

"I could have lost you." The words were barely a whisper, but the pain on his face spoke volumes. His emotions filled me up, and I swallowed against the lump that had formed in my throat.

"I'm still here. Scarred and fabulous." I went to cover the scar with my hand, but Rab took my hand away, pressing a kiss to my palm before dropping it.

Running his hand softly up my side, he cupped my face. "You're the most beautiful woman in the world, Lyra. You're a goddess, bringing light, even in darkness. Knox doesn't have to light Briarhaven. He just needs to send you out in the square and the whole damn town would glow."

"Rab," I whispered, tilting my head up for his kiss. Tears welled. "You're too sweet. It's too much. I should—"

"No, love. Not now. This isn't the time for regrets. We're here now. With each other. And you, Lyra? You are my light."

"You've always been mine, Rab," I said, and he deepened his kiss. "You were the only thing I looked forward to. Every day."

"I know, Lyra. I know. I know what we were to each other." Rab looked up and held my gaze. "And I know what we can be to each other. I love you so much. Do you know that? Can you feel that?"

He took my hand and placed it on his chest, where his heart beat in a heavy rhythm.

"I love you too, Rab. I always have. There's never been another . . . not like you."

"Same, Lyra. Same. Even when I tried to forget you. Goddess knows I tried."

And then his lips were on mine, in the kiss to end all kisses, and I felt his love pour through me, all the way down to the very tips of my toes. My entire body trembled with need, and now that I finally had free rein, I stroked my hands across his chest, loving the feel of his strong muscles under my hands. He was built so exquisitely, a god in his own right, chiseled from stone. I arched backward as he buried his face in my breasts, his hands coming up to cup them, his thumbs stroking my nipples.

I went dizzy with need.

"I think . . . I need to . . ." I gasped, throwing my head back as he kissed my breasts, finding my nipples through the silk, his mouth wetting the material.

"Aye, lass. Settle back." Together, we eased backward onto the bed, Rab crawling after me, and I cried out as he brought his thigh up between my legs. Hard muscles rubbed against my sensitive skin as I rocked against him, and he reached beneath me to unhook my bra.

My breasts spilled free.

"I feel like I should genuflect." Rab's eyes were wide, drunk on the sight of my naked body, and it was the hottest thing I'd ever seen. It had always been him, the one I'd wanted to look at me this way.

"Rab?" I asked sweetly, even though my body throbbed with need.

"Aye?" Rab tore his eyes away from my body and looked up to me.

"Speaking of that condom . . . I hope you have one?" I trailed a finger down his chest and to the waistband of his jeans. "Because I want your mouth on mine and you inside me."

Rab groaned, his hands tightening at my waist, and buried his face in my neck as he shuddered in a deep breath.

"What the lass wants, the lass gets."

Rab rolled off me, and I instantly missed his weight against my body. But I admired the view as he stripped, his bum high and tight, thick muscles banding his shoulders. He protected us with a condom, and then he was back to bed, crawling over me until the delicious weight of him pressed me back into the pillows.

"I've missed you," Rab said. He kissed me, soft and sweet, and I sighed into his mouth, so many emotions playing through me. Desire for him, sadness over time lost together, all the what-ifs spiraling through me. Rab pulled back and his eyes softened. "Och, love. Don't."

"It's hard not to. We've missed out on so much."

"Maybe we had to," Rab said, nibbling at my lower lip. "To bring us back here again."

"That's a nice thought, isn't it?"

"You know what's another nice thought?" Rab asked, and I gasped as he rubbed himself against me. I was slick and ready, desperate to have him inside me.

"What's that?" I whispered against his lips.

"Doing this. Every day. Until the end of time." Rab laughed against my lips and then entered me in one long thrust. I gasped at the intrusion, my body opening and welcoming him in, and then I arched my hips against him. Clenching, I pulled him close, needing him there, and threw my head back against the pillow as he pinned me, refusing to move.

"Rab," I gasped, angling my hips, needing him to move.

"Och, the lass wants more, does she?" Rab angled himself over me and took a nipple into his mouth, biting lightly as I moaned. "Greedy, aren't you?"

"No." I gasped, laughing, and smacked him lightly on the shoulder. My gasp turned into a moan as he rocked, and then neither of us could speak as he thrust into me, sliding so deep that my body shook with need. He rolled his hips, his body hard to my soft, and slid in again, ever so softly, as he crooned words of love at my ear.

I'd craved him. For years. His touch, his laughter, the way he looked at me.

He'd always made me feel like I was the only person that mattered in the world.

Rab's focus was intense, his exploration thorough, his hands touching, stroking, caressing, while his mouth licked, his teeth scraping sensitive skin. And still he rocked into me, his rhythm precise, his control unmatched as he pulled me to the edge with him.

"Rab, I . . ."

"Go over with me, Lyra. Together." It was only then I saw the tic in Rab's jaw, the strain as he held himself back, waiting for me.

He'd always been waiting for me. My body convulsed as waves of pleasure washed through me. "Rab," I cried, needing his kiss, and his lips came down to mine as he found his own release.

"Lyra, it's always been you. Always you."

"Us. It's always been us." I gasped into his kiss.

And we collapsed together, neither of us willing to move apart, to break this moment that had brought us back together.

"Rab."

"Shhh, Lyra. Just a moment longer. Just like this. You and me, me and you. The way it's meant to be."

CHAPTER TWENTY-EIGHT

Lyra

Turns out, eating ice cream in bed after making love is an excellent idea.

As was using that ice cream for more than what would be sanctioned by the judges of *Bewitching Bake Off*. We'd stayed up wildly too late, laughing and indulging in each other, and collapsed in the early hours of the morning, curling into each other as we slept.

Somehow, Rab's spell had worked, and despite my uncontained desire for him, the contents of his house had remained exactly as they should be.

"Filming starts at one today," Rab said, burying his face in my hair as he wrapped his arms around me from the back. "Stay."

"I can't," I said, laughing and leaning back into him. His arms felt perfect around me, like I was home, and I still couldn't believe how much time we had missed out on together. "I need to shower and change. How will that look if I show up to set wearing the same thing as yesterday . . . minus the stockings?"

"Hot." Rab turned me to him and slid his mouth over mine. I leaned into him, craving his touch but hating to break this moment.

"Nope, you'll not distract me." I laughed up at him and pushed back, my hands caressing his chest of their own accord. He looked down at my hands, eyebrow raised. "Damn it, I can't stop touching you. I've missed you, Rab."

"Och, lass. I've missed you too. When you left, it just . . ." Rab stepped back and ran a hand through his hair, making a sound like a balloon deflating. "It took the wind right out of my sails. I had a hard time trusting again, after that. Women, at least."

"And between you and my dad leaving"—I held up a hand when Rab went to speak—"I know that's not the case now, but I thought you had left—I never dated seriously again. It was easy enough to blame the curse for my having to keep moving on. Not the fact that I wanted to leave before someone left me."

"Damn it, Lyra." Rab pulled me close for a hug. "I'd say that I'm upset for all the years you hurt, but a part of me is happy you never got this close to someone else. Not like what we have between us."

"No," I admitted, leaning my face into his shoulder and inhaling his soapy scent. "Never like us."

He held me just like that, rocking slightly back and forth, and happiness filled me as we stood there in his kitchen, Merry and Pippin racing in circles in their pen, the scent of coffee lingering in the air. This was exactly what I had always wanted. Rab, a little place to cook in, and a home base where I could stay and make friends and build a community. The curse had been a convenient excuse to keep running, but now that we finally had a chance to break it, I realized just how much I really wanted to put down roots.

I wanted to bake pies with Marcie.

Argue with my sisters over what to make for Sunday dinner.

Go to holiday-themed parties and be involved in planning community events in Briarhaven year-round.

Settle in with Rab. Maybe even start a family. I'd always wanted a family. Sloane and Nova had adjusted better to traveling all the time than I had, but I'd craved consistency more than anything else. Everywhere we'd landed, I'd always decorate and try to make it a home, even when Sloane had griped at me for spending money on things we couldn't take with us.

At the thought of a wee Rabbie running around, my eyes got a bit misty, and I realized just how far down the line my thoughts had scrambled. What I needed to do was get home, get in the shower, and pick a new outfit for today's filming. They were resetting the set decorations this morning for the final challenge, so we'd be cooking later into the day.

Not that it mattered much, as I glanced outside at the darkness that still hovered over Briarhaven.

"Right, best to crack on." I pulled back, and with one more quick kiss from Rab and a goodbye to Merry and Pippin, I grabbed my coat and purse and headed to the door. I already knew the inquisition that would be waiting for me when I got home, but I was too happy to really care.

"Are you sure I can't drive you?" Rab asked, leaning in the doorway with a cup of coffee in his hand. He looked adorably sleep rumpled.

"No, it's not a far walk, and I like to take in the fresh air."

Plus, I needed just a moment to myself before my sisters pounced on me and demanded every detail.

The morning was cool but not cold, the kind of crisp October air that nipped playfully at my skin and smelled faintly of wood-smoke and damp leaves. Overnight rain had left the pavement dark and glossy, leaves on the branches overhead just turning to gold, with some scattered across the street like confetti. I wandered slowly back home, unconcerned by the breeze tugging at my skirt, enjoying the hush of early morning before Briarhaven fully woke.

Halloween decorations were already out in force. One house had transformed their garden gnomes into a haunted party—tiny witch hats perched on their heads, cauldrons bubbling with fairy lights, and a gnome-sized banquet laid out on a makeshift wooden table. From what I could tell, the guests included everyone from a wizard gnome stirring a potion to an elf gnome offering a serene pumpkin-shaped lantern. Someone had even wired a small speaker beneath the display, and a soft Celtic jig drifted into the morning air, turning the whole scene into a whimsical, slightly chaotic autumn celebration.

Turning down our lane, I paused in front of my childhood home. Warm light spilled from the front windows, Broca's unmistakable touch evident in the enormous wreath bedecked with tiny mirrored pumpkins and dangling moon and star charms. A cluster of carved gourds sat grinning on the steps, and enchanted wisps of purple smoke curled lazily from one of them. We'd had a tough go of it growing up here, but despite everything, I still loved this wee house.

Humming, feeling as relaxed as I'd been in ages, I opened the door to chaos.

"Good—"

"Lyra! Iris is hurt." Nova's head shot up from where they were bent over the kitchen counter, and I slammed the door behind me, dropping my handbag and racing across the room. Iris, Broca's falcon, was a wizened familiar who had been with her for years.

"The owls," Broca said, fear in her eyes. Her thin shoulders trembled as she held her hands around Iris's prone body.

Her expression made my heart drop. Broca had always been our North Star. She was stalwart, pragmatic, and deeply loving. Her ability to find fun in the mundane was unmatched, and even when our parents were at their worst, Broca had provided the consistency we'd needed from an adult in our lives. I could count on one hand the number of times I'd seen her this shaken.

"Raven's on her way," Sloane said, paging through her grimoire. "But I have a spell now that might help."

"Do it," Broca ordered.

"We've got to hold our hands over her and visualize a glowing light surrounding her body."

"Just Sloane," Broca said, making room for me at the counter. I could barely look at wee Iris, her feathers were all in disarray, and blood marred her wing. "Lyra's magick is unreliable and Nova doesn't have hers yet."

I winced, but she was right. This wasn't the time to take chances with my misfiring magick. I took the book from Sloane.

"I'll read it out for you."

Sloane and Broca clasped hands over Iris, and I found the incantation in the book.

"'Life to limb, and breath to bone, mend what's broken, make it whole. From brink to bloom, let spirit rise, by earth and heart, this life be tied.'"

Soft light, like the warm glow of a candle in the window on a rainy night, bloomed from their clasped hands, and surrounded the falcon. At first, nothing happened, and worry dredged through me. Broca would be distraught without Iris.

And I would be to blame because I hadn't broken my curse yet.

Then the falcon shifted, a small movement at first, but enough to have my breath catch in my throat.

"It's working," Nova hissed and wrapped an arm through mine. I leaned into her, waiting and praying that their magick would be enough to bring wee Iris back from the brink of death.

When the falcon rolled and stumbled awkwardly to her feet, Broca let out the softest cry of relief, and tears filled my eyes. The falcon held one wing at an awkward angle, but at least she was alive and well. It was a step in the right direction, and I was certain that if Raven could help heal up my stab wound, she'd certainly be able to assist in setting a broken wing. And if not her, I had faith Henry could do it. I was starting to think that Henry could do anything.

"Oh, Iris. I was so worried," Broca said, reaching out to run a finger down the feathers at Iris's chest. "I know you're not fixed yet, but we'll get you the help you need. Raven's on the way. It's going to be just fine, my sweet old gal. Just fine indeed."

Iris bent and nuzzled her head against Broca's finger, nipping lightly at her hand with her beak, and the door popped open as Raven came in on the fly. Blue jumped up from his spot on the couch, barking out a soft poof of flame in surprise, and then slumped back when he saw who it was.

"I'm sorry, I'm sorry, I got here as soon as I could. I had to rush a few people out of the shop," Raven explained, dropping a large leather satchel on the couch. "Let me see her."

"We just did a rejuvenation spell that I found," Sloane explained, drawing Raven close. "But her wing still seems broken."

"Well done, you two." Raven beamed at Broca and Sloane like they were star pupils. "That's a spell that requires a level of healing that not many can do."

"Unless you love the patient," Broca murmured, still cooing to Iris.

"Also true." Raven pulled out a few bottles from her satchel. "Can I have a small bowl?"

"On it," I said, and dug in the drawers and cabinets for a bowl and spoon. Handing them over, I stepped back. "I'll just stay out of your way since my magick desperately wants to help."

"You can help." Raven looked over her shoulder at me.

"No, best not. I'm still royally messing recipes up. It's not that my magick isn't eager to help, it's just not really working at the moment. I mean, it works, but kind of like opposite day." I didn't want to insult my magick, as I could feel it shriveling inside me at my words, but I also wanted to be realistic with Raven about what the current state of affairs was.

"Luckily, I should be able to handle this on my own." Raven put a few drops into the bowl from a brown tincture bottle and then added a yellow liquid from a small blue bottle. She stirred clockwise with the spoon and muttered some words over it. The liquid shimmered in the bowl and then changed to a glittery poultice. "Come here, sweet thing."

Iris obediently hobbled forward and bent her head to Raven.

Raven crooned soft words, applying the poultice gently to the wing, a glimmer of light surrounding her hands as she did so. When finished, Raven straightened and looked to Broca.

"She'll need time and a safe space to rest while this bone knits back together."

"I have a space for her," Broca said, reaching out her arm so Iris could hop on. Broca steadied the bird with her other hand. "I'll just go get her settled."

Broca left for the back room, where Iris had a lush cage—with no door on it—and relief filled me.

"That would have been—"

"Horrific?" Sloane suggested, turning to me, her face grim. "Lyra, we need to do something. We can't go on like this."

"Don't you think I know?" I demanded, the tears I'd held back during the healing falling down my cheeks. "But I don't know what to do. I haven't had time to do anything. The filming takes up so much time, and the curse is only getting worse and—"

"Shhh, hush now. It's going to be just fine." Nova slung her arm around my shoulders. "Knock it off, Sloane. You know she's overly emotional since she obviously just shagged Rab. You can't dump everything on her right now."

"You shagged Rab?" Raven asked, surprise on her face. "I do believe I need details."

"Details later. Curse first." Sloane walked around the counter and gave me a kiss on the cheek. "Lyra, I love you. You know I love you. But we need you to focus now. I have your grimoire, but it's only revealing spells that it feels like, not anything that has been helpful. Which is typical of grimoires, as they will be tricky with anyone who isn't theirs."

"I need to—"

"You need to take some time over your coffee and see if you can find any spells that will help. Then you can shower and pick out a dress to wear today," Sloane said and handed me the book. Nerves filled me as I took my grimoire to the couch and dropped onto the soft cushions. It had been years since I'd been in school, but the similar feeling of needing to ace an exam settled over my shoulders as I flipped open the book.

For a moment, the words swam before my eyes, a gobbledygook of madness, and I pressed my lips together, tension banding my neck. Pulling my feet up under me, I dragged the soft blanket from the back of the couch over my lap, and Ruth flew downstairs and across the room to land on my lap.

I didn't want to disturb the healing. But is the bird okay?

"Aye, it sounds like she'll be just fine."

And you? Ruth's tiny eyes searched my expression, her little nose sniffing the air as her lavender whiskers wavered.

"I'm great. Was great. I don't know." I lowered my voice as Ruth came over and peered at the pages of the book. "I'm supposed to find a spell in here to break the curse, but I can't even read this."

Can't you?

"I can't . . ."

The words suddenly swam into place on the page, neatly lining themselves up in order so I could decipher them.

"Och, wait a minute. You're right. *I can.* Would you look at this? They're recipes. It's recipes," I turned and cried to my sisters who were huddled in the kitchen. They knew to give me space when I was doing any type of learning, because distractions made it almost impossible for me to focus. "I *can* read them."

"Isn't that grand?" Broca said, coming back into the room. The color had returned to her face, and she looked much more her usual robust self. "I wasn't sure if we'd need a deciphering spell like we did with Sloane's."

"Every grimoire is different," Raven said, packing up her bag. "Will you need me for this? If not, I do need to get back to the store. I just flipped the sign to Closed and ran out when you called."

"It will probably take a while for her to find the spell—er, recipe—needed. If it's in there at all," Sloane said. She gave Raven a hug. "Best for you to crack on and I'll call a meeting of the Charms if more power is needed."

"Good luck."

"Thank you, Raven. You're a miracle worker." Broca hugged Raven.

"Och, I barely did a thing. You'd already patched her up a treat when I came in." Raven paused and leaned over by my head on the way out. "And I'm still going to need those details on Rab."

"They shagged. What more do you need to know?" Nova dropped into a lounge chair, kicking her legs over the arm. "Or do you need a discussion on how babies are made? See, first—"

"I'm well versed in that department, thank you very much." Raven sailed out the door while Nova chuckled, clearly delighted with herself.

"There should be a law about you taking the piss before a certain number of cups of coffee in the morning," I said, glaring at her.

"I'd second that motion." Sloane joined me on the couch, her mug filled to the brim.

"You should try starting your day with a run," Nova suggested. "Wakes you right up so you can start taking the piss out of others almost immediately."

"I wonder if there is a recipe in here to shut up annoying sisters?" I asked and then gasped when the pages flipped of their own accord, landing on a recipe. "Recipe for quieting."

My mouth dropped open.

"Holy shite," Sloane breathed, putting her cup of coffee on the table and leaning forward. "Can you just ask it what you want and get the spell? That's . . . No way. That's so helpful."

"Does yours do this?" I asked, blinking at the recipe in shock.

"I don't think so. I've never tried, I guess." Sloane jumped up and grabbed her book. "Show me a spell for warming a home."

We all stared at the grimoire in her hands.

None of the pages moved.

"Nope, nothing." Sloane came back around the couch, and Broca crossed the room to take a seat.

"Grimoires are highly personalized. They adapt to what their owner needs."

"They do?" I glanced up at Broca, surprised. "I didn't realize."

"We all have strengths, dear. The grimoire will work in the best way possible for its owner. Remember, magick wants to be used."

Excitement coursed through me. Perhaps I'd been subconsciously avoiding this book because I'd been nervous about having to study and learn from it. But now, hearing that the grimoire wanted to work with me? Well, that changed things entirely. For the first time since stepping into my magick, I felt like I might be able to finally harness it in the way that I wanted to.

"Show me the spell for breaking my part of the bloodline curse that has haunted the MacGregors."

Ruth flew up to my shoulder and nestled in while we all waited. At first, nothing happened, but then the pages of the book began to flip slowly in my lap, as though someone were casually perusing the contents. Then, as though it had figured out where the spell was, the pages picked up speed until they stopped suddenly on a recipe with a sketch of a loaf of bread and two candles next to it.

"It's here," I said, bouncing in my seat. "I have it. I have the recipe."

"Is it complicated?" Broca said, leaning forward.

"Let's have a look." I scanned the recipe, noting the ingredients, and then looked up. "Largely, the ingredients are what I have on hand. I do need a black candle and a white candle. But it also says it is a sisterhood recipe. And, well, we'll need a drop of blood from each of the three of us."

"But not the whole town?" Sloane asked. To break her part of the curse, Knox had rounded up the whole town, and everyone had contributed a drop of blood.

"Nope, just us, it says."

"And is there an incantation? Once you've done your recipe?" Broca asked.

"Yes, in two parts. It looks like everything will need to be done in order."

"So? What's stopping us?" Sloane asked. Blue bellied his way over to her on the couch, spreading his back legs out so he was splooted between me and Sloane, the best of both worlds. I scratched his bum while I thought about it, and Sloane rubbed his ears.

"Uh, nothing, I guess? It just feels like . . . Shouldn't we do something more formal? Call the Charms? Make sure the moon is in the right phase? I dunno." I bit my lower lip as nerves made my stomach twist.

"While I understand why you'd say that, Lyra, I do think we need to move as quickly as we can." Broca gave me a sympathetic smile, but it wasn't hard to spot the tension in her face. "Ruth and Iris are particularly vulnerable to the owls at the moment, as I imagine many other familiars are as well. We need get them back up to their normal hunting grounds and on their normal rhythms. They're hurting too."

"Right, okay. Right," I repeated, my thoughts scrambling. "Um."

"Just breathe," Sloane said, knowing how I could get under pressure. "Look at the list of ingredients and tell us what to get."

"Ingredients. Got it." I looked down at the book. "Honey, boiling water, salt, a loaf of bread, a bowl, candles, and, well, our blood."

"I'll get the candles." Nova jumped up and went into the back room, which also doubled as a storage pantry for any overflow. I heard her croon soft words to Iris while she was back there, and then she came out, two pillar candles clasped in her hand.

"I'll put the kettle on," Sloane said and went to the kitchen. Blue, seeing her direction, hopped up and air-waddled after her in hopes of finding cheese.

"We've got a nice baguette. Will that suit? Or do you need a particular type of bread?" Broca rose and followed Sloane to the kitchen.

I checked the recipe, but it did not specify.

Within minutes we were settled around the dining table, with the bread placed between one black and one white pillar candle. A bowl had been placed in front of the bread, silver needles to prick our fingers, a spoon to stir, honey, salt, and a kettle of boiling water at the ready.

I took a seat at the head of the table, facing directly at the bread and candles, while Broca and Sloane sat on one side and Nova on the other.

"Read it out, Lyra." Broca patted my hand gently.

"Right, so first I'll light the black candle to signal strength and power to cut the cord of the curse. And then I'll light the white candle for healing and renewal." I took a deep breath and reached for my magick, and it unfurled inside me, all but dancing to the surface, so that my hands trembled slightly as I struck the match and lit the candles.

"'Next, each sister must place a hand on the bread and speak something about what the curse has taken from them or how it has hurt them. This acknowledges the curse and gives it form,'" I read out. Taking a deep breath, I laid my hand on top of the bread.

"It took years away from my love." I kept my focus on the bread, refusing to let tears fill my eyes, needing to keep a hold on my magick, which was zinging about my body.

"It took my childhood," Nova said, adding her hand on top of mine.

"And it took my freedom of choice." Sloane laid her hand on top. Everyone turned to look at me, but I was still reeling at how heavy their words were. We didn't talk about it, not really, since there had never seemed like there was much we could do about the curse. The past was the past, and we had to look forward, accepting whatever we came up against. So to articulate in such broad but harsh strokes made me understand even more deeply what a burden this curse was to ourselves and others.

"Now we salt the bread together." I indicated the bowl of salt, and we all drizzled salt over the bread while I read out loud. "'No jealousy, no broken vow, we salt the wound and heal it now.'"

The flames grew higher on the candles, and tiny sparks buzzed around the flame.

"Now, a drop of blood each, directly onto the bread," I said. Nova went first, pricking her hand and squeezing a single deep red drop onto the bread. I followed, barely feeling the prick of the needle on my skin, so focused was I on trying to keep my magick in line. It felt like I was trying to net a thousand buzzing bees, zipping around inside me. Sloane followed, pressing the blood into the bread and sealing it.

"Now for honey." Broca passed me a pot of honey, and I took the little wooden spoon and drizzled honey on the bread. "'By blood and sweet, the circle complete. From curse set free, our line shall be.'"

The flames grew even higher, and Nova's eyes widened, but she didn't say anything.

I tore the bread into little pieces and poured the boiling water over it. Reaching for the spoon, I stirred clockwise as I recited the final steps of the recipe.

"'By hearth and hand, by blood and flame, we break the curse and heal our name. From sister to sister, the bond is true. The heart is mended, the bloodline made new.'"

I barely had time to duck when the bowl flipped, flying toward me, splattering boiling hot water across my arms. I shrieked, and Sloane was up, already moving, but there was nothing to be done.

"Ow, ow, ow," I cried, tears springing to my eyes. My skin was scalded and my hopes dashed. "I'm never going to get this right."

"Shhh, it's okay, Lyra. It's okay. Come with me, over to the faucet, now." Sloane dragged me up and over to the kitchen, pushing my arms under the tap. There she ran tepid water over my arms while Nova called Raven.

"I should have cast a circle for protection," Broca said, her hands clasped against her chest. "What was I thinking? I know better."

"It's not your fault," I said, tears streaming down my cheeks and mingling with the water running over my burns. "I'm a failure. I'm never going to learn how to be a real witch. It was stupid of me to be excited about it, and stupid of me to think I could actually learn how to do it well. My magick is messed up for a reason. It knows that I'll never be good enough."

"Wheesht," Broca said, getting up and striding briskly over to the kitchen. She put her arm around my shoulders. "I'll not have you talk about my favorite granddaughter that way."

"Hey!" Sloane and Nova both said, and despite the pain I was in, I choked out a laugh.

"Your magick isn't working because of the curse, Lyra. This has nothing to do with who you are or how you learn. Remember, I said your magick wants to be used. It wants to work with you. Tell me, how does your magick feel inside you right now?"

I closed my eyes while the water ran over my wrists and realized that my magick was no longer zinging happily around inside me. Instead, it had withdrawn, curling back up into a ball, as though it was deeply sad and needed a rest.

"It's sad, I think?"

"Exactly. Your magick is yours to use. It will never deliberately hurt you or put you in harm's way. This has everything do with the curse and nothing to do with you. But the problem is, we have a solution and we don't know how to use it."

"And, um, not to add any stress, but didn't you say you had to film at one o'clock today?" Nova asked, and my head whipped up to see the clock.

"It's almost one o'clock? When did that happen?" I cried, pulling my hands from the water. Large red welts were visible on my skin.

"You can't bake like that, Lyra." Sloane was already moving toward the first aid kit, which was still out on the counter from helping Iris. "Let me bandage you."

"Nova. Go pick a dress, please. I need to take the world's fastest shower and then get ready."

"If you make it a cold one, I'll bandage you after?" Sloane asked, and I nodded. My heart hammered in my chest. There had been just too many things in a short period of time. The memory with Rab, getting stabbed, falling for Rab again, getting burned, Iris getting hurt . . . I wasn't sure how to process any of it. It was like I was watching a movie on fast-forward and didn't know how to react.

How to feel.

All I knew was that I couldn't leave Rab hanging, not again, and I ran upstairs without another word.

CHAPTER TWENTY-NINE

Rab

"We should just film. It's going to be great for the viewers who are watching their romance arc. She doesn't show up? To the final?"

I closed my eyes and pretended not to hear Kelly whispering gleefully with Vaughn behind the cameras.

It was now an hour and a half past when we were meant to film, Lyra hadn't answered any of my—or anyone else's—calls, and Vaughn was livid.

I couldn't lie, it had hurt when she hadn't picked up my call.

Or answered any of my texts.

After all these years of studiously ignoring each other, only to have her be unavailable the first time that I needed to reach her . . . had stung. I was doing my best to not let it show, but Kelly's excited prodding wasn't particularly helping me keep a cool head about it.

"Did you two have a fight?" Kelly came over to my table and asked me the same question she'd already asked me three times. But this time, the cameras were rolling. Apparently, they thought my heartache would increase their ratings. "Trouble in paradise? Let me guess . . . you got her the wrong present for Christmas?" Kelly tapped a red-painted nail to her ring finger and winked at the cameras.

I rolled my eyes. "We didn't have a fight, and no, I haven't gotten her anything for Christmas."

Kelly gave Nevin a knowing look.

"Well, lad, just a tip from your old pal Nevin here." Nevin grinned, hamming it up for the cameras. "Most women are hoping for something glittery under the tree."

"Like a snow globe?" I asked, widening my eyes and pretending to play dumb.

"Well, now, there's nothing wrong with a snow globe for Christmas, is there?" Kelly intercepted what was surely going to be Nevin's teardown of my choice of gifts, gently reminding him he was currently filming a Christmas special, so a snow globe would presumably be very on theme.

"Of course, of course. Much like this beautiful set our decorators have designed for us. Isn't it lovely, everyone?" Nevin held his hands out, and the cameras panned away from me toward the elaborate set that the designers had built for the last day of shooting.

We might as well have been inside a snow globe. The backdrop was rolling hills covered in snow, silvery tinsel with delicate shimmering strands crisscrossed the ceiling, and gorgeous fir trees were clustered behind and thoroughly covered in twinkle lights and silver bows. Occasionally, fake snow was puffed into the air at the side of the room and floated gently down among the tinsel, adding to the sparkling snowy effect in the test kitchen.

Marcie had almost had a fit.

Even now, I could see her just off camera, looking like she was ready to fight Vaughn in a cage match. I got the impression that she hadn't expected her bakery to be so thoroughly transformed, and she was ready to go back to life as usual, without so many people in her space.

"Don't worry, lad." I turned to see Henry, who had sidled around the front of his table and come to my side, while his partner from the bookstore eagerly discussed her favorite holiday recipe books. "She'll show."

"I hope so." I pretended nonchalance, but instead my emotions were swirling like crazy. *It's not the same as before.* But . . . it was taking all of my willpower not to flash back to the boy I'd been at sixteen, waiting on Lyra to show. I'd been so gutted then. And so angry since. Now, though, I was being filmed, and a lot of other people in the magickal world were obsessed with this reality show. *But where is she?*

"She will, lad. She will." Henry patted my arm.

I didn't know what to say. Lyra wouldn't just leave me hanging, not with the whole magickal world watching, but I wasn't sure what to think right now.

I swallowed, worry twisting my stomach. I had to believe that this wasn't intentional, but the timing? A small voice that was becoming increasingly louder as time went on kept insisting she was doing this on purpose.

I hated thinking that about her.

"Lad. I can see you spiraling," Henry whispered, and I snapped back to attention, looking down at the kindhearted ogre. "Don't think about the past. Think of Lyra. In the now. Would she do this to you?"

"No," I said automatically.

"Exactly. So something else is up."

"Maybe she fell asleep?" I said. I had kept her up much of the night, unable to keep my hands off her.

"Henry, how are you feeling about your odds today?" Kelly asked, drawing Henry back to his table and team while I went back to talking myself out of leaving the show to go find Lyra and demand an explanation from her.

"Do yourself a favor and steer clear of the MacGregors," Mandy told me, pitching her voice low as she arranged bowls in a neat little row in front of her. "Messy witches. The whole lot of them."

"I'd rather a messy witch than a bitter one," I said, glaring so hard at Mandy that she shut her mouth and turned her back to me. How dare she insult Lyra? The woman who was sunshine in a bottle?

"Cut!" Vaughn called. "Lyra, we were filming."

"I know, I'm sorry. I didn't want to rush out, but if you haven't started the challenge yet, I'd still like to join," Lyra said.

I whirled to see Lyra just off set, standing in the hallway, wringing her hands. She wore a deep purple long-sleeved dress with sparkly silver threads, and her hair was pulled back from her head in a high ponytail. Worry creased her pretty face.

My heart ballooned.

Vaughn sighed and then looked to Kelly and Nevin.

"It will film better with her on it. The cameras love her, and the viewers will be dying to know if she can get her magick under control enough to finish the contest. I say we let her on," Nevin said, straightening his red tartan bow tie.

"Fine by me." Kelly yawned. "I just want to wrap this up so I can get a cocktail and be done with work for the year."

"We're delighted to hear how enthused you are with your job," Vaughn drawled, and tapped his clipboard with his pen. "Right, let's crack on. Take your place, Lyra."

Lyra rushed forward, her face all apologies, and I didn't even care what had happened, I was just so happy to see her. As soon as she was at the table, I pulled her into my arms and dropped my forehead to hers, brushing a soft kiss over her lips. Cameras be damned.

"Damn it, hold that, hold that," Vaughn ordered, snapping his fingers at the cameras to get them rolling. "Can you do that again?"

"Nope," I said, and Lyra laughed. I kept my voice low. "I called you."

"Phone is dead. You didn't have a charger for it, remember?" Lyra whispered.

Of course. One of the reasons she'd gone home was to charge her phone.

"Lyra," Kelly said, drawing us apart and reminding us we were filming. "A bit of a dramatic entrance today, wouldn't you say? Care to tell us why you were late?"

"My phone died, and I didn't get a lot of sleep last night," Lyra said, and then her cheeks flushed as she realized what she'd admitted to the entire world on camera.

"There's a good lad," Henry called, and I choked back a laugh.

"If it's all the same to you," Kelly said, rolling her eyes at Lyra, "the rest of us wouldn't mind cracking on with today's challenge."

"Of course, please proceed. I'm excited to see what we're making for the final challenge," Lyra said smoothly, fidgeting with her sleeve. I glanced down to see a bandage poking out from the edge of the sleeve before she pulled the fabric down to cover it.

Why was she bandaged? It hadn't been a regular plaster, either, but instead the white surgical wrap used for more serious wounds.

Concern filled me, and I turned to Lyra, whose eyes rounded when she saw the expression on my face.

"Not now. *Please*," Lyra whispered, barely opening her lips, and fury whipped through me. Something had happened. Something that had harmed her.

Dragging a deep breath in through my nostrils, I worked to calm myself down and focus on what Kelly was saying, even though I was more than ready to murder anyone who had hurt Lyra.

"Contestants. Today is your biggest challenge yet. The theme? Twelve Days of Christmas," Nevin called, rubbing his hands together in excitement. "Not only will this be your most complex challenge, but it will also require your very highest levels of magick." Felicity groaned, putting her hands over her face.

Worry shadowed Lyra's face, and I reached out to take her hand while the judges continued to explain the challenge. I didn't care if the cameras were trained on us, or zooming in on our hands. I would shout from the rooftops that Lyra was mine. We'd been apart for too long to be shy about hiding what we were to each other now.

"In honor of the 'Twelve Days of Christmas' song, you'll need to bake twelve different pastries or desserts, all of which perform something magickal when presented to us. You'll be given two extra hours for this challenge today, for a total baking time of five hours." Kelly slanted an annoyed look at Lyra. "Which is why being on time is so important."

"Maybe they should get a penalty for delaying us all?" Mandy suggested.

"Oh, that's a—" Kelly's eyes brightened.

"No," Vaughn called. "Carry on as normal."

"As I said, you'll be given extra time for this challenge, but, with that being said . . . time starts now, everyone," Nevin said, and chaos erupted in the kitchen. "Remember to wow us!"

"Lyra, what—"

"There's no time, and I'm not talking about it here," Lyra whispered, bending to pull spices off the shelves. "I'm fine, I promise you. Let's just get through this."

"You'll tell me, though?"

"Of course." Lyra paused to look up at me. "I wouldn't hide anything from you, Rab. It's just not something I want to discuss on camera."

Relieved that at least I would get the story, I set aside my worries and helped Lyra pull ingredients onto the table. I had no idea how to make a pastry, let alone twelve of them, so I'd be relying heavily on her for help.

"Let's write this down," Lyra decided, grabbing a paper and pen. "Otherwise I'm going to get wildly off track."

"I'll take notes. Just talk it out," I said, knowing Lyra preferred to talk through things rather than write them down.

"I say we stick to the song and try to create stuff themed for that." Lyra looked at me, and I nodded in agreement.

"At least that will give us some framework." How the hell were we going to make twelve different things this quickly?

"It needs to be stuff that we can use a lot of the same ingredients for, but each item has its own magick." Lyra tapped a finger against her lush mouth, and I lost my train of thought as I remembered sinking into all of her softness last night.

"Rab?" Lyra snapped her fingers in my face, and I realized I was just openly staring at her.

"Och, bloody hell. Right, give it to me." I waved the pad of paper in the air.

"Here's what we're going to make: pear hand pies, dove-shaped sugar cookies, mini egg custard tarts, chocolate ganache truffles, shortbread rings, cream-filled pastry puffs, swan profiteroles, milk biscuits, spiced gingerbread cutouts, mini sponge cakes, cinnamon breadsticks, and chocolate drum cakes." Lyra ticked each off on her finger, and I scrambled to keep up with the list.

"This sounds . . . impossible." I looked down at the list in awe. We were just meant to casually make all these and infuse them with a magickal element? Like no big deal? It seemed to me this challenge was deliberately set up for us to fail. And not just our team, but all of us. Was that the entire purpose of reality shows? To delight in people's failures?

"It's not. We've got this." Lyra's brow furrowed as she inventoried her supplies.

Or maybe this was all about rooting for the underdog. And Lyra was most definitely the underdog in this competition. But I could help her win. My competitive spirit rose, and I leaned in, pen at the paper.

"Tell me what you're thinking for the magickal elements," I said.

By the time she'd listed it all off, I was nodding along, but also in complete awe of her ability to come up with these ideas. There was no way that I would have been able to do this competition on my own. Granted, I never would have signed up for this competition if I'd had to bake on my own, but still, Lyra's ideas were incredible.

Just like her.

Leaning over, I kissed her cheek.

"I want you to know that I think you're incredible. Let's do the spell we did last night to contain your magick. I think we can adapt it a bit for this situation, and then, I've noticed that when you use me as a conduit, your magick flows better. I think that I ground you."

Lyra stopped in her tracks, turning to me, her mouth dropped open.

"*You*," Lyra breathed.

"Me," I agreed, tapping a finger at my chest, not certain where was going.

"You. Duh, oh my goddess. *Duh.* Why didn't I see this before? Of course—*you're* the answer."

"Um, I'm not sure what the question is, but I do like being the answer," I admitted. "Care to clue a lad in?"

"I'll tell you later," Lyra said, stacking ingredients and opening spice jars. "We've got to get started."

"Quick, repeat after me." I gripped Lyra's hands and bent down to whisper in her ear. "By root and stone, by breath and flame, I call my power, I call my name. No surge, no spill, let balance stay, my will is steady, night and day."

Lyra repeated the words, and I felt the shift inside me as our magick melded and hers flowed through me. I grounded myself, happy to act as her conduit, and waited for instructions.

"Right, okay." Lyra nodded to herself, blowing out a breath. "This feels good. It feels right. I think we can do this."

"I know we can do this," I amended.

"Let's crack on." Lyra reached for the eggs, and for a second worry flashed across her face, and despite my confidence in her, I did move my head out of firing range when she cracked the first egg into the bowl.

The egg landed with a plop, zero explosions to be had, and Lyra looked up at me, excitement in her eyes.

"Holy shite, Rab, it's working."

"Keep going, love. We've got a lot to do. Order me about."

"Right, grab the flour and a bowl."

Four and a half hours later, the clock was ticking down, and the entire room was in a frenzy. Long ago had we abandoned any semblance of trying to act professional or be polite for the cameras. There was shouting. There was cursing. There were devasting losses as various pastries deflated before they were meant to.

At one point I was certain I'd even seen Mandy wipe a tear away with the back of her hand. When I'd raised an eyebrow at her, she'd only snarled at me.

"It's sweat, okay? Bloody roasting in here."

"Uh-huh," I said, turning back in time to catch a bowl from falling off our table.

Mostly, Lyra's magick held. And bloody hell, did we need it to. Creating this many desserts in this time required a level of magick and spells that was taxing for even the most experienced magickals in the room. We had a few minor mishaps—like when the baking chocolate melted into a puddle—but otherwise, we were cruising along, and Lyra plated the very last dessert just as the timer went.

"That's time! Contestants, step back from your tables," Kelly called. "That means you, Felicity."

"But . . ." Felicity's shoulders slumped, and she backed up.

"We did it." Lyra turned to me, her smile as bright as a lighthouse beacon in the dark night. "I can't believe we finished in time." Tendrils of hair that had escaped her ponytail curled around her face, and sweat dampened her brow. Pink flushed her cheeks, and her lip gloss had long worn off.

She'd never looked sexier to me.

"You did it," I said, turning as the judges approached our table.

"Lyra and Rab," Nevin said, steepling his fingers in front of him and bending over to look at our assortment of treats, "it looks like you took a different tactic this challenge. Care to explain?"

"We've been working on grounding Lyra's magick, to keep it from misfiring. It seemed to serve us really well in this challenge," I said, putting a hand to Lyra's back.

"It is significantly less destroyed in here, which I am sure the set designers are grateful for," Kelly acknowledged, leaning over the table. "Shall we give these a go?"

"Please do." Lyra beamed. "The first is a spiced pear hand pie."

We watched as Kelly and Nevin cut into the pie, and when the steam escaped, it formed the shape of a partridge before flying away.

"Clever," Nevin admitted.

"Next, dove-shaped sugar cookies." Lyra waited until Nevin bit into one and then laughed when the sugar from the cookie exploded into tiny sugar feathers that floated down to the floor.

"That's fun," Kelly said.

"And tasty." Nevin saluted us with the cookie.

"Then we have mini egg custard tarts," I read from the list and waited while the judges cut into the tart to reveal a glowing egg center. Their sounds of approval made a smile bloom on Lyra's face, and I could barely take my eyes off her.

"Next are four chocolate ganache truffles." Lyra waited until the judges bit into them and beautiful birdsong filled the air.

"Singing truffles—aren't those fun?" Kelly asked. She'd transitioned from being snarky to invested in the outcome of this challenge, and I hoped we'd continue to impress her.

"Five golden rings." Lyra pointed to the shortbread rings, which, when activated, floated into the air and did a complicated dance before dropping back to the plate.

"Easy but effective," Nevin decided.

"Six geese a-laying." Lyra indicated the cream puffs, and when the judges bit into them, an explosion of sugar crystals dusted their mouths. This one had them laughing so hard, they both doubled over, slapping each other's backs.

"I so was not expecting that." Nevin wiped his eyes.

"Swan profiteroles." Lyra pointed to where pastries swam in a dish of cream, leaving a trail of red-and-gold-colored waves in their wake.

"Honestly? Stunning." Kelly was starting to become our biggest cheerleader.

"Milk biscuits for eight maids a-milking," I said, pointing to that tray. When the judges bit in, the biscuits began to hum, as though they were humming a song while they worked.

"Spiced gingerbread cutouts," Lyra said, pointing to the gingerbread cookies, which promptly jumped up from the plate and began to dance. "Nine ladies dancing."

"Mini sponge cakes," I added, and the sponge cakes began to pulse and bounce, leaping across the plate.

"Cinnamon breadsticks," Lyra said. We waited until the judges cracked them in half to take a bite, and a haunting piping tune filled the air.

"And finally"—Lyra beamed, offering the plate with the chocolate-covered cakes on it—"twelve drummers drumming."

The cookies began to wobble on the plate, drumbeats filling the air to match the piping, and both judges began to clap.

"Bravo!" Nevin shouted, without a hint of sarcasm in his tone. He seemed to be genuinely pleased with what we'd turned out. "I must say, highly unexpected and wildly effective."

"Well done, you two. I'm impressed," Kelly said, and they moved on to the next table.

"Holy shite, we did it." I whirled to Lyra, who had an expression of disbelief on her face. Grabbing her arms, I shook her in excitement and then stopped when she winced. "Bloody hell, I'm sorry—"

"No, no. It's fine. I promise. I'm so proud of myself. Of us. I can't believe we did it." Lyra took my hands and bounced up and down, and I enjoyed the bouncing a little too much, because she stopped and gave me a stern look.

"Not here, Rab."

"Right, sorry. I'm so proud of you. Just look at this." I gestured to the table of treats. "You did this."

Lyra leaned into me, and I felt like my heart might explode. "No, Rab. We did this."

"Jeez, get a room, you two," Mandy sniped.

"Wheesht, Mandy," Lyra and I said in unison, and we burst out laughing.

CHAPTER THIRTY

Lyra

We didn't win *Bewitching Bake Off*.

Henry edged us out with mince pies that formed a fire-breathing dragon, and honestly? I was happy for him. If we had to lose, it *should* be to Henry. Even so, I couldn't help but feel like I'd won anyway, since finally, *finally*, my magick had worked in tandem with me.

And, goddess, it had felt good.

Now I understood how some witches could get drunk on their power. It had felt incredible to have the magick flow through me and actually do what I instructed it to do. Not only was I happy, but my magick was happy too.

We'd stayed after, having a wrap-up drink with the crew to celebrate, though I could tell that Rab was all but vibrating with the need to pull me out of there. I didn't want to break up the celebration, though, and I just wanted to relish in the moment of finally feeling like a normal witch. Eventually, though, production called it quits.

"All right, everyone, thank you so much for your participation on the show," Vaughn said, raising a glass of whisky to us. "It's going to be a belter of a special, I'll tell you that much. Our editors have already started working on the earlier challenges, and we'll be live just before Christmas."

We all applauded, and then the crew went into break-down mode and people drifted away.

"Lyra." Vaughn caught me as I turned. "I just wanted to say, really well done. Truly. I wasn't sure you'd be able to bring it around, but you had a cracking last round. Well done, you."

"Thank you." I beamed up at him, happiness a fluttery little bird in my chest. "I'm really happy with how it turned out."

"Say, I was wondering . . ." Vaughn cleared his throat as Rab came up and wrapped his arm around my waist.

"Wondering what?" Rab asked, giving Vaughn a pointed look.

"If the pub will still serve food this late?" Vaughn asked, and I bit back a smile as Rab's arm tightened around my waist.

"Should do. They're open until ten."

"Noted. Best to run, then." Vaughn checked his watch and waved us away.

"You wouldn't have gone out with him, would you?" Rab drew me away.

"Honestly? When I first met him, yes, I probably would have." He'd given me the ick after a few days of knowing him, though. But that wasn't what Rab was asking, and I needed to speak into that space. "His biggest appeal was that he didn't live here. I haven't dated since I came back home." I sighed, and Rab stopped me outside the bakery, where a brisk wind whipped my hair back from my face.

"You haven't dated anyone here since you came back? Why?"

"I . . ." I shrugged, feeling awkward. "Because it's a small town. People talk."

"So?"

"And I didn't want you to hear I was dating anyone," I admitted. "And, well, I didn't want to date here. If it wasn't you."

"Lyra." My name on Rab's lips was soft, as was the lingering kiss he pressed to my lips. The show be damned, I could have stood there for hours, safe in his arms. "I couldn't even pretend anyone else would ever matter. You're everything to me."

"I'm so sorry I was late." I drew back, my brow furrowing as I looked up at him in the soft light of the lantern behind the test kitchen. "I know how that must have looked to you . . . like last time."

"I'll admit, it ran through my head a few times," Rab said, turning my hands to press a kiss to each palm. "It didn't help that Kelly was pointing arrows your way the whole time, but I knew it wasn't like all those years ago. We hadn't made specific future plans, you weren't leaving me wondering why you'd left me, and I didn't have my parents in my ear suggesting I didn't know my own heart. It wasn't the same, darling. I wasn't as . . . invested, if that makes sense."

"Yeah, that does make sense. I was just so frustrated when I realized how late I was going to be and that I couldn't reach you. I knew you wouldn't have had your phone on you, too, so I was so worried."

"We're okay. My fears might pop up occasionally in the future. I do trust you—I know that now. I think I was rattled because it was so quick after we'd reunited and, I guess, it's hard to break that pattern of thought."

"I understand," I said, taking his hand and tugging him with me. "I have the same issue. I always want to smooth over any conflict, and I'm half convinced that the people I love will always leave me."

Rab pulled up short at that. We'd just turned the corner onto Main Street, and a few burnished leaves drifted down, nature's glitter, as a soft breeze shook the trees.

"Because of me?" Rab asked, reaching out to brush a leaf from my shoulder.

"Aye. And my dad." I shrugged. Though I tried to be indifferent to the traumas of the past, they'd caught up to me more than I'd care to admit.

"I'd never leave you, Lyra." Rab gripped my hands, his voice resonating through me. "So long as we just talk to each other. All of this could have been avoided if one of us had been bold enough to reach out. To track the other down. That's a huge life lesson to us, isn't it? Don't assume the worst of each other when a conversation could resolve so many misunderstandings?"

"Aye, it is." I didn't miss his meaning and glanced down at my arms. "So . . . I got hurt this morning."

"Who do I have to kill?" Rab asked, his eyes sharpening, his face going devoid of expression. It was actually quite terrifying, and I shivered at the thought of him defending me.

"Um, well, in this case it would be me, or, I guess, a woman long dead," I said. At the question on his face, I rushed forward to explain what had happened. By the time I was finished, Rab was pulling me to him in another hug.

"You poor thing. And you didn't treat your arms?" Rab worried. "Damn it, and I grabbed them by accident. I'm so sorry, Lyra."

"No, it's fine. Really. Raven has dropped a salve she swears by at the house, and I can administer it now." My arms were in pain, there was no denying that, though I thought I'd done a fairly good job of hiding it during filming. But now that the adrenaline rush of the challenge was over, the pain had returned, sharper than before. "I'd like you to come with me, if you wouldn't mind? I think I need your help."

"Can you give me ten minutes to feed Merry and Pippin?" Rab asked, and my heart melted as I realized what a good man he was.

"Of course, a quick pit stop."

I knew the recipe for breaking the curse had called for my sisters' help, but my magick wasn't working unless I was with Rab. The only solution I could see was to use him as my conduit and pray that was enough to change the outcome of the spell. Now I just had to convince him to let me try it again.

A half hour later, after feeding a delighted Merry and Pippin, we were walking into my house, where Sloane, Nova, and Broca all waited for me. Ruth was chilling on Nova's shoulder, arguing with her over something Nova was drawing on her iPad, and Blue popped up from Sloane's lap when we came through the door.

An old episode of *Bewitching Bake Off* ran on the television.

"You're watching the show!" I exclaimed, surprised that my sisters would watch it.

"Of course we are." Broca sniffed. She was curled up in the lounge chair in a screaming-pink jumper and gray wool trousers. "That Kelly is a real bitch."

Rab choked on a laugh next to me, and my smile widened.

"Honestly? Aye, she is." I laughed out loud when my sisters looked at me in shock. It was so rare for me to admit anyone else's faults. Ruth fluttered over and surprised us both when she chose to land on Rab's shoulder.

I like this one, Lyra. You should keep him.

My grin widened.

"How'd it go today?" Sloane jumped up and went to the counter, coming back with a small glass jar. "I was really worried about you."

"She almost didn't let me come in," I explained to Rab and pushed my sleeves up so Sloane could take off my bandages.

"Lyra." Rab sucked in a breath of surprise when he saw the burns. "How on earth were you able to bake for hours with those injuries? You must have been in so much pain."

Angry welts, some blistering, stood out against my skin, but I just shrugged, too happy with the day to let it worry me.

"The show must go on."

"Raven swears by this. She says it heals burns so fast you'll barely notice a mark in a matter of days." Sloane unscrewed the jar and lightly covered my burns with the golden salve. Instantly, my burns tingled and then cooled, as though the salve was sucking the heat from the skin.

"Wow, I can already feel it working. She's incredible, isn't she?"

"The best in the business. And she's still so young," Broca said, turning to me. "Have you had dinner? We put some food on just in case."

"We haven't, but, um . . ." I glanced to Rab and worked myself up for an argument of convincing him to let me try the spell again. "I think we should try the curse-breaking spell. Together."

"Nope," Rab said, shaking his head. "What if the boiling water leaps at you? I can't have you getting burned—"

"Wait, just let me finish." Blue walked across the couch and stretched up so his paws were hanging over the back, his wings tucked down. I scratched his ears, laughing down at his smiling face. "Rab helped me today. He's able to ground me, to act as a conduit for my magick, and we cooked almost flawlessly. With magick."

"*Almost* flawlessly," Sloane said, crossing her arms over her chest.

"Aye, almost. But we have to try. Don't we?" I looked to Broca. "How's Iris?"

"She's much improved." Relief passed over Broca's face. "And you're right. We do have to try. We can't guard ourselves against a potential hurt when the payoff is so great."

"If this means you can live without a curse tainting your bloodline, then I'm happy to help," Rab said, turning me to put his hands on my shoulders. "But I have one caveat . . . you let me stand between you and any harm."

"I can't promise that," I said, my heart filling. "Because I can't anticipate where it will come from. But I'll trust you to do what you think is best."

"Then I'm fine with it. I'd be more than happy to help you."

"He's a good one. I've been telling you that for ages now." Broca winked at Rab. He'd been taking her for weekly walks ever since her hip surgery, and the two had developed a firm friendship.

"Let's crack on, then. I'm hungry," Nova complained.

Once more, we set the spell up, and once more we sat around the table, but this time, Rab sat next to me and Ruth curled into my neck, where I'd put the dragon-scale necklace on. It warmed against my skin, as though sensing it needed to be used, and I reached up to run a finger lightly across the petals of the pendant.

"Let me cast the circle," Broca said. "By salt and flame, by breath and bone, this circle is cast, we stand as one. No harm may enter, none may stay, only light shall guard our way."

"And let me do our spell." Rab squeezed my hand when he said the word "our," and my heart melted a bit. I was head over heels for this man.

"Ready?" I asked when we were finished with Rab's spell.

"Aye." Broca nodded. "This feels good."

Taking a match, I lit the first candle.

And my magick stepped into the light.

I could see it now, though others couldn't: lovely purple silvery threads winding around the table and those I loved, pulling the magick down through the tapestry of time. My hearth witch powers bloomed, and I allowed the magick to connect with those who had come before me, endlessly weaving and interchanging, cutting cords and mending broken threads, and by the time the spell was completed, my magick had cut the bad thread and patched a tear in the fabric of our bloodline.

Closing my eyes, I drew in a deep breath, my body trembling.

We'd done it.

I could feel the change in me, the difference in how my magick moved confidently through me, ready at my fingertips.

When I opened my eyes, a single piece of a broken quartz heart was in the bowl.

"Lyra!" Nova gasped, leaning over.

"Sloane, go get your—"

"Wait," Broca ordered as Sloane moved to stand. "Let me close the circle."

"Och, right." Sloane plopped back down while Broca muttered a closing ritual.

The glowing tapestry of magick that lay before me shimmered and dissolved, and then Broca nodded to Sloane. "Go on, then."

Sloane raced upstairs, and I picked up the piece of pink quartz, still warm to the touch, and turned it over in my hands.

"I could see it," I said, looking up at Broca. "My magick. It was, like, weaving a tapestry. Of sorts. Cutting and mending."

"Hearth witch." Broca nodded. "Of house and home. That's a lovely manifestation of your powers, Lyra."

"Here it is." Sloane bounded back down the stairs with a small velvet pouch, and Blue perked up, clearly hoping she had food. "Not cheese, buddy."

Blue plopped his head back down with a disgruntled sigh, and Ruth flew to his shoulder to stroke the side of his neck.

Sloane pulled her piece of quartz out of the bag and handed it to me.

I fitted it to mine and put it back in the bowl, and we all leaned over to look at it.

A soft light shimmered from where the stone had cracked in two, and then we all jumped as it flashed brightly once.

"It's mended itself," Nova murmured.

I leaned over and picked up the almost-complete heart and held it in the air.

"It's almost complete," I whispered, looking to Nova.

"My turn is next." Nova's shoulders slumped. She just wanted to open a tattoo shop and work on her art, not be caught up in ancient witchy quests. But I knew her. Nova was solid. She'd come through when we needed her.

"If it's any consolation, you hopefully have a little bit of time." Her birthday was still months away.

"And in the meantime, we'll call an emergency meeting of the Charms tomorrow and see what we can do to refresh the wards and keep the curse from returning for as long as we can," Sloane said, jumping up to come give me a hug. "I'm so proud of you."

"Of us," I said, turning to beam up at Rab. "We did this. Together."

"Of course we did, love. Now that we're back together, we're unstoppable." Rab leaned down and gave me a lingering kiss.

"I'm too happy to be grossed out," Nova said, standing and going to the kitchen. "But let the record note . . . ew."

Blue, seeing the refrigerator door open, took off into the air, sending Ruth flying across the room.

"Ruth!" I cried, just as Rab reached out and caught her in midair before she could land with a splat.

"Oh, thank goddess," I said, taking my rattled familiar from Rab's hands.

I'm going to . . . Ruth pulled out her sword.

"Nope, you're not going to hurt Blue," I ordered sternly, and Ruth tilted her head at me, putting on a beguiling look.

What? Me? Hurt anyone? I was just going to help cut the cheese.

"Help cut the cheese, my arse. You're a menace." I laughed. "But you're *my* menace."

"Did someone say 'cheese'?" Rab asked, and I laughed, moving toward the kitchen.

My happy place.

"Out of the way," I said, nudging Nova aside. "I'm in charge here."

EPILOGUE

Lyra

"Shhh, it's starting!" Marcie barked, and we all settled back in our chairs, ready for the Christmas special of *Bewitching Bake Off*. Marcie was hosting a viewing party at Mystic Munchies, complete with several featured desserts from the show, and afterward we all planned to wander over to the Pinecones & Peppermint Fest. The festival was kicking off tonight with a bonfire and fireworks provided by Briarhaven's dragons, and everyone wanted to be there on time.

Everyone from the show was here, including Mandy, though she stayed in the corner and away from us. My family was here, and Knox was tucked next to Sloane, with only Liam missing because he was covering both the festival and the pub.

Drone footage opened the show, sweeping over Briarhaven, the town lit up and looking like the perfect postcard Christmas village.

Knox beamed.

"That should bring in some new visitors."

Though Briarhaven was built for attracting non-magickal tourists to visit, we still got a surprising number of magickals who enjoyed holidaying in the village as well. Turned out, they enjoyed meeting other magickals as well as the freedom of being able to live out in the open without hiding their magick.

"Welcome to our very own Christmas special of *Bewitching Bake Off*." Nevin and Kelly beamed into the cameras. "With our juiciest season ever, we've got love, betrayal, and second chances. Sink your teeth into this sugary-sweet competition as we take you to Briarhaven, Scotland."

I glanced up at Rab to see if he was nervous, but he was relaxed in his seat, his arm casually draped across the back of my chair. I was still getting used to this, to us, and it caught me off guard, every once in a while, that after all these years we could fit so seamlessly into each other's lives again. I still had some nerves around us, and where we were going, but as Nova and Sloane reminded me daily, we had time now to give our relationship an honest chance.

I gasped as my face flashed on the screen, egg exploding in slow motion across my makeup, as the intro rolled into highlights to build everyone's anticipation of the upcoming episodes.

"Oh no," I groaned, as everyone laughed. "This is gonna be a bloodbath."

The room cheered when the screen flashed to Henry proudly presenting his truffles, and he chuckled and wiped his eyes with a handkerchief in the front row.

"I love her." Rab's voice filled the room, and I froze, my eyes caught on the screen, where Rab lifted his chin, looking confidently at the camera.

I turned to look at Rab as his words played in the background.

"Do you know when it's absolutely pissing out, and the clouds have all clustered in and are moody and gray?"

"Aye, that's typical enough Scottish weather," Vaughn said.

"And then, out of nowhere, the clouds will shift, and the loveliest ray of sunshine will pierce through all that gray. It just lights the whole world up in a way that has made poets reach for their pens and painters grab for their brushes in a desperate attempt to capture that moment of stunning, perfect light."

My heart warmed.

"That's Lyra."

My mouth dropped open, and Rab leaned down, brushing a soft kiss across my lips.

"Get a room," Knox called, and we broke apart, laughing. My heart hammered in my chest.

"Rab, I can't believe you said that on camera," I said, blinking back the tears that welled.

"Aye, I surprised myself as well. But then I realized I didn't care who knew it. Not anymore. I'd shout it to the world if I could." Rab threaded his fingers through mine and lifted my hand to kiss my palm.

"But—"

"Shhh," Rab whispered, nodding to the screen, where the show was opening with our personal interviews.

Rab squeezed my hand tighter when it flashed to me speaking about my favorite Christmas with my childhood boyfriend, and Sloane's sigh of happiness brought a smile to my face.

The first show ended just as we were going to be judged for our dishes, leaving the entire room complaining.

"They can't leave it like that! We have to know who wins this round." Henry turned around, appalled.

"Henry, we *know* who wins," I said, amused.

"Still. That's just . . . nobody likes a cliffhanger." Henry crossed his arms, his chin sinking into his chest as he glowered.

"Agreed." Marcie stood, anger on her face. "I'll just be texting Vaughn what I think about this." Despite Marcie's annoyance with the show, she'd struck up an odd friendship with Vaughn, and I was privy to hearing about his catastrophic dating attempts, which Marcie grimly reported to me when it was just us baking in the mornings. True to her word, Marcie had made me a much stronger baker, and I'd found that I loved the routine of going to work each morning. The quiet early hours in the kitchen soothed me, and it was there that I'd come up with some of my best new recipes for my YouTube channel. My follower count had exploded, and Rab was making noises about building me my own set to film on. It was a step too far for me, at the moment, as I liked my life exactly as it was. The idea of any other big changes was just too much to stomach. I wanted routine and normalcy. Well, as normal as life in Briarhaven could be, that is.

"Either way"—Knox stood—"I think we need to get over to the festival. The fireworks will be starting soon."

Leaving the bakery, Rab took my hand and pulled me aside as the rest of the group walked ahead of us toward the main square in town, where the festival was being held. It was a crisp, cold night, but the winds were low, and the sky was clear—a smattering of stars sparkling against the velvet backdrop of night. Music and laughter drifted in the evening air as we followed the stream of people heading toward the brightly lit square.

"Are you okay, lass?" Rab leaned in, his eyes searching my face.

"Me? Of course." I laughed. Sure, it had been embarrassing to see myself flounder on television, but at the same time, I was just too happy to worry much about anything else. Nobody was perfect, so if people needed to see me fail to give them courage to try something new, I was fine to lead as an example. "I'm happy I went on the show—if I hadn't, I'm not sure we'd be where we are now."

"No, I'm not sure we would be either," Rab admitted with a frown. "I do have a streak of stubbornness, I'm afraid to admit."

"As do I. It's part of our Scottish heritage, isn't it?"

"Can I buy you a cup of fancy cocoa or whatever posh cocktail Liam has dreamt up for his booth to make up for it?" Rab asked, and I pursed my lips, pretending to think it over.

"I guessssss so." I fluttered my eyelashes at him.

"And then I'll make up for it . . . later . . . when I have you to myself again." Rab leaned in and kissed my neck, blowing a hot breath against my skin, and I shivered as desire unfurled inside me.

At least I didn't have to worry about turning random objects into hedgies anymore. Once I'd managed to break my part of the curse, that particular annoyance had disappeared, much to Sorcha's relief.

The group split off as we arrived at the festival, where booths lined the square, and the ancient yew tree in the middle was wrapped in sparkling lights. Strands of twinkle lights arched out from the tree and to poles at the corner of the square. A band on a small bandstand in the corner rocked about Grandma getting run over by a reindeer, and the smell of toasted chestnuts wafted in the air.

Sloane and Knox broke off, their arms wrapped around each other, and Knox bent to whisper something in Sloane's ear. By the look on her face, I could guess it was similar to what Rab had just whispered to me, and her cheeks flushed.

Nova stood to the side, alone, scanning the crowd, and my heart twisted. I hadn't much thought about what it would be like for her if both Sloane and I had boyfriends, and I made a mental note to be sure to spend more time with her so she didn't feel like we were leaving her behind.

Not that she much seemed to care. Nova had always been more of a loner, happy to relax away an afternoon sketching in her book.

"Come on, there's Liam." Rab nodded toward the Rune & Rose's decorated booth wrapped in tinsel and twinkle lights, where Liam and another bartender were filling drinks.

Raven appeared, having missed the viewing due to setting up her own apothecary booth, a very handsome man at her side. Tall, with dark-framed glasses, a knit cap pulled over his dark hair, and a short beard shadowing his sharp jawline, he looked to be late twenties and just Raven's type.

Liam dropped a shaker to the counter, the loud clatter drawing our attention, and apologized when I jumped at the noise.

"Sorry. Slippery suckers." Liam nodded to where Raven chatted with the newcomer. "Who's the new guy?"

"Not sure," Rab said, his eyes lighting in his face, and I raised an eyebrow at him as he leaned against the counter. "But he looks just her type, doesn't he? I wonder if she's got a new boyfriend."

I jumped as Liam slammed the shaker onto the counter again and squinted at Rab. What the hell was he doing?

"Uh-oh," Nova singsonged, sidling in next to me. "Looks like Liam might be getting jealous."

"Ohhhh." I finally clued into what was going on, my eyes flying between where Raven laughed at something the man said and Liam's lips drew tight into a flat line.

"Three gingerbread hot cocoas," I said quickly, trying to stave off any issues.

"Everyone, this is Jack. He's just moved to town and is going to buy Gilda's Gifts."

"Is that right? Sell lots of gifts, mate?" Liam said, his tone not remotely as welcoming as it usually was.

Jack flashed a smile that wasn't even close to friendly, and Nova stiffened beside me. I couldn't blame her. The smile took Jack from a nice-looking man to almost predatory—but in the best way possible. The man was hot with a capital *H*.

"Naw, mate. I'll be opening a tattoo shop there."

Nova sucked in a breath. I couldn't tell if she was excited or upset, as opening a shop had always been her dream.

A roar went up from the skies, signaling the start of the fireworks, and Nova took off her gloves to dig in her handbag for cash.

"I've got the drinks. Jack—do you want anything?" Nova looked over her shoulder at Jack as she pulled her money from her pocketbook.

Jack grabbed her wrist, and I gasped.

"What is—"

Rab was already moving forward, but Jack only lifted Nova's arm until her wrist was close to his face.

There the faint lines of one of her tattoos peeked out from beneath her coat sleeve.

And they glowed.

Nova gasped, her eyes moving slowly from her wrist up to where Jack's expression was set in hard lines.

"I've never seen that happen before," Jack said, accusation lacing his tone.

"It never *has* happened before," Nova said, her voice faint.

"It does to mine."

They stared at each other, the moment drawing out, and fireworks exploded above us.

ACKNOWLEDGMENTS

It was such a joy to return to Briarhaven, a place that now feels as familiar to me as an old friend. I always write with the hope that you, too, would want to linger in the worlds I create—to walk their streets, sit by their fires, and feel at home there. I was in a particularly festive frame of mind while writing this story. Having just sold my home in the Caribbean, I'd stepped fully into a nomadic chapter of my life. In many ways, I understood Lyra's push and pull—the longing to build roots and community while also being shaped by years of travel. I hope this story brings you joy and reminds you that home and belonging can be found anywhere . . . Sometimes all it takes is adding a little sparkle of your own.

My heartfelt thanks go to my agent, Christina, for her steady guidance, keen insight, and unwavering belief in my ideas. Thank you to Casey, whose enthusiasm and thoughtful feedback made the drafting process such a pleasure. Ghjulia, your insight and care have helped these stories truly shine, and I can't wait to see where the next adventures take us. I'm also deeply grateful to the entire team at Gallery Books—Carrie, Molly, Sarah, Janet, Fallon, Sally, Mackenzie, Christine, and Olivia—as well as Molly, Gemma, and Sabeh at Simon & Schuster UK. And to Allison, who has been helping to get my books translated into foreign languages—you rock! Seeing these books find readers around the world has been an absolute delight, and I'm so thankful to all of you for helping them sparkle.

Lastly, my deepest thanks go to the Scotsman—and his wonderful family—for always being willing to help me navigate my interpretation of all things Scottish. I was lucky the day I met him, but even luckier the day his family welcomed me with open arms. Found family means the world to me, and I'm endlessly grateful to have them in my life. All my love to you.

And if you're already missing Lyra and Rab, pop on over to my website for a free bonus scene where Lyra and Ruth get into a wee bit of trouble at www.triciaomalley.com/free.

Finished *A Taste of Magic* and want more?
Pick up the first book in The Scottish Charms Series
and dive back into the magic.

Love's A Witch

She's hexed. He's vexed. And for Scotland's most magical small-town, their feud might just spell disaster.

Sloane MacGregor swore she'd never return to Briarhaven, but with her twenty-fifth birthday looming – the day witches come into their magic – her grandmother summons her and her sisters back for one tiny task: break the centuries-old curse haunting their bloodline.

Knox Douglas, Briarhaven's grumpy mayor, has worked tirelessly to make his town a haven for magical folk. The last thing he needs is a cursed MacGregor wreaking havoc. It doesn't matter he once crushed on her. For the sake of Briarhaven, Sloane has to go.

But magic has other plans – and in Briarhaven, love really *is* a witch.

AVAILABLE IN PAPERBACK, EBOOK AND AUDIO

SIMON & SCHUSTER

London · New York · Amsterdam/Antwerp · Sydney/Melbourne · Toronto · New Delhi

ABOUT THE AUTHOR

Tricia O'Malley is a *New York Times*, *USA Today*, and *Wall Street Journal* bestselling author of contemporary, paranormal, and fantasy romance. Her books have sold over three million copies worldwide. When she's not writing, Tricia can be found scuba diving, traveling, or debating the best popcorn topping. She splits her time between Scotland and the Caribbean, loves fun vacation reads, and thinks life is better with a little bit of sparkle. *A Taste of Magic* is the second installment in her national bestselling series, The Scottish Charms.

To see some of her Scotland or island life photos, visit her on Facebook, on Instagram, or at TriciaOMalley.com.